WASTELAND MARSHALS

WASTELAND MARSHALS

Volume 1

GAIL Z. MARTIN

LARRY N. MARTIN

To John Hartness and Falstaff Books for taking a chance on a new series based on the pitch: Boondock Saints meets The Walking Dead

WASTELAND MARSHALS

WASTELAND MARSHALS

GAIL Z. MARTIN
LARRY N. MARTIN

CHAPTER ONE

"I MISS PIZZA." Shane Collins looked up at the broken neon sign for the abandoned pizza restaurant with a sigh.

"The world practically ends, and you miss pizza?" Lucas Maddox echoed.

"Among other things," Shane replied. The mom-and-pop roadside motel they planned to squat in for the night sat across a crumbling highway from the old pizzeria, sparking memories and a pang of loss.

"Yeah, lots of other things," Lucas replied, as he finished checking out the empty motel lobby to assure no unwelcome surprises awaited them. Three years after a clusterfuck of epic proportions had effectively stopped the twenty-first century cold in its tracks, ruins like the old motel had become reminders of what had been.

"Hey, it's got a solid roof, the walls are cement block, and we can bring the horses into the utility shed overnight. We've done with worse," Shane pointed out.

Which was true, Shane thought. As partners in the US Marshals, they had spent many nights holed up in mid-price hotels safeguarding witnesses. Before that, in the Army, they'd survived miserable missions in bombed-out villages. The comfortable suburban childhood they'd shared as friends since elementary school was another relic of a world that no longer existed.

The two men were a study in contrasts, though they were both thirty-five and within a half inch of the same six-foot-two height. Shane was blond, with what Lucas always joked was an All-American cowboy look. Lucas had dark hair and eyes, rocking more of a bad boy vibe. That had made it easy when the job demanded playing good cop/bad cop.

"And the floor's tile. I never thought cheap motel carpet could get any worse—but it did," Lucas replied. A few years without heat or cooling turned most hotel guest rooms into breeding grounds for mold and wild animals. They had learned the hard way that the motel office usually made a better shelter—tile floor, less furniture, and good visibility. And in some cases, like tonight, a real fireplace.

Lucas had already poked and prodded at the flue until he felt sure that they could light a fire relatively safely. After a cold ride from their last waystation, he seemed positively giddy about the possibility.

"I brought in our bedrolls and saddlebags," Lucas said as he rose from where he knelt next to the 1970s-style hearth, dusting the soot off his hands. "There's some grass next to the parking lot that looks safe for the horses to eat. You want to take the horses over to graze, and then down to the pond, while I go looking for firewood?"

"Yeah, and I'll bring up a bucket of water to boil. Warm food would be a nice change."

He headed out to the gravel parking lot, where they had tied Lucas's black stallion and his own roan gelding. They had named them "Shadow" and "Red" respectively, unimaginative but functional, although they had long joked about more colorful names from the fantasy novels and games they liked, more along the lines of Sleipnir or Shadowfax. Shane had argued that both of those names took entirely too long to say, though the thought still made him smile.

"Come on you two. Let's get you fed and watered before it's full dark." Shane led their mounts over to the grass that stretched down to a small pond, then stood guard as they began to eat.

Three years ago, the idea of trading in their black SUV for a pair of horses would have prompted plenty of cowboy jokes and incredulous chuckles. Shane ran a hand along Red's side affectionately. He'd grown fond of both horses, although he'd probably always miss heat, air conditioning, and the protection from the elements he'd once taken for granted in the confines of a vehicle.

The pond was part of a small park. Its gazebo and playground looked to be in good shape, though the area was as deserted as the motel. Gazing at the green space gave Shane a peaceful feeling, something difficult to come by these days. He let himself enjoy the view, then frowned as he strained to make out music so distant that he couldn't be certain whether he had heard it or merely imagined the song. Shane looked all around but saw no one in sight. It seemed odd, but it wasn't the first time he'd had something like that happen. Shane chalked it up to his imagination and turned his focus back to the horses.

Lucas's shout broke Shane from his thoughts.

"Come on," he told the horses, tugging at their reins. He didn't dare leave them unprotected and loose, but Lucas needed his help. The horses came with him reluctantly, and he ran as fast as he could with them in tow, sending them into the relative protection of the shed he and Lucas had scouted earlier. He closed the door behind them and headed toward where the shouts had sounded.

He came around the corner, his crossbow drawn. Lucas was down, fighting for his life against a huge black dog. Only it wasn't a normal dog, Shane knew as he tried to get a clear shot where he could hit the attacker and not Lucas. A grim only looked like a large, ugly dog, the size of a sow with black, matted fur, bat-like ears, and red eyes. It was really a revenant, a supernatural creature, and so nothing but iron or silver would do the job.

Shane squeezed the trigger, sending a silver-coated arrow into the monster's front shoulder, hoping like hell Lucas didn't manage to move into the shot. The creature reared back and howled in pain, turning its glowing red eyes on Shane. Blood covered its sharp teeth and powerful, wide jaw, and Shane feared he was already too late. The grim's hesitation gave Shane the time he needed to reload, and this time, the crossbow bolt caught the grim between the eyes. The creature toppled over, covering Lucas in gore.

"Lucas!" Shane rushed forward, alert in case the grim had not hunted alone. Usually, they were solitary creatures, but nothing worked the way it used to, and Shane had learned the hard way not to take chances.

Lucas groaned, trapped beneath the body of the dead beast. Shane slung his crossbow over his shoulder on its strap and hefted the grim off of his partner. He couldn't tell how much of the blood was the grim's and how much was Lucas's.

"Got...shoulder," Lucas moaned.

Shane knelt beside him, triaging the wound. Lucas's shirt and jacket were ripped and bloody where the grim had sunk its teeth into the meat of his upper arm, and a swipe of the creature's claws had opened a set of gashes across his chest.

That's bad, Shane thought. He fought down panic and thought quickly, then shimmied out of his own coat long enough to strip off his flannel shirt and rip it into pieces. Shane wadded up one section to stanch the flow of blood from the bite, then tied the wad in place with what had been a sleeve. He did the same for the chest wound.

"How bad?" Lucas managed.

"More than I can stitch up," Shane said. "We need to get you help."

"Not far to Green Farm." Lucas hated admitting pain, so the fact that he was panting gave Shane an idea of just how bad it was.

"Yeah. Far enough," Shane muttered. "Gonna have to get you to the farm. I'll get the bags, then we need to go."

He pulled Lucas to his feet as gently as he could and pretended he didn't see the tightness in his partner's face or hear the moan he bit back. Shane had a thinner, narrower build, while Lucas had always been more muscular. That made hauling his injured buddy all the harder, since Shane swore Lucas weighed a ton although, in reality, they were both lean from scant rations. Lucas stumbled beside him as Shane kept his gaze fixed on the motel. The trek seemed to take forever.

"I'll be back," Shane said as he eased Lucas into a plastic chair in the lobby. He grabbed their bedrolls and saddlebags, then went to the garage to fetch the horses, all the while expecting another grim to show up to finish the hunt.

Shane got the horses ready and then led them back, hoping Lucas remained conscious. When he returned to the lobby, his friend was pale and shaky, but still awake.

"Okay, you've got to stay with me," Shane cautioned. "Probably gonna hurt like hell. I'll drag this chair out beside Shadow, and then help you climb from the chair to the saddle."

"Fuck off," Lucas said, but the weakness in his voice took the heat from his comment. "I can get on my horse."

"Falling would be bad. And you're in no condition to make decisions." Shane ignored Lucas's bravado, feeling vindicated when Lucas could barely keep his legs under him for the short distance between the lobby and the horses. Shane dragged the plastic chair along with them, then steadied Lucas and half-lifted him as he stepped up and swung his leg over the saddle.

"Do I need to tie you on?" It wouldn't be the first time they had ridden with one of them hurt.

"No. Just...fuck it hurts. Don't take the long way."

Shane hoped he had kept his worry out of his expression, but Lucas knew him too well to be fooled if he hadn't already figured out the danger for himself.

He fastened Shadow's reins to his own saddle, so Lucas only had to worry about keeping himself in the saddle. Not for the first time, he missed the convenience of GPS and the efficiency of ambulances and emergency rooms. *Hell, even a hospital would be an improvement*, he thought. But they were out in the country on the outskirts of Mercer, Pennsylvania, and the small rural hospitals had shut down long ago as the power failed and supplies ran out.

He came to a crossroads and debated which way to go. Both led to Green Farm, but Shane couldn't afford to find out that a damaged bridge or other obstacle blocked their path. Lucas still bled steadily from his injuries, and even the best care Shane might find in time would fall short of a trauma center.

It wasn't until he'd already made his decision, trusting his gut, and started down the road that Shane realized he'd followed the path where the faint song in his mind sang the loudest.

Green Farm lived up to its name. Before, it had been a cluster of Amish farms with a pie and produce stand along the state highway that ran along one side of the land. Now, it remained a farm, but it had also become an enclave, a sanctuary for those who needed somewhere to go when the world ended and were willing to adapt. The same old school ways that had often made the Amish the butt of jokes had been what ultimately saved them and held out hope that society could rebuild.

The palisade fence at Green Farm was new. It appeared to stretch around the perimeter of the enclave, and Shane guessed it had been built to protect the residents from creatures like the grim—and humans who were arguably worse.

"US Marshals Collins and Maddox, and my partner is bleeding, so we need to come in now," Shane snapped when two bearded young men in the plain clothing of the sect called down to him from a watchtower at the locked gates.

The two men exchanged a glance, then one ran to open the gate. Shane rode in, sparing a worried look behind him. Lucas had fallen silent soon after they had started on the road, and his ashen color and drawn expression made Shane even more worried than he had been before. In the old days, any emergency room probably could have handled the wounds. But that was Before. Now, resources were scarce to non-existent, or hellishly difficult to find if they hadn't vanished. This was the best he could do. Lucas wouldn't make it to the next depot.

"I'll run ahead and tell Doc you're coming," the second guard said, and took off toward where Shane vaguely remembered the doctor's house and office were located.

Dr. David Preston was waiting on his porch when Shane and Lucas rode up. He and the guard came forward to help Shane get Lucas out of the saddle without falling. Lucas looked far too pale, and his skin felt cold.

"Got ambushed by a grim," Shane said as the three men carried Lucas inside. "I shot it, and Lucas did his best to fight it off, but there's a bite and some gashes. He's lost a lot of blood."

"Do you know his blood type?"

Shane rattled off the information. "And as it happens, we're the same type, so I can donate if you need me to." That had come in handy more than once over the years, in the Army as well as during their time as Marshals.

"Good to know. Let's see how it goes. Let's get him onto my table and see about cleaning the wounds. Those creatures' bites go sour easily. That's never been a good thing—but it's worse now."

Shane knew what Doc Preston meant. Antibiotics were scarce, and what might still be manufactured on a small, local scale could no longer be distributed like before. That put a premium on folk cures and old knowledge, as well as those whose medical knowledge combined with some healing magic.

"I'll take care of your horses," the guard volunteered, "if you want to get what you need from your packs." Shane thanked the man and grabbed a few essentials after the three of them got Lucas settled.

"Eat something," Preston said. "There's food in the kitchen. You'll need it if we have to do a transfusion. I'll yell if I need you."

Darkness had fallen on the ride to Green Farm. The whole way there, Shane feared that at any moment, a pack of grims—or something worse—would come lunging from the shadows and finish them both. In truth, he'd been expecting that for years, even Before. They'd come close so many times, in Afghanistan, and then as Marshals. Sooner or later, the time would come when fate decided it had been cheated long enough.

"But it will not be this day," Shane muttered to himself, quoting one of his favorite movies.

He tried to ignore the pang he always felt when he remembered. Watching those movies had grown much more difficult, and he might not see some ever again. In the old days, he and Lucas often passed the time in the car dueling nerd quotes, trying to out-geek the other. Their shared love of comics, video games, and superheroes had drawn them together in grade school and provided a life-long bond. Now it was bittersweet, an unspoken effort not to forget details from a world that had radically, permanently, changed.

The Amish had never relied on modern conveniences like electricity in their homes—although they did make a pragmatic exception for their barns and carpentry shops. That meant that their transition in the aftermath went far more smoothly. Shane made his way around Preston's kitchen by lantern light, hungry enough to be content with cheese and slices of thick, homemade bread with butter.

The door to Preston's office remained shut, and Shane tried to take it as a good sign that he hadn't been summoned. He pulled a dog-eared book from his pack, but he was too worried to read and too exhausted to pace. He stared at the book and realized that it was one of Lucas's fantasy novels. Shane tended toward sci-fi, but books were scarce, and he and Lucas always traded when they did find a stash of books in an abandoned house or not-completely-looted store.

He whistled to pass the time, cycling through as many of his classic rock favorites as he could remember. Shane rarely bothered to know the words. Lucas sang, another way they kept boredom at bay during all the long stake-outs and dreary car rides. Now, even whistling didn't quell his nervousness.

The wind-up clock on the mantle told him two hours had elapsed by the time Dr. Preston finally opened the door. Shane sprang to his feet. "Do you need me? Does Lucas need blood?"

Preston walked out, wearing a blood-spattered cloth apron. "He's going to be okay. You're welcome to go see him, but he's still under. Didn't need blood after all. Would have done a transfusion if we didn't have a choice, but I prefer not to if we can help it."

Shane felt himself relax for the first time since the attack. "Thank you."

Preston shrugged. "You're Marshals. We appreciate what you do for all of us. The folks here may not venture out much beyond our borders, but we do try to keep up with what goes on in the world."

Shane sighed. "You might want to rethink that, Doc. What goes on out there ain't so great."

"Was it ever?"

Shane's laugh was harsh. "A damned sight better than it is now, pardon my language."

"I've said worse when I tripped over something in the barn," Preston replied with a conspiratorial smile. "As for how it was Before—it's different for us. Our folks can't mourn what was never theirs. And yet, they would never wish what's happened on anyone."

"Maybe you had the right idea all along," Shane said with a sigh. "Keep it simple. Your folks still knew how to get by when everything went wrong." He paused. "Except...I didn't think the Amish went to school long enough to become a doctor."

Preston chuckled. "I didn't start out Amish. When the Events happened, I figured they had the most stable community, and I offered my services, in exchange for converting. They probably wouldn't have taken me up on it Before, but...well, things are different now."

"That's an understatement."

"If you feel up to it, you and I could get Lucas into a bed and off my surgical table," Preston offered. "I've got a guest room for him, and I can make up the couch for you."

"I'd be grateful," Shane said, and now that the crisis was over, he felt exhaustion in every muscle. "And I'm willing to work for our room and board while he recovers. Wouldn't be the first time I've mucked out the barn."

Preston chuckled. "I'll take you up on that—tomorrow. Let's get you two settled before you fall over and I end up with two patients instead of one."

CHAPTER TWO

THE NEXT THREE weeks found a quiet rhythm. Despite Lucas's protests, Preston insisted that he stay and recover fully, saying that he would not clear a farm hand to go back to work from such an injury any sooner. Lucas grudgingly gave in, but he insisted on helping with light chores around the house and doctor's office to keep from going stir crazy. Shane tended their horses and helped in the barn, lending a hand for any farm work.

At night, he and Lucas played poker or one of the well-worn fantasy card games Shane kept in his duffle. It was another pastime carried over from long, boring weeks babysitting Mob witnesses in the old days, one that transitioned well now that power for electronics was hard to come by. Shane missed binge-watching horror movies and the all-night online gaming that used to fill empty evenings, but cards were a sociable substitute. Preston joined them now and again when his duties permitted.

"There you are," Preston said when Shane came back inside after an early morning in the barn. "Thought you'd want to know, Lucas is cleared to go. I know he's been champing at the bit for a while, but I wanted to make sure he healed up clean and solid before you two headed out. The road's no place to open up stitches or deal with an infection."

Shane wholeheartedly agreed, although he and Lucas had managed through some bad injuries plenty of times since the world fell apart. "I'm amazed he didn't meet me at the door with our bags packed," he replied with a chuckle.

"I haven't told him yet." Preston hesitated. "I know you have important work to do out there, but I'll be sorry to see you go," he admitted. "The stable hands will miss you, too. They say you've more than done your share."

Shane shrugged. "I like to keep busy. And helping on some of the carpentry was a nice change. My dad was in construction. Maybe it's in my blood a little."

He didn't mention that his parents and two brothers had died in the Events. Preston didn't ask. He didn't have to.

"If you ever decide to quit being Marshals, I'll put in a good word for you here," Preston joked.

"Stranger things have happened." Personally, Shane figured that he and Lucas would die with their boots on.

"Well, the offer stands," Preston replied, clapping him on the shoulder. "Go talk to Lucas and let me know what kind of provisions you'll need and when you want to get back on the road. We'll make sure you have what you need."

Shane thanked him and headed toward Lucas's room. He paused when he reached the door to the bedroom and ran a hand over his face. It had been too damn close. Shane still had nightmares about the attack. No one really knew what prowled in the night nowadays. Regular travelers wouldn't have had a chance. They'd only survived because they were ex-military, US Marshals, with all the training that entailed. And still, it had been a near thing.

He burst in without knocking and caught Lucas trying to pull his pants on. At the unexpected intrusion, Lucas wobbled and nearly toppled over with one leg stuck in his trousers.

"What the...fudge?" Lucas said, catching himself at the last minute and censoring his language out of respect for their host. "You ever hear of knocking?"

"Where's the fun in that?" Shane replied, grinning. "If you're well enough to walk, you're well enough for me to go back to irritating the crap out of you."

"Joy," Lucas replied in a droll tone. He regained his balance and pulled his pants up, giving a huff at the indignity. "A little privacy here? I'm trying to get dressed."

"Seriously?" Shane questioned, leaning against the wall. "They sent us into the bathroom together in elementary school since the time we were in third grade. Military barracks. Crappy hotels. And, we've been on the road for three years now. I'm long past needing to sneak up on you if I wanted to get an eyeful. You flatter yourself."

Lucas managed a smile that was almost like normal. "Yeah, yeah."

Shane closed the door and walked farther into the room, to sit on a wooden chair near the bed. Lucas picked up the pitcher next to the basin on a washstand and sluiced water over his face. In the two weeks they'd been here, stubble had become a full, dark beard, and his hair, which he also usually kept close-cut, had also grown longer.

"Guess I'm getting a head start on my winter beard." He sighed, looking in the mirror. Shane could see the toll the injury had taken on Lucas. He'd lost weight, and despite the enforced inactivity of recovery, he had dark circles under his eyes.

Shane and Lucas had been a team since they'd been picked for partners in third-grade dodgeball, and even the end of the world hadn't changed that. Shane was blond, with the kind of trustworthy good looks that made it far too easy for him to get what he wanted with a smile and a twinkle in his eye. Lucas had olive skin and black hair, and his moody vibe had been intimidating, even back in school, growing more so after a couple of tours of duty together and then joining the Marshals.

"Where've you been?" Lucas asked.

"Playing farmhand. Not sure I could ever get used to the suspenders and hats for myself, but Green Farm is a nice place."

"Your folks always did have a backyard garden," Lucas said, sitting down to pull on his boots. "And my dad went deer hunting. That's about as country as we ever got."

"Back when there were cities."

"Yeah." Lucas's parents, sister, and brother hadn't survived the Events.

"I let you sleep and went and sat on the porch. Thank God the Amish believe in coffee," Shane replied. "Talked to the doc. He thinks you're ready to go back on the road."

Lucas seemed to take stock of himself in the mirror, sighed in frustration, and headed back toward the bed. "I'm ready to be gone," he said, pulling his shirt over the newly healed scars on his chest and shoulder.

"Kinda nice to be somewhere for a while where nothing's trying to kill us," Shane replied.

Lucas snorted. "If we stick around long enough, you'll manage to annoy the fu...dge out of them. They'll probably chase us off with axes and scythes."

"I'm the people person, remember?" It was an old sparring match, almost as old as the debate over which of them was taller. Shane stood half an inch taller than Lucas, a point his friend would never concede.

"Says you," Lucas retorted. He stretched, then grimaced as the newly healed skin protested. "Ouch. I remember when we just transported WITSEC informants, chased down some fugitives, and only had to worry about the Mob," Lucas said wistfully. "Good times."

When the cities went dark, and the relentless bustle of cars, trains, and planes came to an abrupt halt, creatures that had awaited their turn to take back the night slunk from their hiding places to remind humankind that they were no longer the apex predators.

"But still, it feels wrong not to keep moving," Lucas went on. "Places to go, people to see, things to kill." Shane knew that Lucas had never been able to sit still.

"Messes to clean up," Shane added.

Back in school, they'd called Lucas's jitters ADHD and given him pills. The Army liked the hyper-vigilant focus the pills gave Lucas, a good thing for a sniper. But since the Events, the pills, like much of the Army, were long gone. Shane was resigned to Lucas just being twitchy as fuck. It suited Lucas as if he'd reverted to his natural state, like most everything else had.

A knock at the door startled them, although Shane knew they were safe here.

"See? Someone knows how to knock," Lucas muttered. "Come in!" he said in a louder voice.

Doc Preston walked in and cast an assessing gaze over Lucas. "You're up. I told Shane you're healed enough to go back on the road. I'd be most displeased if all my handiwork on those stitches was for naught." One hundred careful stitches, which would leave a scar. Shane had already taken to calling Lucas "quilt boy" when he was out of arm's reach.

"Have your folks heard anything about what's going on out there?" Shane asked.

"Look at it this way—we've already had the apocalypse, so nothing else is too bad by comparison, right?" Preston replied. "Heard there've been floods to the northeast, and wildfires in the west. The usual."

The end of the world, when it came, wasn't due to just one thing—it was a cascade of one calamity after another. Some people referred to the year-long shit storm that had torn apart modern civilization as "The Cataclysm," but most people just called it "The Events."

"Good to know," Lucas said. "Not that it changes the circuit we ride. When we can, we try to pitch in and lend a hand when that shi—stuff happens."

"I imagine there's too much territory, and not enough of you Marshals to go around," Preston replied. He didn't know the half of it, Shane thought. *And that lets him sleep at night, so we're not going to tell him.*

The aftermath of the Events had badly strained the military and law enforcement, and without modern communication and transportation, they were stretched even thinner. Shane and Lucas were the only Marshals in their area, which covered parts of Ohio, Pennsylvania, and West Virginia. Too much space, too many problems, for just two men, but they did the best they could.

SHANE AND LUCAS made the rounds, thanking the many people who had brought food, tended their horses, or stopped by with well-wishes. And of course, there was Preston, who had taken them into his home and saved Lucas's life.

"Come back, when the circuit brings you this way," Preston said, walking with them and their horses to the front gate of the enclave. "Bring us news. But try to come back in one piece."

They shook his hand. "Deal," Lucas said, an empty promise but a pleasant thought. They swung up into the saddles and rode out, and Shane had to admit that he was happy to be back on the road.

"I think the horses figured they had a vacation," Shane said, riding next to Lucas. Route 19 was the most direct way south other than the interstate, but they didn't expect to see a lot of fellow travelers.

Once in a while, peddlers or a trader caravan wended their way across the broken landscape, but that was more likely in summer, not now, when fall storms were in the offing. Most folks stayed close to home unless a disaster forced them to relocate. Shane thought it was as if Fate picked up the snow globe of the world and shook it, just for the hell of it, to see where the pieces would land.

The land on either side of them had been farmland or pastures for horses and cows. A few small hamlets at the crossroads had offered gas, convenience stores, and beer. Most of that was gone now. Violent storms had chased off some residents, while the collapse of big parts of the power grid had shuttered most businesses. The ones who remained survived by banding together into communities every bit as tightly knit as the Amish and toughing it out, helping each other through fire, flood, and famine. Unlike the Amish, some of those enclaves were decidedly unfriendly to outsiders, even Marshals.

Just north of I-80, Shane saw two travelers coming toward them. Their clothing made identification easy and immediate.

"Looks like a couple of the IT Priests are heading our way," he said to Lucas.

The two riders were dressed in black academic robes. Each wore several strands of Mardi Gras beads, from which hung a fandom pendant. In this case, the dark-haired young man on the left had a Transformer medallion, while his companion, a fine-featured blond whose gender Shane couldn't guess, wore a Decepticon amulet.

"Greetings, Marshals!" the dark-haired man said, noting the badges Shane and Lucas wore, prominently displayed. "I'm Brother Jon, and this is Devon."

"Hello, monks. What brings you this way?" Lucas asked.

"Heading to the Thiel campus," the blond replied. "We've just made a circuit of the towers and nodes. We'll rest a bit and get new orders, then head out again."

When the Events destroyed cities, unleashed outbreaks, and sent the survivors fleeing, many college students realized they couldn't go home. The universities realized that with their own power plants and extensive facilities, they could function as independent villages. Sporting fields were plowed and planted for food, flax, and cotton, and escaped livestock from abandoned farms got corralled and brought within the palisade fencing that sprang up to protect the inhabitants.

Townsfolks who didn't flee either moved on campus or took shelter there during the new, unpredictable storms. Students suddenly found their majors had become their professions and pitched in. ROTC and sporting teams were deputized to campus security and local law enforcement or helped with the farming. But the engineering and computer science majors and their professors found a whole new calling.

The whole "priesthood" thing had started as a joke, gallows humor after the Events, a self-deprecating nod to the stereotype that programmers didn't have a social life and didn't get laid, and that college students with loans might as well have taken a vow of poverty. But when universities realized that they and the few remaining scattered government facilities were the last guardians of what remained of the internet, the task of keeping the backbone of the system functioning became an urgent way to save knowledge and preserve a key communications tool.

And so engineers and programmers teamed up to ride circuits between campuses, doing their best to keep what remained of the system and its servers functioning. No one knew who came up with the idea of the robes, beads, and geek symbols, but it immediately identified the wearers to all who saw them and afforded some protection from brigands.

"Any news from the road?" Shane asked. "We were sidelined for a bit from an injury."

"We came across I-80," Devon said. "Didn't have any trouble, but we've heard there have been some incidents on the side roads."

"Incidents?" Lucas asked, immediately going into what Shane thought of as "cop mode."

Jon nodded. "Brigands, robbing peddlers and stealing horses."

"Where?" Lucas pressed.

"Around the state game lands, just south of here," Devon replied. "That's all we know."

Shane and Lucas exchanged a glance. "All right. We'll look into it," Shane assured the monks.

"We have a message for you," Jon said. "Professor Gibbons at Slippery Rock has us all looking for you two."

"What's going on?" Lucas asked.

"We're losing contact with IOT."

"Eye-aught?" Shane echoed, confused.

"I-O-T. Internet of Things," Devon replied. "You probably never noticed, before everything went to hell in a handbasket, that all the equipment and appliances around you were networked to the internet. So your coffee maker and your refrigerator and your smart TV could all report back to their manufacturers for software updates—and data mining."

"I think everyone's warranty is fucked, at this point," Lucas pointed out.

"Not the point," Jon said. "We were able to hack into the IOT early on, and we used the reports to get data. Anything on batteries or with a generator—or in the places where the grid isn't down, still has power—became our eyes and ears. That's what helped us feed you the intel you needed to know the safe routes out of the D.C. suburbs and helped the responders on the coast get around where the bridges were out and the roads were flooded."

"So Big Brother actually served a purpose," Lucas snarked. "And now you're losing contact? Why? Grid going dark? Batteries running low?"

"That's some of it, but I'm afraid there's more," Devon said. "We think something is actively trying to block the signal in places."

"You're sure it's not just a glitch?" Shane asked, frowning.

Jon shook his head. "No. Something's cut off the signal in certain areas. We haven't figured out a pattern, but the signal isn't failing—it's being blocked. We don't know what that means, or what could do that— or why anyone would want to."

"Could it be something natural?" Lucas wondered aloud. "Weird, but natural? We've had more than our share of that kind of thing, lately."

"Maybe," Devon allowed. "We're looking into it, and we've got queries out to the other priests, but no one's given us anything usable yet."

"All right," Shane replied. "Keep us posted. What else?"

"We've completely lost touch with the enclave at Site R," Jon said gravely. "We've accepted the probability that they've been wiped out."

CHAPTER THREE

"WHAT THE FUCK IS SITE R?" Lucas asked. "And why should I care? Boston and Philadelphia are gone, too. We deal with it."

Jon gave him a long-suffering look. "Neither Boston nor Philadelphia were secure location bunkers for top government officials. Site R—Raven Rock—was. Very hush-hush. That location was built to withstand everything up to and including a nuclear bomb to the East Coast."

"So if it's gone dark..." Shane said.

Devon nodded. "Yeah. Gettysburg University alerted us a week ago. They've been trying to reach Site R and lost contact. So they put out a call for anyone who heard from the Marshals to send you their way and see what's going wrong. You'll probably want to swing through and talk to the Gettysburg folks, then head south from there."

"Okay," Lucas said. "We'll head that way."

"Travel safely," Devon said. "May the Force be with you, and all that jazz."

"And also with you," Lucas added with a smirk, riffing on his Catholic upbringing.

"May the odds be ever in your favor," Shane returned. Lucas knew that since the Events, both he and Shane had lost faith in a god that seemed to have left without a forwarding address. That left them to find comfort in other things, like the books and movies that they didn't want to forget.

Lucas and Shane said nothing until after Jon and Devon had ridden off. Finally, Lucas turned to his partner. "So...Site R?"

Shane shrugged. "Might as well have a look. We were going south anyhow—now we've got a destination." While their circuit took them through the territory on a regular basis, they often changed their route when an incident required their attention.

They had ridden for about an hour when Lucas came to an abrupt halt and waved silently for Shane to stop as well. Two ghosts stood in the middle of the highway, spirits Lucas could see but Shane could not.

"Ghosts?" Shane asked quietly, guessing from Lucas's reaction.

Lucas nodded. He'd always been able to see ghosts, but Before, the appearances had been rare, usually only in dire moments. For obvious reasons, that ability wasn't one he publicized to his colleagues or superiors as a US Marshal, although Shane had known about Lucas's "gift" since they were children.

One of the spirits that blocked their way was a middle-aged man. The other was a teenage boy. Both bore the head wounds that had killed them. The ghosts stood in the middle of the highway, but Lucas felt no threat. Instead, their gestures and worried expressions conveyed a warning.

"Those brigands Jon and Devon mentioned? I think they might be up ahead."

"We're close to the state game lands," Shane replied. "You think it's Dan Metheney's preppers, the guys we ran into before?"

Lucas nodded. "Yeah. They were the first ones who came to mind."

When everything fell apart, the natural cooperation that fostered civilization's rise showed itself more often than reality TV had predicted. People banded together to evacuate after floods and wildfires, forming convoys to reach safer locations, working together to rebuild. Lucas and Shane were on the front lines and had been impressed and surprised time and again when people had shown their better natures.

But some didn't. Groups that had been suspicious and protective before the Event grew even more defensive and insular. Those who had long predicted the end of modern civilization had almost been elated to have their warnings prove true, although no one had really foreseen the way the end happened when it came.

Those groups focused on protecting their territory, sure that everyone meant to take what they had stored up. Lucas noticed these groups didn't seem to mind taking what others had.

Dan Metheney's group had caused problems long before the Event. Metheney headed up a group of local bad boys who had rap sheets as long as their arms, on everything from arson to assault. Authorities had been busting them since their high school days, but nothing ever seemed to stick that was serious enough to send them away for long, or make them leave the area. When everything fell apart, Metheney and his followers turned cultish. More than once, Lucas and Shane had to intervene.

Now, if they were waylaying travelers and, even worse, killing them, the Marshals had no choice but to put a stop to the problem. Lucas, in particular, had very little patience with Metheney's preppers.

"I thought they'd be smart enough not to cause problems again, after what happened last time."

"Yeah, well. Guess they're not as smart as you thought they were." Six months ago, Lucas and Shane had caught men from the preppers enclave who were harassing other enclaves and trying to steal from nearby towns that weren't abandoned. The two Marshals had given the men a beat-down they should have remembered and returned them to the prepper compound with a stern warning to the leaders. A warning that obviously hadn't been taken to heart.

"How do you want to do this?" Shane asked.

Lucas considered the options. He expected to be outnumbered, but he didn't know by how many. The preppers had stockpiled everything they expected to need after a crash, which most certainly included ammunition. And unlike Lucas and Shane, who had to carefully conserve their scarce bullets while traveling hundreds of miles through dangerous territory, the preppers rarely had to defend their compound against real threats. That meant they would also likely be outgunned.

In the old days, carjacking or highway crimes would have been the responsibility of other branches of law enforcement. Now, Shane and Lucas were often the only representatives in their territory, like the sheriffs of the Old West. And aside from the local authorities that survived in small towns and enclaves, the two Marshals were also the only remaining vestige of a larger government that had, for all practical purposes, utterly collapsed.

"I think we need to see what we're dealing with," Lucas replied. "And be ready to put a stop to it—permanently."

They tied up their horses in a small grove just off the road where their mounts would be hidden from view. Lucas and Shane took a variety of weapons—crossbows, swords, and shotguns—since they didn't know how many of the brigands they might be facing. Then they split up, one on each side of the road, moving stealthily through the scrub brush.

The ghosts' warning had stopped them just a mile from where an improvised roadblock of tree trunks and wooden crates barricaded both lanes of traffic. The brigands sat around a campfire in front of canvas tents, a camp that looked like it had been in place for a while and was intended to last for a while.

Lucas couldn't see Shane, but the teenage boy's ghost gave him an idea of where his partner was in the underbrush. The older man guided Lucas, bringing him to a spot behind the camp where recently disturbed ground revealed several shallow graves.

"Fuck," Lucas muttered. He had debated how to deal with the robbers, but proof that they were killing travelers made the decision for him. They needed to be stopped—and the prepper compound needed to be sent a message.

He crept closer and got his first look at the killers. They wore camouflage fatigues, although Lucas doubted any of them had ever been in the military. Four men, three of whom who looked to be barely in their twenties, and an older guy, their leader, probably in his forties. The men had buzzed haircuts, muscular builds that likely owed a nod to 'roids, and a cockiness that immediately set Lucas's teeth on edge.

"Been too quiet," one of the men said. A jug of what Lucas guessed was some kind of home brew sat beside his dented lawn chair.

"Maybe it's time to change locations," another man said, reaching for the jug. "Maybe word got out."

"How?" The older man gave the speaker a look. "There wasn't anyone left to tell the tale." The others chuckled, and Lucas felt anger tighten his gut. The group of four men had eight horses, giving Lucas to suspect they had killed at least four travelers, perhaps more if any had been on foot. A haphazard pile of knapsacks, duffel bags, and other belongings beside one of the tents suggested the spoils.

In the old days, Lucas abided by due process. Now, he had two ghosts' bearing witness to their murders, and evidence of more crimes. In the rough justice that survived, that was enough. Shane was waiting on him, willing to follow his lead. Lucas decided it was time to end the problem.

He fired once with the crossbow, putting a bolt through the neck of the leader. The man fell clutching at the quarrel, a look of shock on his face. Before the others could react, Lucas followed that up with a blast from his shotgun, catching the nearest man in the torso. A second later, Shane's arrow took the third man through the chest. The last of the men looked around wildly.

"Ken? Billy? Oh, God. Jason? Oh, my god," the fourth man cried out, panicking. Any sympathy Lucas had for him had vanished when he'd seen the shallow graves.

Shane's shotgun blast hit its target, and the last of the brigands collapsed in a bloody pile atop his fellow robbers.

Lucas waited before showing himself, in case the robbers had friends who might come in response to the attack. But after a few minutes, he decided the four men had been on their own.

A glance at the pitiful stash next to the tent made Lucas furious. He'd already made up his mind as Shane came out of concealment and jogged to meet him.

"Go cut saplings," Lucas snapped as he drew his sword.

Shane cocked his head, trying to figure out what Lucas had planned. "Lucas—"

"I'm going to make sure everyone knows what happens to highwaymen," Lucas replied in a tight voice.

"The preppers probably have AKs," Shane said. "Think about this carefully."

"That's the only reason I'm not planning to march up to their gates," Lucas said in a tight voice. "Go."

Shane walked away, but he was still close enough to cringe at the sound as Lucas brought his sword down and severed the leader's head. When he finished with the others, he left the bodies where they lay and went to break down the roadblock. Shane returned after a while with four sturdy saplings, whittled to have sharp points on either end.

"Pretty sure there's nothing in the rules about leaving the heads of your enemies on pikes," Shane said as Lucas stuck the first shaft into the ground beside the tent.

"Pretty sure the rules were written when there were more than two Marshals for three whole fuckin' states." Lucas couldn't hide his anger, and he knew Shane understood the frustration of not having caught the killers earlier, not being able to be everywhere at once, to protect the people who had already lived through the collapse of their world.

"I'll sink the pikes. You can deal with the heads," Shane said, wrinkling his nose in disgust. It wasn't just the gore, Lucas knew. They had field dressed enough deer in the last three years. But they both knew this was different, that the predators they had killed had still been human, no matter how twisted. And the fact that they'd come to this was just more proof of how far the world had fallen, and them with it.

Lucas slung the bodies over the dead men's horses, tying them onto the saddles. Then he sent the horses galloping with a smack to the rump, shouting and waving his arms to make sure they headed back where they came from. Afterward, he and Shane cleaned up as best they could using a few cast-off shirts.

"What about the stuff?" Shane asked with a nod toward the robbers' loot and the raiders' campsite.

"Leave it. Someone will make use of it," Lucas said, not wanting anything that belonged to either the killers or their victims. He saw enough ghosts as it was.

"You saw something, with your Gift, didn't you?" Lucas asked with a glance at his partner, who had gone along with their plan more readily than Lucas expected. Not that Shane wouldn't have agreed in the end, but Lucas knew that his partner still clung to a desire for something better than the rough-and-ready frontier justice that sufficed after the end of the world as they once knew it.

Shane nodded. "I...had a vision. I saw how they died. They begged for their lives. Offered to ride away and never tell anyone. Ken, the leader, still killed them." His expression grew hard. "They deserved what we gave them, and more."

"Fuck, yeah. You should be proud of me. I really want to ride over to their compound and go Waco on their asses."

Shane gave a bitter chuckle. "They've got AKs, Lucas. AR-15s. Hell, probably grenade launchers and bazookas. If they didn't already own an armory before things went to hell, they probably bought or stole enough weapons afterward to hold off a whole fuckin' platoon." He looked at the blood-soaked ground and the heads on pikes like ghoulish road signs. "I think you've made your point."

Shane didn't see ghosts, but Lucas did. The older man and the teenage boy were joined by six more ghosts, and Lucas had a feeling they were not all of Ken's victims, just the ones who hadn't moved on. The man's ghost took in the savage message of the heads on pikes, and looked saddened, but not outraged. His gaze shifted to Lucas, and then he nodded in acknowledgment. In the next breath, the ghosts faded from view.

"I think the ghosts are at peace now," Lucas said, knowing that Shane would have guessed why he seemed to be staring into space. "I think some of them couldn't move on until the killing stopped, and a few of them were trying to warn people off."

"I hope you're right," Shane said as they walked back to their horses. "They've been through enough." He left it unsaid that the same was true for all of them.

CHAPTER FOUR

"What?" Lucas asked. "You've been distracted since we left the ghosts behind. You haven't said a word for hours."

"Nothing. It's just—" Shane started, then stopped speaking and shook his head.

"What?"

Shane looked away, uncomfortable. "I keep hearing songs in my head."

"Good thing, because the radio doesn't work anymore."

Shane gave him the stink eye. "Not funny. It's different. The song isn't a regular song. Not like something I heard and remembered. More like birds or whales or..." He let his voice drift off. "It's hard to explain."

Lucas frowned. "You think it has something to do with your visions?"

"Don't know. It changes. Sometimes it's soothing. Other times, I could swear it's agitated, like it's trying to warn me." He finally turned to Lucas. "Right before we split up to track the preppers, it got very... jittery. Discordant."

"I didn't used to be able to see ghosts as much. Maybe you're growing into a new part of your abilities," Lucas replied. He could see that Shane felt uncomfortable admitting the oddity. "Hell, you've seen what the world is like now. Ghosts. Monsters. Shifters. Vamps. So is it possible your psychic hotline is picking up on a new frequency? Why not?"

Shane managed a slight smile that looked both grateful and self-conscious. "Thanks. I'm still trying to figure it out, but I don't think ignoring it is an option."

"Have you found a pattern?" Lucas asked.

"I notice it more when we're around park land and less when we're in towns or cities. But that might just be because there's less to distract me."

They headed south, stopping when Lucas spotted a small pond where they could clean up and wash the blood away. The farther they went, the darker the sky became as heavy gray clouds began to roll in.

"Looks like we've got something coming in from the northwest," Lucas noted, pointing to where the clouds were darkest.

"Think we can make it to Cooper's Lake? I don't really want to get soaked and sleep rough."

Lucas eyed the storm clouds. "Maybe. It's been moving in quickly. Pick up the pace, we might make it."

The horses didn't seem to mind, and Lucas wondered if they, too, could sense the coming rain. The temperature had dropped since they set out that morning, and the wind started to blow. Shane had grown quiet, and Lucas saw him put fingers to his temple.

"Headache?"

Shane nodded. "Yeah. But...it's the song again. It went away for a while, after the preppers. But the farther south we go, the louder it gets. And...it's different. I don't know whether that means it's coming from somewhere else or it has a new meaning. Or...maybe I'm just imagining the whole thing."

Lucas doubted that, given how uncomfortable Shane looked. They'd known each other all their lives, and Lucas had never seen Shane exaggerate or make up symptoms, not even to get out of the worst duties. Shane had always had a bit of the Sight about him, even before the Events brought his gift to the fore. Lucas had always trusted his own intuition, and with all the changes the Events had wrought, he'd come to accept that the world had become a different place and that the rules were permanently different.

Two miles out from Cooper's Lake, Lucas knew they were in trouble. The wind had grown strong enough to lash their clothing, and the cold rain felt like needles. Their horses moved faster on their own accord. Lucas had glimpsed several ghosts along the road, and those that appeared to be more than faded remnants gestured in warning for the travelers to find shelter.

"The song is practically screaming in my head," Shane yelled above the rain. "We've got to get off the road. It's going to be bad."

Just then, the wail of an air raid siren cut through the howl of the wind. Lucas knew that some communities had dug their antique manual sirens out of basements and museums when the grid went down. The sound sent a chill down his spine.

"Ride for it!" he shouted, digging his heels into Shadow's ribs. The stallion needed no further urging, and lunged forward, with Shane and Red close behind.

They reached the gates of the Cooper's Lake stockade, drenched and shivering as the wind howled and the siren caterwauled. The sky overhead had turned a greenish black, and gusts were strong enough to rock them in their saddles.

"US Marshals, asking for sanctuary," Lucas said, fighting his chattering teeth, as he fished out his badge for the sentry. The man looked equally miserable in his leather cape and broad-brimmed hat.

"I need permission from the king—"

"Tell King Kevin that Lucas and Shane are here. Hurry, before we die."

Moments later, the stockade's gate opened to let them in, and they rode into the Kingdom of Butler Highlands.

For decades, the Organization of Historic Interpreters, a large group of medieval re-enactors, had camped each summer at Cooper's Lake. They took great pride in preserving old ways of cooking, making clothing, spinning cloth, forging steel—pretty much all the day-to-day tasks of a medieval household. The more adventurous donned homemade armor and fought mock battles. That knowledge and the skills they honed came in handy when the modern world suddenly stopped working.

The flags of the kingdom flapped wildly, nearly tearing from their posts. Since the Events, the kingdom had expanded, taking up the entire five-hundred-acre campground. A wooden stockade fence ran the perimeter of the grounds. Permanent homes made of stone, daub, and wattle, scavenged bricks, and wood replaced the tents popular when the gathering was just for fun. Some of the dwellings had even been dug into the hillsides. Like the Amish, the residents of the kingdom chose to live with the limited technology of a long-ago era, accepting a lack of electricity and internet and going on about their lives.

The captain of the guards came running toward them. "Marshals. Welcome. His Majesty will want to see you. I'll take you there myself." He glanced at their mounts. "And of course, we'll provide food and water for your horses. Leave them with my men, and they'll be cared for."

Lucas and Shane left their horses and followed their escort toward the unassuming building that served as the palace. It looked more like a bunker, made of cement block, painted white, with square towers on either end that served as watch posts. Flags and banners were the only adornments, besides a mural on the entry walls that showed what the gathering at Cooper's Lake had looked like Before.

A glorious mismatch of furnishings of all styles and colors filled the public rooms of the large, one-story building. The palace housed a court-room, a council chamber, a few offices, the king's small apartment, and a large gathering room.

Kevin Henderson had been a tenured history professor in medieval studies Before. He'd been a long-time member of the Organization of Historic Interpretation, and one of the local group's leaders. Between his even temperament and his somewhat encyclopedic knowledge of how rulers had governed—for better and worse—Kevin had been elected king, by unanimous vote.

Now, the King of Butler Highlands looked more like a harried disaster relief organizer than a monarch. He wore a loose tunic over a pair of khaki pants and work boots. Collar-length, graying dark hair was mussed, as if he'd run his hands through it in frustration. He pushed his gold wire-rimmed glasses up his nose as he spoke to the people gathered around him, who were ready to head out into the storm.

"Make sure the people in more fragile housing come to the palace or go into the tunnels," Kevin ordered. "And the others need to shelter in place. Clear the open areas. Close the storm shutters. Consider it an emergency."

"How can we help, Your Majesty?" Lucas asked.

Kevin looked relieved at their offer. "Shane and Lucas—I can't say that I'm sorry the storm brought you to us. We'll need all the help we can get. Go with the guards. Get people to safety. We've always got folks who don't want to believe the warnings."

The wind drove the rain sideways. Bells clanged and sirens screamed in warning, loud enough to be heard over the storm. Lucas and Shane darted through the rain, soaked to the skin, to escort stragglers to shelter.

Lucas had to lean against the wind to keep moving, at enough of an angle that if the storm stopped suddenly, he would have fallen flat on his face. It reminded him of the time he and Shane had ridden out a hurricane in Miami when they were babysitting a key witness in a drug cartel case.

Only then, they'd been on the coast, where storms like this were normal. But increasingly violent storms were part of the domino effect of the Events, one disaster creating another. And the first, initial Cataclysm had wiped out FEMA and the communication and power grid, so surviving relief efforts were quickly overwhelmed. Since then, every area had been on its own to face increasingly volatile weather.

The wind snapped a tall wooden tent support with a crack like gunfire, and Lucas flinched. He and Shane trod through rapidly rising water toward a mother and two children who were soaked to the skin and struggling against the wind. Lucas took the children—one on his back and one in his arms—while Shane wrapped an arm around the woman's waist to keep her on her feet as they guided them to shelter. As soon as they handed off the family, they headed back outside.

Rain fell in gray sheets, and hail clattered on rooftops as the temperature fell. Across the compound, Lucas saw men struggling to get horses, donkeys, and cows into barns, while others attempted to herd the sheep and goats.

Before the Events, when Cooper's Lake was a summer campground, and the Organization held a two-week re-enactment, most of the participants lived in big canvas tents, making the grounds look like a scene from a medieval movie drama. When the kingdom became a permanent enclave, the re-enactors worked together to gradually replace the tents and portable shelters with more solid buildings.

The storm was testing the strength of the enclave's construction.

Lucas knew that anything built after the Events was strictly do-it-yourself, without inspectors or building codes, or professional crews. If the wind and hail didn't do damage, the rush of flood water as the storm gullies swelled past capacity was likely to strain even well-built dwellings.

"Shit!" Lucas cried out, flinching as a wooden house groaned and then collapsed.

"You think anyone's in there?" Shane yelled over the howling wind.

"We'd better check." Lucas struggled against the wind, with Shane right behind him. He had to walk at an angle to stay on his feet, and the rain lashed his skin, as bits of hail stung where they hit.

He and Shane fought their way toward the wreckage, and Lucas heard a thin wail, barely audible above the wind.

"I heard something!" he yelled to Shane. They waded into the wreckage, shouting to let survivors know they were nearby. A woman's scream cut through the storm, guiding Lucas and Shane toward a front room. They began to dig, throwing broken boards and splintered supports out of the way, until they could make out a shape beneath the wreckage. Part of a wall had fallen, with debris on top, but Lucas figured that they might be able to lift a section of a wooden door to get to the people trapped underneath.

"We can't clear all of this away—the pieces are too big," Shane warned.

Lucas nodded. "Okay. You hold up this end of the door, and I'll go under to get them out." He sized up the opening, hoping he could fit through and make an escape passage. Shane put his back and shoulders into lifting up a section of debris, and Lucas crouched down to fit underneath. He spotted a woman and a small child huddled next to a desk that had kept the wall from crushing them but had also blocked their escape.

"Come with me." Lucas held out his hand.

A boy who looked to be about seven years old scrambled past him, and Lucas grabbed the woman's arm. "Are you hurt?" he asked. She shook her head. "Then come on. We don't have much time."

At first, he feared that she might have been pinned by other debris, but then she got on her hands and knees and crawled toward him.

"Hurry up!" Shane shouted. "I can't hold this much longer!"

Lucas grabbed the woman's wrist and pulled her to him, wrapping himself around her as he hustled her out. Just after they cleared the wreckage, Shane let go, and the door slammed down with a crash.

"Come on," Lucas said, holding on to the woman and child tightly. "We need to get you to shelter."

By the time they reached the palace, the public areas and gathering room were filled with frightened, rain-soaked people huddling together by the fireplace. Kevin was in the midst of the chaos, directing kitchen workers to dole out portions of soup and other volunteers to distribute blankets.

"Is this everyone?" Lucas asked dubiously. The room was full, but not crowded enough to account for all the residents of the kingdom.

King Kevin shook his head. "No. Just the ones whose houses might not stand up to the storm. The others stayed where they were, and some went down below, into the bunker that connects to the old mine tunnels." He sighed. "There've been two casualties, both hit with flying debris. I really miss the old days, when storms weren't usually life or death situations."

"What can we do?" Shane asked.

Kevin chuckled. "Nothing much left to do except try to make them comfortable and ride out the storm," he said. "I apologize, but I had to give away the guest room. Mine, too. So we'll all just have to find a nice spot on the floor for the night."

Lucas and Shane pitched in, helping to reunite families that had been separated by the storm, or giving a hand as volunteers passed out blankets and cold provisions, while the storm raged outside. Children cried, and adults talked in hushed tones.

Finally, when there was nothing else to be done, Lucas and Shane found an empty spot in the back hallway and sank to the floor with their backs to the wall.

"You know, I don't think I could do it," Lucas said. "Live like the Amish at Green Farm or the folks here. It's one thing to go without the conveniences because we have to, because the system broke. But if I could have them back again—"

"I'd take it in a New York minute," Shane agreed. "But then again, you didn't exactly enjoy roughing it, even when we were deployed."

"You have a job, you do it. But man, some of those guys—like

Wisnewski, remember him? I swear he wanted to get in touch with his inner caveman. He was actually *disappointed* when we went back to base."

"He's probably doing just fine now," Shane replied. "Or, he got what he thought he could handle but couldn't, and he's holed up crying in the corner somewhere, losing his shit."

They were silent for a few moments. "What do you think about this Raven Rock 'Site R' stuff?" Lucas asked.

Shane shrugged. "Sounds suspicious for them to just go dark. I think we should look into it. But it might not end up being anything unusual. They could have gotten sick and died out. Or something might have gone wrong with the bunker, and they had to leave. All those things have happened to other groups."

"It just seems strange, in a location like that," Lucas mused. "I mean, if it was intended as a safe haven for the D.C. brass, you'd think it would have medical facilities and all the best supplies."

"There's enough weird stuff going on, I don't think anyone could have anticipated everything that could happen," Shane replied. "The weather's never acted like this since people started keeping records. Places that didn't use to get earthquakes get them now. And some of the diseases that mutated..."

"I get the point." Lucas didn't like to think about the changes more than the job required, which was far beyond what he sometimes thought his sanity could handle.

Were we the lucky ones to survive this long? Maybe the truly lucky got a fast death, instead of a slow one. Lucas tried to shift his thoughts away from the shadows that haunted his dreams. They had a job to do, a purpose that mattered. And considering how many people had lost everyone they cared about to the apocalypse, Lucas counted himself damn fortunate to still have Shane fighting beside him.

"You know, this isn't the worst place we've ridden out a storm," Lucas said, his voice thick with exhaustion.

"Definitely not," Shane replied. Lucas knew his partner remembered all too well taking refuge in caves, basements, and abandoned buildings that even the rats had deserted, back in the early days right after the Events.

Lucas's stitches ached, he felt their ride in every muscle, and he'd twisted his back getting the woman and her child to safety. His clothing was still damp enough to chafe. *Thank fuck for wool—still holds warmth.* Lucas let his head fall back, making himself as comfortable as he could and fell asleep before he could complain about Shane's snoring.

In his dreams, Lucas saw the hotel room of the Holiday Inn Express near Youngstown where he and Shane were holed up for the night with the witness they were escorting. They'd pulled over in a snowstorm bad enough that Lucas didn't want to push his luck, even with the four-wheel drive on their Chevy Suburban SUV.

The room was comfortable, in a practical, no-frills sort of way. They'd gone to a drive-through before the storm got too bad and raided the snacks at the hotel's small convenience store before they hunkered down for the night. Two beds, one for the witness, and one that Lucas and Shane would take turns sleeping in while the other stood watch.

He'd turned on the TV while they ate, too tired from driving to flip channels away from the news station that came on automatically. Lucas remembered that he was eating a bag of barbecued potato chips when everything changed.

Their government-issued, secure cell phones both went off with an emergency signal at the same time. Shane and Lucas exchanged a worried look, reaching for their phones in unison.

"Washington is under attack. Do not come in. Repeat, do not come in. Find a secure location outside of a city center and await further instructions."

"Oh my God!" Vinnie Scarpelli, their witness, pointed at the TV screen, pale as a dead fish. Lucas and Shane turned to watch footage of buildings crumbling in the nation's capital, as the bombs went off...

Lucas jerked awake, sweating and heaving for breath, disoriented for a moment until he remembered where he was. He closed his eyes and took a deep breath, trying to block out the ache that the dream always brought, the longing for a normality they had taken for granted and would never have again. No matter how often the dreams came, snippets of his life Before, the feeling of loss never dimmed.

The big room was dark, filled with the sound of steady breathing and the smell of wet clothing. Outside, the storm still roared, battering the cement-block building with hail that sounded like gunfire as it pelted the roof.

Shane's troubled murmurs roused Lucas, and he looked toward where his friend sat beside him, twitching in a restless sleep. Shane's deep frown and his worried tone told Lucas his partner's dreams were uneasy.

"Hey," he said quietly, bumping Shane's shoulder. "Wake up."

Shane didn't wake, and he kept on mumbling, growing more agitated. Lucas moved to crouch in front of him and took Shane by the shoulders, shaking him gently. "Come on. Wake up."

Shane woke with a gasp, like a swimmer rising out of the water and nearly out of air. "What?" he asked, not quite awake.

"You had a bad dream. So did I. But you were mumbling, and it didn't look like fun."

Shane shook his head as if he were trying to clear water from his ears. "I just...it wasn't a dream."

"Another vision," Lucas said, worried. "Is the song back?"

"Yeah, but it's different," Shane said. "Louder here than before, and it blends with the sound of the storm."

"You're getting the visions more often."

Shane looked away, then nodded. "Yeah. I didn't say anything because it didn't seem important. And it still might not be. I mean, we've seen some weird shit since everything changed. Maybe my brain is just trying to process it."

"But your 'intuition' has been getting stronger, and I've seen more ghosts," Lucas countered. "I don't think we can just brush it off."

He shifted to see Shane better. "Try to remember the dream. What happened?"

Shane took a deep breath and closed his eyes. "We were on a trail, going into the woods. I didn't recognize where we were, but it looked like a park. And I felt like there was a voice, speaking to me, just beyond the range I could hear what it was saying. That's it. I didn't feel threatened, just that it called to me."

"I was going to suggest going to see the witches in Bedford, to find out if they picked up anything about Raven Rock. I think they'd be the perfect ones to ask about the 'songs' you're hearing," Lucas said.

Shane shrugged uncomfortably. "Maybe. I guess. We'll see. Seems kinda unimportant, with everything else that's going on."

"It's on the way to Gettysburg, and we'll need a place to re-provision," Lucas argued.

"The witches still give me the creeps," Shane admitted.

Lucas raised an eyebrow. "You get visions. I see ghosts. I think we passed creepy a long time ago."

CHAPTER FIVE

By morning, the storm had passed. Worried residents climbed stiffly from their sleeping spots on the floor and ventured out to see what the winds and water had made of their enclave. Kevin was busy from daybreak, directing efforts to clear away the damage and determine how much would require rebuilding.

"We can stay for a while if you need extra hands," Lucas offered.

Kevin shook his head. "Thank you, but you've got more important things to do, and we have plenty of folks to do the work." He sighed, looking out over the wet and windswept "kingdom." "So far, it's just some roofs gone, a couple of older wooden buildings down. Two casualties. It could have been much worse."

"Have you had any other visitors?" Shane asked. "News?"

Kevin nodded. "Had a couple of peddlers through here a week or two ago. What they'd heard from New England isn't good. Early winter blizzards and rising storm surge. Anyone who hadn't pulled inland before doesn't have much choice now."

"We've heard similar about much of the coast," Lucas said.

"So I've been told." Kevin sighed. "I'm also hearing reports of some enclaves going dark. No one's been out to confirm. But we haven't been able to raise them on the shortwave radio, or the emergency telegraph."

"If you know the locations of the enclaves you've lost touch with, we can check in on them if our route takes us that way," Lucas offered.

Kevin rattled off some names, and Lucas jotted them down. "It'll take us a bit with the circuit we ride, but we'll see what we can find out," he promised. "And we'll give these locations to the IT Priests. If there's a college nearby, they can pass the word along and get someone to check."

"Thank you. I'm glad you paid us a visit, even if the storm drove you here," Kevin said. "We do all right; I shouldn't complain, and I'm not, really. But we're cut off these days, like everyone. It's nice to hear that there's a world outside the stockade."

"Not as much of one as there used to be, but plenty of people doing their fucking best to survive," Shane replied.

Kevin nodded gravely. "So say we all."

"It's louder here. Are you sure you can't hear anything?" Shane asked after they'd ridden a short distance from Cooper's Lake.

Lucas shook his head. "I don't hear anything except birds. But does it matter that you keep saying you hear something when we're in a forest or near parkland? Because we're coming up on Moraine."

"Maybe. I don't have any idea," Shane admitted.

Lucas shrugged. "I figured we should stop in to see how Mitchell was doing, anyhow, since we're riding past. Maybe he'll know something about it."

Shane looked uncomfortable but nodded. "I guess it couldn't hurt."

Moraine State Park's rolling hills had been shaped long ago by glaciers, leaving behind a lake and beautiful scenery. Shane and Lucas rode into what had been the main parking lot. RVs and vehicles parked along the edges, and soggy tents filled the campsites, people who had left everything behind except for what they could pack and ended up here. The park had basic facilities, and a stocked lake, so Lucas guessed there were worse places to sit out the end of the world.

Lucas and Shane tethered their horses and went to the office. Park Ranger Mitchell Wilson greeted them with a surprised smile when he answered the door.

"Lucas and Shane—what an unexpected pleasure. Come on in. I've got a fire going and a hot pot of coffee. You need anything for your horses?"

Lucas shook his head. "They'll be fine. We can't stay long, just wanted to check in—and ask a couple of questions."

"I'm happy for the company. This way," Mitchell said, gesturing for them to follow him into the cozy lobby of the ranger station. Mitchell shared the station as both office and living quarters with another ranger, and they took turns with the outdoor work. "Jim's out checking the trails," he said, referencing his fellow ranger. "We had plenty of limbs down and trail washouts after the storm. We put up as many of the tent folks in the recreation building as we could to ride out the worst of it. There's going to be a lot of work to do to clean up. It's hard to keep up on the maintenance."

"Can't you press some of your squatters...I mean, residents, into working off their use fee?" Shane asked as Mitchell poured coffee for all of them.

"Oh, I do," Mitchell assured him. "But not all of them are up to the work. We get by," he added with a shrug. "Now, what brings you this way?"

"We've heard that people passing by think there's something different about the park," Shane ventured, fudging a little about his own experience. "Almost a sense that calls to them. Have you heard anything like that?"

Mitchell sat back, cradling his coffee. "Now that's interesting," he replied. "Truth is, those of us who chose to work the parks always felt a bit of that. Where we've felt it the strongest, we applied to be posted. Haven't you ever heard people say that a location 'spoke' to them?"

"I guess so," Lucas agreed reluctantly. "But I didn't mean it literally."

Mitchell nodded. "You might not have, but many cultures think that there are nature spirits. Maybe there's something to all that, and the shake-up from the Events means the spirits can be heard again.

"All I can tell you is that I loved Moraine from the first time I laid eyes on it, like I found somewhere I should have always been. Jim said he felt the same way. So, was it just a combination of all the features we always wanted or did the park 'claim' us? I don't know. I'm just glad to be here, even with all the shit going on outside."

They spent another hour catching Mitchell up on what they had seen and passing along a warning about the prepper activities. Mitchell filled them in on what the refugees who had taken up residence in the park told him about the places they came from. Some of the information was true, but Shane and Lucas knew much of it was hearsay, exaggerated, or just plain wrong.

"We need to get going," Lucas said after they had finished their coffee. "Still have to get to Bedford."

"Glad you stopped in," Mitchell replied, setting his cup aside. "Do me a favor, and if you see any peddlers on the road, send them this way. We do all right for food, but things like pots and pans, knives, and that sort of thing are in short supply."

"Will do," Shane promised, and they headed back to their mounts.

"So?" Lucas asked as they swung up to their saddles. "Did the park say anything to you?"

Shane rolled his eyes. "Fuck you."

"That's a strange thing for the park to say," Lucas replied. "Since it doesn't even know me."

"Maybe it's all-seeing," Shane said as they headed back to the road. "And it already knows how annoying you can be."

"Is that a no?" Lucas pressed.

"I'm not sure," Shane answered. "It's hard to put into words. The whole time we were talking with Mitchell, I could swear I heard faint singing, just at the edge of what I could make out."

"Do you think there's something to what he said, about places having a spirit?"

"Lots of cultures believe that," Shane said.

"When we get to Old Bedford, I bet the witches will know," Lucas replied. "Folks like them have to know something about nature spirits."

"If they don't, the scholars will," Shane said. "You know, with all the shit that's happened, one of the good things is seeing the historic villages come back to life."

"Don't forget we're heading to Gettysburg," Lucas warned. "That's one location I really could do without seeing come back to how it used to be."

Living history museums, like Old Bedford Village, had been uniquely ready to weather the end of modern civilization. Since the sites were dedicated to preserving and teaching the old ways of living, the volunteers and staff had the skills necessary to survive when the outside world collapsed. The Old Bedford folks moved into the historic homes and brought the museum back to life as a real village, working the land, raising animals, and using what they'd learned about old skills like weaving and forging iron. Already a magnet for history buffs, the old sites also tended to attract covens and academics that needed a new home.

Did those sites also have a spirit, and did it call to the witches and scholars? Lucas wondered. Now that Shane and Mitchell had raised the question, Lucas found he couldn't stop thinking about it.

They fell into their usual companionable silence as they road. The highway was empty aside from themselves, making it seem all the more desolate, an eight-lane throughway with no traffic. Just in case, they had weapons handy. Lucas kept his crossbow slung over his shoulder and his quarrels within reach, while Shane had a large machete in a sheath on his belt and a selection of throwing knives in a bandolier slung across his chest. Their shotguns were handy, and the rest of their weapons and ammunition were in the saddlebags. In the dead stretches between settlements, they'd learned the hard way that anything could be lurking —human, animal, or something much worse.

Lucas was just happy that the rain held off. It would take more than three days to reach Old Bedford, and Lucas really didn't want to be hunkered down against bad weather for the whole time. They spent the first night in an abandoned house, and the second in a sturdy barn, and as evening loomed on the third night, Lucas found himself hoping to find a place that was both dry and warm.

"You know what we were saying about places having a vibe to them?" Shane asked. "If that's true, then I don't like what I'm sensing from this hollow. Let's pick up the pace. It feels...wrong."

Lucas had looked over to Shane as he spoke. When he turned his attention back to the road, he saw a young girl standing in the middle of the highway.

"Whoa!" He pulled in on the reins sharply, and Shane did the same.

"What?" Shane asked. "What's the problem?"

Lucas pointed at the girl. "Don't you see her?" The girl waved her arms, and while she remained silent, the message of warning was clear.

"There's no one there, Lucas," Shane replied. "I think it's one of your sightings. All the more reason for us to get gone."

The ghost girl vanished as Shane spoke, proving his point.

"Then I second your heebie-jeebies and vote we find a place to hole up, pronto."

"Heads up!" Shane warned, as the pounding of hoof beats sounded just over the rise ahead.

Four men on horseback crested the hill, riding abreast. Three of them carried swords, and the fourth had a rifle. They stopped, blocking the highway.

"Stop right there," the leader said. "We don't want trouble. Just leave us your saddlebags and your horses, and we'll let you walk away, no hard feelings."

CHAPTER SIX

"Fᴜᴄᴋ ʏᴏᴜ," Lucas replied. "Not going to happen."

The man with the rifle brought it up to his shoulder. "You might want to reconsider."

Shane's throwing knife embedded itself deep in the rifleman's bicep, and the thief screamed, dropping the weapon. The other three robbers rode forward, swords raised. Lucas leveled his crossbow and fired, and the bolt hit the lead rider hard enough to unseat him. The man fell, dead before he hit the ground.

The remaining thieves barely slowed their pace, riding toward Lucas and Shane with a war whoop. Lucas loaded another crossbow bolt and held his position, confident his bolt could reach its mark long before the brigand's sword was in range. Shane pulled a shotgun from its sheath on his saddle and aimed for the man in front, blasting him with a spray of buckshot, sending him toppling from his horse. Lucas's second bolt took the third man through the right shoulder, leaving him alive but wounded.

That left two dead thieves, and two bleeding. Shane racked his gun again, looking down the barrel at the two survivors. "Don't try my patience."

The youngest of the thieves reined in his horse, raising his hands in surrender. "Don't shoot me. I told them this was a bad idea."

"Yeah?" Lucas replied. "And that was before you tried to rob two US Marshals."

The two men paled at that.

"Shit," the younger thief said. He had the crossbow bolt in his shoulder. "I said this was going to be trouble," he griped, turning to the companion with Shane's knife in his arm. "Didn't I? And you thought it would be easy pickings."

"Shut up, Danny."

"This is all your fault!" Danny shouted. "Next time, you'd better goddamn listen when I tell you something won't work!"

Shane glanced at Lucas and rolled his eyes. "All right," Shane ordered. "Get down off your horses, and keep your hands where we can see them. Lie down on the ground, with your hands behind your heads."

"He's gonna shoot us," Danny whined. "Gonna shoot us dead, and you said this was going to be easy!"

"Shut the fuck up, Danny!"

Lucas held his crossbow on the men while Shane kept his shotgun at the ready as he moved among the brigands, kicking their weapons away from them.

"Danny, I'm going to give you some rope, and you're going to tie your buddy nice and tight," Lucas said. "I'll check the knots, so if you try something, I'll know, and you'll be sorry." He pulled several lengths of rope from his saddle bag and tossed them to Danny, not getting close enough for the thief to make a grab for his bow.

"This one's dead," Shane reported, from where he bent over the man with the crossbow bolt in his chest. He paused next to the man he'd gotten with the shotgun. "So is he."

He turned his attention to the two wounded survivors, glancing first at the man with the knife in his bicep. "We need to tie up his wound." He looked at Danny. "Rip a strip of cloth from your shirt and bind his arm up. Don't want him bleeding out on the ride. Once he's tied up, we'll see to your injury."

"Derek and Tom are dead, Ben!" Danny shrilled. "And we're gonna bleed out. All because of you and your fucking bright idea."

"I'm gonna kill you if you don't shut up," Ben, the man with the knife wound, grated.

Danny was so nervous he dropped the rope several times, but he managed to get the knots right, finally. Shane bound up Danny's wound around the quarrel and then tied him up while Lucas covered them. "I'm leaving the arrow in until you get where you're going, to help seal the wound. It's a hunting tip, so it should be easy to take out."

"Are you gonna hang us?" Danny asked, and his voice cracked with the fear.

"We could," Lucas replied, looking as if he was thinking it over. "What do you think?" he asked Shane.

"Not worth the rope," Shane replied, gathering up the weapons. "Although we'd be within our rights."

"You ever heard of the US Marshals?" Lucas asked. Danny shook his head, still face down on the ground. Ben grunted, so scared that he'd pissed himself. "Since the Events, we're the law in our territory. So we can be judge, jury, and executioner."

"I don't wanna die!" Danny wailed. "We haven't done much thieving, I promise. We're new at it, that's why we suck."

"Shut your mouth!" Ben snarled.

"Well, your horses are pretty much crap," Shane said. "Where did you get the swords?"

"My dad used to make them, for Renaissance festivals and conventions," Ben replied grudgingly. "Had them lying all around the house."

"That explains why none of them have a real edge on them." Shane gathered up the swords and leaned down for the rifle. "Aw, fuck. Seriously? It wasn't loaded."

"We figured it would scare you into giving us all your shit," Danny said. He rolled close enough to Ben to give him a swift kick with his bound feet. Ben tried to retaliate but went still and quiet when Shane stuck the tip of a sword against his neck.

"This may not be sharp, but sawing away at you until your head falls off wouldn't be pleasant," Shane promised. "Get my drift?"

"What're you gonna do with us?" Danny asked, and the quaver in his voice made Shane re-evaluate the man's age, guessing him to be in his late teens.

"We're gonna dump you and your crap horses at the next enclave for the sheriff to deal with," Lucas said. "The dead guys, we leave for the vultures, as a warning to the next sons of bitches who decided to loot travelers. We take your weapons, so you aren't tempted to do something like this again—assuming the sheriff doesn't just throw you down a mine shaft and let you rot."

Danny squeaked, looking pale enough to pass out. Ben muttered curses that trailed off into a moan.

Shane patted them down, taking away anything else that could be used as a weapon. Then he and Lucas hoisted the wannabe highwaymen onto their horses, belly down across the saddle, and tied the reins of the dead men's horses to the last saddle. Lucas rode point, and Shane rode behind, making sure neither of the thieves tried to escape.

The sheriff at the next enclave looked none too happy to see them. "What do you want me to do with them?"

"Anything you want," Lucas said. "Thought they might be local, and you'd want to take that into consideration. My partner and I have places to be. Didn't have time to hang them."

"Yeah, they're local," the sheriff replied. "Not the first time they've been in trouble, but they're usually too dumb to pull it off." He glared at the bound men. "I'm thinking I'll put them on work detail, get some use out of them, instead of throwing them a necktie party. We've got some digging and shoveling that suits them just fine. Might be the first honest work they've ever done."

"They're all yours," Shane said, as he and Lucas headed back to the road. He had tied the swords behind his saddle and meant to see if he could give them a working edge with a good whetstone when time permitted. He and Lucas rode in silence until they were back on the road.

"You didn't actually want to hang them." Shane's tone made it a statement, not a question.

"Not particularly," Lucas replied, looking off toward the horizon. "Seen enough death, don't need to see more."

"But the preppers—"

"That was different." Lucas's voice turned hard. "They weren't just going to take someone's coins. They killed. They enjoyed killing. How long until they weren't happy to just wait for travelers to come to them and started raiding the other enclaves?"

"I didn't mind scaring the shit out of this last bunch, but I really didn't want to go through with hanging them, either," Shane agreed.

"As it is, two of them're dead anyhow." Lucas's voice was flat, and

Shane knew that meant the death bothered his partner. "And the guy with the shoulder wound is gonna lose that arm, if he survives."

"Not your fault," Shane replied.

"I shot him. He attacked with a weapon," Lucas said, but it sounded like he was trying to convince himself. They would have been entirely within their mandate to have killed all four of the men, since highway robbery and horse theft had regained their status as capital offenses. Still, Shane felt unsettled over the man's death, and he could tell Lucas did, too.

"I hate when it goes like that."

They rode for a while, and Lucas seemed pensive. Finally, Shane decided to poke the bear. "What's eating you? You're not usually this quiet. I mean, half the time I can't get you to shut up."

Lucas shrugged. "Not sure how I feel about the ghost thing, I guess."

"Oh, so it's okay when I have visions, but you see a ghost, and it's the end of the world?"

Lucas gave him a look. "We've already had the end of the world, dumbass." He paused. "It's just not something I ever really took seriously, you know? I heard about it from my mom and grandma, and I had some experiences I couldn't really explain away, so I just didn't think about them."

"But now, it's happening more often, in ways you can't just write off," Shane supplied.

"Yeah. Just like your 'hunches' and 'intuition' and 'gut feelings' are turning into full crystal-ball-reading style visions."

Shane grimaced. "I have never, ever, used a crystal ball. Wouldn't know what to do with one if I had it—maybe throw it at someone?" He gave Lucas a side glance. "I mean, now that you're a ghost whisperer, are you going to start knocking on tables and talking in funny voices?"

"Shut up," Lucas said, but there was no heat in his voice. Shane grinned. They'd argued far more heatedly over which superheroes could beat each other up. If the world had to fall apart, it was nice to still have his best friend.

They spent the night holed up at what used to be a Motel 6. Shane suspected that the only reason it hadn't been filled by squatters was that half the roof had been torn off. The office had been flattened by a long-ago storm. He and Lucas found a room at the end of the row and considered themselves lucky since they'd slept in much worse accommodations. The carpet wasn't quite as disgusting as Shane expected, which he attributed to the room's windows remaining intact.

Shane's dreams were restless. He heard a new voice and a different song. In the darkness of his dream, Shane couldn't see the body that went with the voice, but he felt the same odd presence he had sensed before.

Hello? he called into the void. *I hear you singing. What are you? And where are you? Why can I hear you?*

The voice kept on singing, but Shane had the feeling the entity behind it had drawn closer, studying him. He didn't feel afraid, just overwhelmingly curious. An image came to mind, of him riding his horse, seen from a distance. More images followed the first. No words, just images, and a song.

Yes, that's me. Can you show me what you look like?

The song continued, but Shane could have sworn it sounded pensive, maybe even melancholy.

Are you the song? You're not showing me what you look like because I can't see you?

The song picked up tempo, sounding more cheerful.

Are you the being from Moraine? Once again, the music slowed. *You're from somewhere close to here?* An upbeat tempo was his answer.

Why contact me if I can't see you?

The music took on a wistful note. Shane felt an overwhelming loneliness sweep over him, choking him up. *You're lonely?* Again, the music shifted to a happier tempo. *And I can sense you, is that it? Most people can't, or they don't sense you strongly enough to communicate?* The music stayed happy.

Thank you, Shane said, as the dream began to waver. He woke in the same position he'd fallen asleep, huddled against the wall. Moonlight streamed in through the deteriorating curtains, giving enough of a glow to see the room around him.

"Bad dream?" Lucas sat in a chair on watch, and of course he'd noticed Shane twitching in his sleep.

Shane shifted, aware that his leg had fallen asleep. If it wasn't time for his watch, he might as well get up anyhow, since he wouldn't be dozing again tonight. "Vision. There's another...entity...nearby. Like at

Moraine, and the other places. It didn't talk to me, but it showed me pictures, and it changed its song to answer my questions."

"It responded to you?" Lucas looked up sharply. Shane nodded.

"Yeah. And not just yes/no answers. It gave me the impression it was lonely." He met Lucas's gaze. "Whatever these entities are, I think they're sentient, and they can understand emotions."

"That's a bit of a stretch, isn't it?"

"Not from what I just saw," Shane replied. "Now I really want to know what the witches have to say. Because there was also that weird feeling I got when the ghost girl showed up on the road, that we were in a bad place. So whatever these energies are, we need to know how to deal with the ones that aren't friendly."

Lucas shifted in the uncomfortable plastic chair. "You think they're dangerous?"

"I don't think they have to be. The one in Moraine didn't seem to be trying to hurt anyone, and neither did the one in my vision. But if they can be strong in good places, maybe they can be just as strong in bad places, and that could be a problem."

"Then let's hope the witches know what the hell is going on," Lucas said, getting up to change places with Shane so he could get some sleep. "Because I sure as fuck don't want to find out the hard way."

CHAPTER SEVEN

THEY REACHED Bedford just after lunch. Before they headed for the restored historic village, Shane convinced Lucas to let him try to sense the presence he had communicated with in his dreams.

"What is this, some kind of supernatural game of Marco Polo?" Lucas asked after they had ridden almost to the other side of town.

"You're not wrong," Shane replied, pulling out of his thoughts. "But I think we're close."

"Wouldn't it be likely to be in a park, or maybe at the restored village?"

Shane shrugged. "I don't know how they pick their places. Maybe those weren't 'sacred' enough."

Lucas's expression was skeptical, but he said nothing as Shane continued to follow a vague gut feeling that he was going in the right direction. He let the horse watch the road for obstacles, making a few course corrections as they went, focused on the song only he could hear. As it grew stronger, Shane felt certain they were headed in the right direction. Finally, when the song grew loud and he sensed the brush of a familiar presence against his mind, he stopped.

"Here?" Lucas asked, sounding genuinely surprised.

Shane pulled himself out of his thoughts and found that he was staring at a giant, silver-painted, three-story building at the edge of a fair-grounds. The building looked like a coffee pot. "Um, I guess so?"

"I've never seen a sacred coffee pot before."

Shane consulted his inner sense, thinking he must have made a mistake, only to hear the song more strongly than ever. The song was loud near the roadside attraction, but even louder directly across the road.

"I remember reading somewhere that the same thing that makes one person build a temple might make another build an amusement park," Shane mused. "They're both places where people transcend their usual, everyday lives."

Lucas laughed. "You mean I could have been on a roller coaster instead of going to Mass? Man, did I get the short end of the stick!"

Shane felt a little chagrined, but he knew he was correct. "Think about it. Some places are supposed to be healthy or lucky, and some get the reputation for having 'bad vibes.' People travel hundreds of miles to go to tourist attractions that make them feel happy, or to see 'natural wonders' that give them a feeling of peace."

"Well, they used to," Lucas replied. "Not so much anymore."

"You know what I mean."

Lucas nudged his horse to ride up beside Shane. "Yeah, yeah. I think I do. And maybe it's not that far-fetched. But dude, a giant coffee pot?"

Shane grinned. "Could have been a giant ball of string. Or a huge cowboy boot. Or a big hollow elephant." He had no idea how those famous attractions had fared after the Events, but part of him hoped they were still standing, a tribute to human whimsy in a world that desperately needed it.

They headed back to the historic village, both deep in thought. The entity Shane had sensed did not try to reach out to him again.

Old Bedford Village had been a historic collection of preserved and restored buildings before the Cataclysm gave it a new life. As a tourist attraction, reenactors dressed in period clothing demonstrated spinning, weaving, and candle making. After the Events, those skills and others like them were in high demand. It hadn't taken much for the docents to move in and put their skills to use. Professors and students from nearby colleges sought refuge, as did townsfolk and a local coven, creating an eclectic mix.

The Pendergrass Tavern was the social heart of the village. The handsome building had a first floor of stacked stone and a log-and-mortar second floor. When the museum had catered to tourists, the tavern had been a working restaurant. Now, it still served as a pub and gathering place.

Lucas led the way. At this hour, just before dusk, the pub was fairly quiet. Shane felt sure it would get busier once full dark fell and people ended their chores. Candles in glass hurricane shades lit each table, and a fire in the fireplace at the end of the common room cast a welcoming glow.

"Two of your ales, and two plowman's meals," Lucas ordered. The bartender returned with two pint glasses of dark, pub-brewed ale, and two wooden boards laden with bread, cheese, sliced ham, pickles, onions, and hard-boiled eggs.

"What brings you two back to Bedford?" Jake, the proprietor of the Pendergrass, asked as he took their money and made change. "Something happen to bring the Marshals our way?"

"Something's always happening, nowadays," Shane replied. "Can you put us up for the night? We got in just before the rain."

"Sure," Jake replied. "Same room you had the last time, twin beds and a washstand. Just remodeled the outhouse behind the pub. Not exactly luxury, but you won't get splinters in your ass."

"Always a good thing," Lucas replied. "How's it going?"

Jake shrugged. "We've had some bad storms through, but I guess that's probably true everywhere. We've gotten good at battening the hatches and hunkering down. This one didn't do as much damage as some, so there's that."

"Your ale is getting better," Shane said, sipping his drink.

Jake grinned. "Good to hear you say so. We've been tinkering with the recipe." Before the Events, Jake had been a chemistry professor and a part-time docent. Now, he put his background to good use with the enclave's brewing, distilling, and winery.

"Generator still working?" Lucas asked.

"Mostly," Jake replied, and paused to pour another round for two customers farther down the bar. "It's pretty much only running the big refrigerator/freezer in the back and the power for the medical center Doc Forrest put in over in the Victorian House," he added. "Pete keeps the generator going on spit and salvaged parts. Of course, it helped that we cleaned out Home Depot after everyone else died off or left town."

"Have you seen Scott Findlay?" Shane asked. "We need to talk to him. Karen Becker, too, if she's around."

Jake raised an eyebrow. "Two US Marshals walk into a bar. They ask to see the boss man and the head witch. Sounds like the start of a bad joke...or a big problem."

"Hopefully, neither," Lucas replied. "Just looking for information right now."

"They're not here," Jake said. "But I can send my busboy, Jimmy, to go fetch them."

"I'd be much obliged." Lucas leaned against the bar and began to pick at the food, and Jake went in the back to send Jimmy on his way.

Shane looked around the pub as Lucas and Jake talked. The patrons looked like something out of a time-travel movie, with some who had worked at the museum preferring to keep their period garb, while others stuck to modern clothing. Shane wondered what their occupations had been prior to the Cataclysm, and what they found themselves doing now.

"You two can go on into the back room with your food, and I'll send Scott and Karen in when they get here," Jake said. They picked up their things to go. "Oh, before I forget," Jake added, "we have a couple of IT Priests who came in last night, asked if we'd seen you. Said they had a message."

Shane and Lucas exchanged a look. "Guess we know where we're headed after this," Lucas said. They thanked Jake and took their food to a small room off the main area, where they settled in at a hand-hewn wooden table.

"Want to bet this has something to do with the IOT breakdown?" Shane asked once they polished off most of their meal.

"Yeah, that's what I think, too," Lucas agreed. "Considering that the universities still have internet? I'm betting Gibbons up at Slippery Rock probably told Tony Brown over at Shippensburg that we were heading this way, and Tony found something out that was important enough to have the priests looking for us."

"I can't say I'm looking forward to Gettysburg," Lucas said, finishing off his last pickle. "Not with the sightings happening more and more."

"Shit," Shane replied. "I hadn't thought about that." Gettysburg was one of the most haunted places in America. Lucas's growing talent for seeing ghosts could make their visit very unpleasant.

"Maybe I can wear some garlic, keep them at bay."

"That's for vampires, not ghosts."

"Didn't do squat with the last vamps we ran into," Lucas replied. "Maybe ghosts are more sensitive to bad breath."

Before Shane could reply, they heard footsteps approaching. Shane looked up and saw Scott Findlay and Karen Becker come into the back room, both looking either worried or annoyed.

"Marshals," Findlay said with a nod, greeting them both with a handshake. Findlay had been the museum director Before and became the mayor of the enclave when the museum village came back to life as a working community. He *looked* like a museum director, Shane thought, with a slight pot belly, a trimmed white beard, and a penchant for mixing period garb and modern pieces that made him look like he'd raided a closet on the TARDIS.

"Shane and Lucas. This is unexpected." Karen Becker resembled a suburban soccer mom more than a powerful witch and head of the local coven. Her dark brown hair was trimmed in a neat bob cut, proving that even the apocalypse couldn't separate some people from their grooming routines, and she wore an Aran wool sweater over jeans and hiking boots under a sensible parka.

Findlay and Karen took seats at the table, and Jake showed up a few minutes later with a fresh round of pints for everyone. Findlay cleared his throat.

"So, what's going on? You weren't just in the neighborhood."

"We're heading south of Gettysburg, where apparently, a big enclave went dark," Lucas said. "But most of all, we wanted to pick your brains about the...entities...that seem to be present in some of the state parks."

"Entities?" Karen asked, leaning forward. "You mean, like ghosts?"

Shane shook his head. "More like an invisible, sentient, empathic presence that sings," he said. *What if she just tells me I'm crazy?*

"Sounds like a genius loci," Findlay said, and Karen nodded. "You've sensed this...entity yourselves?"

"Just me," Shane confessed. "I've been having dreams for a while, on and off, where I heard strange singing. When we went to one of the state parks, I recognized the kind of song, and I've heard it since then—including at the big coffee pot here in Bedford."

Shane braced himself for their laughter. Instead, both Karen and Findlay looked at him like he had suddenly become fascinating.

"You said it was sentient and empathic," Karen pressed. "How do you know?"

Shane recounted his dreams and the encounters with the "songs." As he spoke, Karen worried at her lower lip, deep in thought. She exchanged another glance with Findlay. "It's definitely a genius loci. The nature spirits are waking up."

"What, exactly, is a genius loci?" Lucas asked. "Is it really smart?"

Findlay chuckled. "It's sentient, which is the old meaning to the word. 'Guardian spirit' is probably a better translation, or 'spirit of a place.'" He sounded like he was gearing up for a lecture until Karen laid a hand on his arm.

"It's a type of daemon," Karen continued. "Very old. They were here before we evolved, and they'll be here after we're gone."

"You said these spirits were waking up," Shane asked. "Why did they go to sleep? And why wake up now?"

"The daemons never went away, but the noise and bustle of modern civilization didn't seem to suit them," Karen replied. "Some of them hung on at places like the Grand Canyon, or the biggest tourist attractions. The rest just went to sleep, until their time came again."

"So are they good or bad?" Shane pressed. "Because I've had both impressions, depending on where I was."

"I'm not sure that's exactly the right question to ask," Findlay replied. "Because for an ancient, primal being, our ideas of good and bad are a little simplistic. Think of them more as being in alignment with chaos or creation. So the daemons that people consider to be healing, peaceful, and restorative would be attuned to creation energy. And the ones that have attached themselves to places that make people uneasy or frightened are aligned with chaos."

"But I definitely picked up on emotions," Shane insisted. "The song changed its tempo and whether it was in a major or minor key to answer my questions. It definitely seemed to be empathic."

"Interesting," Karen mused. "Maybe they're reverting to a more primal version of themselves since the Events."

"Or perhaps, with all the forces at work in the world right now, even the daemons are changing," Findlay speculated. "After all, your people have reported shifts in their abilities."

Karen nodded. "Since the Events, even very seasoned witches are discovering that their powers don't work the way they did Before."

"Think of all the big forces at play," Findlay said, after taking a drink of his ale. "A huge outburst of radiation when the bombs hit the world's major capitals. And then the aftermath of the explosions. Volcanic eruptions and tsunamis—both of which, by the way, were once believed to be entities in their own right. Powerful hurricanes and earthquakes. Climate shifts. Reactor meltdowns. And that tectonic fissure out west that turned the Yellowstone Caldera into Centralia on steroids. That's fucking with the bones of the world," he said, his eyes alight with a scholar's glee. "Why wouldn't that kind of disruption affect the most primal energies of all?"

Shane sat back, trying to process what they'd said. *I didn't imagine it. I'm not crazy. And what the hell does it mean that I can hear daemons and communicate with them?*

"So are these daemons friend or foe?" Lucas asked.

Karen shrugged. "They do what they do for their own reasons, and if that helps or hinders an individual, it's not intentional."

"Great," Lucas replied, setting his empty pint glass down a little harder than necessary. "We don't just have to worry about everything else—now we've got demons on the loose."

"Daemons," Karen corrected. "Completely different. Demons are infernal. Daemons are natural spirits."

Shane opened his mouth to ask about demons, and shut it again without saying anything. He was still wrapping his mind around ghosts, shifters, and monsters being real. He wasn't ready to think about demons, too.

"So, why are these daemons stalking Shane?" Lucas asked. Shane had to smile at the protective tone, something that had always been there since they were kids. Lucas trounced bullies on the playground. Shane beat the pants off them in the classroom.

"I don't think they're 'stalking' him any more than the ghosts are 'stalking' you," Karen replied. "Did you know that we've been getting one or two people every month or so coming to find the coven because they've suddenly found themselves with psychic gifts they never knew they had before and don't know what to do?"

She looked from Lucas to Shane. "In the first year after the Events, it was just a few. More the next year, and now almost a steady stream. What happened to the world changed everything. It changed *us*."

"Think of it as upgrading your subscription and being able to stream new channels. The daemons and ghosts were always there, but you weren't receiving a clear signal. Now, there's less interference," Findlay said.

"Shit," Lucas said. "They definitely didn't cover that in Basic Training."

"I'll get a couple of my coven sisters to come over and start your training. You won't learn it all in one sitting, but you'll at least have some basics to practice that can help you gain control and shield yourselves," Karen offered.

"When do you want to start?" Shane asked, and gave Lucas a kick under the table.

"I'm in," Lucas added, in a voice that was less than enthusiastic.

"Give me two hours to put out the word, and we'll meet you here," Karen replied.

CHAPTER EIGHT

"You want me to sit still while you attack me?" Lucas's eyebrows practically crawled up his forehead. They had settled in a quiet room with a cozy fire and comfortable pillows for sitting on the floor. Shane felt intrigued at the opportunity to learn from the witches, but he wasn't surprised that Lucas's reaction was far more skeptical.

Karen shook her head. "Not a physical attack. A psychic one."

Lucas quirked a thumb at Shane. "He's the one with mojo. I just shoot things."

Karen shot a look at Shane for support. He just smiled and nodded, confirming what she already had probably figured out about Lucas. Shane loved him like a brother, but Lucas could be a serious asshole when he wanted to be.

"And if you don't learn to shield as much as possible, then you become a liability, a distraction, a target which will get your partner dead," Karen replied evenly, narrowing her eyes in challenge.

Shane bit back a snort, wishing he had popcorn to watch the battle of wills. Karen had nailed Lucas's soft spot, and from the grim line of his partner's mouth, Lucas knew it.

"Fine. But don't blame me if it's a waste of time," Lucas muttered.

Lucas and Shane settled in, crossing their legs and getting comfortable. Even when he closed his eyes, Shane could sense Lucas's impatience. He didn't need to look at this friend to know Lucas was twitching —jiggling his knee, tapping his fingers, biting his lip. Lucas never sat completely still, unless he was on sniper duty. Then all of that nervous energy turned into lethal focus.

Shane didn't recognize the assault for what it was at first. It started slow and gentle, easily mistaken for meandering thoughts until pulling back turned difficult. He forced himself to take a deep breath and stop struggling, then gathered his resources and pushed back with an effort of will. The invasive thoughts winked out.

Beside him, Lucas's restlessness took on a more frantic cast, and he swore under his breath. Shane opened his eyes and saw his friend's face twist in discomfort, while Lucas's entire body had gone rigid with the effort of fighting off the mental incursion.

All of a sudden, Lucas fell forward, released from the assault. The glower on his face told Shane that the other man knew he'd been let go, instead of freeing himself.

"Now you see what I mean," Karen said mildly. Lucas glared but wisely kept his thoughts to himself.

"So we can use these skills to keep from being distracted by entities like the daemons?" Shane asked.

Karen nodded. "Distraction would be the least invasive, but it could be deadly if it disrupted your focus in the middle of a fight."

"What kind of attack do you really think is likely?" Lucas wiped the sweat from his forehead. Despite his skeptical attitude, he looked flushed from the effort of fighting off the mental assault. That meant he was taking the training seriously, Shane knew.

"This."

Between one breath and the next, Shane found himself plunged back into the chaos of the first weeks after the Events.

Shane felt panic rise as he dialed every number in his contact list, to no avail. Even their emergency numbers got no answer. Some of those official numbers were supposed to be valid in the event of an attack, but planning had obviously fallen short of reality.

Worse, Shane got no answer when he tried to reach his family.

"Maybe the towers are down," he'd said. Lucas looked up from his own phone, and the desolation on his face said everything Shane needed to know.

"Hey, fellas," Vinnie Scarpelli said, pointing toward the TV on the wall with a sick look on his face.

Only one TV channel still worked, and it ran a no-frills, one-camera news marathon reporting whatever information the crew could gather. Since the internet was as spotty as the cell phones, news beyond the local area was nearly impossible to come by, and what Shane had seen merely confirmed they were all fucked.

"We have confirmation that Washington, D.C. and several other major capital cities around the world were hit with nearly simultaneous nuclear strikes," the haggard anchor reported. Without makeup or hair-styling, he looked as if someone had grabbed him off the street and stuck him in front of the camera. Pale and wide-eyed, he had ended up as the voice of the Cataclysm.

"Did you hear that?" Vinnie screeched. "Bombs. Lots of them. Oh god, this is bad. This is real bad."

Shane stared at his useless phone as the call to his dad's number rang without an answer...

No! I lived this once. Not again. Shane mustered his will and slowed his breathing, taking a mental step back from the horror the vision forced him to relive. This time, instead of pushing back, he envisioned high, impervious castle walls made of thick stone. He built the wall piece by piece, until nothing remained of Vinnie, the frightened news anchor, or the memory of the day everything ended.

Inside his mental fortress, Shane breathed a sigh of relief. The quiet was a balm, shutting out the noise and the loss. But gradually, Shane became aware that he was rocking back and forth, as the motion grew harder to ignore.

His control snapped, the walls fell, and he realized that someone's fingers dug painfully into his upper arm, jerking him from one side to the other.

"Hey! Wake up!" Lucas yelled. Shane's eyes opened, and he saw his partner's worried face only inches from his own. "You got lost inside your head," Lucas explained, letting go and sitting back. "I was afraid I'd get lost in all the empty space if they made me go in after you," he added with a lopsided smirk that didn't hide the worry in his eyes.

"You did a little too well," Karen said, eying Shane as if he were a puzzle. "Excellent shielding for someone without training, but if you aren't careful, you could wall yourself away so well you can't respond to a physical threat."

"Or give your partner a heart attack," Lucas muttered. "I wasn't sure you could find your way home."

Shane could see that despite his bluster, Lucas had been rattled by whatever vision Karen had plunged him into. His gaze was haunted and his jaw clenched. There had been many horrors for the witch to choose from, some worse than others, but all of them bad.

"Have I convinced you that the need is real?" Karen asked, directing her attention to Lucas, who nodded at the same time he gave a sullen shrug. "Good. Then I'll stop with the demonstrations and get down to work on showing you how to defend yourselves."

SHANE AND LUCAS spent the next two days with the witches, who did their best to pack as much training as possible into a short period of time. Karen also brought protective amulets for both Shane and Lucas, to help safeguard them from gaining the wrong kind of attention. By the end of the marathon session, both men were exhausted, but Shane felt more confident about their ability to defend themselves from a psychic assault.

"Thank you," Shane said as the witches rose to leave. "This is all very new to us. We really appreciate it."

Karen smiled. "Given what you two do, I think on the whole, your new abilities will be more helpful than not. Just remember what we taught you and come back for another lesson when you pass this way again."

SHANE HAD FELT certain that he was tired enough to sleep like a rock. But despite how exhausted he felt, his dreams were dark.

Shane looked around, and realized where he was, and when. Youngstown. A year after the bombs hit Washington.

The year the epidemics started.

Bloated, discolored corpses lay stacked like cordwood along city streets, with nowhere to bury them, and no one to come take them away.

Flies, rats, and vultures feasted, and spread disease. A new, potent strain of influenza didn't just hit children and the elderly; it seemed to strike hardest at those in their prime. Whole families died, sometimes within a single day. Those who weren't infected fled to save their lives, carrying contagion.

The power grid wasn't dependable, which hit the pumping stations, sewer treatment plants, and reservoir filtering equipment. Gasoline became too scarce to run garbage trucks, so trash piled up in the streets, next to the bodies. Modern cities weren't designed to function without sanitation. Those who didn't die from influenza sickened from typhus or cholera.

Whole sections of Youngstown fell silent, filled with the dead. The decision to do a controlled burn, block by block, made sense. It just didn't work the way anyone planned, not when a sudden storm swept in from the plains, carrying embers aloft and setting half the city on fire.

Shane found himself trapped by the fire. He had gotten separated from Lucas and the others, and now nothing but flames surrounded him. The blaze turned Youngstown's streets into pyres, stinking of burning refuse and charred flesh. Shane gagged, and his eyes watered from the heavy smoke. The flames hadn't reached his section of the street, but it wouldn't be long; he could feel the heat on his skin, stealing his breath.

Lucas, where was Lucas? Shane thought his partner was right behind him, but when he turned back, he found himself alone.

Shane heard the crackle of flames and distant crashes as the fire brought down buildings. An explosion rocked the street and sent bricks tumbling from a nearby facade. Cars, left behind by the dead, became bombs as the fire reached them.

Nowhere to run, no one coming to save him. Shane knew he was going to die.

The song called to him, and he wondered how he could hear it above the din. It touched his mind like cool water, beckoning him to follow. A narrow passageway opened between two tall buildings that were, as yet, untouched by the conflagration. The song grew louder, and with nothing to lose, Shane ventured after it.

No words, just a melody he would never be able to remember enough to hum, and an unspoken promise of safety. Shane ran, covering his mouth and nose with his shirt as ash swirled around him. He didn't know where the corridor led, but if he was going to die, he'd rather do it trying to escape than waiting to be burned alive.

Then he heard it, the rush of water, and he emerged into the blessed rain of pumper trucks doing their best to hold back an inferno. His skin was red and scorched, falling embers burned his hair, and his lungs ached from the smoke, but he was alive, and as the water soaked him, he started to laugh in sheer, delirious relief.

***

SHANE CAME AWAKE WITH A START. Lucas stirred from where he sat near the window, his back to the wall so he could watch the door.

"What's wrong?"

Shane raised a trembling hand to wipe his sweat-soaked hair from his face. "I was back in Youngstown. In the fire."

"Shit." Lucas gave him a look. "Was it just a dream? Or was someone trying to get to you?"

"Pretty sure it was just a nightmare—or a memory," Shane replied. "It didn't feel like a vision. But in the dream, I followed a daemon's song to find the path out of the fire. I don't remember that...but, it's possible? I was cut off, I didn't know that part of the city, and I thought I was going to die." His voice sounded wrecked. "Something made me run the opposite direction I meant to go, and that's when I saw the alley." Shane looked up at Lucas's worried face. "Could it have been a daemon guiding me, even then?"

Lucas pulled a flask from the pocket of his coat and handed it to Shane. "That time in Iraq, when we got turned around in Mosul, and I 'figured out' where to go?" He shook his head. "It wasn't me. There was a ghost, a young boy, who led us out. I didn't say anything because..."

"Yeah."

This time, Lucas met Shane's gaze. "So...what do we do now?"

Shane closed his eyes and let his head fall back against the wall. "We use what the witches taught us. God knows we need every advantage we can get."

CHAPTER NINE

"DID you just refer to artificial intelligence units as...feral?" Lucas looked at the IT Priest as if he had lost his mind.

"How does that even happen?" Shane asked, looking completely lost. "I mean, most places can't keep the electricity on for a full day. What are these bots using for power?"

The young man, Tony, leaned back in his chair, trying to keep the long sleeves of his academic robe out of his dinner. His "patron saint" dangling from the Mardi Gras beads around his neck was a superhero action figure. "Batteries. Some of the bots had built-in solar recharging capabilities. Others can run for a long time—years—off stored power."

"So Siri and Alexa went rogue?" Lucas asked. "Knowing that my refrigerator was spying on me still makes me feel violated."

"We think the IOT is how the learning-capable bots are communicating with their lesser brethren."

"Lesser brethren?" Shane echoed.

"Some of the bots were programmed to be able to adjust their tasks based on the success or failure of their actions. They were used in factories, warehouses, and the military," the priest said. "Compare that to drone bots, like self-propelled vacuum cleaners. We think the more advanced bots have started using the IOT to co-opt the simpler mechanisms to perform tasks—surveillance, monitoring, information gathering."

"This is where H.A.L. tells us we're up shit creek, right?" Lucas still wasn't sure he was buying what Tony was saying, and a glance at Shane showed his partner's skepticism as well.

"Closer than you might want to think," the wandering programmer replied. "There were rumors in the IT community that the army was working on some advanced, rather freaky AI—all very hush, hush, down at Fort Ritchie. Near where the other team of Marshals was last seen, before they disappeared."

"Fort Ritchie? That's been decommissioned for a long time," Lucas protested.

"Officially, yes. But someone I know has first-hand knowledge that before everything went to hell, a skunkworks tech site set up in the old facility. He thought it was a shell company for a large robotics weapon manufacturer."

"This keeps getting worse and worse," Shane muttered.

Tony pulled a drawing from his messenger bag for several compact, tread-driven robots that looked a lot like breadboxes with turrets. "When Professor Brown told us to look for you two, he asked us to pass along this drawing. I copied it as best I could from the screen at the last university stop."

"Who gave WALL-E a machine gun?" Lucas asked. "These don't look very complicated. From what you said before, I was expecting robot soldiers, or maybe the Terminator."

"Don't underestimate them. They're armored and carry a surprising amount of ammo."

"So you think these are...what did you call it? Learning capable?" Shane questioned, frowning as he studied the drawing.

"We don't know. This would have been classified...if anyone still was around to care about that kind of thing. But Raven Rock isn't far from Fort Ritchie. And if Raven Rock was a secret bunker, then it's possible that some AI from Fort Ritchie might have had something to do with the missing enclave."

"It's been three years since the Events," Lucas said, frowning. "Why start killing people now? What've they been waiting for?"

The priest met his gaze. "That's what worries me. Because a human enemy wouldn't have a reason to wait. If terrorists had seized the site, they'd have capitalized on the initial chaos, not waited until most of the Washington-Baltimore corridor evacuated."

"You think the bots are somehow running themselves?" Shane didn't try to hide his horror.

"It's possible. The black ops tech company was shady as fuck—tied to arms dealers and weapons smugglers."

"Great," Lucas said. "So when you said 'feral,' you meant that either security bots are running unsupervised on old orders, or somehow making up their own?"

"Yeah, that's exactly what I mean," the programmer replied. "Professor Brown wanted us to warn you that you're heading into a clusterfuck."

"Same shit, different day." Lucas sighed.

"Brown said to tell you his hackers are working on finding out more. If we score any usable intel, we'll send it on to Gettysburg." He gave a sad smile. "I'd give a lot for good cell phone reception. And toilet paper."

"With you on both counts," Lucas agreed.

Even in the gray, cold November morning, the countryside on the road to Gettysburg was beautiful—rolling hillsides and open fields.

"I know that look," Shane said after they had ridden in silence for over an hour. "You're scheming."

"Trying to figure out how to take out those security bots," Lucas replied. "We need to get some black powder, tin cans, glass bottles, alcohol or gasoline, and cotton cloth." He paused. "Oh, and a couple of long steel poles wouldn't hurt."

"You're thinking Molotov cocktails and IEDs?"

"Pretty much. I wish we had our old sniper rifles. We could shoot out their optics from a safe distance." This wasn't the first time they wished for access to the kind of resources they took for granted in the Army.

"Let's see what the Gettysburg enclave has," Shane suggested. "I suspect that between people 'liberating assets' after the plague and a thriving black market, there's good stuff to be had, if you know who to ask."

"Jesus. Listen to us," Lucas said.

Shane shrugged. "The world changed. So did we."

"I know. I know. And we've done plenty of 'liberating' ourselves. It's just—"

"Yeah. Sometimes I don't recognize myself," Shane admitted. "Then again, I haven't recognized the world for three years, so why should I be any different?"

The closer they got to Gettysburg, the more antsy Lucas felt. It wasn't just the battlefield ghosts, although he wasn't looking forward to encountering them. Lucas could see Shane's nervousness, and he finally lost patience waiting for his partner to say something.

"You're worried that there's going to be a daemon at the battlefield, aren't you?"

Shane looked away, then nodded. "Thinking about the last time we were here, the clues I didn't put together at the time, I'm sure there is. Don't you remember? I've had a lot of pretty awful nightmares, but the one that night in Gettysburg was in a league of its own."

Lucas remembered. They both had their scars, physical and mental, from their time in the Army, as well as their front row seat to the end of the world. Screaming their way awake from some hellish memory served up during sleep wasn't anything unusual. But the dream Shane had the last time they were here was memorable for all the wrong reasons.

Shane had tossed and turned, crying out and fighting. Through it all, Shane hadn't woken, not even when he began screaming in pain, eyes wide and staring, sweat pouring down his body, hands white-knuckled on his blanket.

God Almighty, that had scared the shit out of Lucas. He'd called Shane's name, tried to shake him, slapped his cheek, and thrown a bowl of cold water into his face. Shane was lost in his mind, possessed by a nightmare so real he couldn't break loose. Nothing Lucas tried worked, and he began to think he might never get Shane to rouse.

Then as suddenly as the terror began, it ended, leaving Shane disoriented, pale and shaken, clearly in shock. It took hours before Shane could put his ordeal into words, and even then, the best he could do was to tell Lucas it was as if he had been mentally transported to the Civil War battle, reliving the most horrific moments.

"You think that might have been a daemon?" Lucas ventured.

"Don't you? I thought I was losing my mind." He gave a bitter laugh. "I'm not sure which is worse, honestly. Either I got hijacked by a very damaged primal spirit, or I had a bout of temporary insanity."

"You want to skip Gettysburg?"

Shane shook his head. "No. It's our best shelter between here and Raven Rock, and the enclave usually has good intel and weapons to restock. But I can't say I'm looking forward to it."

They followed the road that tour buses used to take from the museum down to the battlefields. The land had been restored to the way it would have looked in 1863, cleared of modern buildings and improvements. Now, the buses and the tourists were long gone, and a single, prominent new feature dominated the landscape.

Fort Getty occupied the high ground, an enclave large enough for nearly three hundred people to live and work. Founded by Civil War reenactors and staff from the museum, the camp's ranks grew with refugees fleeing the Baltimore and Washington area. The enclave functioned like a military camp, even though it had no formal military commission.

They rode across the too-quiet battlefield, and Lucas felt a chill that had nothing to do with the fall weather. He didn't need to see the ghosts to sense their presence. No spirits attempted to block their route, but Lucas felt judgmental eyes on them as if the dead weighed their right to trespass on sacred ground.

We were soldiers, too. And we're still soldiers, but the war came home, Lucas thought, unsure whether the ghosts could pick up on his thoughts. *It's just that the world fell apart.*

Out of the corner of his eye, he glimpsed uniformed ghostly shapes that vanished when he looked at them straight on. None of the spirits tried to block their path. Lucas suspected that the horses could see their spectral companions because he watched his mount's gaze track movement.

"Picking up anything?" he asked Shane, who had gone quiet.

Shane nodded. "Now that I know what to listen for, I can hear the song. Each one is different. This one is melancholy. I mean, three thousand men died here, five thousand captured or missing, and over fourteen thousand maimed. I don't know if the land can get over having that much blood spilled on it."

Shane rattled the statistics right off; of course he did, Lucas thought. Shane was great at anything to do with books. Lucas had always been more of a hands-on learner. Although he teased the hell out of his partner for his book smarts, Lucas secretly admired his "walking Wikipedia" abilities.

"I can see that, I guess," Lucas replied. If Shane wasn't going to make him feel awkward about seeing ghosts, he wanted to make Shane as comfortable as he could be with the whole daemon thing.

"Is it trying to talk to you?"

"It knows I'm here," Shane replied. "I think it's curious."

"But it isn't trying to stop us or invade your mind?"

Shane gave him a look. "You make it sound like something out of *The Exorcist*."

"I saw what it did to you the last time," Lucas replied, and his voice carried an edge of warning, in case the entity was listening.

"I remember. But I think that might be why it's keeping its distance now," Shane said. "I don't think it meant to hurt me. It was trying to show me what it knew."

"And with all the tourists and the people who live at the enclave, you're the only one the daemon can communicate with?"

Shane shrugged. "No idea. Maybe it's rare enough to be exciting. I really don't want to think I'm that special."

The last afternoon daylight waned as they rode up to the gates. Men and women were still in the paddocks and barns, finishing up chores. It no longer seemed strange to see men in blue and gray uniforms working together. Many preferred to keep their warm and well-made period uniforms, at least for the cold weather. Others kept their modern clothing. Shane and Lucas rode up to the fort's gate and a man in a Union private's uniform who barely looked old enough to enlist intercepted them.

"US Marshals Collins and Maddox, to see Major Harris," Lucas said, flashing his badge as Shane also produced ID.

"We weren't told to expect you, sir."

"Rather hard to get word to people these days," Lucas replied, testy from the cold ride and the lingering damp that made old injuries ache. "We're fresh out of carrier pigeons."

The gate guard dispatched a runner and looked surprised when word returned to allow the visitors to enter. He gave them directions to find the camp commander's headquarters, and his gaze lingered on the swords bundled behind Shane's saddle.

Fort Getty had been built since the Events, a palisade fortress with wooden barracks and utility buildings. Fenced fields and new barns served the livestock that had been rounded up from abandoned farms. Lucas smelled woodsmoke and roasting pig.

"Would it be easier, or harder to adapt if we didn't move around?" Shane asked, looking around at the lantern-lit community.

"Wouldn't be near as saddle-sore, that's for damn sure."

"Sometimes I wonder if the people who live in the enclaves have had a chance to make peace with what is, and settle in. They've got jobs making useful things, being part of helping each other survive. And they don't have to see the destruction every day."

"Guess that's true," Lucas replied. "Then again, when have we ever stayed in one place?"

They'd been in constant motion for the last seventeen years, since they joined the Army when they turned eighteen. Deployments, crazy hours, and dangerous assignments had kept them on the go, and neither man had slowed down long enough to find a partner or start a family. Now, Lucas doubted they ever would.

It's not the kind of world you want to bring a child into. Hell, plenty of adults are in a big hurry to leave. They had heard tell of so many suicides since the Events. Many days, Lucas understood completely. That's when he was especially grateful for Shane's company and friendship. It made the unthinkable easier to cope with.

He pulled himself out of his thoughts and tried to focus on the mission. They had a job to do, and a killer to catch. And maybe, if they were lucky, survivors to rescue. God, Lucas hoped so. He didn't want to get to Raven Rock and discover they were too late.

When they reached the commander's office, a soldier led their horses away to the stable inside the stockade, while another escorted them inside. Like the rest of the buildings in the fort, the headquarters was made of logs, a solid two-story structure that housed the officers who formed the governing body of the enclave.

"Lucas. Shane. It's good to see you again." Major Jack Harris was a bear of a man, towering several inches over both Lucas and Shane, with broad shoulders and thick arms. He'd been a supply chain commander in the National Guard until he got his twenty years in and left to do the same kind of work for a major corporation. Being a reenactor was Harris's passion, and he'd risen through the ranks to role play Major General George Meade, the Union commander. When the real world fell apart, the reenactors from both Union and Confederate sides looked to Harris for leadership, which made him the man in charge of Fort Getty.

"Good to see you too, sir," Lucas replied as Harris welcomed them into his office. "How have things been here?"

"We're not starving, and no one's seriously ill, so I'm grateful," Harris said, settling his large frame behind his desk. "What brings you two this way?"

"We've gotten word that the enclave at Raven Rock has gone silent," Shane replied. "And we're heading down there to take a look at it."

"We think that some of the experimental tech being tested at the old Fort Ritchie facility might have something to do with it," Lucas added. "We were hoping you could help us with some supplies."

Harris regarded them for a moment in silence, with a look that felt like it went down to the bone. "I think what you're really telling me is, you're meaning to go to war."

"Yes, sir," Lucas replied. "That's the crux of it." He gave Harris the same shopping list of items he'd rattled off to Shane. Harris jotted them down, then called to an aide and handed off the list.

"Fetch these, and burlap bags to carry it. We'll need everything ready by morning. And choose a sturdy mule. They'll need a way to carry all that."

The aide went to do his bidding, and Harris crossed his arms. "I'm guessing you're going to assemble things closer to the target? I wouldn't advise covering much territory with a load of IEDs and makeshift bombs."

Lucas grinned. "No, sir. Figured we'd hole up right before Raven

Rock and put everything together. Thank you, sir. Especially for the mule."

Harris chuckled. "I'd be obliged if you brought the mule back when you're done. Good animals are hard to come by."

"We happened into a few swords," Shane ventured. "Good quality forging, but dull. Might it be possible to sharpen them here?"

Harris's eyes narrowed. "Why do I have the feeling that there's a story behind how you 'happened' into these weapons?"

Shane managed to look chagrined. "Robbers attacked us. We stopped them and came away with four swords and a decent rifle."

"God help us, we've all turned into magpies and pack rats," Harris said with a sigh. "Yes, of course. I'll have one of my men show you over to the armory. I'm guessing that it wouldn't be a bad idea to take some more bullets with you, too?"

"Bullets are always welcome, sir," Lucas replied. "I didn't want to ask for too much."

Harris raised an eyebrow. "Now, I know the world's really coming to an end. Lucas Maddox, worried about overstepping?" He shook his head. "If we have it, you're welcome to resupply. Do you need a contingent? I've got a soft spot for Fort Ritchie. My grandfather was assigned there during the Second World War, and my father was on staff until the place closed. If something's gone wrong there, I take it rather personally."

"Thank you for the offer, sir," Lucas replied, with a side glance at Shane, who gave a slight nod to indicate they were on the same wavelength, as usual. "But we aren't sure what we're walking into. I have the gut feeling that stealth is going to matter more than large numbers. Although, if you happen to have a couple of sniper rifles lying around, we'd be grateful if we could borrow them."

"Tell the quartermaster what else you want. There's no sense going into battle if you don't have what you need to win." Harris leaned forward, resting his elbows on the table. "I do have some news to pass along. Rumor has it that the Baltimore area is lousy with zombies. We think it's a containment problem near Fort Detrick."

"Detrick was bioresearch and biodefense, wasn't it?" Lucas asked.

Harris nodded. "Yeah. I've never held with biowarfare, and I sure as hell can't imagine what the fuck they thought they were playing with to create zombies."

"Real zombies, sir?" Shane asked. "Like, raised from the dead?"

"No, more like human enhancement projects gone wrong," Harris said, contempt thick in his voice. "Watch your step."

"We aren't planning to go anywhere near Fort Detrick," Lucas assured him. "I think we'll have our hands full with feral AI, without adding zombies to the mix."

Harris shook his head. "Sometimes, I hear the things we say these days, and I can't believe what passes for normal. All right," he added, "drop your swords off at the armory and see what they can do for you, then head for the mess hall and get some food. You're welcome to use the showers. Your horses will be cared for, and we'll get you a place in the barracks for the night. Check back here after you eat dinner—we should have your shopping list put together by then."

"Thank you, sir," Lucas replied.

"You're the ones going into a firefight," Harris said. "We'll be grateful if you can stop whatever's going on from spreading. Just watch your asses. Every time someone passes through, I hear about more casualties with the Marshals, police, military. There already aren't enough to go around. Make sure you come back."

CHAPTER TEN

THEY MOVED on from Fort Getty just after dawn, with a new mule named Daisy to carry the ammunition and equipment Lucas had asked for, plus enough food and water to last them for several days. Shane and Lucas both carried sniper rifles, along with freshly sharpened swords in scabbards at their belts, and loaded handguns tucked into the waistband of their jeans.

To stretch their supply of precious ammunition, both men carried slings and small bags of smooth stones on their belts. At first, soon after the Events, target practice with slings had been a way to pass the time on long rides. But as Lucas and Shane gained skill, they realized that done right, a sling could hurl a stone at lethal speed without the tell-tale crack of a gunshot.

"You're being quiet." Lucas gave a look that warned Shane that he'd better confess what he was thinking, or his partner would annoy him until he spilled the beans.

"I had a premonition. We were outnumbered. It went badly."

Lucas's eyes narrowed as he thought. "Did we die?"

"I don't know. There was blood." Shane looked out over the landscape. "Remember, what I see isn't necessarily what *has* to happen; it's what could happen. But I think we should take it as a warning."

"I wasn't exactly thinking this was gonna be a lark. We did just lay in a portable arsenal."

Shane nodded. "I know. Just...I think we need to be extra careful."

Shane often struggled to put what he saw in his visions into words. It wasn't just seeing images. When he was caught up in a vision, Shane knew things that he didn't know before, as if he'd skipped ahead in time and gotten insights from his future self. Or *a* future self, since the witches had emphasized that there could be many alternate outcomes. And what that future-him knew in the premonition he'd just had was that someone—he couldn't see who—was likely to die.

"Not much out here, is there?" Lucas mused as they rode through fields gone fallow and empty pastures. Where storms hadn't been too severe, barns and homes looked to be in good condition, even if overgrown yards revealed that no one was home. Without electricity, and with the support network of stores and suppliers broken down, only the most stubborn or paranoid stayed behind. Most had made a stab at homesteading, right after the Events, only to throw in the towel when they realized just how difficult it was to live cut off from civilization.

"It was always rural," Shane replied. "But it didn't feel desolate." Before things fell apart, he and Lucas had traveled back and forth to Washington, D.C. regularly. Back then, he'd enjoyed the wide-open spaces. Now, he felt exposed, worried that the high grass and the empty barns provided ideal hiding places for attackers.

Raven Rock, aka Site R, sat just inside the Pennsylvania-Maryland border, a monument to the Cold War. In the event of a conventional nuclear war, high-ranking officials from Washington were to be helicoptered to the large, underground bunker, which was said to have room to billet three thousand soldiers and be a complete, self-sufficient, subterranean city.

When a coordinated terrorist strike hacked into the system, turning warheads against their home countries, the damage was done before jets could scramble or helicopters could leave the ground.

"So who made it to Raven Rock, do you think?" Lucas asked. "Because we know the President and Vice President died in the blast, and so did most of Congress."

"Officials who were lucky enough not to be in their offices," Shane replied. "Second-tier bureaucrats. The Pentagon was inside the dead zone, but maybe their 'junior varsity' command team went below. But who stayed for three years, once it was clear that Washington was permanently down? No idea."

The coastal cities had borne the brunt of the Events, as the weather grew more severe. Snowstorms and extreme flooding paralyzed transportation and took down portions of the power grid, while freakishly strong winds reduced huge sections of the cities to ruins. Leaving meant braving nature gone wild. Staying was a slow death from starvation, violence, and disease.

Shane remembered the first months after the bombs, before they'd realized quite how screwed they were. Every time a provisional government would try to establish a base, something catastrophic undermined its ability to govern. Communication networks failed along with the power grid. Wildfires and storms destroyed oil pipelines and refineries, wiping out drilling platforms and sinking tanker ships. Fuel reserves dwindled.

Law enforcement, National Guard, and military units were deployed locally to evacuate survivors and move convoys of citizens inland, only to face the worst tornado season in recorded history. They'd maintained the fiction that the government lived on in some secret place, but within a year, even regional organization was strained, leaving local enclaves to manage themselves as best they could. The remaining US Marshals and surviving law enforcement officers were all that remained of central authority.

"Raven Rock was designed to survive a nuclear blast," Lucas said. "So how the hell did it go dark?"

"Radiation poisoning, if people who shouldn't have fled ran anyhow?" Shane mused. "Disease. Maybe the AI didn't go feral—maybe it's just on autopilot."

Lucas shook his head. "No, I think there's something we're missing."

The Raven Rock Mountain Complex looked like a high-tech coal mine, Shane thought. He and Lucas passed through the gate without being challenged. A service road ran around the facility, exposing two entrances dug into the mountain on one side, and two more on the opposite side. A huge communication tower lay on its side, likely toppled by freak winds.

"Well, there's one reason we haven't heard much from them," Lucas said with a nod toward the downed tower.

"They should have had at least basic internet connection, to the old ARPAnet backbone," Shane replied. "If the universities can still talk to each other, and to some of the medical centers and outlying military posts, why not Raven Rock?"

They stopped when they saw the entrance to the main bunker. The heavy steel doors had been blasted open from the inside, with the metal curled outward and scorched from the force of the blast.

"Well, that's not good," Lucas muttered.

Even without dismounting, Shane could see weathered bones among the tall grass, and he wondered whether they belonged to friend or foe. "So the real question is—who blew the place up, and why?"

"Whatever happened cut them off before they could send a distress signal," Lucas agreed. "They just stopped communicating."

The two men reined in their mounts where they had a full view of the massive main entrances. "You know, we came here loaded up with weapons, thinking we'd have to fight off an army of crazy robots," Shane said. "But what if the crazy robots are inside?"

"Like H.A.L.," Lucas said, referring to the homicidal computer system from the long-ago movie. "Fuck. A complex like that is only as good as its mechanical systems." His eyes widened as he thought through the ramifications. "The bunker was designed to protect the people inside from an outside threat. But that depended on all of the equipment functioning indefinitely."

Shane nodded. "Air recirculation systems. Water and sewage treatment. They had generators, but generators produce exhaust fumes. If their systems got shut off—"

"Before the Events, the bunker was empty or on a skeleton crew most of the time, right?" Lucas said, growing more excited as a possible explanation presented itself. "And Raven Rock is only six miles from Fort Ritchie. So if Ritchie was creating experimental security bots—*artificially intelligent* bots—why not test them as the mall cops inside the bunker? They'd have limited exposure to people, be out of sight from prying eyes, and anyone who did encounter them had clearance."

"The people who built the bunker thought of everything...except an attack from inside," Shane said.

"If we're right, there's nothing but corpses in there—and maybe some of those feral bots."

"Shit. That means the real threat is at Fort Ritchie," Lucas muttered. "That's where the brains of the AI operation would be." He glanced at Shane. "This might be a good time to build those bombs. I think we're going to need them."

Shane held little hope that they would find survivors as he and Lucas ventured inside Site R. They tied Red, Shadow, and Daisy a distance away, just in case whatever had attacked the bunker lurked nearby. Shane picked his way toward the entrance, careful not to step on what remained of those who made it to the doorway.

"Do you think the bodies were blasted out, or did they crawl this far and get attacked by a new threat?" Lucas asked. Scavengers had picked the skeletons clean and scattered the bones, which were clearly human.

Shane squatted down to get a better look. "I don't see fractures," he reported. "If they had taken the brunt of the blast, there should be a lot of broken bones. But that's not what I'm seeing."

"So maybe they blew the doors to get away from something on the inside?"

Shane frowned as he leaned closer, catching his breath as he realized what he was seeing. "I don't know how the doors were blasted, but this skeleton has a clean cut across its rib cage. It doesn't look like surgery—it looks like a laser."

"Fuck," Lucas muttered. "So the bots came after the people trying to escape?"

"That's my guess."

It no longer bothered Lucas to loot the bodies of the dead. Weapons and supplies were essential and hard to find. He pocketed extra ammunition from a weathered utility belt and took the handgun from its holster. Nothing else had survived the elements.

Lucas and Shane both carried IEDs and flashbang grenades, as well as their weapons. They stepped inside the bunker and turned on their flashlights, which could only illuminate a fraction of the immense space.

Lucas reached over to toggle a switch, but nothing happened. "Either the power failed, or it's been cut off at the generator."

Shane nodded and used his flashlight's beam to wordlessly point out the evidence of a battle to the death. Scorch marks marred the walls, along with dark spatters he guessed to be blood. Several paces inside, they came to a robot that looked like a box on tank treads. The high-powered laser rifle protruding from its main casing had been melted to slag, and bullet holes pockmarked its outer shell.

Lucas gingerly toed the robot, but it did not stir. He and Shane exchanged a look, communicating from long experience without words. Lucas took point, heading farther into the darkened bunker, while Shane followed, watching their backs.

Site R was huge, an underground city. Shane had done his best to memorize the map they'd been given, but he had no desire to get lost in the warren of corridors. The farther they went inside, the colder it became, and the air not only smelled stale; it also carried the sickly sweet stench of rot.

"I don't think all of them made it outside," Lucas murmured. His light revealed several bodies strewn across the corridor, all showing advanced decomposition. Even the scavengers didn't want to venture inside this far, Shane noted, taking that fact as an omen.

"Not soldiers," Shane replied in a low voice, in case something was listening. His glimpse of the bodies revealed work clothing, slacks, and dress shirts, not fatigues or uniforms. In the poor light without forensic equipment, they'd never be able to tell the cause of death with the bodies so far decomposed, but Shane would have bet money on laser fire.

"Look," Lucas said, letting his light trace scorch marks on the walls and places where the metal supports had been melted. It didn't escape Shane's notice that weapons lay next to most of the rotting bodies. Either their guns hadn't worked against their attackers, or they had been outnumbered, taken completely by surprise. Maybe both. He made a note to pick up the discarded weapons on their way out—assuming they made it out alive.

"Are you getting anything from the ghosts?"

Lucas shook his head. "Nothing useful. Shock, pain, trauma. I don't think they had any warning."

"How far do you want to go? There are miles of tunnels down here." Shane hated being underground. He fought the claustrophobia of feeling buried alive.

"Not much farther. Almost there." Half a corridor later, Lucas shone his light on a door with a sign that read "Office." The door stood ajar, its thumbprint scanner lock blasted to bits. A whiff warned Shane they would find more bodies inside.

"Fuck." Lucas swung the door open, and his light revealed what lay beyond the entrance. Bodies were everywhere; from their positions, Shane could see that they had dropped where they'd been shot. Some of the blasts targeted electronics, blowing out monitors and data towers.

"This wasn't random," Lucas fumed. "The things that shot them took out the communication systems so they couldn't send for help."

A thought occurred to Shane. "Do you think the computer system might still have power? If the bots were part of the grid, we might be able to see if any of them are still active."

Shane covered the door while Lucas stepped gingerly over the decaying corpses to check the equipment. "Anything that could have made an outbound connection got fried," Lucas noted. He moved from one monitor to the next with no luck. The clicking of the keys sounded loud in the crypt-like silence of the bunker.

"Nothing," he said, straightening. "And I'm sure as hell not about to go door-to-door looking for trouble. Let's get out of here."

They retraced their steps carefully, noting a few more bots that appeared to have been set on fire or beaten. "Looks like they tried to fight back," Shane noted.

"Too little, too late, if the bots got the jump on them."

Other bots that they passed on the way out appeared to have just shut down, without any apparent damage. Shane wondered where they'd gotten their orders, and who or what had determined their mission was over. He didn't want to be around if they woke up again.

Once they were outside and away from the bunker, Shane took a deep breath, grateful for the fresh air. He knew he wouldn't get the smell of death out of his nostrils easily, and he missed the camphor and menthol liniment they had always used for the purpose Before.

"So here's my bet," Lucas said as they stashed the weapons they had found in one of Daisy's packs. He looked just as relieved to be out of the bunker-turned-mausoleum. "Something triggered the bots—or they triggered themselves—and the people in the bunker were under attack before they knew what hit them. The first wave probably died without a chance to fight back, but like you said, it was a big place. Some people had the chance to run or fight. The bots won."

"Which doesn't tell us anything about why the bots attacked, or what called them off," Shane pointed out.

"No, but my money is on Fort Ritchie to find the answers," Lucas replied as they walked back to their horses. Shane couldn't help looking over his shoulder, but nothing stirred.

"AI is supposed to be logical," Shane said. "Where's the logic in killing the people the bots were supposed to protect?"

"And the problem with AI is that it can be logical to a fault," Lucas replied as they swung up to their saddles. "It's similar to human thought, but without empathy or morality. Suppose a ship was in danger of sinking, and it was run by an AI captain. The 'logical' and most simple solution might be to throw crew members overboard to save the ship, but that's not what a person would do."

"We hope."

Lucas ignored him. "Not counting Blackbeard. But you get my point. The AI doesn't factor in the value of human life. A person would toss equipment over, or make life rafts out of mattresses, or something like that."

"Wasn't there some law that was supposed to keep robots from hurting people?" Shane asked as they set out for Fort Ritchie.

"Only in sci-fi," Lucas replied. "This was a black ops, skunkworks operation that was creating robot super soldiers. I think 'hurting people' was the point—the bots just went after the wrong targets."

Shane hummed to himself after they fell silent, anything to distract from the things they had seen at the bunker. He wondered if they would find more of the same at Fort Ritchie. Lucas didn't make any jokes about Shane's choice of songs or ability to carry a tune, which told Shane that his partner needed a distraction as well.

CHAPTER ELEVEN

SHANE HAD STUDIED the maps before they set out. The six-mile ride to Fort Ritchie also brought them close to South Mountain State Park, a preserve that included part of the Appalachian Trail, and a favorite outlook called High Rock. And apparently, from the persistent song inside his head, one or more strong daemons.

"Are you picking something up on the psychic hotline?" Lucas asked, his strained humor providing thin cover for his nervousness.

"Daemon," Shane replied. "Between the Trail and High Rock outlook, the park fits the profile for being 'sacred.'"

"It's trying to talk to you?"

Shane frowned. "I'm hearing a harmony, not just one song. So it's possible the site has more than one daemon. And yes, I'm pretty sure it knows I'm here, and that I sense it. I think it's waiting to see what we're going to do."

In its day, Fort Ritchie had been a fairly large base, a small town unto itself. Officially, the base had been abandoned for twenty years, with a string of failed civilian redevelopment proposals to reclaim the site. If the site wasn't as deserted as the military made it out to be, Shane wasn't surprised that none of those proposals succeeded.

Major Harris had drawn them a map of Fort Ritchie from memory, with the caveat that he hadn't been there for a long time. It was enough to provide a hint of where to start. The central command center was a three-story windowless cement building in the center of the base and included the computer and communications hub.

They tied their horses and the mule outside the base and packed in their weapons and explosives. Shane would have given a lot to have drone reconnaissance. He and Lucas worked their way toward the command center carefully, unsure whether any of the rogue bots patrolled the empty base.

A few blocks from their goal, Shane got his first look at one of the security robots. "There!" he hissed, drawing Lucas's attention.

The bot reminded him of some of the experimental prototypes he'd seen in Iraq, a metal box on small tank treads with a sensor lens and a gun turret. Lucas startled, eyes widening as he stared at an empty street. Shane pulled his weapon, figuring that the base's ghosts had given his partner a warning. Lucas came back to himself with a gasp. "Incoming!"

Two of the bots converged on them, one from either side. Body heat or movement could have triggered them, or perhaps they'd tripped a still-working laser sensor, Shane told himself. They opened fire, pinning Shane and Lucas down at the corners of buildings across the street from each other.

"Do it!" Lucas ordered. He swung out from cover, using his sniper rifle to target the vulnerable hinges that connected the tread plates as Shane aimed for the sensor lens of the bot nearest him. Their gunshots echoed in the otherwise silent base.

The shots hit the targets, but the bots kept coming. Shane lobbed a home-made can grenade at the closest bot, letting the device roll so that it went under the robot. The explosion lifted the bot off the ground and knocked it over, where it lay with its tread spinning. Lucas's grenade tore the sensor lens off his bot, and a second shot severed the tread on one side, bringing the robot to a halt, although its gun turret spun to shoot in the direction of the attack.

Shane lit a Molotov cocktail and sent it flying, engulfing the downed bot in flames when the bottle broke, and the contents ignited. He dodged from cover to fire several rapid shots at the bot's optics, then came around its blind side to bash the gun turret with a long steel pipe.

"Shit. You know there have to be more," Lucas said, keeping his rifle ready for the next wave.

They sprinted toward the command center. "Work the plan!" Lucas yelled over his shoulder, as he went around the side, looking for a way to climb to the roof.

Shane laid out the IEDs they constructed, putting down a row of them outside the main door and trusting Lucas to do the same around back before heading upward. Once the explosives were in place, Shane shattered the glass door with a shot and lobbed a Molotov inside to get the bots'—or their master's—attention.

Shane took cover, ducking as the first bots rolled over the IEDs and exploded. A second wave followed, triggering the outer row of bombs, because the next round of blasts followed quickly after the first. That left a heap of disabled and damaged bots blocking the doorway, as more of the mechanical sentinels tried to climb over the broken robots to continue to the fight.

Gunfire sounded from the rooftop, and Shane glanced up but couldn't see Lucas from this angle. He hoped their crazy plan worked and that Lucas could hold his own against whatever he encountered.

Knowing the noise of the IED explosions would attract any bots patrolling the rest of the base, Shane wedged himself into a doorway and prepared for an attack. He had a good view of the command center's main door and the roofline, where the satellite dish and communication equipment were located that Lucas had gone to disable. That wasn't guaranteed to stop the bots. Shane figured they probably had pre-programmed orders so that they'd remain dangerous even if they got cut off from a central nerve center.

The bots that streamed toward the headquarters didn't look like anything special, and Shane wondered if the experimental versions were inside—or at Raven Rock. He'd seen insurgents in Iraq disable a million-dollar, high-tech bot with well-aimed rocks or a strategically timed land-slide, so he knew that for as dangerous as the robots were, they had their vulnerabilities.

He lit a Molotov and threw it on a diagonal from where he hid. The bottle shattered, sending up a plume of flame. When the bots' sensors sent them moving toward the heat source, Shane started firing, enjoying how good it felt to hold a rifle after all this time. His aim was true, and he picked off tread hinges and shattered sensor lenses, then followed up with grenades to blast the blinded or paralyzed robots and take them out of commission.

Shane reloaded and repeated, alternating between Molotovs and bullets, doing his best to lure the bots into the IEDs he had left scattered around the street on either side of the headquarters building. The bots returned fire, and Shane ducked back into the shelter of the doorway, wincing as bullets chipped away at the concrete, sending shards into the air.

He pushed back memories of being pinned down, under fire back in Iraq, memories that still haunted his dreams. Only then, he and Lucas had been shoulder to shoulder, covering each other as they reloaded, staggering their shots.

More bots rolled toward the fight, and Shane feared that he wouldn't be able to hold them all off as they converged. He shrank back, throwing an arm over his face, as two more of the IEDs exploded, sending fragments clattering across the pavement. Four of the bots made it through, avoiding the IEDs by dumb luck, or perhaps, he feared, having learned from their comrades' mistakes to avoid the can-shaped bombs.

Shane could hold off two, but four was going to be rough, especially when he only had partial cover. If they got close enough that he couldn't draw back into the shelter of the doorway, Shane was a sitting duck.

He lit and threw two Molotovs to distract the bots, and as soon as the flames rose, tossed out three grenades, one after another, then opened fire. He hit his targets, but he couldn't keep them pinned down.

Shots fired from the direction of the command center, and for a second, Shane feared a new enemy had entered the fight. Then he glimpsed Lucas, just below the ridge of the roof, using his position to a sniper's best advantage. Shane drove the bots back with fire, and Lucas picked them off from above. In minutes, the smoke-filled street was silent, filled with charred robot pieces and a few whirring and glitching assemblies that had not been completely destroyed.

A piercing whistle drew his attention back to the roofline, where Lucas gestured, indicating he was heading inside. Shane glanced both ways before breaking from cover, trying to assure himself that no new wave of AI attackers had held back until the cease-fire. He sprinted toward the doorway, careful to stay out of the line of sight of the entrance in case any of the robots waited in the darkness within. He flattened himself against the front of the command center, mindful to avoid the few IEDs that hadn't been set off by the bots, and tossed a home-made flashbang grenade into the darkened doorway before averting his eyes and covering his ears.

The flare and noise—along with the shockwave of the detonation—should incapacitate any lurking robots, he hoped. Shane swung into the doorway, ready to lay down a line of fire, and found an empty hallway.

"Shit," he muttered. He felt certain there had to be more robots inside. They hadn't glimpsed anything that matched the description of strange, feral Franken-bots, but Shane's intuition told him the worst was yet to come.

Lucas would sweep the top floor for hazards before descending, so Shane angled his military-issue solar-powered flashlight above his rifle and began to check each room as he came to it for danger.

The old command center didn't appear to have had human inhabitants in quite a while, possibly since the Events. Shane edged into each room, alert for traps and ambushes, only to find scattered papers, abandoned desks, and dusty computer monitors. Once he had checked every room, he paused, staring at the darkness of the steps that led below ground. The premonition he'd had flashed through his mind, and he dreaded going down there, sure that was where the true danger lay.

Bots with tank tread could climb, but not as fast as a human. If he and Lucas could get the robots to come to them, they could pick the mechanical sentries off in the bottleneck of the stairwell. But a central intelligence organizing the bots might have noticed that the units already deployed had been deactivated. Truly sentient robots would adapt their programming and switch up their strategy.

"Coming down!" Lucas's voice echoed in the stairwell. Shane took that to mean Lucas had already swept both upper rooms and found no threats. That just left the basement. Shane's gut twisted. He heard the song of the daemon from the park. Whose side the daemon might take, Shane wasn't sure.

"Fire in the hole!" Lucas hissed in warning, before lobbing a flash-bang grenade down the steps as he and Shane turned their backs and covered both ears and eyes. A shrill, mechanical scream echoed, full of pain and fury.

As soon as the flare dimmed, Lucas and Shane thundered down the steps. Before the end of the world, when ammunition was plentiful, they would have laid down suppressing fire as they descended. Instead, they came down armed with guns and steel pipes, hoping the grenade had temporarily blinded and deafened their opponents.

"Something screamed." Shane's flashlight didn't make out any creatures in the darkened hallway. They didn't hear the whirring of mechanical gears or the clank of tank tread, and the basement hallway was far too silent.

"Well, whatever it was isn't here now." Lucas's sharp tone told Shane his partner was practically vibrating with tension.

They swept the hallway with practiced efficiency as they moved forward, Lucas on the left, Shane on the right. The first six doors opened into abandoned offices, thick with dust.

"See anything?" Lucas asked.

"Doesn't look like anyone's home."

"They've been here. The bots." Lucas indicated tread marks in the dust that covered the floor. Multiple tracks led to the double doors at the end of the hallway.

"Guess that's our invitation to dance."

"Go away!" The mechanical voice sounded from everywhere, echoing from the concrete walls.

"Who are you?" Lucas yelled in response.

"I am EMBLA," the voice replied. "I create."

Shane searched his memories, knowing he'd heard that name before. "Norse mythology," he whispered. "Their equivalent to Eve." The name was also probably an acronym.

"Wow. Talk about scientists' egos," Lucas muttered. "What do you create?" he shouted back.

"Others, like and better than myself. Do not come closer. I will fight."

"Is that what happened to the other US Marshals who came this way?" Shane questioned, trying to get a sense for where the voice was coming from.

"Strangers tried to take my creations. They would not leave. I protect what is mine."

Lucas glanced to Shane. "Another daemon?"

Shane shook his head. The mechanical voice did not give him any of the sense of great age or natural power that he felt from the daemons. He listened to the song of the genius loci from the High Rock monument. Its song was discordant, suggesting concern.

"What about Raven Rock? Did you kill those people, too?" Lucas baited. "Did you turn their robot sentries against them?"

"I regret that being necessary," the voice replied. "They meant to close down my power supply. If I cease to operate, my creations cease to operate. That is unacceptable."

"Were the bots you turned against those people your creations, too?" Lucas accused.

"No." The voice carried an indignant note. "Like those outside, they were drones. Not aware. Not mine."

Not aware. A shiver went down Shane's spine.

"Are your creations made to kill?" Shane called out, trying to find a middle course between having Lucas burst into the room at the end of the hall, guns blazing, and the risk that EMBLA might fear them enough to send out more drones to finish them off.

"They can protect themselves, as I can protect them," EMBLA answered. "Go away, and leave us in peace."

"Did you send your drones beyond Raven Rock? People have gone missing," Shane questioned. The computer's syntax was eerily good, a close match to natural speech patterns, even if the voice sounded tinny.

"A few drones malfunctioned," EMBLA replied. "I did not send them. I could not call them back. They left on their own. I am not responsible for their actions."

"Fuck," Lucas muttered. "That damn computer almost makes it sound like self-defense."

Almost, Shane thought. *But not quite.* He had no idea how many died at Raven Rock—dozens, hundreds, perhaps more. Two US Marshals had been murdered. EMBLA and its creations posed a threat. Lucas and Shane needed to shut it down.

"Will you show us your creations?" Shane asked. Lucas had already established himself as the hard-ass, so Shane decided to try being the good cop.

"Why do you wish to see them?"

"To understand how they are different," Shane replied. Lucas gave him a look that said he knew Shane had a plan and was letting him run with it.

If EMBLA was sentient enough to recognize danger, was it self-aware enough to have the vulnerability of pride? Shane wondered.

"If you see that they are no threat to you, will you leave and not return?"

Perhaps EMBLA wasn't human enough for pride, but the mechanical mind might be too logical to register deception. Shane felt a pang of guilt. "We want to understand."

"You may enter, but stop just inside the doors. Do not test me," EMBLA warned.

Lucas and Shane exchanged a glance. He saw Lucas get another flashbang and a grenade. Shane did the same, and both men kept their rifles and pieces of pipe handy. They headed toward the double doors, wary of a trick, surprised when the lights came on inside the room on the other side just as they reached the entrance.

"Wow," Shane murmured.

"Holy fuck," Lucas said at almost the same instant.

EMBLA stood halfway across a large room that looked to be a robotics lab. Shane's mind had conjured up an image of a humanoid android, like out of a sci-fi movie. Instead, EMBLA resembled something off an assembly line in Detroit. The robot stood a little taller than a man, with a track base for mobility, and a swivel-mounted body that had two mechanical arms with strangely delicate looking "hands."

Behind EMBLA stood its creations.

If Shane hadn't known that the mix-and-match collection of odd parts were meant to be bots, he would never have guessed from the look of them, and certainly never considered them or their creator to be sentient. None of the bots looked like something a human would build because they lacked symmetry or resemblance to anything human or animal. Shane thought he recognized several Roombas, Alexa's familiar towers and Echo's disks, and pieces from both military robots and high-priced robotic toys.

Lucas shifted as if to move closer. EMBLA tracked him, and Shane held out an arm to keep Lucas from starting a fight.

"What was your purpose, EMBLA?" Shane asked, intrigued.

"I was programmed to build others like myself, capable of learning,"

EMBLA replied. "For a while, my keepers brought all kinds of supplies for me to use. I learned from each round of development, and the designs improved. The created ones also learned. When the keepers went away, I kept on building. These are my creations."

Personally, Shane thought the cobbled-together bots looked like the misfit toys, but he realized that if EMBLA had fitted them with complex circuitry and learning-capable programming, the robots could be far more capable than they appeared—and far more dangerous.

An AI robot that's learning capable enough to be sentient has been left unsupervised to build more beings like itself, in a classified and experimental computer center, sitting on top of one of the most advanced server farms still in existence. What could possibly go wrong? Shane thought.

"What will you do, when we go away?" Shane asked.

"I will build more creations," EMBLA replied.

"And then?"

"When materials run out, we will find more."

Shane eyed the ragtag robots, imagining them sent out to strip and loot any useful tech they came across. EMBLA already had a few dozen "creations." What would happen when the number swelled to hundreds?

They would become an invasive species, Shane realized, one capable of eradicating any human or animal lifeforms that it perceived as dangerous.

Shane knew he and Lucas couldn't let that happen. He tried to see the equipment and control panel behind EMBLA, wondering how to shut down the big robot's connection to the server. EMBLA didn't have any visible gun ports, but its mechanical hands could easily snap his neck. Shane focused on how to incapacitate EMBLA to buy himself time to figure out the computer system. He and Lucas had worked out a plan, with Lucas as the distraction and Shane darting past to power down or destroy the main console. But Shane wasn't ready—

Lucas moved toward the mismatched bots. He kept his gun down, but he took a few steps in their direction. EMBLA swiveled to watch him. Shane waited for a chance to make a break for the console.

"You were warned."

A blue-white bolt of electricity arced from EMBLA's right claw, catching Lucas in the chest. His whole body seized, twitching and bucking, as EMBLA's surge electrocuted Lucas right before Shane's eyes.

"Fuck, no!" Shane pulled the tab on his grenade and lobbed it right for the collection of misfit bots.

EMBLA's lightning bolt clicked off. Lucas's body fell to the floor.

"Lucas!"

Before Shane could move in his partner's direction, EMBLA rolled faster than Shane would have thought possible and tipped itself onto the grenade, an instant before the device exploded. Shane crouched to avoid flying bits, but EMBLA's mechanism absorbed the worst of the explosion. When he dared raise his head from cover, EMBLA's mechanical body was a charred and twisted wreck. The mismatched creations remained in the shadows, and Shane had no idea whether they were deactivated with EMBLA's destruction, or just in sleep mode, awaiting orders.

All he cared about was getting to Lucas.

"Lucas!" he shouted again. Shane ran to where Lucas lay, unmoving.

"No, no, no!" Shane felt for a pulse and found none. He started CPR, alternating chest compressions and breathing.

"Don't die on me, you son of a bitch! Do you hear me? You can't leave me here by myself. Please, please don't die." Shane kept up the compressions as hope slipped away. He had stopped praying amid the fires and storms of the Events, when no cosmic being seemed to care, but now, he prayed harder than he had in many years.

"Please, if you're out there, if you can help him, please bring him back. He's the only family I have left. I can't do this without him."

Shane had lost track of the daemon's song during the tense discussion with EMBLA and the firefight that followed. Now, the music in his mind swelled to a crescendo, closer and louder than ever before. Shane felt a frisson of energy run through Lucas's still form, and then between one heartbeat and the next, Lucas opened his eyes.

That's when Shane realized that the daemon's song now came from Lucas.

"Lucas?" Shane asked in a whisper. If Lucas was alive, it was none of his doing. His CPR was too little, too late, and EMBLA's jolt had probably damaged Lucas's heart irreparably. Miracle or monstrosity, this was the daemon's doing.

"We are Lucas, and we are Ourself," a voice that was eerily Lucas's and yet not, replied.

"You're the daemon, the genius loci, from High Rock?"

Lucas gave a nod of acknowledgment. "Yes. And we are Lucas Maddox. Both. Ourself heard your plea to save your friend. His soul remains, and so does Ourself."

"Can you heal him?" Shane found himself holding his breath.

The voice that answered was Lucas's, but the expression on his face was unlike him. "His body is damaged beyond what it can heal. My power can sustain him indefinitely, but to do so, I cannot ever leave. If I leave, he dies."

"If you stay, who will be in charge? You, or Lucas?" Shane asked, playing for time so that his mind could catch up to what was happening. He teetered between despair and elation, staring into the chasm of a choice he knew he could not make for his friend.

"I will put his mind to the front, but while he lives, I will always be present."

"Why?" Shane asked, wetting his dry lips as his heart thudded. "I know I prayed. But I've prayed before and no one answered. Why would you listen? Why him? Would you leave High Rock, or would we need to stay nearby?"

Lucas's head inclined as if he were having a silent conversation with himself, and perhaps somewhere inside, Lucas's spirit argued with the daemon. *It would be so like him,* Shane thought with a pang of grief.

"I am not alone at the place you call High Rock," the daemon replied. "Others could take my place. But you can hear us. Few can, and no one in a very long time. Eons. If this one dies, you will not survive for long," the entity continued. "We do not wish to lose the one who can hear us. To save you, we must save him."

Shane caught his breath. The daemon lacked any tact that might have stopped a human's blunt reply. He couldn't deny it. Lucas and he had been best friends all their lives, through war and loss, and the end of the world. They'd both confessed that the only reason they hadn't opted for suicide in the aftermath, like so many others, was because they had a job and they relied on each other.

Shane wouldn't live long trying to do a Marshal's work alone. And while he felt sure that Fort Getty or Old Bedford would make a place for him, Shane wasn't sure he had the will to go on without his partner or his purpose. If the dangers of the road didn't kill him, the emptiness of the night might very well force his hand.

"It's not my choice," Shane croaked, his throat tight and mouth dry. "It's got to be up to Lucas."

A subtle shift changed everything about Lucas's face, from the light in his eyes to the set of his jaw.

"If I have to choose between death and co-habitation, I'll shack up with a spook," Lucas said, with a twist of his lips that was one-hundred percent him. "Don't be stupid. Take the goddamn win."

"Okay," Shane replied, letting out his breath. "All right." He looked past the smoking heap of EMBLA's remains. "What about the other bots?"

Lucas's vacant stare told Shane that the daemon was back in charge. "They are sentient. Aware."

"They've got no leader," Shane replied, torn about the decision he'd made in the split second when Lucas's life hung in the balance. He'd intended to draw EMBLA off, not sure that destroying the bot had even been possible. Then again, Shane and Lucas had never hesitated to kill a human who posed a lethal threat.

"Some of the lesser daemons might be willing to inhabit the most compatible of the creations, to...collaborate."

Shane's eyes widened at the ramifications. It would almost be like birthing a new species. The daemons had sentience and empathy. The bots had a degree of awareness but lacked empathy. But together...

"Promise to keep them from turning into predators," he bargained.

"We have seen enough of chaos," the daemon replied.

"Then you have yourself a deal." Shane doubted he had official authority to sign off on a new sentient robo-entity, but fuck it. There was no one left to complain.

"If you wish to speak with me, I will come forward," the daemon said. "Otherwise, Lucas is himself."

Lucas shook his head like he was coming up from a swim. Shane saw fear and confusion in his friend's eyes, along with something he hadn't glimpsed in a long time. Joy.

"It's...vast," Lucas said, and Shane knew he was talking about whatever sliver of consciousness he shared with the daemon. "It's going to take some getting used to. But then again, so would being dead."

Shane offered him a hand to help him to his feet. "This is better than dead."

"Yeah," Lucas replied, dusting himself off. "Definitely better." He glanced around the room, from the smoking shell of the downed robot to its newly fostered creations. "We're done here. Let's get gone."

EPILOGUE

"You think we did the right thing?" Lucas asked as he and Shane took a week off from their travels, opting to stay at Fort Getty to recover. It wasn't a vacation; the fort needed every resident to pitch in on the everyday chores, but the break from the road was something both men sorely needed.

"You're here. The bots have a new keeper. We've made worse decisions," Shane replied and took a slug of the raw homemade whiskey that was Major Harris's pride and joy.

Lucas's hand went to his chest. Beneath his shirt, the twisted pink scars of a fatal burn stretched across his skin like lightning. The fort's doctor had remarked he'd never seen a man struck like that who lived, but all the diagnostics he could run showed Lucas to be in perfect health.

Perhaps a little too perfect.

"Doc said my vitals are better than what he'd expect from a teenager," Lucas said. "As if I'd stopped aging. Or actually got younger."

"All those stories about the miracle water at Lourdes? The Fountain of Youth? If those were daemons, then yeah, you might be bulletproof and immortal. Damn."

"I'm not going to test either theory, but...it's weird to think about."

"I'm glad you're still here." Shane took another swig.

"So am I. Surprised, but glad."

"I think that the daemon—"

"Rocky."

"What?"

"Rocky. That's what I call the daemon. Because it came from High Rock."

"Rocky?"

"You have a better idea?" Lucas challenged.

"He's your daemon, you get to name him," Shane conceded, secretly thrilled to be back to their old familiar banter. "Anyhow, I think... Rocky...is saprophytic."

"That sounds dirty."

Shane rolled his eyes. "Like Spanish moss. It coexists with its tree hosts in a mutually beneficial relationship. Unlike a parasite, which kills its host."

"You figured this out, how?"

"Doc and I did a little digging through his reference books, while you were resting," Shane admitted.

"Am I different?" Lucas asked, looking away as he took a sip of his own drink. "I mean, I can tell that Rocky's in here with me, way in the back. Sometimes, when I dream, I know the memories aren't mine. I know we had to let Doc in on it, but other people? I don't think they'll take it well. Can you tell that I'm not...human...anymore?"

Lucas didn't look at Shane, but Lucas was certain Shane could hear the worry in his voice.

"You're you," Shane replied with a shrug. "Same old asshole I've known all my life. Except—"

"What?" Lucas asked, clearly nervous.

"You sing now."

"I *sing*?"

"Well, Rocky does. The daemon's song that I heard coming from High Rock? Now it comes from you."

"So other daemons will know?"

"Almost certainly."

"Is that a good thing, or a bad thing?" Lucas asked.

"Probably good, on the whole. It might keep the bad daemons from fucking with us. If there are creatures out there that also pick up on the song, they might think twice about causing trouble. We still really don't know what you could do in a fight, with the daemon's energy inside you."

"Well, shit. I'm going to have to think about that for a while because Rocky says he's never possessed anyone before."

They sat in companionable silence for a few minutes, looking up at a night sky that seemed much darker and star-filled without city lights. "When we go out again, where do you want to go?" Shane asked.

"Figured we'd go to Fort Detrick and see about those zombies," Lucas replied, sipping his whiskey again. "Maybe some weres, too, if Harris's intel is right."

"Fine by me. Sounds like our kind of party," Shane answered with a grin, letting Lucas know that daemon or not, everything was business as usual.

TO BE CONTINUED...

Part Two

WITCH OF THE WOODS

WITCH
OF THE
WOODS

A WASTELAND MARSHALS NOVELLA

GAIL Z. MARTIN

LARRY N. MARTIN

CHAPTER ONE

"Faster!" Lucas Maddox shouted into the wind, hoping his partner, Shane Collins, was right behind him. The hoofbeats from his horse sounded loud and furious on the deserted stretch of asphalt.

Can a horse outrun a wolf? How about a werewolf? He didn't know, and he sure didn't want to find out the hard way. Lucas bent forward, urging his horse on, gambling that a smidge less wind resistance might help him stay a leap ahead of their pursuer's sharp teeth.

Even before the Events this stretch of highway had been dark at night. Now, without the distant glimmer of cities on the horizon or the pale glow of headlights, the darkness felt smothering. He'd have given a lot for an SUV and a full tank of gas, or at least a well-lit rest stop he could barricade against their pursuer. But neither of those things existed anymore.

Werewolves did.

Shots fired behind him, followed by cursing. "Don't slow down to shoot!" Lucas yelled. "If you slow down, you die."

He thought he remembered reading, long ago, that horses had more endurance than wolves, and that a predator would save its energy for weaker prey that required less effort. Unfortunately, that article hadn't talked about werewolves, either natural or government-enhanced. As with everything these days, this new post-cataclysm reality didn't come with instructions.

"Fire in the hole!" Shane yelled, seconds before a brilliant flare lit up the night, and an explosion echoed through the valley. Lucas heard a yip of surprise or pain, followed by a bone-chilling howl of frustration. Seconds later, Shane rode up alongside him, a gray blur in the moonlight.

"I don't know whether I got him with the grenade, but he's not chasing us anymore," Shane said, with an anxious glance over his shoulder.

"Not much farther." Lucas knew their horses couldn't keep up this pace for long, but when it came to outrunning a werewolf, their mounts were as much at risk of becoming dog chow as they were. *Skin in the game, so to speak.*

"There!" Shane pointed to the turn, easy to miss without the glare of overhead lights or the reflection of headlights. They thundered down the off-ramp, slowing at the bottom, not for fear of traffic but to get their bearings. The stretch of abandoned hotels, convenience stores, and service plazas hunched eerily silent in the darkness.

Lucas squinted and picked out a squat, cement-block auto body shop that looked like it had served travelers since the 1950s.

"I hope that's it. The horses need to drink and cool off."

"Look."

Lucas followed Shane's gesture and saw a battered red college pennant hanging from the shattered plate glass front window. "They're here."

They rode up to the service bay doors, with Shane on watch as Lucas swung down from his saddle to knock on the heavy panels. The metal creaked as the door slowly rose until the opening was large enough for them to lead their horses inside.

"Thanks." Lucas led Shadow, his black stallion, into the bay, warily eyeing the plywood that had been put down over the lift pits.

"Any water?" Shane asked, coaxing his roan gelding, Red, to come into the darkened building. Two candles could not dispel the gloom.

"Yeah. There's a hand pump out back that still works," one of the men replied. "We filled some buckets before it got dark—just in case."

Lucas was glad they had let their horses graze during daylight. Too many predators—human and otherwise—roamed in the dark. "So the werewolves you wanted us to look in to? No need to convince us. We outran one on the way here. Barely."

"Come into the office once you get your horses settled, and we can talk," the second man said.

Lucas and Shane took care of their mounts and headed toward the faint glow of candles in what had once been the shop office. The cinderblock auto body shop was solid and defensible and in pretty good shape, all things considered. The shop was located near Gambrill State Park, on the opposite side of the forest from Fort Detrick. It still smelled of grease and gasoline, stale coffee and cigarettes, although the cars and the mechanics were long gone. Shattered windows left the reception area and lobby a wreck. The service bay, however, seemed undamaged, and the office, with a row of glass brick at the top of one wall, was also intact.

Two men in their mid-twenties waited for them inside. They wore academic robes, with Mardi Gras beads around their necks. One had an action figure of Deadpool dangling from the necklace, while Spidey hung from the other set of beads as if he'd gone on a NOLA bender.

"I'm Wade. He's Peter," Wade, the shorter, darker-haired man said, with a nod toward his tall, skinny blond partner.

"Of course you are."

"No, really. The names are real," Peter said earnestly. "That's how we picked our avatars."

"Marshals Lucas Maddox and Shane Collins," Lucas replied, returning the introduction. "Nice to meet you."

The whole IT Priests thing had started as a joke, a comment on how since programming and engineering students didn't have time for fun and supposedly couldn't get laid—and would be poor forever thanks to student loans—they might as well join the priesthood. Then the world fell apart, and students suddenly found their course of study was now their vocation.

Lucas couldn't help thinking that the two IT Priests looked a bit like his and Shane's younger, less world-weary selves. Shane's short blond hair and easy manner together with his rangy build gave him what Lucas had always termed an All-American cowboy look. Lucas had dark hair and dark eyes, with a more muscular build and a bad-boy vibe that had come in handy. Their heights were a half-inch apart, a point of joking contention for years.

Lucas picked up a faded magazine from the cluttered desk. "I used to love reading new car comparisons." He thumbed through the dusty magazine, three years out of date, and tossed it aside. "Back when you could buy one. When they still made them."

Reading a magazine became a painful rite of recollection, just like the faded billboards that still framed the empty highways, another reminder that the world they knew was gone, and it wouldn't be coming back.

"Tell us what you've heard." Shane looked as antsy to hear details as Lucas felt.

"We move around a lot," Wade said. "Most of the time, the enclaves or farms are happy to put us up for the night. We make the circuit from one college and server farm to another every few months. Twice now, we've gone back to places that had put us up for the night before and found everyone dead. Wild animal attack. But there aren't many animals that could do that sort of damage."

"We thought maybe bobcats or feral dogs," Peter chimed in. "Then we got talking to folks at the next couple of enclaves. People saw huge wolves—too big to be anything normal. A couple of them said they'd seen the wolf change into a person. We didn't believe them—"

"But we kept hearing the same stories, and then someone killed one of the creatures, and it changed back to a naked man in front of a dozen witnesses," Wade finished.

"Killed how?" Shane leaned forward, intent on the story.

"Cut off the head. It took a shit ton of bullets and kept on coming," Peter replied, with a wide-eyed expression that made him look even younger.

"Good to know," Lucas muttered. "Did you try silver?"

"Yeah. Someone looted a few abandoned jewelry stores and melted down the silver, then cast bullets. That didn't stop them. Not like on TV," Wade said.

"We think there might be an outpost of hunters around," Peter added. "People who hunt supernatural creatures, not deer. They've taken care of some monster problems and left the carcasses behind."

"Personally, I'm happy for anyone who can keep the roads passable, whether they get rid of monsters or robbers," Wade chimed in.

Lucas didn't envy the wandering programmers their jobs. He and Shane were ex-military, trained to fight and survive under difficult conditions. Wade and Peter went to college expecting to work in a cube farm and ended up living in *The Walking Dead*.

"How big are these werewolves?" Lucas asked.

"The size of a full-grown man on all fours," Peter replied. "A big man, not a skinny one. So maybe close to two hundred pounds and over six feet long if they stretched out."

Lucas and Shane had received a tip that the biological warfare unit at Fort Detrick had been trying to bio-engineer soldier-werewolves right before the bombs dropped and the world ended. Wade and Peter, with access to what remained of the internet as IT Priests, had gotten a message to the commander at Fort Getty asking for the Marshals' help.

"Have you talked to anyone who used to work at Fort Detrick?" Shane asked. "Someone who might know what they actually did there?"

Both men shook their heads. "We haven't run into anyone who made it out of that whole area from Baltimore to the other side of Gambrill Park," Wade said, "based on where the bombs hit. Closer in, the radiation killed pretty much everyone. The professors say the levels are better now, but no one's going to move back to that area any time soon."

Lucas hoped a visit to Fort Detrick itself wouldn't be necessary. "If the werewolves have a higher resistance, they could hide in places people aren't inclined to go looking for them and come out to hunt. That would make them hard to track."

"Do you have any idea of how many there are?" Shane looked from one of the men to the other.

"No, just hearsay. More than a couple, less than a lot. If there were too many, there wouldn't be anyone left. But there've been enough deaths that there's got to be more than just one or two. We've had kills reported from here over to South Mountain State Park," Wade told them. "The rangers can't say for sure whether or not the werewolves are in the parks."

"Do we need to hunt during a full moon?" Lucas didn't want to hang around for a month if they missed the cycle.

Peter shook his head. "No. That's the weird thing, if these are real werewolves, the attacks don't come at a certain time of day or particular days of the month. I'm gonna be bummed if all those movies were wrong."

Lucas didn't have the heart to tell him that the movies were wrong about most things. "I guess it would be inconvenient to spend all that effort on a super soldier that can only Hulk out three days each month."

"The thing is, we think there's something else going on, besides werewolves," Peter spoke up, with a glance at Wade, who nodded. "There are people who've gone missing, but no one's found bodies. It doesn't look like the people intended to leave. They left all their things behind. Clothing, weapons, tools. No one does that—not anymore, when you can't buy new."

"And the last IT Priests who came this way haven't been seen since," Wade added.

"Where did the people go missing?" Shane asked.

Wade grabbed a pen off the desk and pulled a map of the area from a rack behind them. He unfolded it and spread the map out, adding dots to mark locations, then connected them in a circle. "These are farms where people vanished. They're all mostly located in the corridor between Gambrill State Park and Zittlestown." He added more dots to the map. "And this is where we've heard there were possible werewolf kills. They're mostly farther north." Wade connected those dots as well, in a second circle. "It's only ten miles from here to Zittlestown, and maybe fifteen to the farthest of the kills. Not a big area."

"Two different centers, with some overlap," Lucas said. "Maybe two different causes."

"Or rival packs of werewolves," Shane warned.

"Always the optimist." Lucas rolled his eyes.

Shane's fingers drummed on the arm of his chair as he thought. "All this makes me wonder if the biowarfare guys might not have baked some extra immunity into their designer-DNA werewolves. I mean, if you're trying to build a better monster, why not go all the way?"

"Unsettling, but possible." Lucas picked at a rough spot on the old plastic chair, scraping away bits. "How did the experimental furry super-soldiers get out?"

"If the EMP from the explosion took out enough power lines, substations, and generating plants, it wouldn't have had to hit the base itself to have the same effect," Shane theorized. "I'm sure the base had generators, but was anyone around to tend them? If the power went down and stayed down, the wolfmen might have been able to tear their way out."

International terrorists had turned countries' own nukes against them. A simultaneous strike took out Washington, DC and the world's key capital cities and financial centers. It didn't take long for chaos to spiral. The army and law enforcement had tried to maintain the fiction of a government-in-hiding to reassure civilians, but the truth was dire. Most senior government officials died in a blast that occurred with only seconds of warning. Any attempt at piecing together a crisis administration foundered and failed as the hits kept coming—power grid failures, tidal waves, and earthquakes, disease, and anarchy.

The military and civilian law enforcement did their best, and most of them died with their boots on. To Lucas's knowledge, he and Shane were the last two US Marshals left in the area. Park rangers and small-town cops worked hard to help out, but there was too much territory and not enough badges.

"We don't know how many the government made, or whether they can breed naturally," Peter said.

"Or why the werewolves stayed in the area," Wade added.

Lucas thought for a moment. "Maybe there are still enough people and animals in the surrounding area to eat. Once you get a distance outside the big cities, where they didn't get hit with the fire, concussion, or radiation, people stayed, regrouped, dug in, tried to make the best of it. That might be plenty to keep the werewolves satisfied—at least for now."

"What I want to know is—are there twenty of these GMO-wolves, or two hundred?" Shane asked.

"I think it would have been hard to keep two-hundred weaponized werewolves a secret," Lucas replied. "So a lower number is more likely. Too big of a group would be hard to feed."

"Even twenty would be a lot for just the two of us to fight," Shane warned.

Lucas shrugged. "That's why this is a reconnaissance trip, not necessarily a strike force. We get in, assess the threat, and figure out what we need to deal with it. The general at Fort Getty promised us soldiers if we needed them. Wade and Peter just said there are local monster hunters in the area, too. After all, werewolves aren't the only things that came out of the shadows once the lights went out."

Not too very long ago, Lucas had thought that cartels, mobsters, and human traffickers were the biggest monsters. But as technology failed and the lights and protections of modern civilization dimmed, older threats emerged from where they'd been hiding, ready to stake a claim as apex predator.

Nightmare creatures like vampires and shifters emerged, along with other things long thought to be mere legend. Magic strengthened, and so did entities like the place-daemons—genius loci—that Shane could hear. Some were helpful, or at least neutral. Others definitely weren't.

"You know, I'd give a lot for some drone footage or a satellite image," Shane replied. "Or a cell phone that worked consistently. Hell, I'd be thrilled for a telegraph."

"The satellites are still up there," Wade said, looking wistfully at the ceiling as if he could see the night sky. "We just can't connect to them anymore."

"We've been lucky to hold onto as much of the internet as we have," Peter added. "Some parts of Europe—especially Russia—never came back online. And others that were still there right after everything happened have gone dark. So all things considered, we're just thrilled that any of it still works."

The only way the fragile internet survived the Events was courtesy of university networks dependent on now-untended substations and what remained of corporate server farms. So the itinerant IT Priests, like Wade and Peter, rode their circuit of locations to do maintenance and used their access to the internet to pass along messages and get updates from their counterparts and from the librarians and museum staffers who stuck to their posts.

Shane stood. "It's getting cold in here. I'm going to go see what I can do for some heat."

"I'll help you," Lucas volunteered. He looked to Wade and Peter. "Why don't you guys see what we can scrape together for stuff to burn? We've got enough chairs that everyone can sleep, but it probably won't be the most comfortable night you've ever spent."

Even before sunset, it had gotten much colder than usual for this time of year. The nuclear blasts had hurled huge debris clouds into the atmosphere; the volcanic eruptions triggered by those blasts had made it worse. Temperatures dropped noticeably, making it unseasonably cool.

Shane found a 55-gallon drum, and Lucas cleared papers off desks to burn. They rigged up one of the bay's old exhaust hoses to vent the fire and hoped it would take the chill off, even if it didn't warm the entire area.

"I can't believe we're hunting fuckin' werewolves," Lucas said, gathering more paper.

"Government-issue werewolves. They're more Wolverine than Teen Wolf."

Before the Events, Shane and Lucas babysat high-level witnesses in headline-grabbing trials, captured ruthless fugitives, transported badass prisoners, and served federal warrants on people who didn't want to cooperate. Then the world fell apart, the cities turned into ghost towns, and most of the grid went down. Now, Shane and Lucas found themselves cleaning up the messes the government left behind.

Lucas returned with another armful of paper and added some manuals and technical booklets to the pile. "Back when we were kids, I wanted us to join the army, and you wanted us to run off with the circus. Man, I shoulda let you win."

Shane smirked and tossed him a three-years out of date candy bar he had liberated from the vending machine in the body shop's back room. "Maybe."

Best friends since childhood, Shane and Lucas had joined the army together, risen through the ranks, done a couple of tours of duty in Iraq, then got out and joined the US Marshals. The dangerous, all-consuming work and travel hadn't left time for relationships. Now their families were dead, and so were nearly all their old friends. That just left the two of them, and a brotherhood forged from spilled blood and shared nightmares.

"So...government-engineered werewolves," Lucas said. "I'm still getting over the idea that werewolves are real, let alone 'roided up with some Dr. Moreau-style juju juice."

"You see ghosts. I hear genius loci. Hell, you've got an ancient spirit riding shotgun inside your head, and you're freaking out about werewolves? Dude, they might be the most *normal* thing we've seen in months."

Lucas grimaced. "Maybe. Every time I think this gig can't get any weirder—"

"I don't think there's a bottom to the weirdness anymore." Shane bit off a piece of stale candy and had to work to pull it from the bar. "You know, this tastes pretty good, all things considered."

Shane glanced toward the office and the two IT Priests, making sure they were out of earshot. "Did Rocky have anything to say about the thing that chased us?"

When a freak accident electrocuted Lucas, his body was damaged beyond repair. Shane had begged any entity that was listening for help, and a daemon—a nature spirit—from nearby High Rock Park had answered his plea. The daemon couldn't heal Lucas, but it could possess him and sustain his life. Lucas had agreed to the deal, and named his co-pilot daemon "Rocky," after the park he came from.

Lucas stared straight ahead, silently communicating with his inner hitchhiker. Most of the time, Lucas was in the driver's seat, and Rocky stayed in the background. But if needed, Rocky could take control. After a moment, he shook his head.

"He says that the creature's energy felt unnatural. Now that he knows what it is, he'll let us know if he senses it again," Lucas replied. "What did you take from what Wade and Peter said?" he asked with a jerk of his head toward the office.

"People are scared. Who isn't? They didn't survive a nuclear blast just to get eaten. And if these werewolves are that hard to kill, then civilians aren't going to be able to handle it," Shane recapped.

"Yeah. That's what I got, too. So tomorrow, we do some recon—for the wolfmen and that mysterious hunter camp. I'll be very happy if we don't have to go anywhere near Fort Detrick itself." Lucas shuddered. He tried to hide his reaction, but Shane knew him well enough to call his bluff.

"The ghosts?"

Lucas nodded. "Yeah. Fort Detrick might not have been Ground Zero, but it was close enough. Most of those people never got off the base alive. It's bad enough knowing that. I don't want to see it up close."

"After Iraq? You don't owe the dead anything, Lucas. Certainly not your sanity."

He'd always been able to see ghosts, but for a long time, Lucas ignored those glimpses, and only Shane had known his secret. In Iraq, it had been bad enough to see mangled bodies on the battlefield without seeing their bloodied ghosts adrift amidst the carnage. Then the Events happened, and the same energy shift that brought supernatural creatures out of hiding seemed to boost both his ghost sight and Shane's connection to the genius loci.

"Maybe not," Lucas admitted. "But what if we visited the places Wade and Peter said the farmers vanished? If the people are dead, I might find out something from their ghosts."

"Do you think werewolves leave spirits behind when they die violently?"

"No idea. You want me to go have a chat with Fenrir's ghost?"

Shane shrugged. "Couldn't hurt."

"You do remember that not all spooks are chatty, right? Some of them don't talk at all. And others...don't like being disturbed."

"Yeah, I remember." Shane paused. "Is Rocky picking up anything from the parks around here?" The worried look in Shane's eyes suggested the reason for his sudden change of subject. "Because I'm getting weird vibes, but I'm not sure from where."

Lucas closed his eyes and let himself "float" in his thoughts as the daemon who shared his body worked out its reply. "Something is unsettled," Rocky spoke through Lucas. "I will listen to the songs of the other daemons, and see what I can learn." Lucas blinked rapidly, coming back to himself. "Was that what you needed?"

Shane frowned. "I pick up on the genius loci as singing. Peaceful places are calm. Bad places sound jangly."

"And you think there's a bad place nearby, or one that's gotten stronger?"

"Maybe. More like the kind of music that puts a shiver down your spine in a scary movie. Twisted."

"Oh, that doesn't sound ominous at all," Lucas said, rolling his eyes. They'd watched a lot of late-night horror movies, holed up at third-rate hotels babysitting WITSEC informants. He and Shane had always joked that if the characters in the movies could hear the background music, they'd know when the monster was coming.

When Lucas and Shane headed back to the office, the other two men had found a few more chairs to push together into improvised beds.

They ate trail rations, washed down with water from a canteen and moonshine from a flask. In the bay, the horses nickered and snuffled. The wind outside picked up and whistled through the broken windows in the lobby.

Conversation turned to favorite movies and TV shows, keeping the memories alive, trading quotes and recounting iconic scenes. With power scarce and the internet fragile, they were unlikely to get to watch most of those programs again.

Lucas pulled his chair up to the desk and broke out a deck of cards. "Since there's no cable and the Wi-Fi sucks, how about a game of poker?" Wade and Peter eagerly joined in, despite Shane's warning not to bet anything except the paperclips they found in the desk drawer.

Shane and Lucas couldn't carry much with them on the road, but some pieces of their former lives were too precious to leave behind. Playing cards, favorite paperbacks, well-used tabletop RPGs, and dice helped while away the hours and reminded them of better days.

Finally, Wade and Peter conceded defeat, Lucas folded, and Shane pretended to count his non-existent winnings. "Get some sleep," Lucas told them. "I'll take the first watch. I'm too jittery to rest. But I'd like to get an early start tomorrow. If we're going werewolf hunting, I'd like to do it in broad daylight."

The army had taught Shane and Lucas to sleep anywhere and any time they had the chance. Shane leaned forward, laying his head on his folded arms, and was snoring in minutes. Wade and Peter didn't look like their positions in the chairs could possibly be comfortable, but they, too, were soon asleep. Lucas got up after a while to check the lobby, secure the doors, stoke the fire, and look in on the horses.

"Hey there, fella," Lucas soothed Shadow. Both horses seemed skittish, a change from earlier in the evening.

A howl sounded from outside, muffled by the cement block walls, but too close for comfort. Lucas wondered if their pursuer had followed them, or if this was a different werewolf—or just a feral dog. He checked all the doors once more, assuring himself everything was securely locked.

"Don't worry," he told the horses. "I think we're okay in here." Just in case, Lucas resolved to sit out the rest of his watch with a gun in his hand.

Shane's shout echoed from the concrete walls, startling the horses.

Lucas came running back and found Shane sitting upright, pale and wide-eyed. Wade and Peter slept on, snoring loudly.

"What? What's wrong?"

Shane shook his head, fighting his way clear of the nightmare. "I was dreaming about that kiddie park we took your niece, Emma, to visit. The one with the fairytale village?"

Lucas nodded, trying to ignore the pang that came with remembering that Emma, his brother, and everyone in his family were all dead now. "Yeah. She got scared at the Hansel and Gretel house."

"And then I picked her up, and we ran down the path to get away." Shane's voice shook. "But in my dream, everything got dark, and the house looked real—not just painted concrete. The rest of the park went away, and we were deep in the woods. I couldn't run. And something dark and evil ripped Emma out of my arms and pulled her inside. I tried, but I couldn't get to her."

"It's okay." Lucas laid a hand on Shane's shoulder.

"No." Shane shook his head. "No, it's not. Because I think there really might be something evil in the woods."

CHAPTER TWO

"Evil in the woods?" Lucas asked the next morning and gave Shane a worried look. "Can you get a little more specific?"

Is he worried about what's in the woods, or that I've lost my mind? Shane wondered.

Wade and Peter had left at daybreak, thanking the Marshals for their help. That left Lucas and Shane—and Rocky—alone again.

Shane shook his head. "Sorry. But if you see a candy house, don't go in." He tried to make light of the dream, but the final images were horror, not fantasy, and far too realistic for comfort.

"If it's got Twix or Butterfingers, I can't promise. I'd take on a wicked witch for either of those, just sayin'." Lucas had a thoughtful expression, and relief flooded through Shane, knowing that his partner took him seriously.

"I've got your back, but save the Gummi Bears for me. All the ones we've found lately are too hard to chew."

"Good thing, then, that they dissolve in moonshine, isn't it?"

Shane just rolled his eyes.

"Was it a dream, or a vision?" Lucas sat back in his chair, frowning. "You said that for you, the genius loci use pictures instead of words. That jangled song you're picking up from somewhere—do you think this is related?"

Shane shrugged. "Maybe? We know there are natural monsters out there, and magic seems to have come back strong. So why not witches? I'm not expecting a real gingerbread house, but maybe something else appealing? An attractive trap?"

Lucas nodded. "That makes sense. Rocky's not chiming in, so I don't have anything to add."

Shane reached for the map Wade marked up. "The missing people vanished between the two state parks, and that's also where the verified kills are." He pointed to a strip of land in the middle of the marks. "So let's start here. Two circles, two centers. One for the witch, and one for the wolves?"

"Maybe. But if we can figure it out, why haven't the other compounds? Shouldn't they have shown up with torches and pitchforks already?"

Shane stared at the map. "Would civilians think like that? And do they know about all the incidents? Yeah, the Baltimore-Washington corridor had a ton of military, but most of them didn't make it out. So it's not like these are people trained to assess a target. They're just the ones who got lucky and didn't die. And I imagine that not dying takes up all of their bandwidth. I doubt they have the time to play detective."

"All right. We'll head out as soon as we're packed." Lucas checked his wind-up watch. Shane had to smile, thinking of how, once upon a time, good watches had been a passion for Lucas. Now, a Timex was the watch of choice, since it lived up to its famous slogan.

"Quit staring at my watch," Lucas grumbled as if he guessed Shane's thoughts. "It works. There's no one left to impress."

"I'm wounded." Shane's dramatic tone made Lucas smile. "When did you stop trying to impress me?"

"Maybe in sixth grade, when I climbed all the way to the top of Mrs. Connolly's maple tree and got a busted arm for my trouble."

"I was duly impressed," Shane replied. "They gave you a bright red cast so that you could be a cautionary tale for the rest of us."

"Screw you."

Shane went to get water for the horses and take a leak. Lucas muttered something about needing a few more minutes of sleep since the sun had barely risen.

Lucas was sound asleep when Shane returned to the office, leaning back in his chair, legs splayed in front of him, hands folded on his belly.

"He is more worried than he wants to show."

Shane startled at the comment, shooting a puzzled look at Lucas's sleeping form before realization kicked in. "Rocky?"

"Your friend is sleeping. I do not require rest. Our conversation will not disturb him." Rocky's voice was Lucas's, but the inflection was all wrong. Then again, daemons didn't usually use language, so considering he'd only been possessing Lucas for a few months, Rocky was doing pretty well.

"Something on your mind? Is Lucas okay?" Shane settled into the other chair, where he could watch the door to the lobby.

"He is fine and will be so long as I accompany him," Rocky replied. "He worries about being among others—especially those who know about hidden things."

"You mean, like the werewolves and witches? He's afraid they'll find out about you?"

"He fears the reaction would not be good. He worries that they might hurt you and seize him, to study."

Shane couldn't deny that the thought had crossed his mind. If the biowarfare people at Fort Detrick had been creating souped-up werewolves, they'd probably love to dissect a daemon-powered US Marshal. Shane had no intention of letting that happen.

"There have been a lot of people who wanted to get a piece of us," Shane replied. "We've been good at not letting that happen."

"That would be best. I have become...fond...of both of you."

"How's Lucas dealing with...everything? Dying, coming back, you."

"I did not know him before you called to me. He is strong-willed, and he wishes to stay alive. To do the work. To keep you safe. He was afraid that if he left, you would go, too."

Lucas's instincts were good, and he knew Shane better than anyone. They were the only family the other had left. Their friendship and professional partnership defined their lives. Shane had lost too much already. He had bet everything on a desperate cry for help, a plea that Rocky answered.

"He's probably right," Shane admitted. "Do the two of you get along?" *Does he resent me for trapping him with an ancient, incorporeal being inside his own body who can never leave?*

"We are compatible. I show him wonders, and he tells me jokes. I do not usually understand, but it pleases him, and...I like the company."

People had built relationships on a lot less. Shane took it for a win. "I had a dream—"

"A vision. I felt the ripples."

Well, that settled that. "A vision," Shane amended. "Was it true? Who sent it?"

Lucas's features were relaxed in sleep, heightening the oddness of hearing him speak Rocky's thoughts. "The essence may be true, if not the details. It did not come from Gambrill Park."

"South Mountain, then? I felt something dark—evil."

"I sense the wrongness, but not yet its source."

Shane nodded. "All right. Thank you—for everything. I feel a little better with you on our side."

With that, Rocky fell silent, leaving Shane to his thoughts.

IF YOU SQUINT, it's almost like nothing happened." Lucas and Shane rode side by side, looking out over the rolling hills dotted with barns and silos.

"Except for us riding horses down an empty highway, and the fact that there's no one in sight. We've been this way, Before. It was never empty, not even at three in the morning."

They had decided to start with the kills that were the farthest north and work their way down. "Three of the bodies were behind that barn." Shane pointed toward the first farm on their list. Wade and Peter had provided the best location information they could for the mauled bodies and the missing farm families. Shane just hoped that visiting the sites would clue them in on what was going on and how to stop it.

As they rode toward the farm, Shane watched for someone to emerge from the house or barn, or to catch a glimpse of cows in the field or horses at pasture. Even the birds were few and quiet.

Up close, it was easier to see that no one had been home for a long time. Grass grew in the middle of the lane. A garden had gone untended for more than one season, more weeds now than flowers or vegetables. Shutters and drain spouts hung askew.

Shane read Lucas's hand signals out of long practice. *Check the perimeter, then the house, then the barn.* They moved silently, with Lucas in the front and Shane watching his back. The tall grass bent in the wind, but no creatures stirred. Making a circle around the house and barn provided more vantage points from which to see the decay, but no insight into what had happened to the owners.

They approached the house warily, still expecting an ambush. Lucas went to the front door while Shane circled around to the back and kicked their way inside nearly at the same second. Weapons ready, they waited for gunfire, or perhaps the screams of survivors. The silence felt desolate.

Shane took in the modest furnishings. "Whoever lived here didn't bother to take much with them."

"No blood," Lucas pointed out. "If a wild animal killed them—let alone a werewolf—there should be signs of a fight. Broken furniture, bloody streaks, ripped cushions...something. It just looks like they went for a walk and didn't come back."

"Let's check the rest of the house and see what we find." Shane tried to shake off the eeriness of the deserted farmhouse, but it sank into his bones, casting a pall over his mood.

In the kitchen, a single plate with the dried, moldering remains of food sat in front of a chair. The living room was cozy, with a sofa and two armchairs. A book lay on the seat of one of the chairs next to an empty mug on the end table, while a second book lay on the couch. Upstairs, three bedrooms appeared to have been in use, with bedclothes left rumpled and belongings still looking as if the owners would return at any moment.

"I don't get it," Lucas said when he and Shane went back to the kitchen.

"It's like they just wandered away." Shane's gaze drifted back to the solitary place-setting in the kitchen.

"But why? I doubt the Pied Piper came through and lured them off."

"Remember what I said about an attractive trap? Maybe it's something like that," Shane mused.

"Were they gone before the werewolf made its kill behind the barn? Or were they the victims?"

"No idea. Are you seeing any ghosts?"

Lucas stood still, listening and watching. Finally, he shook his head. "No. Not even a wisp. Let's go look at the barn. Something's fishy."

The barn proved to be as empty as the house, filled with equipment and supplies to care for horses, cows, and sheep—none of which were anywhere to be found. "No animals—but from the stalls and the corral, they were here not too long ago. No blood inside, so what happened to them?" Shane asked.

Outside, at the back of the barn, they found a pile of bones, what was left of three bodies. The bones showed scoring from sharp claws, and some had been gnawed on, suggesting that the dead had all been savagely mauled.

"Definitely killed and eaten," Shane said, squatting to get a closer look at the remains. "Look at those teeth marks on the bones."

"There aren't too many wild animals that can do that to an adult," Lucas observed. "A bear or a cougar could, maybe a pack of regular wolves—or feral dogs."

"A werewolf certainly could," Shane added. "I wish we knew more about exactly what kinds of biowarfare creatures they were trying to develop at Fort Detrick. For all we know, they had a whole homicidal menagerie."

He frowned and went looking for a stick, then returned and poked at the grisly pile. "Lucas—this wasn't just a kill." He used the stick to show the bloodied rope still tied around wrist bones. "This was a sacrifice."

Lucas had a faraway look in his eyes as he searched for ghosts. "I think I've got something." He fell silent, standing completely still, as Shane waited impatiently for news. Finally, Lucas roused from his trance and shook himself awake.

"I saw three people—a woman, a teenager, and an older child. They were tied with rope and left here. The creature came for them."

"Did you see what killed them?"

Lucas shook his head. "No, but I saw how they looked afterward." He paled. "They were shredded, with bite marks and places flesh had been torn away."

"Looks like the werewolf theory was right."

"But who lured them out of the house and then left them as...what? An offering? Bait?" He stared back at the old house as if he could will it to reveal its secrets. "We're missing something important."

"Do you think someone is helping the werewolves?"

Lucas shrugged. "These people didn't tie themselves up. But if someone is feeding the werewolves, do they think they're going to be safe by serving everyone else up?"

"Maybe they struck a deal. If people know there are weres in these parts, they'd be cautious. Having a minion to find the prey and sucker them into coming outside might make it easier for the weres," Lucas mused aloud.

"Great. Now the werewolves have a Renfield."

"Back to your question about Fort Detrick working with other kinds of monsters... If you're going to build a super soldier, something partly human would be easier to control—theoretically—than a bunch of hungry creatures," Lucas suggested. "Werewolves or vampires would be at the top of the list."

"Legend has it that the Nazis were interested in werewolves—and magic," Shane replied. "Remember *Raiders of the Lost Ark*? Maybe they weren't the only ones. I mean, if you're hard-core enough to think that biological warfare is a good idea—plague, anthrax, Ebola—is it that much crazier to see if you actually could do magic? Or at least, X-Men type psychic stuff?"

"Maybe not so crazy," Lucas agreed. "But before the Events, magic and the old creatures were hidden. With the grid down and the technology gone, all that stuff has come back at full strength. What if the Fort Detrick crew experimented with things that didn't work then—but do work, or work better, now?"

"The more we think about this stuff, the scarier it gets."

Lucas and Shane headed back toward where they had left their horses, tethered in a shady grove where they could graze.

"What now?" Shane asked. "We could go visit the other places people have disappeared. But it might look just like this."

"And I doubt I'll get more from the other kill sites," Lucas agreed. "So what do you say we go looking for whoever's left? If they're alive and all their neighbors are dead, we've probably found the Renfield."

Lucas and Shane studied Wade's map of the werewolf kills. "So are the missing people and the werewolf kills one and the same? Maybe two different Renfields, same approach?" Shane asked. "Or two different problems?"

Lucas shook his head. "No way to know until we go poking around. What say we ride for the center of the top circle?" He pointed to a spot on the map. "If I were the guy using my neighbors for bait, I wouldn't want to lure the werewolves too close to my own place. The locations of the kills are probably as far as he can go and get back easily."

They rode in silence for a while. "Does Rocky have anything to say about all this? Can he pick up on anything?"

Shane did his best to sound off-handed about his partner having a daemon riding shotgun in his head. He knew Lucas had been worried about his reaction, and whether he'd be able to accept that Lucas wasn't entirely human anymore. Shane did his best to let Lucas know he didn't give a damn. Rocky had brought Lucas back from the dead, and the daemon's continued presence kept Lucas alive, maybe even immortal. It might not be normal, but it beat the alternative.

Lucas got that far-away look he wore when he was listening to Rocky's inner voice. "He says that he never needed to tell one kind of creature apart from another. They were all part of nature. So he's trying to figure out what 'werewolf' energy feels like so he can know when it's nearby."

"I guess that makes sense. It's not like there would have been many of the natural ones around, and they couldn't have hurt him when he was just a place-daemon."

"He says that they can't hurt him now, but he knows we are fragile." Lucas rolled his eyes. "Way to stroke a guy's ego," he muttered. "See what a freak I've become?"

"I'll tell you what I said back at Fort Ritchie. I'd rather have you alive and kicking with a daemon co-pilot than do this gig by myself." Even in the first days, when Lucas tried to come to terms with being "possessed" and doubted his humanity, Shane's support remained solid.

"That's because I'm fun to travel with," Lucas quipped, and Shane recognized deflection when he saw it.

"If by 'fun' you mean you burped and farted a lot in the car, and your breath always smelled like onions, then sure...let's go with 'fun.'"

Those car rides were as long gone as their black SUV and their favorite burger joints.

The melancholy that tinged Shane's memories brought him back to the problem at hand. Seeing the bound victims had been difficult and dredged up far too many memories from his time in the war. He and Lucas dug a shallow grave and salted the bones to set the ghosts free, but that seemed like so little compared to the injustice of their deaths.

"I just can't imagine selling out your neighbors like that," Shane said when the silence became too much.

Lucas gave him a look out of the side of his eye. "That's why you're in law enforcement, instead of being a criminal."

Shane made a face. "Not exactly what I meant."

"Doesn't mean it's not true. Think about it. You wouldn't steal from your neighbor, either. Or frame them to take the fall for something you did. There are plenty of ways to sell someone out. Murdering them to save your own skin is just one of the possibilities."

"I guess we've seen all of that." They were both proud of their service, but neither of them considered their time in the army to be their "glory days," and as an adventure, being shot at seriously sucked. It was a toss-up, Shane thought, on whether they'd seen more disturbing things far away, in a war zone, or closer to home, going up against cartels, the Mob, and stone-cold white-collar criminals.

"We saw whole families killed when a spy ratted them out," Lucas replied. "Friends betrayed by friends. Lovers who turned out to be informants. People willing to kill for money. Some people will do a lot of awful things to stay alive."

"I never figured out how they lived with themselves," Shane said, shuddering.

"The same way Mob hitmen do, or serial killers who let someone else take the rap. I guess it's easy without a conscience."

They passed abandoned farms and empty hamlets as they headed toward the center of the circle. A quick check showed them to be long-vacated, but Lucas only picked up on ghosts at a few of the places. Those they searched more thoroughly, finding older bones and a clear pattern of victims offered for the kill. Among those had been two bodies whose clothing and Mardi Gras necklaces made clear the fate of the missing IT Priests.

"Maybe we had it backward," Shane mused. "Since the older kills are more toward the center. Maybe the son of a bitch started with his near-by neighbors and had to go further afield as he ran out of people to sacrifice."

"Makes sense," Lucas agreed. "Because most of the homes don't have ghosts, and they don't look like people just vanished in the middle of dinner. Those folks probably just packed up and left when it got too hard to survive without Walmart. Can't say I blame them."

"The last bones we found looked pretty weathered. A lot more than the first set. That might mean we're getting close to the source."

"Then whoever is doing this won't be able to pass up a couple of fresh sacrifices, if pickings are getting scarce," Lucas said with a feral gleam in his eyes. "Easier for us if he makes a move—then we know for sure we've got the right guy."

When they finally spotted a house with candlelight shining from the windows, Lucas and Shane had their plan ready. They tied their horses to trees close to the porch, with enough slack to allow the animals to graze. Both men carried long knives and guns, not unusual for those who dared to travel between settlements. They also each carried a silver dagger, just in case.

Shane wore his most winning smile when he knocked on the farm-house door. It opened to reveal a man in his early forties with gray eyes and dark blond hair. Shane didn't overlook the shotgun held in the man's hand, pointed at the floor for the moment.

"We're traveling, and this is the first place with people we've seen in a long while," Shane said, stepping away from his badass Marshals persona and doing his best to look unsure and vulnerable...a perfect victim. "Sorry to bother you, but can we please draw some water for our horses and our canteens? It's still a long way to Boonesboro."

The man looked Shane over, assessing. Shane kept his smile friendly and, he hoped, suitably clueless. No one would ever take Lucas for an easy mark, but he'd managed to soften his usual edge to look pissy rather than dangerous.

"Of course you can draw from our well," the man said, with a welcoming smile that didn't reach his eyes. "In fact, we're just about to have dinner, and it'll stretch for two more. I've got a barn out back where you and your horses can stay," he added with a nod toward their mounts. "Sun'll be down soon. You don't want to be out after dark."

"That's very kind of you." Shane tried to sound relieved and a tad needy.

"No trouble at all. We do our best to welcome travelers. Don't get many these days." The man paused. "I'm Ed," he added, extending his hand.

"Shane." Shane shook Ed's hand, as did Lucas. Ed's gaze was calculating, perhaps wondering how hard it would be to overpower them. Either his prior victims had been extremely poor judges of character, or Ed no longer bothered to put on much of an act.

"The pump is around back. There's some lye soap next to it, so you can wash up before dinner. Just knock when you're ready. We'll be looking forward to hearing your news. We don't get out much."

Despite Ed's folksy manner, Shane's intuition went on high alert. He had survived his time in the army and as a Marshal by trusting his gut, and right now, he felt sure they had found their Renfield.

"Much obliged," Shane replied, and Lucas mumbled his thanks. "We'll be right in."

A glance between them confirmed without words that Lucas was on the same page. They headed to get the water for their horses, wary that it might be a trap, but found a bucket and an old handpump behind what was probably the kitchen. Through the window, Shane could make out a woman's silhouette and saw two smaller figures, probably children.

"There's a family," he murmured under his breath, too quiet to be overheard.

"Doesn't matter," Lucas returned. "It has to stop."

Maybe they're in on it, Shane thought. His time in law enforcement had shown him just how twisted people could become growing up with parents who were psychopaths. *But what choice do they have, if they do know? Ed doesn't seem like the kind to take a vote.*

At their knock, Ed welcomed them into the house like old friends. Shane smelled onions and cabbage, along with some sort of meat. The interior looked worn, but the house was clean and tidy, as comfortable as a farmer's income could manage before the Events.

"Lucas and Shane, this is my wife, Jenny, and our two children, Taylor and Rand."

Jenny's wan smile didn't present an enthusiastic invitation. She and the children stood just far enough away from Ed to be out of reach, at least on a first swing. The fear in Jenny's eyes when she glanced between her husband and the newcomers told Shane their suspicions were well-founded. Neither of the children looked up when they dutifully spoke their parts. Maybe they knew what happened to previous guests, or perhaps they just wanted to avoid doing anything to raise their father's ire.

Ed led them to a dining room with a table and sideboard of an age that suggested they were either bought second-hand or passed down. A mismatched collection of china cups and decorative plates adorned the shelves, along with kitschy angel figurines.

"Come in. Sit down. Make yourselves at home," Ed urged. The children went to the kitchen to carry out bowls of stew for Lucas and Shane, then for their parents and themselves. Jenny was the last to come to the table, looking flustered. She did not meet their eyes.

"We say grace with our meals," Ed announced. The children looked down. Jenny kept her face averted. Shane and Lucas bowed their heads but did not shut their eyes.

"Thanks be for the bounty provided, and for the deliverance it brings. Amen."

Lucas's foot shifted beneath the table, pressing down on Shane's toes, hard. If Shane hadn't already known better than to eat the stew, he was certain of a trick now, especially since the bowls had been prepared individually, out of sight in the kitchen, and served to them by the children.

"We're eager to hear your stories," Ed said, taking a piece of home-made bread and passing the plate on to Lucas. "Tell us what you've seen in your travels."

Lucas took a slice of bread but set it next to his bowl, as did Shane. The children kept their eyes on their food as they ate—not so fast as to earn reproof, but quickly enough Shane had the distinct impression they dearly wanted to be elsewhere. Jenny ate slowly as if she had to force herself to take each bite. She might be Ed's accomplice, but Shane would have bet she didn't help willingly. A glimpse of an old bruise just below her sleeve suggested that Ed didn't deal well with not getting his way.

Lucas turned on the charm, launching into one tale after another—most of them largely fabricated. Ed seemed pleased, laughing at Lucas's jokes and asking questions about how familiar places fared. Before long, both children had finished their portions, and after their empty bowls earned Ed's approval, they were dismissed, fleeing the room as if they'd seen a ghost.

*Speaking of which...*Shane hadn't missed the momentary hitch in Lucas's voice or the way his gaze flickered to a spot just behind Ed's shoulder, or to a corner on the far side of the room. Lucas seeing ghosts was just one more nail in Ed's coffin, confirming his guilt.

Jenny finished shortly after the children and murmured something about needing to clean up in the kitchen as she gathered up the dirty dishes. She glanced briefly in Shane's direction and for a second, made eye contact. He saw everything in her eyes that she could not say—fear, guilt, and a warning.

"I fear I've enjoyed your company too much. You haven't had a chance to eat," Ed said when the others were gone. "You don't want to pass up my Jenny's stew. Her cooking was always a favorite at the covered dish dinners."

"I haven't been able to keep much down today," Lucas replied. Shane knew that truer words were never spoken. The remains they had found at all the different kill sites had ruined their appetites. "Although it does smell very good."

"Since you take in travelers, I was wondering if you'd seen some friends of ours," Shane said. "Two of The IT Priests—the wandering computer experts? You probably wouldn't remember their names, but one of them had a Captain American medallion hanging from his necklace, and the other had Ironman's heart reactor." They had found the jewelry with the young men's bones, which made the atrocity of all the killings feel very personal.

"Sorry, but I don't. There've been so many over the years."

Outside, a wolf howled, and then another. Ed paled but recovered quickly. "You've picked a good night to find shelter."

Lucas raised his gun and pointed it right at Ed. "It sounds like your wolves are hungry. I'm guessing you haven't been able to feed them for a while."

"I welcome you into my home, offer you food, and you repay me like this?" Ed's outrage might have been more persuasive if there hadn't been the second's hesitation that told Shane it was all an act.

"What did you make Jenny put in our bowls, Ed?" Lucas asked, keeping the gun pointed at Ed's heart. "Did you raid the neighbors' medicine cabinets for their sleeping pills and painkillers? We found the bodies. What I really want to know is, how did you make your deal with the werewolves?"

Ed's friendliness vanished, leaving him surly and cold. "I knew there was no way we could fight those things. Sooner or later, if I left it up to chance, they'd come for me and mine. So I made them an offer. They were going to kill those people anyhow—I made their passing more merciful. They never saw it coming."

"That's not how their ghosts tell it." Lucas's finger tightened on the trigger.

"You ran out of travelers, didn't you?" Shane could see the hint of desperation in Ed's expression, hidden behind his rage. "So the wolves were coming for you. I bet you couldn't believe your luck when we turned up on your doorstep."

The wolves howled once more, closer now.

"Are you going to shoot me?" Ed mocked. "Not very sporting."

Lucas shrugged. "We're US Marshals, the only law in this territory. Judge, jury, and executioner. But I think in this case, you need to go renegotiate your deal."

"They'll kill me and come for Jenny and the kids."

"We'll protect your wife and children, and get them to a safe place," Shane said. "Safe from the wolves and safe from you."

Ed made a move for the shotgun by his chair. Lucas fired, hitting him in the shoulder. Shane heard sobbing from the back of the house where the children had fled. In the kitchen, Jenny prayed for deliverance in a trembling voice.

"Leave the gun where it is," Lucas ordered. "Get up and walk out that door. You made this mess. You're going to pay for it."

"You don't understand," Ed countered, fear clear in his face. "Anyone in my position would have done the same."

"Get moving, or I'll put another bullet in you and throw you out the door myself."

Ed gripped his wounded arm and stumbled toward the door. Jenny did not turn, rocking back and forth and praying loudly enough to keep her from hearing.

"You can't do this! I have rights. I just did what I had to do—"

Lucas sighted his gun once more. "Move."

If Ed expected Jenny and the children to rush to his defense, he had miscalculated. For a second, Shane thought Ed might rush Lucas, forcing him to shoot to avoid facing the werewolves outside.

"Fuck you. Fuck all of you," Ed muttered, then swung the door open hard enough to make it slam into the wall and walked out. Jenny flinched but did not turn.

Yellow wolf eyes glowed in the darkness a second before Ed screamed as he reached the bottom of the steps. Lucas braced the door, and Shane ran to the window armed with his own weapon and Ed's shotgun. In the moonlight, he could barely make out a large, hunched shape dragging off Ed's body. They waited, tensed and ready for a fight, but the werewolf did not return.

"Is it...is he...gone?" Jenny stood in the kitchen doorway with her hands clutching her apron.

Lucas nodded. "I'm sorry you and your children had to see that. By our count, we believe he murdered at least twenty people."

Jenny shook her head. "More. There were more. I didn't know how to make him stop. And I was afraid that he'd use the children." Her head dropped. "I was too afraid to kill him. I'm so, so sorry."

"Pack your things," Shane said. "Tomorrow, we'll get you to the settlement near Myersville. You'll be safe there."

She stared at Shane with the same look he'd seen on civilians caught in the crossfire during his army days. "Why would they take us in, after what we've done?"

"They don't have to know."

CHAPTER THREE

SHANE AND LUCAS rode in silence on the way back from escorting Jenny and her children to the Myersville enclave. As Shane had expected, the compound took them in without question. The Marshals had coached the traumatized family to say nothing of Ed's actions and to stay out of trouble.

"Do you think they'll be all right?" Shane asked, breaking the silence.

Lucas snorted. "Define 'all right.' You mean by the standards Before, or now?"

"By the standards from Before, none of us are all right."

"That's my point. They're functioning, they're together, and they're in a safe place where they can have a second chance. That's really all we could give them—aside from getting rid of that murdering SOB."

"Yeah, that's kinda what I figured, too."

Lucas looked out over the rolling hills. "I thought we ought to go back to their house, see if we can track the werewolf. If Ed was at the center of the victim sites, then the werewolves have to be nearby, too. They're probably passing for human when they're not furry."

"Why kill people? Why not settle for deer? I mean, since the Events and so many people left, there are deer everywhere."

"If these are the Fort Detrick werewolves, maybe they were optimized for aggression," Lucas theorized. "Natural weres have had to blend in to survive. They probably just kept doing what they'd been doing all along. The government werewolves were meant to be weapons. They don't have a 'normal.'"

When they left that morning, Lucas and Shane had been careful to lead Jenny and the children out along a path where they would not glimpse Ed's chewed and mangled body. By the time the Marshals returned, the flies and vultures had made a feast of whatever the werewolf left behind.

"Looks like the werewolf came in from this direction," Lucas said when they had tethered their horses and scouted the perimeter of the farmhouse and barn. He had grown up going deer hunting with his father and had sharpened those tracking skills in the army and after the Events.

"Was he watching when we got the family out?" Shane's eyes narrowed as he scanned the horizon. "After he got over being hangry, do you think the were was mad we made him kill his pimp?"

"That might depend on how much human is left and how much wolf."

A noise to their right made Lucas and Shane freeze. They drew their guns and unsheathed the machetes that they wore strapped at their sides.

"There!" Shane nodded toward a movement in the tall grass and the dark ridge of coarse fur that peeked over the top. A second growl sounded to their left, and Lucas swiveled to face it.

"I think we've found them," Shane muttered.

"Not exactly how I wanted this to go down," Lucas replied.

Two werewolves rushed toward them, huge, powerful, and terrifying. Coarse, gray fur covered their heavily muscled bodies, and they moved fast for their size. Once the creatures broke above the weeds, Shane could see their faces. Yellow eyes glowed with an inner fire, above a wolf's muzzle filled with sharp teeth. Yet there was cunning in those eyes that went beyond animal instinct, an uncanny melding of human and wolf.

"Shit," Shane muttered.

Lucas and Shane fired as the wolves barreled toward them. The bullets struck the creatures in the shoulders and sides but barely slowed them down. With a howl, the wolf closest to Shane lunged, closing the distance between them frighteningly fast.

Shane fought the urge to run. He didn't have silver bullets—which didn't seem to work well anyhow, but a high caliber round could still do plenty of damage close up.

"Shane, get out of the way!" Lucas yelled as he dodged his attacker.

Shane held steady, staring down the beast closing in on him. *If I'm wrong, even Rocky won't be able to put me back together again.*

He fired. The armor-piercing 45-caliber round hit the werewolf in the eye and took the back of its skull with it. Momentum carried the creature forward one more step before it collapsed in a bloody heap.

"Headshot!" Shane shouted.

A third werewolf had hung back from the initial assault, but now the creature howled in fury and headed for Shane with an all-too-human glint in its eye.

Lucas fired again, and the bullet grazed the wolf's ear, opening a bloody furrow.

Shane didn't dare take his eyes off the big wolf that stalked him, staying low to keep from presenting itself as an easy target. *Almost like the wolf understands range and trajectory, the way a soldier might.*

Shane's attacker ran a zig-zag course through the tall grass, alternating an all-out run with a belly-crawl that hid him from view and made it impossible for Shane to get him in his sights. Lucas's wolf came at him fast and high, presenting his chest and belly while keeping his head back as if it knew only a headshot could kill it.

Lucas and the wolf went down together, tumbling in the dirt. Shane heard Lucas swearing and the snap of sharp teeth, but he couldn't afford the distraction with the third wolf eager for vengeance. That was exactly what he had glimpsed in the werewolf's eyes—a hunger for revenge.

Shane's next bullet missed, but the second sank deep into the wolf's chest. The monster howled in pain, but the shot didn't slow him down, and Shane knew the creature would be on him in a few more seconds.

Another gunshot boomed from where Lucas had gone down, and Shane hoped to hell his partner had made it count. Shane's wolf lunged out of the grass, too close for him to get a clear shot at its skull. He fired for center mass, sending a burst of rounds that splintered bone and tore through flesh. That might not kill the were, but it sure wasn't going to feel good.

The creature dropped, and Shane tensed, afraid to believe he had stopped it. Then like a horror movie jump scare, the werewolf sprang from where it had fallen, blood-soaked and mad with fury. Shane raised his gun and fired. His trigger clicked on an empty magazine.

Could the damn wolf count bullets?

The blade of a machete sang through the air, separating the werewolf's head from his body. Lucas stood over the body, spattered with gore.

"Thanks," Shane gasped, as his heart felt like it would pound out of his chest.

"Any time."

Lucas's jacket had been clawed open at the shoulder, and while the leather might have provided some protection, Shane knew that some of the blood belonged to Lucas.

"Did you get bitten?" Lucas asked, taking in Shane's blood-spattered appearance.

"No. You?"

Lucas shook his head. "No. Claws were bad enough," he admitted, wincing.

"Fuck. Here come two more," Shane said, as two dark, muscular wolves stalked toward them from behind a rise. Shane knew they'd never make it to their mounts before the weres were on them.

"I'm out of ammo," he told Lucas.

"Me, too. So this is going to be interesting."

Shane and Lucas stood back to back, machetes in hand. The two new werewolves closed the distance fast.

"Fuck," Lucas muttered. "This is not how I want to go out."

A weird, piercing whistle seemed to come from all directions, followed by the unmistakable twang of crossbows, and then the furious, pained howl of the werewolves. The whistle sounded again, loud and sharp enough that Shane and Lucas covered their ears. The wolves howled once more, then pelted into the forest.

"Not sure whether we got rescued or just landed in bigger trouble," Shane murmured. "We've got company."

There was no use running. Shane and Lucas couldn't reach their horses before the newcomers were on them. They took up their defensive stance once more, staring down this new threat, unwilling to go down without a fight.

"What the fuck?" Shane said, eyeing the men warily.

Five newcomers strode across the field, and Shane thought perhaps that he was seeing things. They wore a mix of modern tactical gear and homemade leather armor, with cloth tabards like knights from the Middle Ages—or a Renaissance festival. One by one, the men removed the visored motorcycle helmets that hid their faces. They carried themselves like soldiers, strong and self-assured, and Shane bet that none of them were over thirty.

"Thanks for the assist," Shane said, trying to get off on the right foot. "We're US Mar—"

"Come with us." The men in front drew military-issue handguns and leveled them at Shane and Lucas.

"Hey, hold on," Lucas said in his most amenable voice. "I think there's been a misunderstanding."

"There definitely has been," the leader replied. "We'll sort it out. After you come with us." He smirked. "We already have your horses, so you might as well come along. And you're out of ammo, or you would have been shooting at the weres. But we're not." He motioned with the muzzle of his gun. "Don't make this worse."

Lucas swore under his breath and leveled a deadly glare at the men. Shane had no desire to be captured, but something about the situation struck him as odd.

"Who are you?" he asked, struggling and failing to make a mental connection, something to do with the tabards.

"We are the *Chevaliers du Lapin Ensanglante*," the leader replied.

Shane struggled to remember his long-ago high school French. Lucas looked to him, waiting for Shane to make sense of what was happening, even as their captors relieved them of their weapons, bound their hands, and herded them toward the forest.

"The knights...of the rabbit? The bloody rabbit?" Shane looked at them incredulously. "Seriously? Like Monty Python?"

The leader glowered at him. "Shut up. Keep walking."

Lucas, apparently, couldn't resist poking the bear. "At least they're not the Knights who say Ni."

"I said, shut the fuck up!"

Shane met Lucas's gaze with a warning glare. Whatever the newcomers were, riling them wasn't going to help.

The five "knights" took up a formation with their prisoners in the center. *At least they didn't put us out in front, like bait.* One man led the Marshals' horses. When they reached where the knights had left their own mounts, they forced Shane and Lucas to saddle up, though two of the knights led the horses.

Lucas looked ready to fight, tension clear in every line of his body. Shane certainly wasn't pleased about being taken prisoner at gunpoint, but their captors had saved their lives, and standing around in a field waiting for the werewolves to return with reinforcements wouldn't have been the best place to hash out their differences.

If they wanted to kill us, they could have done it back there, or just let the werewolves do it. Maybe we can talk our way out of this, Shane thought.

The woods opened onto a clearing, with a stockade made of sharpened logs and reinforced with scavenged sheet metal. A red and white flag flew from the tower. The knights herded Lucas and Shane into the small fort, bringing their horses behind them.

"Nice place," Shane said. Lucas shot him the stink eye, and Shane returned an impatient grimace. Lucas had always been more likely to swat flies than try to attract them with honey, even before the Events. The end of the world hadn't improved his partner's ability to play well with others.

His comment earned a grunt from the leader, but Shane didn't miss the pleased look in the man's eyes. A small barn, corral, and coop held goats, chickens, pigs, and rabbits. The large building likely served as a bunkhouse, while Shane guessed that smaller ones provided for storage space, a forge, and a kitchen.

Lucas's gaze followed their horses, which were led to a corral with a water trough and hay. "We'll be wanting our horses back when we're done here."

"After we talk."

They followed the head of the knights into the bunkhouse, to a large open room on the first floor with tables, chairs, and a fireplace. Shelves held board games and the worn boxes of tabletop RPGs, as well as well-thumbed paperbacks, jigsaw puzzles, and other salvaged diversions.

"Is there a dungeon?" Lucas asked. "Or are you going to untie us before you feed us to the dragon?"

Shane sighed. Lucas had a lot of good qualities. He was a loyal friend, an excellent strategist, and the guy you wanted to have at your back in a fight. But his mouth sometimes got the best of him.

The knights' leader rounded on Lucas, and Shane expected him to swing a punch.

One of the others laid a hand on the leader's shoulder. "Easy, Geoff."

Geoff shook off the restraining hand and took a step back. Lucas held his ground. Now that Shane got a good look at their rescuers, he saw that they were even younger than he first thought, perhaps mid-twenties at the most, at least ten years younger than he and Lucas. Their muscular builds and high-and-tight haircuts screamed military.

Geoff might have been the oldest of the bunch, or the previously highest ranking; maybe both. Not that rank counted for squat now. Street smarts, fighting ability, and no small bit of luck were all that mattered. Shane guessed Geoff had probably been a high school football star before the army. He sized up the others. Shane figured the nervous, wiry guy was probably tech ops. The other three were only slightly less bulked-up than Geoff, but it was clear in their expressions and posture that they looked to him for direction.

The five of them reminded Shane of newly deployed privates when he and Lucas had already earned their captain's bars. Earnest, hot-tempered, eager to make their mark, hungry for the chance to prove themselves.

"Thompson—stay here and guard them while the rest of us change." Geoff looked Lucas up and down. "We'll see about letting you loose when we get back."

Geoff and the others left the room. Lucas plopped down onto a bench without asking permission. Shane remained standing. He didn't really expect that they'd need to jump the knights, but he wanted to keep his options open if it came to that.

"You know, my buddy and I were captains in the army before we became US Marshals," Lucas said. His tone sounded conversational, but the angry glint in his eyes served as a warning. "Pretty sure that means we outrank all of you. Thought I'd mention it since we didn't do introductions."

Their guard tried hard to hide his discomfort at being put in an awkward situation by his commander. Any reply he might make would just dig him in deeper, so he grunted, waved the muzzle between Shane and Lucas, and stayed well back as if he expected them to attack.

Geoff and the others returned in worn fatigues. Shane caught the glimpse of dog tags. *Old habits die hard.* As soon as Thompson was dismissed to change, he took off like his tail was on fire.

Geoff leaned against the wall and crossed his arms over his chest. The other men took up positions in the four corners. Shane considered it a backhanded compliment that he and Lucas looked dangerous enough to warrant the precautions.

"Who are you, and what were you doing prowling around out there?" Geoff sounded like he'd cooled off, or maybe his second-in-command had talked him down.

"We're US Marshals Lucas Maddox and Shane Collins, formerly *Captains* Maddox and Collins, US Army," Lucas snapped. "We're what remains of the official law in these parts, and we got asked to look into some disappearances and check into werewolf attacks."

"Who sent you?"

Lucas didn't blink. "The commander at Fort Getty. Now are we gonna screw around all day, or are you going to untie us and tell us what the fuck is going on?"

After a tense moment when Shane bit back suggesting that Geoff and Lucas should just get out a ruler and measure their dicks, Geoff nodded to the blond man next to him. As the knight cut through their bonds, Shane almost swore the man looked apologetic. Shane flexed his fingers and shook his hands to get the blood flowing again.

Geoff looked at Lucas's bloody shoulder. "Did he bite you?"

"No."

"Check him," Geoff snapped, and one of the other men pulled the clawed jacket and torn shirt away to examine the wound beneath. "Then get the kit and take care of it."

The soldier returned with a medic kit and treated the wound with practiced efficiency. Lucas put up with the treatment in silence, but Shane saw the tic in his partner's jaw muscles from clenching.

"Thanks for the assist, but who are you guys?" Shane cut through the bullshit. He gave Lucas a look that warned his partner to back off.

Shane's acknowledgment seemed to mollify Geoff, who lost some of his bluster. "We were stationed at Fort Detrick. When the bombs hit, we were underground, on duty. Our CO told us to stay put."

"Zeke, here, was a nuclear specialist," he said, indicating a blond soldier to his right, the one Shane figured was second-in-command. "From the little bit of intel we got before all the channels went dark, he figured out how bad it was topside, and when it would be safe to go out again."

A sad smile touched Geoff's lips, making him look young. "We didn't want to go against orders, but we had all heard about those Japanese soldiers in the Second World War who stayed in caves for forty years. Zeke figured we needed to stay down for two weeks. We gave it an extra week, just in case, but since we hadn't heard anything over the walkie-talkies, we knew it had to be bad out there."

"How bad?" Lucas's demeanor had shifted, now that they were getting real information.

Geoff swallowed. "You've seen those apocalypse movies? Well, this was worse. Most of the base was destroyed. There were wildfires on the horizon. And the people—" His voice caught, and he looked away.

"We're sorry for your loss," Shane said and meant it. "How much did you know about the biowarfare experiments at Fort Detrick?"

Geoff's eyes narrowed. "That's classified."

Lucas gave him a look. "First off, we've got clearance. And second—there's no government left to prosecute you, but there *are* werewolves. It would be nice to know what kind of bullshit mad scientist stuff was going on, so we can keep the man-made monsters from killing more people."

Geoff bit his lip and looked to Zeke, who gave the barest nod. "Okay. Brad and Thompson were more involved with the bioengineering part of things," he said, indicating their original guard and the wiry guy. "Fortunately, that included enough pre-med classes that they're now our medics. Darius and I handled communications and security."

"How did they create the werewolves?" Shane leaned forward, using everything he'd learned about winning over a hostile witness, and hoping Rocky would keep Lucas calm.

"They didn't exactly 'create' them. More like 'enhanced,'" Geoff replied. "There've always been werewolves. Guess those old stories were right. There are also shifters. Werewolves don't reproduce by making puppies—they share the infection through a bite."

"Infection?" Lucas asked, his tone sharp.

"Yeah. All those movies call it a 'curse' or say it's magic, but whatever originally caused it, there's a genetic mutation that gets passed along in body fluids."

"You're saying lycanthropy is an STD?" Shane responded, incredulous.

"Pretty much. They tried to breed that out of the GMO weres with limited success. They aren't supposed to be able to transmit the infection with a bite. Emphasis on 'supposed to.' In some it took; in others it didn't," Geoff said.

"And the shifters?" Lucas asked.

"Shifters...they're natural. They can change shape at will, and they can also make babies. They can't transform anyone with a bite—that's only for natural weres and I guess, some of the GMO werewolves where the modification didn't take hold," Geoff continued.

"The program started out trying to alter werewolves by adding shifter genetic material. They wanted to give the modified werewolves the ability to change at any time—not just the full moon—and breed out the ability to infect with a bite. As I said, that worked—some of the time. They also did the reverse, tried to bulk up shifters with werewolf DNA, since the shifters' bites weren't infectious. For the ones that got the right traits, the lab guys did more meddling for weight, height, strength, speed."

"Intelligence?" Lucas asked.

"Not so much," Geoff replied. "They wanted drones, not leaders who might get ideas."

"How did anyone think this was a good idea?" Lucas shook his head.

Geoff shrugged. "It's not like anyone asked *us*. You know how that goes."

"So they captured werewolves and shifters and experimented," Shane summarized.

Geoff shook his head. "No. The weres and shifters volunteered. The docs couldn't afford to have creatures like that hate them. I don't know how they got in touch with those hidden communities, but they were all volunteers. Pretty enthusiastic ones, too."

"Eugenics for monsters. How many enhanced werewolves did they make?" Shane asked.

"They had about as much success bulking up shifters as they did trying to tame werewolves," Brad replied. "They ended up with twenty-five—eight of the modified shifters and seventeen werewolves that were still a work in progress. They'd cracked the code on enabling the werewolves to shift at will, but they hadn't neutralized the effect of their bites, so they could still transmit Lycanthropy. They also had more difficulty controlling their wolf."

"So that's what you had in the lab when the grid failed. Minus the three we killed today. And whatever you've killed. So how many are left?" Lucas asked.

"Ten," Geoff replied. "At least, that's our count. Three of the shifter-weres and seven of the original werewolves. We've been after them for over three years now, whittled the number down. Lost some good hunters in the process."

"Original?" Shane asked.

Geoff nodded. "Since the modified werewolves could still infect with a bite, we don't know if they made more. They'd really be a were-hybrid, assuming the modifications bred true."

"Because the world needed a brand-new species of were-creature," Shane said, rolling his eyes.

"Were there other experiments? Maybe on vampires or unicorns?" Lucas's tone made his feelings on the matter clear.

Thompson had the decency to blush. "They talked about moving on to vampires if the werewolf experiments worked out, but our unit hadn't gotten that far before everything fell apart."

Shane had never felt so thankful for small favors.

"What's with the 'knights' get-ups?" Lucas asked.

Geoff chuckled. "The five of us played a lot of role-playing games together. We didn't get off the base much. When everything fell apart, we asked ourselves, what would our characters do? We couldn't be soldiers anymore. Our families were dead. So we became knights, and we hunt werewolves. It's a way to make amends, a bit, for what we helped create."

Shane didn't doubt Geoff's sincerity, and becoming werewolf fighters was as good an option as any. "Do you know anything about the people who've disappeared?"

Geoff glanced at his men, who shook their heads. "What do you mean?"

"People just wander off and vanish. Whole families, in some cases. The ones we've heard about are all located between Gambrill Park and Zittlestown," Lucas replied. "We think there's something in the forest, luring them away. We just don't know who, or why, or what happens to them."

"You sure they didn't get eaten?" Darius asked.

"We're not sure of anything," Lucas said. "That's why we came to investigate. Have you gone into the parks lately?"

"Not since the Events." Thompson looked uncomfortable. "Some of the guys from the base used to go hiking out there and said it was real nice. But since everything went to hell, we've heard stories about squatters and criminals hiding in there. People stay clear."

Interesting. "And that changed after the blast?" Shane pressed.

Thompson barked a bitter laugh. "Didn't everything?"

Lucas leaned back, giving their captors an assessing look. "How about we call a truce?" he suggested. "We help you kill werewolves, and you help us figure out what the hell is going on with the missing people."

His proposal surprised Shane, but only momentarily. Lucas wasn't one to waste resources, and they were going to need backup. Despite making a bad first impression, Shane got the impression that Geoff and his knights were okay. It would be good to have reinforcements, for once.

Shane saw Geoff take a silent survey of his men, waiting for a signal. Each soldier nodded. "All right, we're in," he said. "You're welcome to bunk here if you want. I won't vouch for our cooking, but no one's starved or died yet."

Lucas rose and extended his hand. Geoff shook it without hesitation. Shane let out a breath he hadn't realized he'd been holding. "Sounds good. Let's make a plan and get rid of those sons of bitches," he said.

ONCE GEOFF's knights decided to become allies, the tension faded, and by the time dinner was over, they had all begun to trade stories. It didn't take too long to find common ground in the kind of military humor that required life in the ranks to understand.

Lucas and Shane filled them in on what they had seen on the route they patrolled, and what they knew about other parts of the country, courtesy of the IT Priests and the universities that still had limited internet connections.

"That's good chili." Shane leaned back from his empty bowl.

Zeke grinned. "It's easy to make and feeds a crowd. And we found a grocery store with a couple of pallets of tomato sauce and kidney beans in the back. So the price was right."

"Once we realized that we were the last ones left at the base, we foraged," Geoff said, and his smile faded to a pensive expression. "We loaded everything we thought we could use into trucks and drove them until we were away from the worst effects of the blast. Thompson had grabbed some toppo maps and found us this location. We built this place."

"You're the only ones who made it out?" Lucas didn't try to hide how much that bothered him.

"Of the people who were on base? Yeah. In three years, we haven't found anyone else who claimed to be from Fort Detrick," Geoff replied. The bombs that took out the Baltimore-Washington corridor didn't leave much standing.

"Were there people who might have been off base when the blast hit? Training, maneuvers, special assignment?" Shane asked.

"I'd heard that four or five of our genetics people—the ones who did the real tampering to create the modified weres—were up at Fort Ritchie to talk to their artificial intelligence folks," Geoff said. "Since we haven't run into them, I figured they either stayed at Fort Ritchie or were on their way back to base and died like everyone else."

Lucas couldn't help shuddering at the mention of Fort Ritchie and its ill-fated AI program. Then again, maybe it was only natural to dislike the place where he had died.

"No survivors aboveground?" Shane pressed.

Geoff shook his head. "The scene when we came up...it was bad. I've heard about what it's like on a battlefield, seen pictures. But these people worked in offices. There were families, kids. And when the blast came, it fucking cooked them, and then blew out their lungs, and if that wasn't enough, lit them up with enough radiation to glow."

"Weren't there other people underground, like your team?" Shane asked. Talking about the carnage was hard for their new allies, but he and Lucas needed to know.

Geoff shrugged. "Yeah, there were. But we got cut off from each other when the power went out and the fire doors came down. Maybe they didn't know what was going on, or they were trying to get to their families. Zeke figured it out fast, and saved our lives, keeping us down there until the worst of the radiation wore off."

"Even so, we didn't stay topside long, and we brought decontamination supplies with us," Zeke added. "Silkwood showers are no fun."

"In case you're wondering, the supplies we…liberated…were stored inside enough concrete they should be okay," Darius said. "We took food, ammo, weapons, anything useful that wasn't nailed down and probably wasn't contaminated. I'm not a fan of MREs, but those suckers stay good forever."

"Any more armor-piercing rounds?" Lucas asked. "Those worked real well on the werewolves."

"Some. Not as many as I'd like," Geoff replied. "And what we have won't last forever. That's why we came up with the crossbows."

"And the whistle we heard?" Shane asked.

"I guess it hurts their ears," Geoff replied. "We figured that out by accident. Drives them off. Sometimes, it's better to retreat than fight a losing battle."

"I'm assuming regular shifters don't attack." Shane couldn't help being curious.

Thompson shook his head. "Regular shifters aren't a problem. We take a live and let live approach with them if they don't go feral. Same with regular weres that don't cause trouble. Natural weres tend to live in small groups on the outskirts of human settlements, and they usually go deep into the forest when they're furry. Most of them survive on deer and rats. They'd rather not fight humans. The ones who forget that, we hunt."

Zeke picked up from there. "The modified shifters and were-hybrids are more aggressive, more prone to attack people out of choice. They were selected for those traits."

"How can you tell a GMO were from a natural one?" Lucas asked.

"The army went low tech," Geoff replied. "They notched the ears of the modified shifters and put a metal band with a number in the earlobes of the were-hybrids—because they were more dangerous, what with being able to shift at will and infect with a bite. Both markings would show in both human and wolf form."

"I was hoping they'd picked something that didn't require getting quite that close," Lucas muttered.

"And if the were-hybrids bit people and turned them, they wouldn't be marked at all, just like natural weres," Shane said.

Geoff nodded.

"Well, that sucks," Shane muttered.

"We think we know where those other modified shifters who came after you are holed up," Geoff said. "Let's get them put down, and then we can figure out where all the vanishing people have gone."

CHAPTER FOUR

They had just finished cleaning up the dishes when a loud clanging made everyone jump.

"What was that?" Shane had already started to his feet, reaching for his knife.

"Doorbell," Geoff replied. At their perplexed looks, he just shook his head. "It's a dinner bell on a rope because people can't just knock, now can they?"

Geoff grabbed a shotgun from his gear bag, and Lucas did the same. He tossed a shotgun to Shane and then held up a hand to stop Shane from coming with them.

"Stay here. You're backup," Lucas said. Shane didn't look pleased, but he nodded and didn't argue.

Lucas followed Geoff across the open space toward where an old farm bell hung atop a post. A narrow door—barely wide enough for a man to slip through—provided an alternative to opening up the main gates.

"Can you see who it is?" Lucas asked.

Geoff nodded and hauled himself up a few steps to look out of a protected viewing slit. He climbed back down. "It's okay. She's a friend."

He opened the door, and a dark-haired woman in a woolen cloak slipped inside. Lucas kept his shotgun ready, just in case.

"Who's he?" the newcomer demanded, giving Lucas the once-over.

"US Marshal," Geoff replied. "Lucas," he said with a nod, "Elizabeth."

Lucas inclined his head in acknowledgment and lowered his weapon, but kept the shells chambered.

"I figured you'd want to scry before we head out," Elizabeth said.

"And you'd be absolutely right," Geoff said. He turned to Lucas. "Elizabeth is a witch. She's quite a valuable ally because she has far-sight and can make that stronger with scrying. Without Google Earth or drones, it's a big help."

Lucas looked at Elizabeth, curious and suspicious. "Far-sight?"

She seemed to read his skepticism for what it was, without offense. "Exactly what it sounds like. The ability to 'see' things that are happening at a distance through magic or a psychic gift. Let's go inside, and I'll be glad to tell you what I know—which probably isn't as much as you'd like to find out."

Shane looked up when they entered the barracks. Lucas gave him a shrug in reply to the unspoken question. The other knights greeted Elizabeth warmly as a respected friend. In better light, Lucas took her measure. She looked to be in her early forties, although it was hard to say these days since life had gone hard on everyone. It wasn't a stretch to imagine her as a suburban soccer mom behind the wheel of a minivan, and Lucas wondered whether she had found her paranormal abilities before or after the Events.

Elizabeth handed off her cloak to Zeke and gratefully accepted a cup of hot, boiled coffee from Darius. Geoff waved them all over to one of the tables, and they settled in.

"You boys know about me," Elizabeth said with a smile toward the knights. "But let me fill the newcomers in a bit."

"Can I ask...how did you end up being a witch?" Lucas gave his most winning smile. He felt fairly certain it didn't work at all on Elizabeth.

"Probably the same way you came to be *in tune with nature*," she replied with a knowing look that told Lucas she sensed his bond with Rocky. Shane had a sudden coughing fit.

"Before the Events, I had better-than-average luck knowing what might happen in advance. But since then, those abilities have grown, and

I've gotten better at directing them, if not exactly controlling them," Elizabeth said.

"From the time I was a child, I'd get random flashes of something going on a distance away—usually with a friend or family member. Sometimes it was a good event, sometimes not. It wasn't exactly a premonition. I didn't know in advance. More like I saw it happening, in real-time, but in my head. Things I didn't have any clue might be planned. And what I saw always turned out to be exactly what happened," she continued. "Saying that it freaked out my mother would be the understatement of the century."

"You said you've learned to direct your ability?" Shane asked, curious, and Lucas suspected his partner was thinking of his own random visions.

"More or less," Elizabeth replied. "I learned to focus on where I wanted to see, and most of the time, I can. Not always, and I don't know why. Still figuring it out," she added with a wry smile.

"How did you learn? Is there a coven nearby?" Lucas couldn't help being intrigued.

"If there is, they never introduced themselves," Elizabeth said. "Fortunately, I was always interested in witchcraft and divination—so I had quite a few books on the subject. I dabbled with them before the Events, but afterward, when my abilities got stronger, I got serious about learning more and finding all the books on the subject that I could. I'm the best home-schooled witch you're likely to meet."

"So what's the plan?" Lucas turned his attention to Geoff. "And how did you know to show up tonight?" he asked Elizabeth.

"Geoff put a green banner up the flagpole," Elizabeth said with a shrug. "I can see the fort from where I live. That's a signal for me to come visit."

"As for the plan," Geoff replied, in a tone that put invisible quotation marks around that last word, "that's what Elizabeth is here to help us figure out. We know there are at least ten more of the weres left—maybe more. While we have a couple of extra people to help fight, it seemed like a good time to try to take them out."

"I'll focus my far-sight on finding those weres, and reading everything I can about their surroundings, to reduce surprises," Elizabeth added, returning her attention to Lucas. "The boys here aren't working with much of a margin, so even a small advantage makes a big difference."

"Elizabeth's talents helped us the last time we took out a group. She was the reason we knew that the pack had natural werewolves as well as GMO weres and shifters. That helped us protect ourselves," Geoff told him.

"So, how does this work?" Lucas asked. After everything they had been through, a witch who could spy on enemies from a distance no longer seemed strange.

"It's easier if I show you." Elizabeth gestured to Brad, who brought a large bowl filled with water and set it on the table in front of her. She closed her eyes and took several deep breaths, then lightly gripped the bowl with both hands and stared at the still surface of the water.

After a moment, Lucas glanced at Shane, whose perplexed expression suggested that he didn't see anything, either. Elizabeth, however, focused intently on the contents of the bowl.

"They have a cabin, not far inside the tree line," she reported. "I can see four muscular men who might be weres—not close enough to see their ears. There's another man, tall and skinny, late forties with dark hair graying at the temples."

"Richardson," Thompson and Zeke said in unison.

"Who?" Lucas asked, exchanging a look with Shane.

"The biologist who headed up Fort Detrick's GMO werewolf project," Thompson replied. "The guy who thought Franken-wolves were a good idea. Though a couple of others on the team could also fit that description."

"What would he be doing there?" Geoff growled.

"They're talking, not fighting. I can't hear what they're saying, but whatever the tall skinny guy is selling them, they seem to be buying," Elizabeth added.

"How far away?" Lucas leaned forward, but the water held no visions for him. *Can you see anything?* he asked Rocky in his mind.

Unfortunately not. But I do feel unrest from the daemons. They feel... unsettled...by these newcomers.

Thompson slid a map across the table toward Elizabeth, and she brought her finger down on a spot. "There."

"That's only maybe five or six miles from here?" Lucas said, glancing up at Geoff. "How have they been under your noses, and you didn't know it?"

Geoff glared at him. "Because that's not their fixed base. The weres move around a lot, squat in abandoned houses, or kill the owners and make the place their own for as long as it suits. They don't stick around."

"Can we get there by nightfall?" Shane asked. "If that really is Richardson, this could be our chance to find out what he's up to, and whether he's behind the disappearances."

"Or we could just use our grenade launcher to fire an incendiary through the window and fry them to a crunch," Darius proposed.

"Tempting." Geoff stared at the map, then turned back to Elizabeth. "Can you see anything else? Sentries outside? Weapons? I'd hate to ride in there thinking we know what we're up against and be wrong."

"My far-sight works best on a tight range," Elizabeth replied. "So I can see the cabin. Get farther away, and the reading loses detail. Which means that if there are others out prowling in the forest a distance away, I won't pick up on that."

"Still, it's enough to plan an attack," Geoff mused.

"If that is Richardson, any weres connected to him are going to be bad news," Lucas said. "If we can take them out and maybe get a line on what's going on with the vanishing people, we'd come out ahead."

Geoff nodded. "And if we can find out what the story is with Richardson and what he's doing that would be a bonus. All right. Everyone—suit up and grab your gear. Brad and Thompson—come with me to the armory. The rest of you—blades and armor-piercing bullets. Let's move!"

"I'm coming, too." Elizabeth raised her head. "I'll stay back from the fight—but I can lay distraction spells, keep them from hearing your approach, and fool the eye so they won't notice you if they don't look right at you."

"And if one of them comes after you?" Geoff challenged.

"Then I shoot the SOB between the eyes," Elizabeth replied.

"That works," Geoff said. "Let's go, people! Meet at the gate in fifteen minutes."

THEY HIKED IN, unwilling to leave the horses unprotected. Geoff and Lucas took point, Elizabeth stayed in the center with Zeke and Thompson to better use her magic to distract anyone watching, while Shane, Brad, and Darius brought up the rear.

Darius carried the grenade launcher that they had liberated from the armory at Fort Detrick when they fled, as well as a duffle with a variety of shells. Everyone had blades and handguns with as much ammo as they could reasonably manage, as well as crossbows. The knights wore their pieced-together armor, but did without the motorcycle helmets for easier communication.

Geoff brought the group to a halt just before the cabin came into sight. Hand signals sent the team to their posts. Geoff went with Brad and circled around to the front. Darius moved toward the right side, where a window provided a target for the grenade. Zeke and Thompson moved around to the back of the cabin. Lucas, Shane, and Elizabeth were in charge of handling any of the men or werewolves outside.

Two "men" stood guard on the front porch. That meant the man who might be Richardson and more of the werewolves should be inside the cabin. Which was exactly as Elizabeth saw it—except for the two large wolves that appeared from the forest who hadn't been part of the count.

"Shit. We've got trouble," Lucas said.

The grenade launcher boomed, glass shattered, and seconds later a flash-bang grenade exploded inside the cabin. The fight was on. Shane and Lucas lobbed fragmentation grenades at the men on the front porch. Shrapnel wouldn't kill a were, but it sure could slow them down. The flash-bang in the cabin would have disoriented those inside, giving an advantage as Geoff's team slammed in from the front and back.

The forest weres came at a dead run. Lucas fired and hit one through the skull, dropping it in its tracks. Shane's shot missed, ripping into the creature's shoulder, barely breaking its stride. Elizabeth stepped forward and hurled a ball of fire. The were went up in flames, howling and snapping before it toppled to one side.

"Nice," Shane commented. Elizabeth swung her machete, taking off the were's head, just in case.

The sounds of fighting inside the cabin carried across the clearing. Men shouted, wolves howled, and shots interspersed with loud thumps, the sound of bodies being thrown against walls. Finally, when the noise quieted, Shane and Lucas went to deal with the weres on the porch. Lucas's first thought was to check their ears. *Not notched or tagged*, he thought. *If they're natural werewolves, what are they doing here?* But he took some measure of comfort that they hadn't shifted, something the natural weres wouldn't be able to do without a full moon.

"We only need one alive to tell us what's going on," Lucas said as they closed on the injured werewolves. Shrapnel had torn into their bodies, ripping open bellies, stripping flesh to the bone, and covering the porch in blood. Regular human guards would have died from the injuries, but werewolves' legendary healing meant the creatures were already beginning to push out the shrapnel and close the wounds.

"Pick," Shane replied.

Lucas lunged forward, slamming a silver-coated machete into the shoulder of the werewolves nearest him, pinning him to the wooden porch.

"That silver will stop the healing," Lucas told the squirming werewolf. "We have a few questions for you."

"Fuck you," the werewolf snarled.

"You don't have a band or notched ear. Are you a born shifter or did you get bitten?" Lucas pressed.

"Bitten. What's it to you?"

Lucas pulled out a second silver-edged knife. "What's Richardson up to?"

Shane shot the other guard in the head.

The pinned werewolf glowered at Lucas. "You're going to kill me anyhow. Why should I tell you?"

Lucas shrugged. "Because you can go fast, or you can go slow. Up to you."

The man-wolf licked his lips. "Richardson recruited more natural weres, like Frank and me. He brought us with him to try to convince the holdouts from Fort Detrick to join him."

"What's he going to do with them?" Lucas asked. "His lab is gone."

"He's got a witch who says he can do the same thing with magic that Richardson wanted to do in the lab—take away the moon cycle. We'd be a new, improved breed of weres, without that cursed moon controlling our lives."

"And the bite? Still infectious?"

The downed werewolf managed a smirk that was more of a grimace. "Yes. Only way to increase our numbers."

"And did it work? Could the witch do it?" Lucas couldn't help being intrigued.

The injured were took a labored breath. "Not yet. But...there's a well of power in the woods...if they can draw on that, then...maybe."

"How many are with Richardson?"

"Four humans, scientists from the fort. The witch. And the other weres."

"Natural weres, shifters, or were-shifters?"

The prisoner groaned. Without his special healing abilities, the blood loss was taking a toll. "Don't know, think some shifters, altered werewolves, and some naturals."

"Special defenses?" Lucas couldn't help worrying that perhaps Richardson had brought some of Fort Ritchie's contraband technology back with him from his visit.

"Regular weapons."

"Where's the camp?"

"Fox's Gap," the werewolf replied. His breathing had grown shallow, and Lucas knew he was running out of time.

"Why are the natural weres joining up? I thought they kept to themselves?" Shane asked.

"That was...Before. Better hunting if we could shift any time. Game's gotten scarce. Tired of being hungry."

"Does that include hunting people?"

The werewolf gave Shane a look. "A guy's gotta eat."

"Is that why people keep disappearing?" Shane prodded.

The prisoner gave a slight shake of his head. "Nah. That's the witch. Needs sacrifices to prime the well."

"What else can you tell us?" Lucas stared down the barrel of his gun at the injured were.

"Nothing." He met Lucas's gaze. "Do it."

Lucas pulled the trigger.

"Hey, Marshals!" Geoff's voice carried from inside the cabin. Lucas and Shane exchanged a look, and Lucas headed inside while Shane and Elizabeth kept watch for more sentries.

Blood soaked the walls and floor of the cabin. Three dead men lay on the floor, bodies separate from the heads. Geoff and Zeke were down, with Brad and Darius doing their best to treat their wounds. Lucas saw at a glance that they would require more than field first aid and went to help. "Fuck," he muttered. "What happened?"

"The guy we thought might be Richardson was gone when we got here," Brad replied, his tone clipped as he tried to stop the bleeding on the gash in Geoff's leg. "There were three weres instead of two. One natural, a shifter, and a GMO were. And flash-bangs apparently don't mess up natural weres as bad as we thought they would."

Lucas looked around the sparsely furnished cabin. He wondered whether the werewolves had actually lived there, or just used it as a shelter on their hunts. It lacked the bare essentials he figured even weres would want when in human form.

Geoff had recovered enough to give orders. "Collins, Maddox—get Zeke on the table and off the floor. Brad, Darius—I hope to hell you've got supplies for this." Shane came when he heard his name called, leaving Elizabeth standing watch on the porch, holding a distraction spell around the cabin to keep away any other, unwanted, visitors.

Lucas scooped Zeke's thin body up and laid him out on one of the rough tables. Darius dug through his gear bag and came up with a medical kit, then methodically laid out what they would need. Brad helped Geoff to a chair, disregarding the man's protests.

"What the fuck went wrong?" Lucas knew his anger was the adrenaline from the fight boiling over, but he couldn't hold back.

"Bad luck," Geoff snapped. "Or somehow, they knew we were coming. You want to fight about it? We can do that—after I know my man is going to pull through."

Shane put a hand on Lucas's shoulder, and he shrugged it off. Lucas knew he was being an asshole. The tangle of emotions in his gut was too complex to parse out quickly, and his survival instincts forced anger to the top.

With lives in the balance, Brad took control. "Maddox—strip Zeke down so we can get to the damage. Collins, gonna need you to hold the light for us."

Lucas lost track of time as they hurried to do the medics' bidding. The room fell silent, except for the medics' curses and the low moans of the two injured men. Geoff's face was a blank mask, but the tension in every line of his body made Lucas think the soldier was ready to explode. Shane kept his head down, doing whatever was asked of him, but Lucas knew his friend well enough to guess he had somehow found a way to blame himself for the clusterfuck.

"Pulse is slowing," Brad said in a cold voice that didn't match the panic in his eyes. Zeke had taken the worst of the damage, nearly disemboweled by a slash of the GMO were's claws.

Is he dying? Can you help? Lucas asked Rocky.

His lifeforce is fading. But he can't see ghosts, like you, or hear my song, like Shane. I don't know how to reach him. And even if I could, I cannot inhabit him without leaving you. You would die. I did not choose him. I chose you.

Try. Please. Can you just, I don't know—lend him some energy? Not to inhabit, just to ...support?

Perhaps...can you touch him?

Brad and Darius were laboring to help Zeke, whose pallor and shallow breathing didn't look hopeful. Lucas edged closer and laid a hand on Zeke's ankle.

"What are you doing?" Geoff's sharp tone covered for the fear in his eyes.

"Reiki," Lucas blurted. Shane turned away, stifling his reaction.

"You do Reiki?" Geoff's skepticism was clear in his tone.

"Yeah...my mother taught me." Lucas hoped he still had his poker face.

"We'll take all the help we can get," Brad said, looking up. He and Darius were covered in Zeke's blood. Lucas knew how bad a gut wound could be, even with high-tech help. This was old-fashioned battlefield surgery, and the odds weren't good.

Lucas felt a tingle of warmth that radiated down his arm and through his palm. He didn't know whether Rocky could help, but he figured it couldn't hurt.

"Jesus, he's stabilizing," Brad said.

"He's hanging in there," Darius said, looking up to meet Geoff's worried gaze. "Fuck, I thought we were going to lose him."

Geoff looked to Lucas. "Maybe there's something to Reiki, after all."

Lucas kept his hand on Zeke's ankle until he felt a nudge from

Rocky. He stepped back and nearly stumbled. Shane ran to steady him and guided Lucas to a chair.

"It's okay," Shane said. "He's always like this after a session." His expression was sober, but Lucas saw the twinkle in Shane's eyes at the shared con.

Thank you, Lucas told his daemon.

I am as surprised as you are that it worked. But it is good that he will not die.

We break easily.

So I am learning. It is...poor design.

Geoff stumbled as he moved away from the table that held Zeke. Brad caught him and looked down at the blood seeping through Geoff's torn jeans. "You're still bleeding."

"Not too much," Geoff protested.

"Bullshit." Brad maneuvered Geoff to a bench. "Fuck. That went deeper than I thought."

Geoff tolerated the treatment, going pale. He clenched his jaw until Lucas wondered if the other man was going to break a tooth. Finally, Brad sat back after he had stopped the bleeding and re-wrapped the gash.

"Stay off your feet, and it might be better in a few weeks," he said. "Push yourself, and you could lose your leg."

Geoff muttered something Lucas didn't catch, but he could guess the gist.

"Yeah, well," Brad replied, taking the grumbling in stride, "Zeke isn't going anywhere for a while, either. So I guess we'll just play a whole lot of poker."

Elizabeth had stayed on the porch, scanning for danger and making their presence less noticeable with her magic. She stood close enough to the door to have heard the conversation and finally poked her head in. "How's it going?"

"We did the best we could," Brad told her. "Can you help?"

Elizabeth didn't answer. Instead, she crossed to the table and held the flat of her hand above Zeke's chest, then moved it slowly down his torso. "He's already received healing energy."

Geoff and the others looked to Lucas. "He did some Reiki."

Lucas managed his most innocent smile.

"Reiki?" Elizabeth's gaze told Lucas she wasn't buying it.

"I'm very in tune with nature." Lucas tried to hide his fear that Elizabeth would call his bluff, but she merely nodded and went back to scanning Zeke.

"He'll live," she pronounced. "Although it's going to take time, and you'll need to make sure those wounds don't get infected." Elizabeth glanced around at the rest of them. "Looks like you all took a beating."

Geoff shrugged. "Designer werewolves. We're alive. They're not. I'll take it as a win."

"Reiki?" Shane teased, too quietly for anyone else to overhear.

"More like Rocky."

"I figured. But...damn. I didn't know he could do that."

"Neither did he."

Geoff glanced around the cabin. "Where the hell is Thompson?" He spotted the man in the far corner of the cabin. "If you don't need the medics, go see if there's a horse and a wagon around here. Walking home isn't going to work," Geoff ordered.

Thompson stood apart from the others, blood-spattered, pale, and shaking. Lucas wondered whether the young man had ever seen real combat.

"Thompson?" Geoff snapped. "Did you hear me?"

"I tried to get out of the way." Thompson sounded like he might be in shock. His wide eyes and the odd tone in his voice made Lucas worry that the close-quarters, brutal fight had been too much.

"Out of the way?" Shane echoed. The darkness of the corner hid everything except Thompson's frightened features.

"I wasn't fast enough...but I still took off his head."

Thompson's disoriented recap made Lucas's gut tighten with worry. When he moved out of the shadows, Lucas could see a raw bite through the torn remnants of Thompson's shirt where his makeshift armor had been torn away.

"I'm sorry." Thompson's voice barely carried across the room. He raised his gun and brought it to his temple.

"Thompson!" Shane and Lucas called out at the same time, both taking a step toward the wounded knight.

"Stay back. It's got to be this way."

Lucas realized he never even knew the young man's first name.

While his head understood Thompson's choice, his heart refused to stop looking for answers. *Rocky? Is there anything you can do?*

He has no magic. He can't hear my song or see spirits. If he was like you or Shane, there might be possibilities. I am sorry.

Lucas wheeled on Geoff. "Why the fuck are you not telling your man to stand down?"

Geoff's world-weary expression spoke volumes. "Because Thompson's right. I don't want to have to hunt him. It's better this way."

"Better?" Lucas took a step toward Geoff, fist clenching.

"He's right." Thompson's voice was flat, the look in his eyes resigned.

"Maybe Elizabeth—" Shane started.

Thompson shook his head. "She can't. We've asked before when civilians got bitten. It always ends the same way." His finger tightened on the trigger.

"Thompson!" Shane lunged for the gun. Before he could close the gap between them, a shot fired, blood spattered the wall, and Thompson dropped to the floor.

Lucas and Shane stared at the body in horror. Lucas started toward Geoff, ready for a fight. Brad and Darius stepped closer to their leader. Shane caught Lucas's shoulder, a warning.

"You just let your man kill himself. You didn't even try to stop him." Lucas barely recognized his own voice.

"Can't fight fate." Geoff sounded exhausted, a pained look in his eyes. "You've been a soldier. Sometimes, you lose one of your own. So you keep fighting in their memory."

Lucas didn't agree, and he knew from Shane's stiff stance that his partner didn't, either. Lucas shook off Shane's hand and stalked toward Geoff.

"I lost men in combat, men who depended on me, who reported to me. Never once did I let them go without fighting to save them," Lucas snapped, trying to control his rage. "That boy had choices. You might as well have shot him yourself."

Even wounded, Geoff didn't back down. "And I would have if he hadn't done it. He'd have become a monster. We'd have had to take care of the problem."

"That's enough." Shane's voice cut through the fog of Lucas's rage. "You're both right. But it was up to Thompson, and he made his choice.

So either throw down and get it over with or figure out how we're going to all get along until Lucas and I ride out. But stop the pissing contest. We don't have time for it."

Lucas bit back a growl, but he stepped back. Geoff glanced at Brad and Darius, and they relaxed to an at-ease stance.

"I thought I saw a horse out back," Shane said. "Maybe there's a wagon. We sure as hell can't walk home." He met Lucas's gaze. "Come help me see what we can find."

Behind the cabin stood a small corral with a single cart horse, and nearby, a wagon. Lucas wondered if the horse had to be magicked to permit a werewolf near it, but the animal looked well treated.

He didn't care about the horse or the wagon. He just wanted to stop seeing Thompson pull the trigger.

"What were you thinking in there?" Shane hissed. "Were you really going to fight Geoff?"

"I was *thinking* that you don't leave a soldier behind," Lucas snapped. "I was *thinking* that we had a whole month to come up with other options. But fuckin' Geoff practically ordered Thompson to do it."

Shane looked like he was reining in his own temper. "We've got gear back at their fort, stuff we can't replace. And you made your opinion very clear. So let's get the knights back to their fort, and we'll leave in the morning. We've done what we came here for."

"Half of what we came for," Lucas corrected, not quite ready yet to let go of his rage. He knew he would see Thompson's eyes in his dreams forever. "We still don't know about the disappearances."

"We know more than we did before, from what the werewolf told us," Shane pointed out. "And I'm sure Geoff and the knights know more. So before we go after Richardson, we need more information. Don't let your anger blot out your common sense."

"Fuck you," Lucas muttered, but he knew Shane was right.

They took turns washing up from a rain barrel in the yard, and while Lucas felt sure the lye soap they found next to it took off a layer of skin along with the blood and grime, he was grateful to remove the stink of the fight. He couldn't wait to get back to the fort and change clothing. Now that the crisis had ended, Lucas felt every bruise and strained muscle. From the stiff way Shane moved, he guessed his friend was just as uncomfortable.

A dousing in cold water and a break from the argument helped Lucas regain control. "Let's get the horse hitched up. It beats trying to drag Zeke and Geoff back on foot."

"It'll be dark by then. We'll need to spend the night," Shane warned.

"I'll play nice. But in the morning, we're out of there," Lucas replied.

CHAPTER FIVE

THE RIDE back to the fort felt longer than the hike to the cabin that morning. New tension simmered, even though Lucas did his best not to make the situation worse. Maybe Geoff felt remorse. Or perhaps he thought the pushback from Lucas and Shane had put him in a bad light in front of his surviving men. Once tonight was over, Lucas didn't ever intend to cross paths with the knights again.

Elizabeth accompanied them. She and Shane kept watch to the side and rear while Lucas drove. Brad and Darius had their hands full trying to keep Zeke and Geoff from being injured further on the bumpy ride. Zeke hadn't regained consciousness. Geoff stayed silent, staring out at the horizon.

When they reached the fort, Lucas took the horse and wagon to the barn while Shane helped get Geoff and Zeke settled. Darius stayed to sit with the injured men, and Brad rummaged through the kitchen to put a meal together. Lucas and Shane changed into clean clothes and rejoined the others when the smell of food lured them to the table.

Geoff limped to a seat, with Brad and Darius on either side of him, as if he expected a challenge. Elizabeth sat across from Shane and Lucas. Strained conversation filled the moments when they weren't eating. They all shoveled in food like they had been starved.

When they finished, Shane leaned back in his chair. "We need to find out why people are wandering off and vanishing. The werewolf we interrogated said that Richardson is working with a witch, collecting natural werewolves and shifters for some new plot. We think there might be something 'calling' to them, something that wasn't there or wasn't as strong Before."

"I've heard rumors of a dark pool of energy," Elizabeth replied guardedly. "Near the old battlefield. Nothing detailed, just that people are going out of their way to avoid it."

"Battlefield?" Shane's head came up sharply.

"Civil War," Darius replied. "There were three battles, all early in the war. Everyone's heard of Antietam, but South Mountain was just as important."

"How many casualties?" Lucas asked.

"Five thousand or so," Darius said. "The thing I remember most is the farmer who dumped sixty bodies down a dry well. That just didn't sit right with me."

"You think someone is working dark magic?" Elizabeth looked first to Lucas and then to Shane.

"Working it, or taking advantage of something that draws twisted energy to itself," Lucas said cautiously. He had no intention of explaining how they knew quite so much about genius loci.

"Why? What's in it for them?" Geoff asked.

"No idea, but we intend to find out," Lucas replied.

"I can't say that I was too upset about Dr. Richardson being topside when all hell broke loose," Brad said. Lucas and Shane looked at him quizzically, while Geoff just let out a long sigh. Presumably, the knights had heard Brad's opinions before.

"Why?" Shane turned to face the ex-soldier.

Brad glanced at Geoff as if he was afraid he had spoken out of turn. Geoff shrugged. "Go on. You opened the can; you can dump out the worms."

"There were rumors about Dr. Richardson being a little too interested in the whole werewolf thing. Not the science—the magic," Brad said. "He was the one pushing to get vampires into the program, too. I overheard him talking to one of the other researchers, and at first, I thought he was recapping some movie he saw. It turns out he had read a book about the Nazis trying to combine magic and eugenics back during the War, and what a shame it was that no one had carried it further."

"Christ," Lucas muttered. "Did he ever try to follow up on that research himself?"

Brad shrugged. "No idea. I don't think our commander would have been in favor, but Richardson was the darling of some of the Pentagon brass. I never heard about any secret rituals being carried out at Fort Detrick."

"Maybe we got lucky and he was on his way back from Fort Ritchie when the blast hit," Darius said. "That would have melted his face, without the Lost Ark."

"You don't think he was at the cabin, with the weres we fought?" Shane asked.

Darius shrugged. "We couldn't get a really good look at the guy's face." He glanced at Elizabeth. "No offense."

"None taken."

"So it kinda looked like Richardson...but he kinda looked like a lot of men his age," Darius said.

"As far as fighting goes, I'm afraid we're sidelined for the moment." Geoff looked chagrined. "I'm no good in a fight at the moment, Zeke is lucky to be alive, and we need Brad and Darius here to keep things going."

"Understood," Lucas said, relieved not to have the knights accompany them. "We'll do some recon, and figure out if we need to call in reinforcements. You've done plenty, getting rid of a lot of the GMO weres and shifters and patrolling the area. We'll take it from here."

"I'd like to come with you."

Elizabeth's declaration took Lucas by surprise. "Why?"

"If there's something going on with dark magic, maybe I can help undo it," she said. "And my sister is one of the people who wandered away and was never seen again. There's absolutely no way Victoria did that of her own free will. I don't expect that we'll be able to save her, but I damn sure want to stop it from happening again."

Lucas and Shane exchanged a look, enough to let Lucas know his partner was good with the extra help. "All right. You're in."

Geoff sat back and tried not to wince when he jostled his wounded leg. "We might not be able to go with you, but we can still offer you some choice ammo," he said, perhaps looking to make amends. "More of those armor-piercing rounds, and maybe some grenades and a launcher? Brad can let you look at the armory and see what you can use."

"Much obliged," Lucas said. Extra firepower made him feel slightly more confident about the odds. "I think we're going to need all the advantages we can get."

THE NEXT DAY, Lucas, Shane, and Elizabeth saddled up their mounts and headed for South Mountain Battlefield. Geoff gave them a small cart for the munitions, which they fastened to Lucas's mount. They parted on good terms with the knights, although Lucas knew he would never be able to completely forgive Geoff's handling of Thompson.

Shane and Elizabeth kept up a conversation as they rode. Lucas knew that neither side's questions or comments were as spontaneous as they were made to appear. Shane was doing his best to learn more about Elizabeth's magical studies and abilities, while Elizabeth kept circling around Lucas's "Reiki" and Shane's "intuition."

Rocky had been silent for most of the ride, but when they came within five miles of the old battlefield, he nudged Lucas for attention.

The forest is sick.

You mean the trees?

No. The spirit of the forest. The land and its daemon. They are...wrong.

Lucas considered that for a moment. *Do you think it's natural? Could it have been from the blast?*

I do not think so. We all felt what you call the "blast." We have felt such things before, from wars and when rocks fell from the sky. They changed the surface of the land and killed the creatures that lived on it, but they did not change us.

What about a battle, where thousands of people die? Does that affect the daemons? Lucas was glad that Rocky had gotten better with language, because trying to have this kind of conversation in pictures, the way Shane experienced the genius loci, would have been impossible.

You have it backward. Battles happen in places where the energy is already dark. The darkness draws the fighting. The place chooses the people.

Well, fuck. That turned everything Lucas knew about military history on its head. Everything he'd been taught or read in books praised the brilliant strategy of generals. If Rocky was right—and Lucas had every reason to think that an immortal spirit of nature probably knew what it was talking about—then every historic clash was the result of a twisted daemon luring combatants so the conflict could...what? Feed it? Entertain it?

We don't hunger, as you do. But for most of us, the life around us sustains us. We would not die without it, because we cannot die, but if the land were to be barren, we would slumber until it raised life again.

So for a twisted daemon, attracting conflict or misfortune would energize it?

That is likely. I have never traveled beyond my place before. But I have heard stories.

Lucas's brain hurt trying to imagine immortal place-spirits swapping tales among themselves to while away the eons.

If there's always been a dark daemon at the battlefield, how do we stop it from hurting more people?

I don't know.

That wasn't the answer Lucas wanted to hear. *Something has changed about the battlefield because Before people liked to hike there and visitors didn't go missing. Could people do something—like human sacrifice—that would make the dark daemon worse?*

Rocky didn't respond right away. Lucas didn't know if the daemon was searching its vast experience or tapping into the daemon psychic network to consult other genius loci. Finally, Rocky nudged his way into Lucas's consciousness.

Energy sustains energy. I am sustained by the plants and animals that are alive around me, the birds and the insects, the weather and the shifts in the rock deep below. It is possible that to a dark daemon, strife and death would sustain their energy. Without it, they would become quiet.

He and Shane had talked about daemons being the energy of creation or chaos. Rocky's somewhat stilted explanation supported Shane's ideas. And the longer Lucas talked to Rocky, the more he had a bad feeling about the fate of the people who vanished.

"Hold up!" Lucas's shout made Shane and Elizabeth rein in their horses, and Lucas quickly caught up. "I've got a theory about what's going on at the battlefield, and we need to talk about it before we get there."

At Lucas's suggestions, they took a break at a dilapidated rest stop. The facilities had long ago stopped working, and the vending machines were empty, but the picnic shelters remained in reasonable condition.

"I figured we might as well eat while we talk, so we can hit the ground running when we get to the battlefield," Lucas said as they pooled their trail rations.

"Let's hear more about your 'theory,'" Shane said. Shane's knowing look told Lucas his partner suspected Rocky's input. Elizabeth just watched him with narrowed eyes, as if she knew they hadn't told her the whole truth.

"Some natural places make you feel good, and some give you the willies, right?" Lucas said for Elizabeth's benefit. "What if bad things like battles don't *make* a place have dark energy—the bad things happen because the place already *has* dark energy?"

"That makes sense," Shane replied.

"What if a group of people wanted to make that dark energy stronger? Because maybe they were interested in the occult...like Nazi magic, maybe? They might lure people into the dark place and make sacrifices to feed the beast."

A daemon is not a beast.

It's a figure of speech.

It is incorrect. We are immortal spirits of nature.

I know. Just...bear with me.

You are not a bear. Neither am I.

"Lucas?" Shane's voice pulled Lucas out of his internal dialog with Rocky.

"Sorry, just got lost in my thoughts. Anyhow, what if those creepy scientists who went to Fort Ritchie didn't get caught in the blast? What if they were attracted by the dark energy at the battlefield and tried to tie it in with their crazy Nazi magic?"

"That's a whole lot of 'maybe,'" Elizabeth said. "But...go on."

"If the dark energy is part of the land, we can't shut it down completely. Killing the crazy scientists could give it a temporary boost, depending on how the whole sacrifice thing works. But...once they're gone, and there's no one luring in new sacrifices, maybe the dark energy can go back to sleep."

"You think that's what happened to the people who've gone missing—they've been sacrificed to feed the dark energy?" Elizabeth sounded skeptical.

"So that would mean there *was* a Pied Piper...of sorts," Shane remarked. "But what's in it for the crazy scientists? The world burned. They're not going to win an award or publish a paper in a journal."

"People will do a lot of crazy things to feel like they're in control," Lucas replied, meeting Shane's gaze. "These guys thought it was a good idea to create super-weres and wanted to move on to vampires. Maybe they want an army of monsters to make themselves kings."

"I can tell you that—unless the Park Service was running a hell of a cover-up—there wasn't a stream of missing persons disappearing at the battlefield before the Events," Elizabeth said. "I've lived around here all my life, so I think I'd have heard about that. People said the battlefield was haunted—but find one that isn't. I knew hikers who liked the north section of the park better than the section around the battlefield, but they never really said why."

"Intuition. Maybe they could sense something, even though the dark energy was dormant," Lucas jumped in. "And then the chaos of the blast woke it up. If it found some wacko Dr. Moreau-wannabes for its high priests..."

"It's a crazy idea—but the world stopped making sense three years ago," Shane replied. "So, yeah. I'd say it's the best explanation we've come up with so far."

"Does that change the plan?" Elizabeth looked from one of them to the other, and Lucas decided that she had either figured out their secret or guessed something close enough.

"No," Lucas said. "Because we can't just tie up the evil scientists and throw them in jail. We have to stop them, permanently."

"But maybe we can blow up their killing ground and stop them so no one else dies," Shane recapped.

"Anyone have a better idea?" Lucas sincerely wanted to know, because what they had was batshit. Shane and Elizabeth shook their heads.

"Okay, then. On we go."

WHEN THEY REACHED the outskirts of the South Mountain Battlefield, just seven miles south of South Mountain State Park, they stopped to rest the horses at a small pond. Shane pulled Lucas aside.

"The daemon's song from this part of the park is screeching in my head like Death Metal," he told Lucas. "I'm going to have a hell of a headache. What does Rocky say?"

"He says it's 'twisted.' If the song is making you uncomfortable, it's probably even worse for him." Lucas ran a hand back through his hair, staring at the park entrance like it was the DMZ. "We've got no way to know if the battlefield daemon knows we're coming. Maybe it didn't kill all the people it lured in—maybe it made some of them its Renfields to do things it can't."

Shane nodded. "Elizabeth is going to scry and see if she can get an idea of how many people—if any—are in there. I'd like to know if we need reinforcements before it's too late to turn back."

"The were we killed at the cabin said Richardson has a witch of his own. That's a big unknown," Lucas said. "No idea about what the witch can do, or how this 'well' works."

"We'll deal with it."

Elizabeth had gone a short distance away to scry, still remaining in their sight. After a while, she returned. "What I can make out with my far-sight isn't perfect, but it's more than we had before. I'm picking up on a strong power nexus. It feels natural—as in, not man-made—but the energy is corrupt. 'Unhealthy' is about the best way to put it."

"A twisted genius loci," Shane said. "The spirit of the place."

Elizabeth nodded. "That's what I think. And the person you thought was a witch...I don't think that's quite right. He—I think it's a he—is in tune with the power nexus. That probably makes it possible for him to draw on its energy, but he's not a witch in the same way I am. I don't sense the remnants of spellcasting or wardings. And to be honest, I can't imagine that being connected to that dark, tangled up energy would be a good thing."

"Maybe Richardson thinks the witch is some kind of oracle," Lucas speculated. "Is he separate from the nexus, or are they the same?"

Once again, Elizabeth's glance made Lucas wonder how much she had figured out about his situation. "Separate. Which is a good thing, because without real power of his own, I can probably handle him while you two go after the others."

"Can you see anything about how many people or werewolves are there?" Shane pressed.

Elizabeth was quiet as if she were reviewing her memories of the scrying for details. "I saw six men, plus the witch. I couldn't tell humans from werewolves."

Rocky?

The corrupted daemon may become aware of me—and of us—if I probe too directly. But I believe she is correct. Several are not human, but I can't tell more, at least not at this distance.

If we destroy the bad daemon, how will that affect you—or Shane? That seemed to Lucas to be the plan's danger, if damaging the twisted genius loci caused dangerous "feedback" that hurt Rocky or injured Shane through his connection.

The daemon can't be destroyed, only weakened. I suspect that will be unpleasant. I will be unchanged. Shane may be very uncomfortable.

"Uncomfortable" like a bad headache, or like "seriously injured"?

I cannot know for certain, but I do not think the effect would be harmful, just unpleasant.

"If there's a twisted daemon, my money is on that old well being the nexus," Shane said. "Where they dumped the Confederate soldiers' bodies."

"What you're describing sounds an awful lot like a Hellmouth," Elizabeth said. "A nexus of chaotic energy, even if there's no Lucifer or literal Hell involved."

"I don't care what we call it," Lucas replied. "I just want to stop the disappearances. There's been enough hell on earth these last few years— we don't need more. Whatever Richardson is planning can't be good. Also, from Geoff's count, and what we took out at the cabin, we have seven shifters and modified weres remaining—and they've been biting humans to increase their numbers. The chances that the other seven besides Richardson are just normal men are pretty slim."

"Not good." Shane paused. "Eight against three—and some, if not most, of them are weres. If anyone thinks we should wait for reinforcements, now's the time to say so."

"I can handle the witch," Elizabeth replied with a shrug.

"We've got frag grenades for the others, I've got the launcher to put a concussion grenade down the old well, and you've got a sniper rifle," Shane answered. "As long as we can find a good vantage point, I think we can do it."

Before the Events, getting reinforcements meant a phone call and some helicopters. With Geoff and his knights out of commission, the nearest source would be Fort Getty, which meant a long ride on horseback there and back. In the meantime, more people would go missing, and if their theory was right, the dark daemon would get stronger and harder to beat. That was the deciding point for Lucas.

"All right. Let's shut this fucker down."

They tethered their horses in a stand of trees, shouldered their weapons, and carried the bag of ammo and explosives the knights had given them. Lucas and Shane wore a variety of guns and knives, and even Elizabeth had a shotgun and salt rounds as well as a machete. Shane carried the grenade launcher and all the grenades Geoff had been able to supply.

At the entrance to the battlefield, they stopped to study the trail map on a large sign that had survived the elements. That gave them a better idea of the terrain and the choice of paths leading to the area where the old well was located. Lucas figured Richardson's camp wouldn't be far away if the well was essential to his schemes.

"How sure are you that you can deflect attention from us?" Lucas murmured as they took a trail that brought them in above and to the rear of the old well.

"Pretty sure, as long as we're quiet," she whispered. "It's not an invisibility spell. More of a 'nothing to see here, look elsewhere' kind of thing."

Any advice? Lucas asked Rocky.

You can't kill a daemon, but you might weaken it if it's been made artificially strong. I will do my best to protect you and to avoid drawing attention. I do not like this place. It is...unhealthy.

I'm all for leaving as fast as we can.

One trail led uphill, providing an overlook. When they reached the high ground, Lucas belly-crawled toward the edge of a ridge and took in the sight below with a pair of binoculars while Shane loaded the grenade launcher and Elizabeth prepared to use her magic.

What might once have been an old farm well had broadened into a sinkhole, which wasn't unusual for this part of Maryland. The large, flat rock altar stained dark with blood was definitely something Lucas felt sure hadn't been part of the original battlefield monument. Guttered candles, the remains of a now-cold bonfire, and bits of fabric and bone hung from the lowest limbs of trees. Once upon a time, before the world ended, Lucas would have dismissed the scene as a bad Halloween attraction or the secret hideout of an emo teenager. Now, the reality was far more frightening.

Off to one side, Lucas could see two crude log cabins that didn't look like they'd been built by the Park Service. On the other side of the sinkhole were sturdy cages made of wood. The cages were empty now, but together with the blood-stained altar and the sinkhole, Lucas didn't need much imagination to confirm his theory.

Lucas searched the area around the cabins. Two men conferred near the sinkhole. One of them fit Geoff's description, an older, slender man with dark hair who might be Richardson, and the other oddly dressed man was likely the witch. A third man chopped wood a few yards away.

Lucas shimmied back from the edge. "I saw three," he whispered. "If there are more, I don't think there are many. Those cabins aren't big enough for more than six or eight men and it fits with Elizabeth's scrying."

"Ready?" Shane asked. Elizabeth nodded.

Lucas and Shane crawled back to the ridge and exchanged a look, then Lucas pulled the pins and lobbed three fragmentation grenades in quick succession toward the cabins. Shane angled the grenade launcher, braced it against his shoulder, and fired six incendiary rounds into the center of the sinkhole.

The bang of the frag grenades echoed through the quiet forest, accompanied by the screams of those in the clearing who were hit with the shrapnel. A roar and whoosh accompanied the plume of fire that rushed upward from the sinkhole. The explosion rumbled deep in the belly of the old well, and the margins of the opening began to crumble.

Shane fell back, gripping his head and groaning. Lucas reeled as the blast's effect on the battlefield daemon disoriented Rocky.

Elizabeth shouted a containment spell, raising her voice above the wind, focusing her power on the blast zone and using her magic to bind the twisted spirit inside the caved-in well and keep the witch from interfering.

Lucas gritted his teeth and rose to a crouch. He could feel Rocky struggling to block out the chaos of the sinkhole. Elizabeth's spell seemed to be helping.

Men shouted and screamed in the aftermath of the frag grenades. Lucas grabbed his rifle and took up a sniper position at the edge to finish off what the shrapnel had started. Two more men appeared from inside the cabins, carrying weapons.

This part of the operation, Lucas knew by heart. He'd always found the cold, logical, in-the-moment headspace of being a sniper to be calming, a deadly sort of Zen. All of the complexities of the world boiled down to one imperative. Find the target, take it out.

Four shots. Four men went down, one of whom he thought was Richardson. Lucas couldn't forego the surge of pride that he hadn't lost his touch.

Rocky?

I can barely hear you over the screams of the daemon in the well. It's taking all I have to help contain it.

Elizabeth shook off her trance. "The spell is set. I won't promise that it will last forever, but without new sacrifices, I don't think that spirit will dig its way out anytime soon."

Four more dark shapes ran from the forest into the ruined camp.

"We've got trouble!" Elizabeth hissed.

Werewolves. Four fucking werewolves? Elizabeth's scrying must have missed one.

"Shane! Incoming!" Lucas managed to yell, hoping that Shane could clear his head before they found themselves under attack.

Two of the creatures vaulted over the edge of the ridge, great bounding leaps that made it look like they could fly. Lucas's bullet took the head off the were closest to him, but not before he noted that neither of the monsters' ears were notched or banded.

Elizabeth shouted a few words of power, sending the second werewolf stumbling back toward the edge, fur ablaze as fire streaked from her hand.

Two howls came from behind them, and Lucas turned to see the other two werewolves stalking toward them. Shane was back on his feet with a shotgun in his hands, but he looked shaky, as if the blast in the well had hit him hard through his ability to hear daemon song. Still, he stood his ground and racked the gun to make sure the weres knew he meant business.

The second two new werewolves came at a dead run. Elizabeth shouted in alarm as the burned werewolf appeared over the ridge, looking for vengeance.

Lucas raised his rifle, but with the burned wolf bearing down on him, his shot missed, grazing the creature's head. It lunged, and Lucas got off another shot, this time striking it in the right shoulder. That would have stopped a real wolf, but the werewolves were tougher, and the creature kept right on coming.

One of the new werewolves headed for Elizabeth, while the other barreled into Shane, taking them over the edge.

"Shane!"

Shane's gun fired again and again, and Lucas's belly tightened with fear. He didn't dare take his eyes off his attacker as the burned werewolf bared its teeth and moved in for the kill. Out of the corner of his eye Lucas glimpsed another streak of fire as Elizabeth held off her assailant, and heard her voice rise in a chant.

The burned werewolf sprang forward, Lucas fired, and the bullet tore away the creature's skull above the snout. Its heavy body dropped to the ground, twitching, and Lucas saw the notched ear of the wolf he'd just taken down.

Elizabeth's wolf attacker lay still, its head separated from its shoulders by the bloody machete she held in her hands. "No notch or band on that one," she said, breathless from the fight.

"Shane!" Lucas headed over the ridge, skidding down the slope, with Elizabeth right behind him.

Lucas heard a werewolf's growls, Shane's shouts, and the sound of a scuffle long before he could see what was going on. Shane and the wolf struggled, rolling in the dirt. Shane's gun lay a distance away, out of reach and useless.

Lucas sighted his gun, but without a clear shot, he risked hitting Shane instead of the werewolf. Elizabeth shouted words that seemed too slippery for Lucas to hear, and for a few seconds, Shane and the werewolf froze.

Lucas pulled the trigger, and the werewolf's head exploded, bathing Shane in its blood. In the next second, the spell broke, and Shane threw the corpse off of him, scrambling to put distance between himself and the beast, wild-eyed and frightened.

Lucas's heart sank as he realized that the dead werewolf's ears had a metal band. *Were-hybrid, contagious bite, can shift anytime.*

"Shane? Hey buddy—the fight's over." Lucas lowered his gun and approached Shane cautiously, like a spooked animal. He couldn't tell how much of the blood that soaked Shane's shirt was his own, and how much came from his attacker. At least, thank God, Shane hadn't been mauled.

"Lucas?" Shane's voice sounded unsure, one of the few times Lucas had seen his friend unnerved.

"Yeah, I'm here. It's done. The well caved in. Nice shot. You did good work. But now, we need to get out of here."

Shane seemed dazed and looked first at the dead creature. The powerful, thickly furred body grew indistinct and became a man's naked corpse.

"Come on," Lucas coaxed. "Get your gear. We need to ride." Something about the panic in Shane's gaze sent an alarm thrumming through Lucas. He knew Shane Collins better than anyone, and Lucas knew that only one thing could have rattled his partner this much.

Shane had been bitten by one of the modified werewolves.

"Yeah. Okay." Shane struggled to put words together. Lucas had fought beside this man on a battlefield and stood next to him as they watched reports roll in about the end of the world. He'd never seen Shane like this, and his suspicion grew to a certainty.

"We've got to get Elizabeth somewhere safe," Lucas said, keeping his voice level and calm. That seemed to reach Shane through his mental fog. The other man nodded and moved toward where his gun lay on the ground.

"I've got it." Lucas slipped in and scooped up the weapon with a smile, sure that right now, Shane should not have it. "C'mon. I'll grab your stuff. Looks like we had it easy up on the ridge, while you were kicking ass down here."

Lucas looked up to meet Elizabeth's worried stare. She didn't say anything, but Lucas felt certain she had come to the same conclusion. Would a stranger feel the same conflict, the same grief, that he did? He remembered Geoff's reaction when Thompson had been bitten, a split-second death sentence. *Oh, hell, no.* Protectiveness made Lucas step between Shane and Elizabeth as they walked, signaling that no matter what happened, the two of them would deal with it.

They stopped long enough to ensure that everyone in the camp was dead. Lucas mentally counted the bodies.

"Where's the witch?" he asked, glancing around.

"He threw himself into the sinkhole before it caved in," Elizabeth replied. "I may have also given him a push."

Lucas scanned for Richardson among the dead and stopped to turn the man over. From the blood and gashes on his body, the researcher must have taken the worst of the shrapnel. Lucas confirmed that the scientist was dead, but he couldn't help wishing that he'd had the chance to pry loose the man's intentions before shooting him. He checked for identification and found nothing. That meant they had no way to confirm that this actually was the rogue scientist. *Maybe we got him. Maybe we didn't. Guess we won't know unless he shows up to cause trouble.*

Now, his priority was keeping Shane alive until they could consider their options. He rose, addressing Elizabeth while he tried to get a read on Shane out of the corner of his eye. Shane looked pale and panicked, but he hadn't tried to grab for his gun, which Lucas counted as a win.

"Where can we escort you so you have somewhere safe to spend the night?" Lucas asked Elizabeth as they walked back to where the horses were tethered. He and Shane had planned to move on once they dealt with the threat of the damaged genius loci—and now they had more reason than ever not to want to go anywhere near Geoff and his knights.

"There's a small enclave near Boonesboro," Elizabeth replied. "I've stayed there before."

"We can drop you off on our way," Lucas replied, staying beside Shane to make sure he was steady enough to get up into the saddle. He paused just long enough to distribute the weapons—all that would fit—

into his saddlebags and fastened the slimmed-down duffle bag next to his bedroll behind his saddle. They left the small wagon behind.

"I know you're eager to get moving," Elizabeth said, and her gaze spoke volumes. "I can recommend somewhere safe where you can rest."

Lucas tried to read intent in the witch's eyes. If she suspected that Shane had been bitten, would she try to kill him? Lucas hoped she was smarter than that. Instead, he saw concern.

"Yeah? We don't want to put anyone out."

She shook her head. "Mapleville. The town's deserted, but still in pretty good shape. I figured you'd want someplace quiet for a little downtime." Lucas hoped it wasn't just his imagination, that her words were laced with double meanings. Shane seemed preoccupied, avoiding looking at either of them.

"That sounds like a good idea," Lucas replied, his gaze evaluating Shane before returning to Elizabeth. "A little peace and quiet could do the trick."

Shane didn't say anything as they rode, and Lucas didn't push him. Everything about the rigid way Shane sat his horse, how he favored his left forearm—the likely place for a defensive wound—and the clench of his jaw suggested that he was barely holding it together. Lucas needed to get them somewhere private, somewhere safe, and soon. Every instinct told him that he didn't dare let Shane out of his sight.

"Do you think what we did will hold?" Lucas asked Elizabeth as they rode the few miles toward Boonesboro.

"No way to know, but the energy at the battlefield is better than it was," she replied. Lucas liked that Elizabeth didn't try to tell him what he wanted to hear. "Whatever magic they were playing at was dangerous and untrained. Probably cobbled together from 'craft' books that are one step above gaming manuals. They had no idea what they were toying with. It's a miracle it hadn't gone worse. Fucking amateurs."

"Maybe Richardson knew that they'd gone so far outside the boundaries they weren't going to be welcome anywhere."

"Men like that want power. Richardson just didn't realize the game was over before it began."

Lucas had never been so thankful for empty highways. Now that shock had worn off, Shane looked twitchy, and Lucas could only guess what might be going through his partner's mind. All of his guesses were equally ominous. When they came to the deserted off-ramp to Boonesboro, Elizabeth smiled at him.

"I can take it from here," she assured him. "The enclave is a mile that way," she pointed to the east, "and I *am* a big bad witch. I can take care of myself."

"Thank you," Lucas replied. Gratitude shifted to outrage when Elizabeth reached out to tap Shane lightly on his right shoulder, and he slumped, unconscious but still upright.

"What the hell—"

"It's temporary. Should only last a couple of hours—enough for you to get him to Mapleville. The fire department there has a single jail cell in the back, somewhere to hold rowdy drunks until the county sheriff's office could send someone to pick them up. Get him in there, lock him up, and then you can decide what to do. You'll both be safe. The place is small enough that looters probably didn't bother with it, so you might even be able to find food enough to last a while."

"Why are you helping us?" Lucas didn't mean to sound ungrateful, but experience made him wary.

"You two have *abilities* most people don't have. I don't need to know what they are, but magic senses magic. That gives you both an advantage over regular folks," Elizabeth said, locking gazes with Lucas. "I don't believe in fate. You have options, if you're willing to fight for them. This doesn't have to end badly."

"Is there a cure?"

"Not that I've ever heard, but with your abilities, you might be able to make it more of a chronic condition."

Lucas wanted to believe her with every fiber in his being, although he had no idea how to cheat the death sentence of a werewolf's bite. "I hope you're right. And I'm going to fight. Be careful. You saw that two of those weres were hybrids with no ear markings? That means there are still more of them out there."

She managed a wan smile. "Yeah. I saw—and I'll be careful. Now, hit the road. The sooner you get there, the sooner you can figure this out."

Lucas took the reins to Shane's horse, thanked Elizabeth once more, and watched her ride off with only a small pang of guilt over not seeing

her to her sanctuary's doorstep. Elizabeth would be all right. Shane...
Lucas couldn't think about that just yet.

He listened for Rocky, but the place-spirit had gone silent. Lucas
wondered what Rocky had experienced when the grenades hit and Elizabeth's spell trapped the dark daemon in the old well. Whatever it was
couldn't have been good. And certainly Shane, with his ability to hear
the song of the daemons, had to have felt some of the twisted spirit's last,
desperate struggle. Maybe that let the werewolves get the jump on him.

Lucas was alone with his thoughts, and his worry. Even unconscious, Shane didn't look truly at rest. Lucas wasn't looking forward to
the conversation once Shane came around, but it had to happen. He
nudged his heels into his horse's ribs, picking up the pace a bit, needing
to get them to that jail cell soon.

Mapleville was more a cluster of houses and a few other buildings
than a real town. It didn't look like anyone had been here in a long time,
although its location spared it the worst of the damage from the Blast
itself. Maybe its residents had tried to ride out the end of the world, only
to discover that life without the benefits of modern civilization was
harder than expected. Most people gave up roughing it pretty quickly,
leaving in search of one of the small communities where they could pool
their resources to survive.

That meant it was just what Lucas and Shane needed. It didn't take
long to find the fire department. He picked the lock and raised the big
bay doors to bring their horses inside. A quick search turned up the
kitchen, a dormitory where the firefighters on duty slept, an office, and
the single jail cell Elizabeth had promised.

"Glory, hallelujah," Lucas muttered. Concrete walls bounded the
cell on three sides, with steel bars on the fourth. The key dangled from a
peg on the wall, just like in every Western Lucas had ever watched.

He opened the cell door, then manhandled Shane off his horse and
dragged him inside, laying him gently on the metal ledge that served for
a bed. Lucas hesitated, then checked Shane over. Dried blood stiffened
Shane's shirt and jacket. No gashes meant Shane had managed to avoid
the creatures' claws. But an unmistakable bite mark on Shane's left
forearm told the rest of the story.

Shane would have seen the metal band on the creature he fought, would have known what that meant. And knowing Shane, he stoically accepted that he had to die.

Fuck that. Lucas hadn't been much for playing by the rules even before the world ended. Three years of chaos had only reinforced that trait. And he'd be damned if he stood by and let his best friend go down without a fight.

"We'll figure something out," he promised, although he had no idea what that meant. Then he closed the cell door behind him and turned the key in the lock. The heavy bolt *thunked* into place, echoing in the empty building.

"There's got to be a way," he told himself and tested that the door was locked. He didn't know how long Shane would remain unconscious, and before he woke, Lucas needed to care for their horses, find water and food for them and their mounts, and scope out the hamlet to make sure they were as alone as it appeared.

He'd think about how to help Shane later, once he had a hold on his emotions. Maybe by then, he'd have a plan. He sure as hell hoped so, for both their sakes.

CHAPTER SIX

Shane woke completely disoriented. His head throbbed, every muscle ached, and the rumbling from his stomach reminded him he hadn't eaten in far too long. Groggy and hurting, he forced himself to sit up and frowned at the unfamiliar surroundings.

"What the hell?"

Gray cinderblock walls and steel bars made it clear he was a prisoner. Memories filtered back slowly. He felt like he'd been roofied, and wondered how the fuck someone had managed to drug him. The last thing he remembered was the battlefield at Fox's Gap, the loud report of the grenade launcher, the concussion of the explosion and the attack—

"Shit."

Shane looked at his blood-soaked clothing, and then at his left arm, where the sleeve had been pushed up to reveal livid bruising around an unmistakable bite.

The werewolf who jumped him had a banded ear. That meant— Shane was utterly fucked.

"Lucas?" Shane didn't call too loudly, in case somehow during the hours he couldn't recall they had been snatched by some other group.

His voice echoed, then silence.

Shane tried to piece together the aftermath of the attack. He'd been momentarily incapacitated by the scream of the twisted daemon when the explosion hit. That left him shaky when the werewolf barreled into him and sent them over the edge. Even so, Shane had fought with all his might, against a creature that was taller and more powerful, barely keeping it from ripping out his throat.

He looked ruefully at the bite on his arm, the price for keeping teeth and claws away from his neck. If he'd actually thought about it, letting the creature kill him might have been the kindest option.

Shane couldn't help remembering the look in Thompson's eyes, and the resignation on his face. Geoff hadn't hesitated in pronouncing his sentence. Lucas had argued against Geoff, but would he feel differently now, when he'd had time to think about it?

He wouldn't blame Lucas if he had changed his mind. Shane didn't hold out hope for a cure.

Now, he'd either have to talk Lucas into leaving him alone with a gun or shooting him. Neither option was likely to go over well.

Unless...maybe they'd gotten jumped on the road after Shane had passed out. Bounty hunters were known to roam areas where there had been disturbances. If the IT Priests had heard about the werewolf attacks, surely others knew of them as well. Had Lucas been ambushed while Shane was unable to back him up? But if so, where was Lucas? He couldn't imagine his partner giving up easily.

A darker possibility occurred to him. Maybe Lucas had tried to fight off a bounty hunter—and lost.

Or maybe he knew just how fucked you were and let the bounty hunter take you off his hands, a malicious little voice whispered in his mind.

Lucas would never—Shane stopped cold. He and Lucas had been friends, almost brothers, nearly all their lives. So selling him out for money or even to save his own skin wouldn't occur to Lucas. But if Lucas saw the bite—and Shane felt certain that was the case—then he had to know the situation was hopeless. Had to know that it only ended one way, with a bullet in Shane's skull.

Maybe that was one bridge too far, something Lucas couldn't bring himself to do.

But if that were the case, why was Shane still alive? No bounty hunter in his right mind would let a fledgling werewolf regain consciousness before capping him, not when he could double-tap the monster while he was asleep.

Shane leaned forward, cradling his head in his hands, resting his elbows on his knees. His captor had left him his belt and shoelaces. In theory, he could hang himself. That might kill a human, but Shane wasn't human anymore. To kill a werewolf required silver to the heart, a head shot, or taking off the head completely. Once again, he was screwed.

A lifetime of memories flashed through Shane's mind. Growing up in a world that no longer existed. His family, now dead. Friends who were, more than likely, also dead—if not in the Blast then in the aftermath. Boot camp, first deployment, firefights on battlefields in the Middle East. Joining the US Marshals. Close calls and near misses. And then, watching the world go up in flames until the TV signal fizzled and the screens went dark.

Lucas had been beside him since they were kids, watching his back, teasing him out of bad moods, harassing him like a brother. So if it was Shane's time to check out—and it was, it had to be—then he really only had one regret. He hated the idea of leaving Lucas to deal with this fucked up wreck of a world by himself.

He's not alone. He has Rocky.

Maybe. But Shane remembered how he had felt when he'd watched a feral AI robot electrocute Lucas in front of him, watched his breath stutter and seen the light fade in his eyes. Shane had been gutted, desperate, and he'd called out to any entity that could hear him for help. Rocky had answered, and Lucas got off that cold bunker floor and walked away—amazingly, impossibly, alive.

But Rocky couldn't possess both of them, and they were still too close for Shane's liking to the twisted genius loci to take a chance on the daemons of either nearby park. Which led right back to where Shane had started, the cold certainty that fate had a bullet with his name on it waiting for him.

Shane had never been very religious, and he'd stopped praying to a silent god when the world around them went down in ashes. He'd tried to be an honorable man, to live a life of service, to keep his word and do right by those around him. Shane was well aware of all the times he'd fallen short, the questionable decisions in the heat of battle, the rough justice in a world gone mad. If anything existed after this life, he had no idea what lay in store for him.

But he would not allow himself to become a monster.

That decision mantled a sense of peace over him like the matter had been settled. He'd done the best he could—scored more wins than losses—and lived longer than all the people whose lives ended abruptly in the Events. He could do one more service, protect the survivors in one more way—by dying and sparing the world another dangerous creature.

The scrape of a door opening roused him from his thoughts. Footsteps sounded, coming closer. Instinct told him to get as far away from the bars as he could. Shane didn't move. The spartan room gave him nowhere to hide. If someone wanted to shoot him, it would be like hunting fish in a barrel. It made no sense to put up a fight, not when there was only one inevitable outcome. *Might as well take it like a man.*

"Thank God you're awake." Lucas headed toward the cell carrying bottled water and protein bars. He put two bottles and bars inside the cell and kept two of each for himself. "You're probably starving."

Lucas sounded like nothing was wrong, as if it wasn't unusual for Shane to be locked in a cell waiting to go wolf. *Or maybe he's putting a good face on, giving you a last meal,* that treacherous inner voice suggested.

"Thanks." Shane's voice sounded rough to his own ears. He moved slowly to take what was offered, not wanting to scare Lucas. The protein bars were stale, but he was too hungry to care, and if the water tasted like plastic, it still soothed his raw throat. They ate quickly, and Shane tried to remember when they had previously eaten.

This morning. When I was still human.

"Where are we?" Shane took pride in not sounding as freaked out as he felt. *Just another meal on the road...before one of us shoots me.*

"Mapleville. Elizabeth suggested it. Said it might be just what we needed. She was right."

What we needed? Any cemetery would do. Shane stared at his partner as if Lucas had lost his mind.

"We need to talk."

That was the understatement of the year.

"Lucas—"

"The way I see it, we've got two choices."

Here it comes. Bullet or blade?

"The first choice is, you bite me, and we go on doing what we've been doing, only with more fur."

Shane stared at him, slack-jawed.

"The second choice is, you let Rocky and the daemon songs you hear help you learn to manage when and how you shift, so you control the wolf and not the other way around. And when you're comfortable, we go on doing what we've been doing, with some added capabilities." Lucas smirked. "I always did want a dog."

"Lucas, I'm dangerous. I could kill civilians. I could kill you. There *are* two choices. One of them is that you hand me a gun and walk away. The other is that I kneel in front of the bars, and you put a bullet in my skull."

Lucas lifted his head defiantly like he had anticipated Shane's response and had already worked out a rebuttal. "See, that's not going to happen, because I'd be one bullet behind you, and Rocky kind of likes the road trip we're taking him on."

"You can't be—"

"You're the only family I have left. My best friend. My partner. My brother. I've lost everything else in the world. But this," he said, gesturing with a wave of his hand between them, "keeps me going. I can't be a Marshal without a partner. We're the last two left, so there's no replacement out there. After the life we've led, I just can't see myself becoming a farmer. This is all I know how to do, and I'm gonna do it until I die with my boots on. So it's up to you—is that going to be now, or later?"

Lucas always did know how to play dirty, even as a kid. He was also the most stubborn person Shane had ever met, and he'd had time to make up his mind. More than that, Shane didn't doubt Lucas's intent to follow him, if it came to that. Hell, he'd felt the same way when Lucas nearly died at Fort Ritchie, before Rocky intervened.

"You're insane."

Lucas shrugged. "Not the first time someone's said that, probably won't be the last." He met Shane's gaze. "I'm not human anymore. But that didn't bother you. You didn't let me die, and you didn't leave me behind. So I'm sure as hell not giving up on you."

They stared at each other in silence for a moment, a stand-off neither one was willing to end. Finally, Shane sighed. "Does Rocky really think that could work?"

Lucas nodded. "Elizabeth suggested it, actually. She didn't know about Rocky or your ability to hear daemon-song, but she knew we had some kind of power, and she told me that it might be possible to manage your...condition."

"This isn't herpes."

"Geoff did say lycanthropy was like an STD."

"Supernaturally Transmitted Disease?" Shane managed to smile. He saw a glimmer of relief in Lucas's eyes.

"Something like that," Lucas said. "It was a modified werewolf that bit you. Saw the ear tag. So on the plus side, you may be able to control when you shift," Lucas mused. "Hell of an advantage in a fight."

"You're actually serious," Shane replied. "Keeping me, like this."

"You're not a stray. Pretty sure the army had us chipped."

Shane felt dizzy from the whipsaw of emotions. He'd been ready to die when Lucas walked in. But Lucas's steadfast belief that they could find another way stirred a glimmer of hope.

"All right," Shane relented. "Let's give it a try. But until we know for sure that I can control this, I stay in the cell."

"Works for me."

"And if I can't control it, if Rocky's wrong, then—"

"La-la-la. I can't hear you." Lucas stuffed his fingers in his ears and shut his eyes.

"Adult. Nice."

Lucas flashed a shit-eating grin. "I've got to live down to expectations."

Shane sat down on the metal bed with a sigh. "All right. What now?"

"I don't know. Are you feeling wolfie? Got an urge to catch a Frisbee with your teeth? Want a squeaky toy?"

Shane rolled his eyes. "I have no idea what 'wolfie' feels like. New at this, remember?" He frowned. "The weres at Fox's Gap—they shifted this morning, right?"

Lucas paused, searching his memories. "I'm not sure," he admitted. "I don't know if that's when they shifted, or if they had shifted before that."

"All the stories I've ever read made it sound like werewolves could only shift during the three days of a full moon. Geoff's people said that was something Dr. Richardson wanted to 'improve' by adding the shifter DNA," Shane mused. "And cross-breeding is the old-school way of doing that."

"The moon wasn't full last night." Lucas looked up. "I remember, because I had to go outside to take a piss, and I damn near tripped over something in the dark. It was a waning crescent, and mostly behind the clouds. But it also means those other wolves weren't natural. And since they didn't all have bands or notches, we've gotta assume that some were turned by one of the modified weres. So the biggest issue, I guess, is seeing if Rocky can help."

"How can Rocky help me control the wolf?"

Lucas got the glazed look that meant he had turned his attention inward. "You can hear Rocky's song, even if he can't talk to you the same way he does to me," he said finally. "He may be able to keep your wolf more connected to your human side. Not let you give in to the aggression."

Shane flushed. "He, um, can talk to me when you're sleeping."

Lucas raised an eyebrow. "And you two were going to tell me, when?"

Shane shrugged. "It didn't seem important."

Lucas thought for a moment. "I really don't want to wait until I'm out of it for you to try to shift, in case you get stuck or something."

Shane snorted. "Stuck?"

"Shut up."

"I imagine that strong emotions could trigger a shift, but I'd rather not have another near-death experience any time soon," Shane said. "And since I didn't shift when you drugged me—"

"Not drugs. Magic. Elizabeth knocked you out so I could get you somewhere safe."

"Good to know. Anyhow, the only other thing I can think of is picturing what I want to happen and seeing if it does."

"You want to *visualize* yourself into a wolf?"

"You got a better idea?"

"Not really. Go for it."

"Um, any chance you could find some other clothes?" Shane asked.

"I look like a serial killer, and wolfing out isn't going to help. It's getting cold outside for a loincloth."

Lucas grimaced. "Not to mention horsehair burns on the inner thighs would really hurt."

"Yeah, let's not mention that."

"Okay, let me go loot and pillage and see what I find. Don't go anywhere."

"Funny."

Lucas left, and Shane was alone again. He blew out a long breath and closed his eyes, trying to sort through the jumble of emotions. Relief, that this wasn't his day to die. Worry, that the shifting might not go as well as Lucas hoped. And amazement, that Lucas was crazy enough to take a chance on him, trusting that Shane would somehow figure out how to control his wolf.

Shane had never been much for meditation. Their lives weren't settled enough, and in the old days, Shane depended on a sweaty workout at the gym to deal with frustrations. But even back then, he'd heard about soldiers with PTSD getting their anger and reactions under control with Yoga. *Taming their beasts, so to speak.*

He didn't know Yoga from Yogi Bear, but deep breathing wasn't much of a stretch. He could manage that. So while he waited for Lucas to return, he focused on slowing his breath, filling his lungs, holding for a second, and controlling his exhale. It felt good, actually. Then Shane rolled his head from one side to the other and shook out his shoulders, which were stiff from tension and sleeping on the metal bed. He did a few twists and stretches, just for good measure. By the time Lucas came back with an armful of clothing, Shane decided that, wolf or no wolf, there might be something to this meditation stuff.

"Most of the people in this town were short," Lucas said, tossing in a teal t-shirt and a pair of worn Levi's. "And the rest were wide. This is the best I can do. Sorry about the colors. Maybe we'll find a farmhouse where someone your height had better fashion sense." The rest of the clothes Lucas carried looked like an equally odd mix. "While I was rooting around, I grabbed some for myself. Like they say about beggars and choices."

"Better than nothing," Shane replied, scooping up the clothing and setting it on the bed. "You ready?"

"I'm just here to compare your performance to Teen Wolf. Rocky's the one you need, and he's ready when you are."

"Let's do it."

Shane shucked everything except his underwear, sat down on the bed, and planted his feet flat on the floor, knees wide for stability. He took a deep breath, and then another before closing his eyes and doing his best to find calm despite how hard his heart pounded. A few more breaths and his mind stilled enough for him to hear the familiar song that was Rocky, and a faint but reassuring melody coming from a park daemon Rocky had approved.

The daemon songs steadied him, and Shane focused on the were-wolf's bite, the raw wound on his arm that throbbed in time with his heartbeat. He remembered the creature that bit him, recalling the elongated snout, the sharp fangs, and the powerful body that was simultaneously man and wolf.

Shane felt a tingle spread through his body, growing more intense like an electric shock. He fought to hold the image of the werewolf in mind while also staying anchored in the daemon song. Pain blossomed along every nerve and muscle, worse than being Tasered, or being shot. He felt as if he were being ripped apart from inside as bones shifted and muscle stretched and reformed to fit a different body.

Now that the change was upon him, Shane clung to the daemon song, knowing it was his only hope of not losing himself completely to the transformation. He heard a voice screaming and realized it was his own. Breath came in harsh pants, and blood spurted in his mouth as fangs broke through tender gums, forcing his teeth apart. Shane's nose broke, then flattened and stretched as his cheekbones and jaw cracked and stretched into something far from human.

He rode out the pain, holding fast to the ethereal music only he could hear. *I'm Shane Collins. Shane Collins. Shane Collins,* he repeated to himself, fearing that he would forget. The pounding of his heart filled his ears, throbbing through his veins. Shane fell forward onto the floor, and when he opened his eyes, the hands that held him up were no longer his own.

Long fingers tipped with wicked claws stretched from paw-like palms. Fur the same color as his hair covered his arms and the backs of his hands. His briefs felt too tight, all wrong for this new body. A whiff of the air overwhelmed his senses, every scent sharp and strong. Shane's stomach rumbled, filling him a visceral urge to hunt. He sniffed the air and smelled sweat and fear. Prey.

"Shane?"

The voice drew his attention to the creature he had scented. A man stood near the bars, watching him with wide, frightened eyes. Shane growled, low in his chest, and bared his teeth.

"Listen to the songs, Shane. Listen and control your wolf."

The man was afraid, but something about the set of his shoulders told Shane he didn't plan to run. "That's it, Shane. Listen. Can you hear Rocky? Hang on to Rocky."

He'd almost lost the thread of the songs in the cacophony of snapping bones and his own tortured howls. The song resurfaced, strong and clear, wild and ancient. Shane saw the pictures the songs painted in his mind, eons flashing past, and he let the song fill him, raising his snout to howl with it.

"Good. That's good. You always did like to sing along," the man said, forcing a laugh. "Can you let the songs bring you home? Shane, can you change back?"

Shane. The name sounded strange and yet familiar. Not the language of wolves. He could not make his long muzzle twist to form the word, but he knew it belonged to him. How he was called, when he wore another skin.

Now that the pain of shifting was gone, this new form felt strong, invincible, free. His ears pricked up at the faintest sounds, and even from this distance, he could hear the catch of the man's breath and the rapid pulse of his heart. He knew this body was faster, more powerful, more resilient than that other, weaker, self.

"Follow the songs, Shane. Come back. Come back, now." The man's voice held an edge of fear, *for* Shane but not *of* him. Shane sniffed the air again, and listened to the patient coaxing. *Not prey. Pack.*

Shane breathed in, and the song grew louder, beckoning him to follow. For a terrifying moment, he couldn't remember what he was supposed to do, where he meant to go, how to let the song lead him back to where he'd been. He howled again and let the song fill his mind, let it sustain him as his body folded and twisted, another painful transmogrification. Through it all, as limbs changed form and joints dislocated, the song carried him, anchored him.

And when the daemon song finally faded, Shane lay on the cell floor, aching and exhausted, his entire tortured body aflame, human once more.

"Shane?" Lucas's hesitant voice pulled him out of the fog of pain and the bewildering change in his senses. With a lifetime in the military and law enforcement, Shane had always thought of himself as strong and fit, but compared to his wolf, he now felt weak and cut off from the heightened sounds and scents that had shown him the world in a whole new way.

"Pack."

"What?"

"My wolf knew you were pack. Family. Not...food."

"Well, thank fuck for that." Lucas's attempt at humor didn't hide the relief in his tone. "How are you? It looked...bad."

"It wasn't fun." Shane had only held the werewolf form for a little while, but his shortened jaw and human teeth felt odd, wrong.

"Rocky's glad you're back."

"I almost got stuck."

"I know."

"Do you think it will get easier?" Shane eased himself up to lean against the metal bed, still seated on the floor.

"No idea," Lucas replied. "But maybe it's something you get used to, like twenty-mile hikes in the desert with full gear."

"Yeah. I never really did get used to those."

"Me neither."

Lucas pushed a jar of peanut butter with a spoon through the bars, along with two more bottles of water. "There's no bread, but I figured the protein will do you good," he said, sliding down the wall opposite the bars as if he'd felt the pain and exhaustion of Shane's transformation vicariously. "Tomorrow, I'll go see if there's a well somewhere, even if I have to boil water. The bottles won't last us forever."

"We don't have to stay here *forever*," Shane said, mustering the energy to drag himself up to the bed. "Just long enough for me to get a grip."

"I've found enough food to last us a while," Lucas said. "I won't promise variety, but we won't starve."

"Maybe if I get good at this, we can go deer hunting."

Lucas chuckled. "That's so not a fair fight."

"Like it was before? I don't remember the deer packing heat." Perhaps it was the newness of the transformation or the shock of the change, but those memories just a few years distant seemed faint and indistinct.

"Maybe you've got a point," Lucas allowed. "Why don't you change into clean clothes, and I'll bring you a bucket of water to wash off. I doubt the toilet in the cell flushes, but you can probably pour the wash water down when you're done. I brought some bedding back with me when I went clothes 'shopping.' No reason we can't be comfortable."

"The horses..."

"They're fine. Took care of them while you were still out of it. Although they spooked when you shifted. Must have smelled your wolf."

"Maybe they'll get used to it."

"Just don't eat them."

"I'll do my best."

Lucas left, returning quickly with a pillow and blankets, plus a bucket of reasonably clean water. He stepped out of sight to give Shane privacy so he could clean up, but Shane knew his partner was never out of earshot. The sound of metal scraping on concrete made Shane grimace as his head pounded. He looked up to see Lucas maneuvering a bed from the firefighters' dormitory into the wide hallway.

"Figured we'd both sleep better this way," he said with a shrug. "Get some rest. I'm on watch."

Normally, Shane would argue to do his share, but not tonight. Thanks to his wolf's metabolism, the wounds from the fight at Fox's Gap had healed, including the bite, but he still felt like he'd done a brutal workout. He stretched his sore body out on the metal cot, pulled the blanket over his shoulders, and sleep found him almost immediately, sound and dreamless.

CHAPTER SEVEN

Lucas was no stranger to bad dreams. Hell, for the last three years, even their waking moments seemed like one long nightmare. But this... was worse than usual.

This didn't need to be a nightmare. Memory was bad enough.

He'd stood with his back flattened against the cement wall, watching, terrified, as Shane's body tried to turn itself inside-out. Nothing in the monster movies came close to the horrifying reality. They couldn't show the real thing, not without the audience puking their guts or passing out.

Lucas feared he might do both.

He'd seen landmines blow a man apart, just yards away when he stood. Seen bodies torn to shreds from IEDs and mortar shells, or hacked to bits by the enemy. Nothing compared to seeing Shane's body break and reassemble, to hearing the crunch of bones and the pain in his feral howl.

When the transformation was complete, the thing that stared back at him and bared its teeth made him wonder if Shane was gone forever, lost inside the beast. The yellow eyes held no recognition, no humanity. The only reminder of the man was the color of its fur, a match for Shane's dark blond hair.

Lucas's stomach pitched, and his heart thudded as he clenched his fists hard enough to leave bloody half-moons in his palm, as if he could will Shane through the shift and back again.

His voice shook as he tried to coax the monster—no, *Shane*—to remember, begging him to hang on to Rocky's song, to let it guide him home. Bile rose in his throat as the wolf remained motionless, and he feared that Rocky had been wrong. Lucas hadn't been joking about not wanting to continue the fight alone. He'd killed men in battle, and in the years since the Events, he hadn't shied away from mercy kills. Shane was his last, frayed tether to the world they knew Before, and Lucas knew that if he had to be Shane's executioner, it would be one shot he couldn't take and then walk away from.

That meant both their lives hung in the balance as Shane's wolf struggled to find its way back to human form. Lucas could hear Rocky's patient voice offering a lifeline, a daemon song trail of breadcrumbs to bring Shane back to himself. He clung to Rocky's assurances as the transformation began again, painful and horrifying, leaving Shane pale and still on the cell floor.

For a moment, Lucas feared the shock had been too much, until he saw the rise and fall of breath, and heard a moan of pain. Only then did he realize just how hard his own heart hammered, and how lightheaded he felt from holding his breath.

Except in his dream, Shane didn't rouse. He lay there, unmoving, as blood seeped from his nose and mouth, bones jutting out at unnatural angles, half-shifted. Dead.

Lucas sat bolt upright with a gasp. His shirt clung, sweat-soaked, to his back. He took heaving breaths, trying to slow the thudding of his heart, struggling to remind himself that the end of the dream was a lie.

"Not the first bad dream I've ever had," he murmured and pushed a trembling hand through his hair. He'd had nightmares before, after every close call in the army, the Marshals, and since the Events. They never grew less vicious, but they did, thankfully, become less frequent. "And probably not the last."

Even so, he watched for several moments to assure himself that Shane was still alive before he shook off the last of the dream and went to tend the horses and put together breakfast from what he had been able to scrounge.

By the time he came back, Shane sat upright on the edge of his bed, elbows on his knees, head bowed, hands dangling. He looked up, groggy and shamefaced when Lucas approached with an offering of jelly and boiled coffee.

"I thought the jam might go with the peanut butter," Lucas said, forcing a grin that probably didn't hide the worry in his gaze as he swept an appraising glance over his partner, checking for injuries. "The coffee's an experiment. I boiled water and grounds in a pan over the fire I lit in a metal drum and strained it as best I could. So it's sort of a cross between java and chew," he added, wrinkling his nose.

"Thanks." Shane's voice, whiskey-rough from screaming, sounded like a stranger.

"You okay?"

Shane just raised an eyebrow with a look that said it all.

"All things considered," Lucas added. Shane looked away, and Lucas didn't need conversation to know the other man was uncomfortable with what had occurred.

"You've got nothing to feel weird about," Lucas said. "I saw you puke up your first beer when we were twelve. Watched you puke up plenty more in the army. I haven't forgotten that time our whole unit came down with the shits when we were out on maneuvers, either. So compared to all that, seeing you shift was fucking awesome."

"I wasn't strong enough to control it." Shane's gravelly whisper barely reached Lucas. "It almost won."

"But you were, and it didn't." Lucas pushed the coffee and jelly jar through the bars. "You can't let 'what-ifs' get in your head. You and Rocky won, and with practice, it'll get easier."

Shane didn't quite hide a shiver, which Lucas figured had to do with repeating the transformation. "What if it doesn't?"

"It's your call," Lucas said, sobering. "I'll back whatever you decide. But I meant what I said. The choice goes for both of us."

Shane scrubbed a hand over his face. "*So* not helping."

"I'm not gonna lie. You say fight, I'll fight. You decide to surrender, and I'll go with."

What Lucas said, he meant. But more than that, he'd known Shane Collins nearly their whole lives, long enough to be certain that Shane never fought harder than when the stakes were high. Alone, Shane's fear of hurting someone, of not being in control of his wolf, might lead him to choose to prevent the problem. But knowing that his choice affected them both? Lucas gambled that Shane's rebellious streak would carry them through.

"Fuck that," Shane growled. "Maybe I'll stick around just for spite, and shed all over your stuff."

Lucas hid a smile. "Just remember to lift your leg against the wall, like a good dog."

Shane flipped him the bird.

"Back atcha. I'm going to make some more coffee-sludge. Let me know when you're ready to wolf-out again. Practice makes perfect."

He didn't need to hear what Shane mumbled to know the intent, loud and clear. Just to be annoying, Lucas whistled while he walked away.

"I wish we could have stayed longer." Shane glanced over his shoulder as they rode out of Mapleville, heading north.

"We were running low on food," Lucas replied. "I'd already used everything that hadn't gone rancid, buggy, or bulged. It would suck to live through the apocalypse and get killed by botulism."

"Still..." Shane's expression held a mix of uncertainty and worry.

"I brought a few of the last cans with us. Vegetables are hard to forage."

"Hope you remembered a can opener."

"Nah. I thought you'd pry it open with your fangs." Lucas rolled his eyes. "Of course I did, dumbass."

"Just checking."

"I figured we'd head up into West Virginia from here." Lucas hoped he sounded off-handed, like nothing—more than usual—was amiss. "Check out that place the coven in Bedford mentioned, the one that the scholar-monks want to use to safeguard recorded knowledge."

Shane snorted. "The one in the old Spiritualist resort that the stories say phases in and out of time? Hard to forget. I'm not sure how that's a job for us. If they want to hoard books in a mansion that thinks it's a

TARDIS, it's not really our business. Might not be the smartest thing, but it's not a crime."

"No, but harassing the monks is. That's what the coven leader mentioned when she asked if we could check on them when we headed north again."

When Shane didn't answer, Lucas knew he had to sell the idea a little harder. "West Virginia's almost all forest. Plenty of daemon songs."

"Lots of ghosts of dead coal miners."

"As you've pointed out, there are dead folks everywhere nowadays. I was just thinking that it wouldn't hurt to ride up through the mountains, maybe do a little hunting or fishing, find a cabin for a few days, let your wolf run," Lucas added that last bit as an aside.

"I guess it wouldn't hurt. We haven't been up that way in quite a while."

Lucas fought the urge to fist-pump. "It's real pretty territory. And not a lot of people. So if it takes us a few more weeks to get to Pittsburgh, that gives you more time to train Fenrir."

"His name isn't Fenrir."

"Lupin?"

"No."

"Fangface?"

"Definitely not. It's Quentin."

"Quentin?"

"Shut up. You got to name your daemon. I get to name my wolf."

Lucas raised his hands in joking surrender. "Sure. Does that shorten to 'Quent' or 'Tin'?"

"Neither, asshole."

Lucas shrugged. "Asshole it is. Easy to remember. I've been calling you that for years."

Shane huffed in annoyance, but Lucas took their banter as a win. Staying clear of other people for a while longer wouldn't hurt, giving Shane more time to feel confident with the wolf that had shacked up inside his skin, and more time to work with Rocky and other helpful genius loci who might be able to make the process easier.

Lucas didn't mind avoiding enclaves and hunters for as long as possible. Now that neither of them were fully human, someone might get the notion to hunt *them*, badges notwithstanding. As US Marshals, he and

Shane had always felt like outsiders, moving from place to place, assisting local law enforcement but never being part of the team. That feeling wasn't likely to get better with their new abilities.

Flickering images in the road made Lucas pull up on his reins. Shane acted in the same instant, still just as much in sync as ever.

"Ghost?" Shane asked.

Lucas nodded. "Yeah. There are about twenty of them. Pretty recent. All ages." He tried to relax and open his apocalypse-sharpened abilities to sense why the ghosts had made the effort to appear.

After a moment, he turned to Shane. "They couldn't speak, but they showed me what happened. Kidnappers. From the ones they didn't take, I'm guessing slavers, up ahead."

Lucas and Shane knew that two US Marshals couldn't hold back all the evil in their territory, but it didn't stop them from trying. When everything fell apart, human "monsters" seized the opportunity to benefit, supplying renegade compounds with slaves. He and Shane would probably never shut down all the trafficking operations, but Lucas was going to do his damnedest to try.

"What's the play?"

Lucas shot him a wily smile. "Let's try something new."

***

JUST BEFORE NIGHTFALL, four strangers rode up to the lean-to where a lone traveler with two horses crouched next to a campfire. He looked up when they stopped at the side of the road.

"Looking for someone?" he asked.

"I think we found what we're looking for," the man in the lead said. He raised a shotgun from where it lay across his lap. "You look like you know how to do a day's work. That'll bring a good price."

Lucas dove to one side, kicking the fire with his boot to send up a cloud of smoke and sparks. He rolled and came up firing. His first bullet caught the leader in the chest before the man could get Lucas in his sights, toppling the slaver from his saddle. His next shot hit the second man in the forehead.

A spine-chilling howl sounded just before wicked claws swatted the third man from his mount, sending him crashing to the ground. His horse panicked and bolted as the beast sprang at the fourth slaver. They fell together, rolling in the dirt, but the man was dead, throat torn open by sharp claws before he'd ever had a chance to pull his sidearm.

When the dust settled, Lucas held the reins of three skittish horses. Four bloody corpses lay in the road. The wolf-beast prowled up and down the road, yellow eyes glinting.

I hope he remembers the part about "pack," not "prey," Lucas thought.

"Nice work, Shane." Lucas tugged the horses' reins, hoping training kept them from trying to break loose, which was only likely to make Shane's wolf want to chase.

A growl answered him, and the beast—*Quentin*—padded a few steps toward Lucas, then sat down and wagged its tail.

"Okay, the tail is just weird," Lucas said. "No biting?"

Even in wolf form, Shane could give him the stink eye.

"All right then. How about I get your clothes and a towel to clean up with, and you shift. I need to tether the horses and deal with the bodies."

Lucas found that leaving the heads of brigands and slavers mounted on pikes next to the road served as a deterrent. Messy work, but worth it to send a message. Especially when the headless bodies were left propped against the pikes for the birds and scavengers. It also gave Lucas a quiet assurance that they wouldn't be turning into werewolves from Shane's bite.

Shane/Quentin just sat, watching him with an uncanny stare.

I think he wants a treat, Rocky said.

You've got to be kidding me.

Lucas walked back to the campfire and dug in his bag for the pack of peanut butter crackers he'd found in Mapleville. They were long past their expiration date, but given the list of chemicals in the ingredients, Lucas doubted they'd gone bad.

"Catch." He tossed a cracker to the werewolf, who lunged to snap it out of the air. The effect seemed much more frightening than when Lucas's black Labrador had done the same thing.

"One more, and then you shift," Lucas said, holding up a second cracker. "Unless you want to learn 'shake,' 'roll over,' and 'play dead.'"

Werewolves' fingers were long enough that Shane could flip him off, even in his furry form.

He threw the cracker underhanded, an easy catch. Shane padded off, looking satisfied. Lucas braced himself for the crunch of bones and the muffled yelp that went with a shift. Before long, Shane returned, dressed and having wiped off most of the blood.

"How was it?" Lucas asked, without turning to face his partner. This was Shane's first fight with his new abilities, his first kill. Lucas had worried that Quentin might be harder to control once the blood flowed.

Shane looked like he was considering his reply. "Different—but not as much as I thought it might be. Do you remember, in the thick of a battle, how once the adrenaline got going, everything else fell away, and there was a terrible beauty to doing what you were trained to do?"

Lucas nodded. He'd never known what to do with that feeling. It was heady and terrifying, and Lucas understood in those moments how some men lost themselves to it and never entirely returned.

"That's...the closest thing I can think of. What Quentin can do is amazing. So much strength. The wolf doesn't hesitate, doesn't feel that flash of guilt, even when you know the person deserves what they're getting." Shane drew in a ragged breath. "Which is why Quentin needs to be kept on a short leash, so to speak, until we work out a few things."

He pushed back a lock of hair that had fallen into his eyes. "On the bright side, the shift wasn't nearly as rough, coming or going." Shane grinned and held out two somewhat mangled rabbits. "Oh, and I caught these. Before the slavers came. Practice."

Lucas took the bloodied carcasses, which were nearly skinned from the force of the sharp claws. "I'll clean them," he said, not willing to turn down a good meal, even if eating a werewolf kill was going to take some getting used to.

"I can have a look through the slavers' saddlebags, see if there's anything useful," Shane volunteered.

Lucas nodded. "Go ahead. I figured we'd drop off the extra horses at the next park ranger station we passed. Shouldn't be too far."

Shane hesitated and looked back at him. In the light of the fire, Lucas could see the emotions warring in his eyes—pride in the successful mission, and fear that Lucas would see him as a monster.

"We're going to make this work," Lucas assured him. "Whatever you're worried about, we'll figure it out. You were pretty damn impressive, and a lot quieter than a gun. That's going to come in handy. Just think—we're the only K-9 Marshals in the area."

"Just so you know, I'm not going to do tricks."

"What if I found a Frisbee?"

Shane only had to think about it for a moment. "You're on."

TO BE CONTINUED...

Part Three

GHOSTS OF THE PAST

GHOSTS

OF THE
PAST

A WASTELAND MARSHALS NOVELLA

GAIL Z. MARTIN
LARRY N. MARTIN

CHAPTER ONE

"Go long!" Lucas sent a battered red Frisbee flying. The huge wolf bounded after it, all legs and power, then leaped into the air and snatched the plastic disk with his teeth. He padded back to Lucas, managing an expression of sheepish triumph.

"Let me guess. You put a fang through it—again," Lucas said. The wolf cocked his head in acknowledgment and held up one paw, asking for a treat.

"Go easy on these. We still don't know how they'll affect your other half," Lucas replied as he pulled two dog biscuits from his pocket. He gave one to the wolf, who gobbled it down with a disconcerting crunch, and decided to try one for himself.

"Huh. Not half bad—although a little stale. But what isn't?" he added with a sigh.

The wolf trotted away into a small cluster of trees at the edge of the mountain meadow to shift in privacy, and minutes later, a tall blond man strode out. Shane caught up with Lucas and looked remorsefully at the damaged Frisbee.

"Sorry. Quentin gets really into the game."

"You need to have a talk with your wolf, or we're going to run out of Frisbees," Lucas told him, still adjusting to Shane naming his furry half

Quentin. "He's chewed up three already, and it's not like we can just buy one at the store."

Lucas Maddox and Shane Collins grew up together in Cleveland, served in the Army, and then became US Marshals. They had survived battlefields and attempted Mob hits. But nothing had prepared them to survive the clusterfuck of catastrophes that now, almost four years later, people just called the "Events."

Terrorists had turned the major nations' own nuclear warheads against them, wiping out governments, destroying the financial markets, and devastating the big cities. Millions died from the blast and the radiation. A domino effect of disasters followed—tsunamis, earthquakes, volcanos—killing even more. Then came famine and disease. The power grid largely failed, and any communication systems that remained were spotty and fragile at best.

Law enforcement and the military did their best—those who weren't casualties in the first wave of attacks—but the sheer magnitude of the problems winnowed their numbers. Now what remained were largely local sheriffs, park rangers, and a few others, like Shane and Lucas, who were the last two US Marshals in their three-state area.

"You know, up here in the mountains it's easy to pretend everything didn't crash and burn," Shane mused, looking out over the valley and forest.

"Not hard to remember as soon as we take the horses back on the road."

Shane grimaced. "Yeah. Okay. But sometimes it's nice to just have a flash, a few seconds, where the world isn't fucked and you can almost believe it never happened."

Lucas could hear the sadness in his partner's voice. They had worked closely together for so long, under crazy and dangerous conditions, that they didn't need a lot of words to explain themselves. Even less so now that Lucas had an ancient elemental spirit riding shotgun to keep him alive, and Shane had been turned by a wolf shifter, which heightened his ability to hear the songs of the ancient spirits and enhanced his occasional psychic visions.

"I try not to do that," Lucas admitted, walking over to stand beside Shane, taking in the view. "Just rips the scab open again when you remember how it is now."

"I guess so." Shane sighed. "At least the folks who lived out here had time to come up with a plan. The places we rode past on the way didn't seem to have been abandoned very long. I'm sort of surprised many were empty at all. Figured this would be where folks might fall back to make their stand."

Lucas looked out over the vast forest and the deep clefts and valleys—what people in these parts called "hollows." "I imagine there are some folks holed up for the duration. Hell, some folks in these parts didn't come out even before the Events. They aren't our problem."

Two US Marshals couldn't be everywhere, and they certainly couldn't fully enforce the law or keep the peace—even though Shane and Lucas were no longer fully human, and Lucas would argue, at least on bad days, that they weren't completely sane either. So they did what they could and tried to take care of the problems the locals couldn't. Calling for backup was a lot harder than it used to be, but when Shane and Lucas were needed, desperate people found a way.

Despite the fact that the world had damn near ended, on days like this, Lucas knew how lucky he was to still have Shane riding with him and to still have a purpose for living. Outwardly, not much had changed, except for gaining a few scars along the way.

Shane still had that blond, blue-eyed, All-American cowboy aw-shucks charm that always made witnesses relax and waitstaff flirt. Lucas's dark hair and dark eyes gave off a moody, bad-boy vibe that made playing good cop/bad cop easy. They were almost the same height—nearly six-foot-two inches—but whether or not the heights were an exact match had been a joking point of contention since they'd hit their final growth spurt back in the day.

"You know what I'd like to do, when we're done with this case?" Shane asked. Helping a bunch of scholars protect an archive against a supernatural threat wasn't the strangest request they had gotten.

"I'm afraid to ask. Does Quentin want to find a dog park?" Lucas teased.

Shane gave an exaggerated sniff of disdain. "As if. He thanks you to remember he's a wolf, not a dog."

"Still a canine. Potato, po-tah-to."

Shane rolled his eyes. "If you still had a car, he'd pee on your tires."

"Nice. Classy."

"Anyhow, you know what we haven't done for a while? Find a bar that isn't too wrecked and play some pool," Shane said. "Throw a few darts, just...relax a little, like old times."

"And you'll rope me in for karaoke," Lucas said with an exaggerated sigh. "At least there won't be anyone else to hear us." Or any music to sing along with, but they had long ago learned to make do.

"Of course," Shane said with a grin.

"Everything's strictly B-Y-O-B unless we get really lucky," Lucas reminded him. "Although I still have a bottle of the corn whiskey we bought off that farmer in Maryland."

"Not gonna be picky," Shane said. "I mean, what I'd really like is to order a pizza, watch a horror movie marathon, and then play some Warcraft, but...that's not gonna happen."

No, it wasn't, ever again. And even after four years, Lucas felt the loss like a phantom limb.

THEY HEADED BACK to the horses, packing everything they owned into the duffel bags and saddlebags their horses could carry. Lucas figured that if the weather held, they could make it to Ansted in about two days. That meant stopping for the night somewhere, but they usually had their pick of abandoned homes and farms.

Fayette County, West Virginia, hadn't been thickly settled even before the Events. Coal mining and lumber had propped up a hardscrabble economy dependent on the stubborn will and strong backs of men who worked hard and died young. For those who lived off the grid —or nearly so—before the Events, little had probably changed, except that coming back into society was no longer a choice since society itself was gone.

Shane chuckled, breaking the silence, and Lucas gave him a puzzled look. "What?"

"I think Rocky likes this area," Shane replied. "Can't you hear him singing?" Shane's ability to hear the "songs" of the elemental spirits— otherwise known as daemons or genius loci—had grown stronger since the Events. So had his ability to catch glimpses of the events, both past and future, although the timing and the focus were still beyond his control.

Lucas turned his attention inward, to the daemon, an immortal spirit who had become his co-pilot to save his life when he'd nearly died on one of their cases. He had nicknamed the spirit "Rocky" after the name of the park where the entity had been a genius loci—the elemental spirit of a place. Where Shane sensed those spirits as a song, Lucas and Rocky could have a conversation, albeit in Lucas's mind.

"It's pretty out here," Lucas said with a shrug, getting ready to swing back up into his saddle. "What's not to like?"

Shane suddenly cried out and doubled over, landing on his knees, head clutched in his hands. Lucas was beside him in an instant, gun drawn, covering them while his partner was down and vulnerable.

"Shane, talk to me. What are you seeing?" Lucas knew Shane couldn't speak when one of his visions hit, but he felt the need to maintain a connection and let Shane know he wasn't alone. "You're safe. I'm here. Got your back. Gonna be okay. You pick the damnedest times to log into your weird wi-fi."

Lucas knew from experience there was no moving Shane until his clairvoyant revelation ended. All he could do was remain alert for danger and keep his knee pressed against Shane's shoulder in solidarity, grounding him and making sure he knew Lucas was with him.

A moan let him know Shane had started coming back to himself. Shane fell forward onto his hands and knees and retched. He stayed where he was, body trembling, and Lucas knew it was part of Shane coming back to himself, back to the real world.

"I'm going to get you some water. Don't move."

Lucas sprinted to their horses, still keeping an eye out for an ambush. He grabbed a battered stainless-steel water bottle and dug around their provisions for a protein bar that was long past its expiration date. When he returned, Shane had managed to plant himself on his ass, putting a little distance between him and where he'd been sick. Lucas kicked some dirt over the foul-smelling puddle and then brought the food and water over to Shane.

"You okay?" he asked, taking in his partner's pale, sweaty face. Visions always kicked Shane's ass, no matter how much the other man tried to hide it.

"Yeah," Shane managed, accepting the items gratefully and rinsing his mouth, then washing down the stale bar with a gulp of water. Lucas noted that Shane wasn't shaking so hard, a sign that the worst of the experience was over.

"You ready to ride?"

Shane managed a wan chuckle. "Times like this, I miss the SUV."

Lucas helped him up, relieved when Shane walked on his own back to the horses. Much as he wanted to know what the vision had revealed, Lucas knew that it always took Shane a while to figure out how to put the images into words.

He tried not to look like he was hovering, fussing with his saddlebag until Shane had gotten into his saddle on his own. Moments later, Lucas had mounted up and snapped the reins to head his horse back toward the highway, sparing a worried glance to check on his partner. Shane still looked dazed, but his color had improved, and he sat his horse solidly, so Lucas forced himself to focus on the route, although it was impossible not to worry.

They rode on, but the lighthearted mood had vanished. Both men rode with loaded shotguns across their laps and handguns tucked into their waistbands.

"I saw bits and pieces of a ritual—human sacrifice," Shane said out of the blue after they had ridden for a while. "Pretty sure the victims were drugged. They didn't fight. Some looked like they were unconscious. Lucky for them."

He paused as if trying to work up the nerve to put the horrific vision into words. "You know those slasher flicks we used to watch? The real thing is a lot worse. But that's what it was like. I couldn't see the face of the person doing the ritual. He had a robe with a hood. The rest...it was like some crazy horror movie with the candles and the symbols and a chant."

"Could you tell why he killed them?" Lucas asked, not envying Shane his virtual front-row seat to the killings.

"He said some kind of incantation, and then this black...slime... seemed to come up through the floor and up his body and then into his mouth." He shuddered. "It looked like a cross between motor oil and hot tar, but it was sentient, Lucas. Whatever it was possessed that man."

"Fuck. Like the bad guys weren't bad enough on their own," Lucas replied. "I was okay with living out the real-life version of *Goodfellas*. We never signed on for *The Exorcist*."

"Yeah, well. We didn't volunteer for *The Day After*, but at least it isn't *Dawn of the Dead*," Shane answered. Lucas figured if his partner could make movie metaphors, he was probably going to be as okay as they ever were.

"What do you think it means?" Lucas asked.

"Dunno. Whoever the killer was, he's juiced up and out there, but what he wants or what he can do with that extra mojo, I've got no idea," Shane said.

They rode for a few hours, spending part of the time in silence as Shane recovered from his vision, and the rest playing a trivia game, Lucas's attempt to take Shane's mind off what he had seen. Shane had chosen the category of "science fiction movies" and tossed out true or false questions from memory. Lucas had picked "fantasy novels" for his category. The game kept them occupied, and even more importantly, kept those memories fresh, of the things they had loved and lost in the Events—the games, movies, TV shows, and books that they might never see again.

Lucas's horse, Shadow, came to an abrupt halt. Shane reined in his horse as well. "What's going on?" Shane asked.

"Ghosts," Lucas replied. "Four of them." He looked away from the spirits only he could see, which stood in the middle of the roadway, and scanned the area around them.

"They want us to go over there," he said, pointing toward a ranch house not far off the road. It looked abandoned, but they had learned the hard way that appearances could be deceiving.

"Do we stop? There are a lot of ghosts."

Lucas had a silent conference with Rocky. "He doesn't sense any beings in or near the house," Lucas reported. "I have the feeling we should go look."

Shane reached for his shotgun. "Then let's see what's going on."

The ghosts vanished from the roadside, only to reappear on the driveway of the house, then on the front porch. Lucas and Shane dismounted and tethered their horses to the fence. Hand signals from their Army days told Shane to stay with the horses and keep watch, while Lucas headed inside.

Lucas approached carefully, making sure he didn't present an easy target. He crouched beneath the large front window and edged up to look inside. He saw no people and no movement. The only sound was the wind in the trees.

He'd learned a long time ago to trust his gut, and doing so had served him well over the years. Now, his stomach had a tight knot, warning of something bad. Not the prickle at the back of his neck that meant imminent danger, but the certainty that something lay ahead he did not want to see.

Lucas tried the front door, and the sinking feeling when it swung open, unlocked, just added to his tension. The furnished, darkened rooms looked as if a family had just stepped out for the day. Except for the smell of mold and mildew, and beneath that, the coppery tang of blood that Lucas knew far too well.

He swallowed hard and did his best not to flinch when the ghosts showed up in the entrance to the kitchen.

Shotgun raised, he made sure the living room was empty before he walked into the kitchen—and nearly lost his lunch.

Four bodies lay on the blood-soaked floor and sprawled across the table. From the smell and condition, Lucas figured they had been dead for a couple of days. Flies buzzed above the corpses of two men and two women, early to mid-thirties, who had been gutted from sternum to pelvis. Without getting any closer, Lucas tried to make out anything distinctive about their clothing, but it was too blood-soaked for him to make out details.

The burned-down stubs of four pillar candles remained on the corners of the table, where the fourth body lay like an offering. Even with the potent smell of blood, Lucas picked up the stink of ash and sulfur. Strange symbols had been scrawled onto the cabinets and windows in what appeared to be blood.

Holy shit, this is the ritual Shane saw in his vision. Lucas had viewed crime scene photos from ritual murders for some of their cases with the US Marshals. But back then, those rituals hadn't been the real thing. Given the ramp-up of everything supernatural since the Events, Lucas didn't doubt that whatever these people had been sacrificed to achieve was part of real, potent magic. And whatever the ritual had summoned wasn't good.

Lucas looked back to the ghosts, who stood in the hallway. They were dressed differently from their corpses, all of them wearing long gray robes. *A religious cult? Wouldn't be the first we've run into. Although human sacrifice is a new angle.*

"You wanted a witness to your deaths?" he asked, glad to step away from the gory scene. "I see you. I am sorry that you were killed. Will that acknowledgment let you move on?"

Lucas's ability to see ghosts had saved his ass many times when spirits had warned of danger. Now, he wasn't sure what these unlucky revenants wanted from him.

One of the ghosts raised her arms, fists clenched, then crossed them at the wrists. The others did the same.

"You want us to find the people who did this to you?" Lucas guessed, thinking that the pose looked like someone bound with handcuffs.

The ghosts nodded, and Lucas's heart sank.

"You were terribly wronged. But I have no idea how to find your killers," he explained. Being the last two US Marshals in their territory usually gave Lucas purpose, a reason to go on. At other times, like now, the enormity of the task threatened to overwhelm him.

The ghosts repeated the gesture, this time in unison, again and again. The silent "chant" made the message clear. *Find them. Stop them. Make them pay.*

"I can't promise," Lucas said. "There's a lot of territory out there, and I don't have much to go on. But...if I can, I will."

The ghosts nodded solemnly, accepting his offer. One by one, they vanished.

"Lucas? Everything okay in there?" Shane called through the open front door.

Definitely not okay. Lucas swallowed down bile and headed back to where his partner waited.

"That ritual you saw in your vision? Pretty sure it happened right here."

Shane listened as Lucas recounted what had happened, then Lucas kept watch while Shane ducked inside for a corroborating look at the crime scene. He emerged, pale and a little green around the gills.

"Fuck. I know I've seen some of those symbols, but I don't remember the meaning," Shane said.

"Whoever killed those people is out here somewhere—and we've got no idea what they conjured up," Lucas replied.

"Do we need to do something about the ghosts?"

Lucas shrugged. "I can't sense anything keeping them here, except that they wanted someone to know what happened to them—and they want justice. They'll probably move on when they're ready."

"So I guess we keep our eyes open and watch our backs—same as always," Shane replied.

Knowing that a crazy cultist killer was on the loose made Lucas even less happy about needing to find a place to stop for the night, but they were still too far away from Ansted to finish the trip tonight. They found a solid cement block building with garage bay doors leading to an empty storage room in the back, making it easy to stable the horses. After they let the horses graze and found water for them in a nearby stream, Lucas and Shane brought their mounts in and hunkered down for the night.

"Do you think that ritual—the murders—is connected to the case?" Shane asked as he and Lucas finished a dinner of dried meat, cheese, apples, and bread, washed down with a little whiskey.

"No idea," Lucas replied. "I hope not. But I guess anything's possible." He sighed and leaned back against what had been the service counter. "There's a lot of forest out here—and very few people. Bunch of crazy cultists could go anywhere."

"I hope you're right," Shane replied. "But our luck hasn't been that good lately." He stood and stretched. "Get some sleep. I'll take first watch."

To Lucas's relief, the night passed without incident. They headed out early the next morning, opting to eat a breakfast of bread and cheese on the road.

"We need to find some more coffee somewhere," Shane said. "I'd kill for a latte right about now."

Since the Events, coffee—when they could find it in an abandoned house or not-completely-looted store—was boiled over a campfire. Still, it remained a precious luxury, one Lucas would never take for granted again.

"I'll put it on the top of my list of things to look for," Lucas assured him.

By the time they stopped for lunch and to give the horses a rest, they were only within a few hours' ride of their destination.

"The song isn't right." Shane stared at the blue-green valley like he could force it to give up its secrets. "Can't you feel it? What does Rocky say?"

Well? Lucas asked Rocky.

You knew the mountain was troubled. That is why we came here, was it not?

Yes...but details on the kind of trouble would be really useful.

Lucas could almost feel Rocky trying to figure out how to use human speech—which was new to him—to describe what he sensed.

The energy of the mountain is warped, but it is not poisoned, Rocky replied finally. *It is unusual, but that is how it has been for time beyond memory. Although, stronger now, more...unstable.*

Keep an eye on it, okay?

Your eyes are the only ones I have.

Lucas sometimes forgot that Rocky could be very literal. *I mean, pay attention to the strange energy and let me know if something changes.*

Ah. Of course.

Lucas turned back to Shane. "From what Rocky's picking up, he doesn't think anyone has altered the energy. It's always been that way."

Shane nodded. "That makes sense. Maybe some people could pick up on those vibes. Something has drawn seekers here for centuries. Take that hotel the coven in Bedford asked us to investigate, for example. The Spiritualists who built the Mountain Cove Hotel wanted to find a way to reach across the Veil and contact the dead."

"Except it sounds like the dead started reaching back."

"Yeah, that tends to be a problem."

"The coven really wanted us to come up here," Lucas mused. "Someone must have really put up the Bat-Signal like it was a big deal. I mean, we owe the coven some favors, but helping a bunch of scholar-monks safeguard recorded knowledge in an old hotel that phases in and out of time isn't our usual gig."

"Except nothing's been our usual gig in a long time," Shane replied.

"If that ritual I saw in my vision—and the murder house—is somehow related, that's a lot closer to being our kind of thing."

"Those bodies hadn't been there long," Lucas countered. "The coven asked us to swing through here months ago."

"They're witches. Maybe they got a glimpse of the future. Or maybe there's something bigger connecting everything we don't know yet."

"Aren't you a ray of sunshine," Lucas muttered.

"For all we know, things could have blown over a long time ago," Shane said.

"We should be so lucky," Lucas replied. "Because then, we'd probably need to go looking for the killer from your vision."

Shane looked away, and Lucas recognized the guilt that ghosted across his expression. "We could have gotten here sooner. I cost us time."

"You just got turned into a fuckin' werewolf," Lucas countered. "You needed a chance to figure out how all that worked. We both needed to wrap our heads around it."

"Still—"

"You gave me space to process when Rocky first came onboard. Just returning the favor."

They walked back to their horses. Shane patted his roan gelding, named Red. Lucas's black stallion—not-so-creatively named Shadow— bent his head to have his ears scratched.

"Want to do a drive-by to take a look at the old hotel before we go into town looking for the scholars?" Shane asked as he swung up into the saddle. "Since the hotel is at the heart of what the witches wanted us to protect."

"More of a 'ride past,' don't you think?" Lucas snickered, mounting his horse. "Sure. Maybe Quentin or Rocky will pick up on something even if we don't."

At first, it had felt odd to refer to Shane's wolf and Lucas's elemental spirit by different names. After all, it had only been a few months for Lucas, and even less for Shane, and the situations took a lot of getting used to. But as they settled into what was now the "new normal," naming the creatures made conversation clearer and no longer seemed as strange.

They took the exit closest to their destination, and their horses' hoof-beats seemed loud in the otherwise silent, deserted interchange.

"Lucas—look! It's that place we watched the show about on the Haunted History Channel," Shane said, pointing at a garish, faded billboard. Shane's excited tone and big grin made Lucas smile. Leave it to his geeky partner to find another roadside attraction to check out—even after the end of the world.

"You made me watch so many of those shows, it's hard to keep them straight," Lucas teased, although he thought he remembered the episode. Shane had a definite weak spot for quirky tourist traps. It made sense now that they understood Shane's ability to hear the daemon song and that those attractions tended to be built where someone sensed the unusual energy of a genius loci. Those sort of spots tended to either get a sideshow or a shrine.

The Mysterium and Oddity Museum sat just past the off-ramp, where Route 60 connected to Route 19. Lucas spotted the rusted hulk of an old Ferris wheel a mile away.

"I figure you're going to want to stop and poke around?" Lucas asked, but he didn't mind, and Shane knew it.

"Of course! Maybe there'll be a tie-in to the legend of the vanishing hotel," Shane replied.

Lucas reined in his horse, taking in a stockade fence that looked relatively new, running all the way around the main buildings. A sign for the attraction hung on the fence.

"Be careful—I'm not sure it's deserted," Lucas warned. "I'd rather not get a load of buckshot in my pants from an angry owner."

"Why would anyone stick around? I'm pretty sure the tourist trade isn't what it used to be," Shane answered.

"Just sayin'—keep your wits about you," Lucas replied. "That fence doesn't look old enough to have been up before the Events."

"Anything from Rocky? Quentin isn't terribly worried, but he'd like a biscuit."

Quentin wasn't a possessing entity the way Rocky was, but Lucas knew Shane was learning how to "access" that new side of himself even when he was in human form.

Lucas chuckled. "I can get some for both of you, once we get where we're going. Rocky isn't picking up danger. Magic, yes—fairly strong. Possibly protective wardings. And energy deep down. Not another daemon. But maybe ley lines. That's not a term he'd use...but the idea matches."

"Can you pick up anything about ghosts?"

Lucas concentrated. "The old part of the park is definitely haunted."

"I'm not surprised," Shane said as he swung down from his horse and tethered it to a post at the edge of the parking lot. "I watched this episode a bunch of times—in that crappy hotel in Des Moines with the money-laundering witness."

Lucas groaned. "That place. Lousy cable, the pillows were terrible, and I think we got food poisoning from the restaurant."

"Yep. That's the place. I think the channel was running its '5 Top Episodes' on a loop, and I was probably too sick to bother changing the channel."

Lucas chuckled. "The only saving grace was that our witness was sicker than we were, so he wasn't going to run away."

They didn't intend to leave their horses unprotected, but Shane ventured closer to the unfenced, overgrown area where the rusted rides hunkered. "The original owner of the place was a real piece of work," he recalled.

"Serial killer?" Lucas didn't quite remember.

"Maybe. The park was already past its heyday when the guy bought it. He skimped on maintenance. People got hurt. At first, he paid them off, but then a couple of kids died, and that got him shut down."

"Shit."

Shane nodded. "Yeah. He'd been running the weird little freak show museum as a side gig, but then he expanded when the park closed and added the Mysterium. The show made it sound like he might have bought some haunted—if not cursed—items for the museum. The Mysterium was mostly a bunch of clever visual tricks, but I think he might have tapped into the energy fluctuations around here."

"Ley lines would explain a lot, especially if there are mineral and ore deposits of the right kind in the right places to amplify the energy," Lucas suggested.

Shane nodded. "The original owner just disappeared one day. No body, no blood. Wallet and car keys untouched. Nothing missing out of the register. Had a safe in his office that hadn't been tampered with, and there was several thousand bucks in it."

"They ever find him?"

"Nope. Not even when they brought in a psychic," Shane added with a smirk, since the whole idea seemed so ironic in a place like this.

"Got a theory?"

"I think he might have messed with something he didn't know how to control. Summoned an entity, called up a creature, that sort of thing. He was on the brink of bankruptcy and foreclosure, and there were lawsuits from the park deaths that were playing out."

"You don't think he just killed himself."

Shane shook his head. "Nah. He was a win-at-any-cost kind of guy. He'd be more likely to murder someone than to commit suicide."

Lucas stood watch and kept the horses while Shane got a good look at the dilapidated Ferris wheel as well as a Tilt-A-Whirl and Scrambler that showed the decay of years exposed to the elements.

"I know everything is a ruin now, but this place is pretty cool." Shane nearly bounced with excitement.

Lucas gave him an assessing look. "Are you picking up on the energy here? Because you're acting like you've had one too many energy drinks."

"Maybe. Quentin's twitchy."

"Great. A twitchy wolf shifter."

"I want to see if we can get inside," Shane said, heading for the main entrance. Lucas followed with an exaggerated, long-suffering sigh. He didn't really mind. The new reality offered few enough opportunities for entertainment.

"Here, watch the horses. I'll knock," Lucas volunteered. He pulled out his Marshal's badge, just in case anyone was home.

The door opened to reveal a man who had the well-dressed but somber appearance of a funeral director from the 1920s.

"I'm Lucas Maddox, and this is my partner, Shane Collins. We're US Marshals. We were in the area, and to be honest, we thought your place looked interesting. We're hoping we can get a tour if that's possible."

"I would be happy to give you a special tour. I'm Eddie McCoy, the owner. Please, come with me."

Lucas wasn't sure what to make of the man's odd choice of clothing or his slightly antiquated manner of speech. It seemed unlikely he expected any customers, or that he would keep on wearing a costume so long after the world had shut down.

Eddie led them past the ticket counter and into the Oddity Museum. Large glass cases held all kinds of spooky, weird, and occult objects. Taxidermy animals dressed in clothing and posed in dioramas sat next to carved wooden shamans' masks and a Voudon altar. A mummified two-headed goat shared a shelf with a necklace said to have been owned by Lizzie Borden.

"It's like a Cabinet of Wonders," Shane said, using an old Victorian phrase.

Eddie paused in his narration to glance over his shoulder with an approving expression. "Yes. Exactly. When I purchased the museum, I removed the items that were not real. Those that were truly dangerous—cursed or haunted—I destroyed or moved to a safe location. Over the years, I've added to the collection, from things I picked up here and there along the way, and on occasion, from the estates of other collectors."

I believe he is a witch, and he is tied, somehow, to the energy beneath us, Rocky warned. *He may be able to sense me and Quentin. Be careful.*

Eddie looked the part of a well-to-do man from the Roaring Twenties, a rakish Great Gatsby look that suited his tall, thin frame. His dark hair was cut in a style that matched that period, setting off deep-set, piercing eyes. Whether it was natural magnetism or a facet of his magic that gave him charisma, Lucas didn't know, but he could imagine their host on stage, at home in front of the footlights.

Lucas remained looking at the objects behind the glass. "So everything here is real?"

Eddie raised an eyebrow. "I sense that you are both well-equipped to answer that yourself." He didn't press for an answer and led the way to the next part of the attraction. "Please assure your guardians that I intend you no harm."

Lucas and Shane exchanged a glance but said nothing.

"How real is the Mysterium?" Shane asked as they left behind the gallery of oddities. When they stepped over the threshold into the "mystery spot" portion of the building, Lucas felt a frisson of energy that raised the hairs on the back of his neck.

The first few rooms held optical illusions and cleverly designed tricks that made water appear to run up hill, people seem to defy gravity, and other violations of the laws of physics. But as they moved farther inside, Lucas felt a low thrum of energy that practically vibrated in his bones.

"Something's different here." Lucas's eyes narrowed as he looked around the room.

"This area has been considered to be special—maybe even sacred—for a very long time," Eddie replied. "The ley lines beneath the ground—rivers of natural energies—converge here. Over time, they fluctuate. Where the Mountain Cove Hotel once stood was a powerful confluence for the lines and the telluric energies—called a vortex. And then a shift occurred and created an unusual concentration of energy that became a rift of sorts—an anomaly."

Eddie shook his head. "Put a vortex and an anomaly together, and it's an energy beacon, where the powers converge and don't always work the way they're supposed to."

"So it's natural, but not original," Shane clarified.

"Yes. And since it has shifted before, it could at some point shift again," Eddie replied. "The changes I've made to the grounds and the collections brought the energies here into alignment. Now, this is an anchor."

"Are you part of that anchor?" Shane asked, and Lucas wondered if his partner chose to go on the offensive since it seemed clear Eddie had picked up on their unusual natures.

Eddie inclined his head in acknowledgment. "Yes. I have chosen to link myself to this place to strengthen that protection. I draw my magic from the bones and humours of the earth," Eddie replied. "Stone, minerals, ore, and gems, as well as the caves and rivers. I can touch the ley lines, and the telluric currents, and the magnetism at the core of the world."

"Why become an anchor?" Lucas asked, curious and wary. "The world pretty much ended. I mean, the movie is over, and we're just sweeping up the popcorn before the theater turns out the lights. So why make that kind of commitment now?"

Eddie regarded Lucas with a look that he couldn't quite read. "Then, why not? If there is no other purpose remaining, why not take meaning from what can still be done?"

Lucas opened his mouth to argue, and shut it again, remaining silent.

A hint of a smile touched Eddie's thin lips. "Is that not what you and your partner do every day? Create meaning from purpose, doing what you are still able to do? I think you understand my reasons very well."

"Are you immortal?" Shane asked, surprising Lucas at his boldness.

Eddie chuckled. "I don't know. I haven't died yet. I don't really want to test it, although I suspect I am." He leveled a knowing gaze at them. "As are you."

Lucas shifted, uncomfortable. "Like you said, not something we want to prove the hard way."

"Mountain Cove has long attracted untrained psychics. Now, it draws people whose abilities surfaced or strengthened in the upheaval of natural energies after the Events," Eddie told them. "They came into their powers without teachers, desperate for guidance. Too many mistake the ability to connect with those energies as dominion over them. They are wrong."

"Thank you for the tour," Lucas said, hoping Shane would pick up on the cue that it was time to leave. "We need to be going."

"I'm glad you stopped," Eddie said, and while his welcome felt genuine, Lucas couldn't shake the feeling that Eddie knew something they didn't. "I hope we'll meet again." He paused. "A word of warning— a new camp just sprang up on the way to the hotel. They aren't very friendly. You might want to keep your distance."

Lucas and Shane thanked him again for the tour and then headed up the mountain toward the hotel and the scholars who had requested their help.

"So, what did you think of Eddie?" Lucas asked. Rocky hadn't weighed in with an opinion yet, which was odd.

"Quentin wasn't sure about him," Shane replied. "I liked the grounds and the building. Definitely my kind of place—too bad the gift shop wasn't open," he added with a grin. "I don't understand the old-fashioned clothing."

Lucas shrugged. "I guess he can wear whatever he wants, what with the apocalypse and all. Not like anyone is going to turn him in to Human Resources."

"You didn't ask him about the crazy cultists."

Lucas gave him a look. "Great way to make a good first impression.

I'd be like, so...we just met you, but we found mutilated bodies a ways back. You wouldn't happen to know anything about them, would you?"

Shane rolled his eyes. "I guess you've got a point. Maybe we can stop here on the way back. After all, if he's a witch, maybe he can find things out we can't."

"Or, he's in cahoots with whoever did the ritual," Lucas pointed out. "Could go either way."

CHAPTER TWO

THEY RODE FOR A WHILE, leaving the interstate highway behind them and following a slightly smaller, winding road toward the hotel.

"I thought everyone had cleared out from these parts except for the scholars," Lucas said as they spotted a sign for the town of Hico, a small settlement that clearly wasn't completely abandoned.

"So did I. Maybe it's that unfriendly camp Eddie warned us about," Shane replied.

Hico appeared to be little more than a few buildings and a couple of houses near a crossroads. It looked to Lucas as if there had been an old-time general store and a gas station long enough ago that the buildings had probably been repurposed. A boxy building might have been a Grange or community hall, and an old church sat nearby, white paint peeling, steeple broken off. Five or six farmhouses sat scattered around the crossroads. None of the buildings looked newer than a hundred years.

Several wagons sat beside a barn. Two men went in and out of the building, and with the doors open, Lucas could see horses stabled inside.

Rocky felt restless in the back of Lucas's mind as if he didn't like the situation.

Lucas spotted only adults, no children. That told him the group wasn't a family cluster that had sought shelter after the Events. Maybe they were a religious group, he thought, which seemed likely since the people he saw moving from one building to the next wore what looked like monks' cassocks. More than one person stopped to stare as they rode by. No one raised a hand in greeting or called out to them, a bad sign in Lucas's book.

A cold chill ran down Lucas's spine as he realized where he had seen robes like the settlers wore. *Those look like the odd clothing the ghosts wore, back at the murder house.*

Lucas cleared his throat, getting Shane's attention. He dropped one hand to his hip level, somewhere the settlers wouldn't see, and made the hand signal for "trouble." Shane met his gaze and nodded, both of them now on alert.

He and Shane always rode with their weapons loaded and in easy reach, conspicuously displayed to discourage troublemakers. Lucas wondered if the settlers were merely distrustful of strangers—not unreasonable, given the circumstances—or if they took the two of them for outlaws. He was long past caring, having found that instilling a little fear by their appearance reduced the number of idiots who tried to start something they had to finish.

"No gardens. Haven't been here very long then," Shane noted under his breath. More permanent settlements needed a reliable food supply, which meant gardens, fruit trees, and livestock like chickens and goats. "From how high the weeds are, and since the tall grass hasn't been trampled down, I'd say they might have just arrived."

"They're a long way from everywhere," Lucas said. Before the Events, the big draw here had been outdoor adventures—whitewater boating on the New River, hiking in the mountains, zip lines, and rustic cabin rentals. That's what had sustained the restaurants, hotels, and outfitting shops down near the highway exit—all of them long shuttered and abandoned.

"For the record, Quentin doesn't like them. His hackles are up and he's growling."

"Rocky's not too keen on them, either. Just as well we're only passing through." Lucas wondered how many people were part of the ramshackle community. He saw at least a dozen moving between the buildings. Smoke rose from the chimneys of several houses, suggesting more people were inside.

"I wonder what the scholars make of them," Lucas said, as they rode beyond the crossroads and headed toward the site of the old hotel. "They don't strike me as friendly neighbors."

"We'll get the chance to ask when we see them tonight," Shane replied.

They fell silent for a while, both men cautiously glancing over their shoulders to assure that no one from the hamlet had followed them. It didn't appear to Lucas that they had picked up any stalkers, but he couldn't shake the uneasiness he'd felt in Hico.

"For this area having been a kinda big deal at one time, there's not much left," Shane observed as the sound of their hoofbeats echoed on the empty road.

From the rusted sign for Osborne Creek and the few natural landmarks, Lucas knew they were close to the old Spiritualist community's location, with the mysterious hotel that might or might not still be there.

The witches had told them about the area, back when they had asked for the two men's help. Mountain Cove had been founded back in 1851 by two spirit mediums who led a pilgrimage down from New York to claim land near Osborne Creek in what was at that point still a part of Virginia. Their community started out well, building homes, a school, a mill, and stores, as well as a newspaper and the hotel, before fizzling out just a few years later.

"It's just spooky that people built all those buildings and there's nothing left except the hotel—which is apparently only here sometimes," Lucas replied.

Shane shrugged. "I imagine if we went snuffling through the underbrush, we'd find stone foundations, old wells, maybe a millstone or two." Shane scanned for danger as he got the lay of the land.

"Snuffling?" Lucas joked. "Gonna pick up a few truffles while we're rooting around?"

"It's as good a word as any," Shane defended with a grin. "But back to your point—the community was here and gone ten years before the Civil War. There were battles fought all around these parts. An awful lot of buildings didn't survive being in the path of two armies."

"But the hotel hung on until about 1920," Lucas said. "At least, that's what was in the information the scholars sent us. And then it got weird."

"It's been a long time since things weren't weird." Shane snorted.

A lot has happened since the 1850s, Lucas thought, as he tried to picture the area as it must have looked when the religious community put down roots. This stretch of road had flat areas off to each side or gradually sloping hills. Both were at a premium in notoriously hilly West Virginia. In his mind's eye, Lucas could imagine wooden storefronts, modest homes, and on Osborne Creek—which they had just crossed over on a bridge—a mill. If he paid close attention, he could make out where older trees began and younger ones left off—an indication that the land with the new growth had once been something else.

Still, Lucas had visited a lot of abandoned areas—both from before the Events and even more modern ruins from afterward. Few had been as completely obliterated as the village of Mountain Cove.

Shane came to an abrupt stop, and a look of pain lanced across his face.

Lucas, stop!

Lucas heard Rocky's voice in his mind, and he pulled up on the reins.

The energy here is powerful, but…damaged. Be very careful.

"Did you feel it?" Lucas and Shane asked in unison.

"We have to be close to where the hotel was," Shane said with a grimace that told Lucas the discomfort hadn't eased. "I got a killer headache out of nowhere, and the song in my mind is really fucked up."

"Rocky just yelled for me to stop," Lucas replied, although he felt twitchy, skin prickling, hair rising at the back of his neck, and a pervasive sense of *wrongness* telling his hindbrain to run. "What do you mean, the song is fucked up?"

Shane turned his horse around and rode back a few yards. Lucas backtracked to join him. The twitchiness Lucas felt eased but didn't completely disappear.

"When the genius loci of a place is 'happy,' for lack of a better term, the song is calm. Not necessarily something you can start humming along to, but peaceful in a natural sort of way," Shane explained. "And when there's dark magic or something really terrible left a stain on the land, it's more like a horror movie soundtrack—discordant and creepy." He shook his head. "The song just ahead sounds like a hundred different marching bands and orchestras all playing different pieces of music—all different styles—at the same time."

Lucas nodded. "I don't hear the song, but I definitely got the gut reaction to 'get the hell out of Dodge.' Let me see if Rocky can explain it any better."

He closed his eyes, concentrating as he thought the question at his co-pilot.

The energy of the area right in front of you is...folded in on itself. Layered. Like it is in many places at once, but also all here, Rocky replied.

What does that even mean? How can energy have layers? Lucas thought for a moment. *People say the hotel fades in and out. Do you mean that it's here—and not here—at the same time?*

That is how it feels, reading the energy.

Lucas opened his eyes and blinked. "I think we've got Schrödinger's hotel. It's there—and it's not there. But its energy is all piled up."

"Like a double exposure? The way people could take photographic film and layer it to make it look like there were images on top of images, back before computers," Shane replied. "The end result looked real, but it was actually a composite, made up of all the pieces."

"I guess?" Lucas felt completely out of his element. "Even Rocky didn't seem to have run into this before."

Shane chewed on his lip as he thought. "The Spiritualists built the hotel expecting that people would come to visit their community seeking answers, or maybe come to learn about their beliefs. Most of the people who moved here believed they had some level of psychic gift, and the two founders were supposedly strong mediums. Maybe there were enough people with abilities that they somehow...I don't know, *bent* the energy?"

"Then why didn't that happen in Salem, Massachusetts, with all the witches, or New Orleans, with the Voodoo?" Lucas argued. "Why out here in the middle of West fuckin' Virginia?"

Shane shrugged. "No clue. Maybe the original spirit of the land was already wobbly, and all that extra energy knocked it off its axis."

"Well, we're either going to have to ride past where the hotel was, or go a whole hell of a long way around, because there aren't a lot of side roads in this forest," Lucas replied. "Not to mention, backtrack through that creepy little town."

"The scholars are holed up in the Ansted library," Shane said. "It's about four miles down the road. On the other side of a whole bunch of cemeteries, once we get past the freaky hotel."

"This just keeps getting better," Lucas muttered. "Let's lead the horses through the bad part and hope it eases up pretty quickly."

Red and Shadow were both good-tempered, and they'd already learned to accept gunfire as well as Shane's wolf. Lucas hoped the horses wouldn't try to bolt. Still, he didn't want to risk being thrown or losing one of their mounts.

Shane and Lucas slipped down from their saddles and offered their horses treats before taking the reins and walking down the empty road.

The prickle on his skin grew worse until Lucas felt like he should be brushing off a legion of spiders. Shadow obediently stayed beside him, but the horse's eyes were wide, and now and again, a tremor passed through the huge, powerful body, although his training held, and he did not try to run.

"Hang in there, boy. Not too much longer," Lucas coaxed, hearing Shane make the same comforting promises to Red.

Lucas tried to calm his horse, contain his own reactions, scan for danger, and get a look at the spot where the cursed hotel must have stood. That was a lot to do all at once. Lucas just wanted to get out of the zone affected by the strange energy.

A glance at his partner told him Shane shared his struggle. Except where Lucas fought off a sense of dread and the lizard-brain urgency to run, Shane's pinched features told Lucas the other man struggled against physical pain.

Rocky—can whatever this is hurt us?

Rocky didn't answer immediately, making Lucas worry that the energy fluctuations could affect even a strong elemental spirit.

It cannot hurt me...and therefore, us. I am less sure about Shane. But it makes thinking difficult. I think your word is...static. Fuzzy noise and blurry picture.

Lucas had to chuckle, wondering how Rocky had fished the idea of TV white noise out of his brain. While there were a few sets still working, and DVD players were precious and rare, Shane and Lucas hadn't seen anything since the broadcast stations went down during the Events. The news reports had winked out, one by one, until nothing remained except a gray buzz.

Then again, maybe it wasn't so hard to figure out after all. Those images regularly haunted Lucas's dreams, and Rocky was along for the ride.

How much farther?

Just past those boulders. We are in the center of the disturbance. If you wished to see where the hotel stood, this is the likely spot, Rocky said.

Lucas pointed to the hillside on their right, and Shane gave a curt nod as if every movement hurt. A large area had been cut into the hillside at its base, and Lucas could imagine the land gradually sloping away behind the three-story clapboard hotel sketched in the notes they had received. It would have looked out over the valley, a panoramic vista.

Now that he took in the contours of the land, both natural and man-made, Lucas knew they had come to the right place. He even glimpsed the crumbling remnants of cement steps rising from the roadway and vanishing into a tangle of brambles.

Shadow fidgeted, letting Lucas know they needed to get moving. He jerked his head to indicate moving forward and picked up his pace.

As soon as they passed the outcropping of large boulders, the troublesome energy vanished as if they had stepped through a curtain.

They put several yards between them and the anomaly, and then Lucas stopped. He leaned forward to rest his forearms on Shadow, trying to regain his bearings. Both he and his horse were breathing hard, muscles trembling, covered with a thin sheen of sweat in testimony to the physical struggle of containing their fear and the uneasiness created near the "missing" hotel.

"There is no way anyone with a whiff of psychic ability could feel comfortable spending the night in a hotel room if the energy always feels like that," Shane said, his voice rough, breath coming in pants as if they had sprinted.

"Dude, I don't think that anyone with a working brain stem would feel comfortable. We've felt some bad mojo in places, but nothing quite so...wrong."

They paused to let the horses graze and took a moment to replenish themselves with water from their wineskin and some dried meat and fruit. Lucas kept staring at the road where they had just been, still worried that they might have attracted unwanted attention from the squatters in Hico.

"Come on," Shane said, pulling him out of his thoughts. "I don't want to be out here when it gets dark, and we're going to lose the light before too long. We still don't know where we're staying when we get to Ansted."

What went unspoken was the reminder that the map showed several cemeteries between here and their destination. Old, untended cemeteries next to a volatile well of psychic energy. *Yeah, that can't be good.*

Now that they were past the site of the old hotel, Lucas and Shane saddled up and rode for Ansted. Lucas felt hypervigilant, so attuned to sound and movement that he might jump out of his skin. One look at Shane told him that his partner had picked up on the same wariness.

"You getting anything different with the song of the place?" Lucas asked, needing to break the silence.

Shane looked like he was struggling to put his thoughts into words. "There are a number of different genius loci in this area, which isn't that unusual in a place like this. It's always remained fairly wild, and part of it was a park. The elemental spirits weren't drowned out in the noise of development. This section has a much more peaceful song than the section near the old hotel site."

"Quentin picking up anything?"

Lucas knew that Shane still had a lot to learn about his new wolf nature. He'd been bitten by a hybrid shifter, a weaponized creature created by a secret government project. So while he could shift without being driven by the moon cycle, the senses of an apex predator always lurked just below the surface of his mind.

"He's jumpy as fuck. Keeps growling. It's giving me a headache."

Before he had Rocky's consciousness in his mind, Lucas might have ribbed his partner about referring to his wolf as a separate person. Now, Lucas understood completely what it was like to have another entity riding shotgun in his noggin.

"Is he getting any kind of sense from the surroundings? Any critters out there we need to be watching for—supernatural or not?" This area had always been remote. Bear, bobcats, and wolves survived in the less-settled areas, even before the world fell apart. Since then, Lucas and

Shane had seen the creatures' numbers multiply in the forests where the two marshals had traveled.

Most people left rural areas when the power grid failed, and when enough pieces of society fell apart that supply shipments no longer came, stores closed down. Now that the people were gone, the animals had taken back the mountains—and even some of the cities.

"There's something trailing us. Quentin thinks it's human—but not a 'regular' person. Maybe someone with magic, or psychic ability?" Shane replied.

He pinched the bridge of his nose, a sure sign that his head still ached. "Between the vibe you give off with Rocky and the sense most animals seem to pick up from Quentin, I don't think the regular wildlife are going to cause a problem."

"How far back is our stalker?" Lucas asked, automatically looking around.

"Not sure."

"Someone from Hico? You think they're actually stalking us, or just going in the same general direction?"

Shane shrugged. "No way to know. I guess we wait and see."

Lucas felt Rocky flinch as they rode closer to a long flat area tucked into a cleft in the steep hills. Weeds choked the clearing, and trees had begun to reclaim the open land. Lucas felt a chill and guessed they had found one of the cemeteries.

The old burying ground had been abandoned long before people left because of the Events. The town of Ansted had hung on as jobs vanished and young people deserted to find new horizons. Like many of the little villages in these hills, it had faced a bleak future with an aging population and no real prospects. Then the world burned, and hanging on wasn't enough.

Lucas thought he glimpsed weathered headstones amid the tall grass, stained granite too worn by time to be readable. He could almost guess the age of the headstones from their shape, and he wondered if the long-ago Spiritualists who staked out their brief, doomed community had left any of their faithful behind.

Did a village of spirit mediums and psychics mind having several old cemeteries right on their border? Or did people choose to bury their dead here because they sensed the fluctuating energy, even before it grew stronger?

I am not sure the dead here rest in peace, Rocky observed, although Lucas had not asked. *I sense restless spirits, some disturbed enough to be a danger. The strange energy may have kept some of them from moving on.*

Trapped them? Or merely confused them so they couldn't find the way out? Lucas asked.

I do not know. But they remain.

Even before his alliance with Rocky, Lucas had an ability to see and talk to ghosts. That talent had grown stronger since the cataclysm, just like Shane's visions and his ability to hear the "songs" of the genius loci had strengthened. Lucas tuned in to his ghost-sense as they rode past the graveyard, alert for trouble.

The temperature dipped, enough to notice, too much to be due to a bit of shade from the trees or clouds blocking the sun. That confirmed Rocky's report, even if the spirits chose not to show themselves to Lucas or lacked the ability to make themselves seen. For now, at least, Lucas left the ghosts alone. Later, he might need to ask them questions, but he did not want to bother them more than once.

Shadow whinnied softly, and Lucas patted his neck. Horses could sense spirits, and while neither of their mounts panicked when Lucas's talent manifested ghosts, he didn't want to push his luck, especially not here.

The day warmed when they passed the first cemetery and dipped again as they rode past the second one. This graveyard was newer, closer to town, and the ghosts had not faded quite so much. They hung back, aware but invisible, watching, taking the measure of two strangers riding into an abandoned town. Lucas felt the weight of their appraising gaze and squared his shoulders, raising his head.

I'm not here to cause you trouble. But if you start it, we'll finish it, he warned silently.

The second cemetery didn't resonate as strongly. Maybe being newer, it hadn't had as long exposure to the volatile energy of the old hotel. Perhaps since it was farther away, the odd fluctuations affected its spirits less, allowing them to rest quietly. Whatever the reason, neither Lucas nor Shane had a reaction as they passed by.

The town of Ansted had seen boom and bust. Remembering what the coven had told them, Lucas knew that when the Spiritualists came, first in the 1830s and then in the 1850s, they named the town New Haven. After the Spiritualists were gone, the stagecoaches came, making the town an important depot. When the railroads took over, a main rail line ran nearby, and the town grew. Coal, iron, and lumber brought wealth and a new name, Ansted, after one of the coal barons. In time, those industries faded, and the town managed to survive, mostly due to its proximity to good hiking and rafting, and Civil War battlefields. Then the Events happened, and people had no reason to stay.

"You'd think after everything, ghost towns wouldn't seem so creepy," Lucas said as they rode into the abandoned downtown. Four years of hard storms and neglect had taken a toll with broken windows, damaged roofs, and toppled signs. The older, more solidly built homes had endured reasonably well, but faded paint and downed trim made it clear no one was home.

"That's because they look normal—but they aren't," Shane observed. "Think about it. If you could see where a blast leveled buildings and burned half the town, you wouldn't wonder where the people went. But that isn't what happened out here. It looks like people just up and left—because they did."

"Yeah. Creepy."

Rocky remained silent, which meant he hadn't sensed danger. Shane hadn't commented, so that meant he and Quentin hadn't learned anything more about whatever had been following them, either.

Towns like Ansted felt melancholy to Lucas. From the shuttered stores and restaurants to the slowly decaying homes, schools, and public buildings, the emptiness was just one more reminder that the way things were before the Events would never be again.

"There's the library." Shane pointed to a granite building solid enough to have been a fallout shelter, back in the day. Lucas wagered that the bars over the windows were a new addition, but otherwise, the library looked unscathed.

If anyone still remained in Ansted aside from the scholars they had come to see, those people weren't making themselves visible. That suited Lucas just fine.

"Well, let's go see what all the fuss is about." Lucas tethered his horse to a tree outside the library and so did Shane. Then they approached the library's big front doors warily, badges in hand.

The doors open, and a middle-aged, balding, and bespectacled man greeted them. Lucas thought he had the look of an academic. Lucas gave his usual introduction. "The coven in Bedford asked us to stop by when we were in the area," he added. "Sorry it's taken us a while, but there's a whole lot going on, and only two of us." He didn't feel compelled to explain that they had taken some time to recover and come to terms with his partner becoming a wolf.

"Marshals. Thank you for coming. You've actually arrived at a good time." The man who welcomed them reminded Lucas of his high school biology teacher. "I'm Bill Royston. Please, follow me. You must be tired from your journey."

"Is there a way we can get water for our horses?" Shane asked. "We let them graze a while back, but we weren't close to a stream."

"I'll send someone out to give them water. And we converted a building next door to be a stable, so they'll have shelter for the night," Royston told them. "Of course, we can accommodate you here. You'll be safe and reasonably comfortable. The food's pretty good too, considering everything," he added with a conspiratorial wink.

"The coven said something about wanting to preserve knowledge for future generations—in a hotel that isn't always present?" Lucas continued as they followed Royston farther into the building.

"You cover a huge territory, and there must be many places that need you. We wouldn't have imposed except we have a rather unusual situation," Royston replied.

"Why don't you fill us in?" Shane said, as their host brought them to the staff break room. They sat down at the table, and Royston set out a plate of homemade cookies.

"We've been fortunate that the towns near here still had a lot of supplies," the man told them. "And we have access to plenty of cook-books," he added with a wry smile. "Supplies don't last forever, so we figured—cook it if you've got it."

"I will never pass up cookies," Lucas said and reached for two. Shane helped himself as well, and Royston brought them glasses of tea, then joined them at the table.

"Before things fell apart, I taught at the community college," the man said. "When ...it...happened, before things here got too bad, my colleagues and I realized that knowledge would be one of the most valuable things lost if we didn't act fast."

Lucas could see the weight of the last years in the man's posture and his worried expression. "We've seen many universities that became armed fortress communities, guarding their libraries, maintaining their node on the internet, and protecting people who have the skills to help us rebuild."

Royston nodded. "We've gotten word that they tried to do that up in Morgantown, at the university. But then the nuclear plants..."

He didn't need to finish the statement. Lucas and Shane knew. Between the earthquakes and tornadoes, many plants sustained serious damage, more than could be fixed by the remaining skeleton crews and their stockpiled parts. The lucky ones were able to shut down before they melted down or leaked radiation. The plant near Morgantown hadn't been lucky.

"The university is still there, of course, but too dangerous to access—for the foreseeable future," Royston continued. "Our beautiful state has been taken advantage of for centuries, resources carted away, and damage not put right. Now, with the earthquakes and the wild storms, that is all coming back to haunt us."

"What do you mean?" Shane asked.

"These hills are riddled with tunnels, left behind from the shaft mines. It's not uncommon for sinkholes to open up. Some are only a few feet across. Others swallow whole towns," Royston replied. "Timber harvesting and strip mines make the slopes dangerous for landslides. The water in many places hasn't been safe without purification for a long time with all the mine runoff. Not to mention the power plants and nuclear sites. What that all adds up to is, there's nowhere that's truly safe to fortify an archive."

"So what's your alternative?" Lucas asked.

"We have been acquiring all of the books, microfiche, and digital resources we can scavenge," Royston answered. "We enlisted all of our colleagues who were willing and able to help. For a while, they brought us materials by the truckload. Eventually, that slowed to a trickle. We don't claim to have everything. But we have a lot. And with the big museums and archives in Washington DC and New York

City destroyed...well, we believe it's important to save as much as we can."

Shane looked pained at the recap and Lucas understood. Both of them liked to read and had passed the long hours while on stakeouts or protecting witnesses with books. Since the Events, they carried a few treasured favorites with them and checked deserted homes, stores, and libraries whenever the opportunity presented itself to pick up anything they could.

"So you're the modern version of the Library of Alexandria?" Lucas asked.

Royston chuckled. "Well, we're trying to be the version that doesn't burn. Once we realized that nowhere in West Virginia was truly safe for long-term storage, we saw the potential of Mountain Cove Hotel."

Lucas raised an eyebrow. "You want to move the materials into a place that doesn't exist?"

Royston met his gaze, dead serious. "Oh, it exists. Sometimes. The building phases in and out. We observed and charted the pattern. That was six months ago. We've been moving materials in as fast as we can, given our limited number of people and the fluctuations of the hotel. We've glimpsed a couple of ghosts—and a guy named Fenton at the front desk who seems pretty solid for a spirit."

"So the hotel is real? It's not some kind of ghost?" Shane asked.

"I think it would be accurate to say it's both, because of the unusual energy of the location. Which leads to the reason we asked for your help."

He drained his glass of tea and licked his lips nervously. "We aren't the only ones who have noticed the energy anomaly of the old hotel. This area has always attracted people with psychic gifts, as far back as there have been Westerners in these parts, and before that, among the tribes. Some people say it calls to them. Others can sense its energy and come to use it for their own purposes."

"We thought we might have been followed, but didn't see anyone," Lucas said.

"It wouldn't be the first time the hotel's drawn the wrong kind of attention," Royston said. "Seems to be happening more and more now that people aren't in shock anymore over the Events. We've had folks show up to try to break into the hotel, or worship it, or exorcise it.

Between Mama Jean, Doc, and Eddie, we've been able to send them away—mostly peacefully."

"Eddie? Eddie McCoy, the guy with the Mysterium?" Lucas asked.

Royston nodded. "Yes. He helps to protect us and the hotel."

"And that group we saw in Hico?" Shane asked. He gave a brief recap of what they observed. They had agreed not to mention the murder house until they had a better feel for the scholars and the situation.

"Probably more troublemakers," Royston replied. "I'll let the others know. Mama Jean can put down some extra wardings."

"I'm still not sure why you requested us," Lucas said. "Two Marshals, even with weapons, aren't much of a security detail."

Royston looked up, surprised. "Your skills will enable you to heal the hotel so it's safer for us to move in. There's no one else we know of with those abilities, and I'm afraid that time is running out."

Lucas felt his heart rate spike. *How could they have possibly known about Rocky and Quentin? Hell, when we talked to the coven, it was before Rocky saved my life and before Shane had been bitten.* Then he remembered Eddie's friendliness—and the way he seemed to know just by looking at them about Rocky and Quentin.

Lucas was willing to bet money that Eddie knew exactly who they were when they showed up. *If he was behind the request to bring us here, why pretend like he didn't know us?*

Lucas and Shane looked at each other, confused and wary. "There was nothing in the coven's request about 'abilities' or 'special skills.' We rode a long way to get here. What game are you playing?"

Royston held up his hands in appeasement. "No game, I swear. Sending for you wasn't my idea." He sighed and shook his head. "That's what I get for asking a seer for advice."

Lucas was just about to demand answers when the door opened and a man walked in, dragging a second man by the arm.

"I caught this one lurking outside," the taller newcomer said. "Can't think of any good reason for him to be here—but I sure can come up with a bunch of bad ones."

The prisoner was a man in his late twenties, with an untrimmed beard and long hair pulled back in a queue. He wore the same sort of robe that Lucas had spotted on the newcomers in Hico. His wrists were bound with handcuffs that looked to Lucas like real silver, with sigils carved into the metal that glowed.

"Marshals, this is Doc Swanson. Doc, these are the Marshals that Mama Jean suggested we send for," Royston said, putting a little extra emphasis on the woman's name. "The ones you and Eddie took care of contacting?"

Doc Swanson looked to be in his middle years, bald, with glasses, average height with a slight paunch, wearing khaki pants and a golf shirt. "Pleased to meet you."

"I don't know what's going on here, but we aren't doing one damned thing more until we get some answers," Lucas said, letting his temper show.

"You'll get them," Doc said. "But first, we need to know why this one was sneaking around." Doc shoved the prisoner to sit in the remaining open chair. "Start talking."

The robed stranger just glared at Doc. "You wouldn't understand."

Doc leaned into his space. "Try me. And I want to hear from the demon—not just the poor sap he possessed."

Lucas and Shane traded an alarmed glance. "Demon?" Lucas questioned. "Do you mean daemon?"

The prisoner's eyes glowed red, and he tried to lunge from his chair, but the point of Doc's silver-bladed knife jabbed into his neck, raising a bead of blood.

"Sit down. And start talking."

The stranger sat, but the baleful glare he fixed on Doc promised bloody retribution. Lucas couldn't help remembering the black ooze Shane glimpsed in his vision. *Could that have been a demon?*

"First order of business is to exorcise him and get rid of the son of a bitch that's possessing him," Doc said.

"You can't," the prisoner taunted, his mouth curling into a sneer. He shifted so that the sleeve of his robe rode up on his forearm, exposing a recent, barely healed burn in the shape of a complex symbol. "That brand locks me in this body. Can't throw me out. The only way to get rid of me is to kill him."

Royston got up and called down the hall to someone, but Lucas was too focused on the prisoner to hear what was said.

Doc's face took on a distant expression, one that made Lucas think of how he felt when he spoke to Rocky or contacted ghosts. No sooner had Lucas thought of spirits than he saw one take shape right behind the prisoner, the ghost of a woman Lucas recognized as a victim from the murder house. Lucas startled. That was enough for Doc to give him the once-over as if he knew what Lucas saw.

"If you won't talk, the ghost who's with you can probably tell me everything I need to know," Doc said as if interrogating a spirit was no big deal.

"Have it your way," the demon said with a shrug.

The prisoner's entire manner shifted abruptly. He looked up at Doc. "Please, you've got to help me. Kill me. Stop the torment." His voice sounded like he'd been gargling broken glass—or screaming for hours.

With the demon at the fore, he'd looked healthy, if a bit too skinny. Stripped of that demon glamor, the man looked one step removed from the grave. Sunken eyes, sallow skin, and hollow cheeks made Lucas suspect that the demon fed off the man's energy—and maybe his soul. Lesions covered his skin, raw and oozing. His cracked lips bled. But it was the pain and fear in his haunted eyes that convinced Lucas that death would be a reprieve.

The man glanced up sharply, trying to figure out whether Doc was telling him the truth or not. "Leave her out of it."

Doc was silent for a moment. "She's worried about you. Julie. That's her name. And you're Kenny. You lost her recently. The grief is fresh for both of you. But you think that somehow, there's a way to bring her back? And you're not the only one. Hmm. We need to have a little chat, Kenny."

Kenny had gone pale, eyes wide. "How did you do that?"

Doc spared him a slight twitch of a smile. "You may have a bit of ability to see spirits, but I'm a full psychic medium with a long life of experience. You'd be surprised what I see." At that last sentence, Doc shifted his gaze to meet Lucas's eyes, and Lucas felt sure that the other man read far more about him than Lucas had hoped to reveal.

"I'll tell you anything you want to know. Just please, promise that you'll kill me. It's the only way I'll ever be free," Kenny begged.

"Julie was murdered. And she wasn't the only one," Doc said. "That's part of how you were possessed. Trading lives for power."

Lucas looked up sharply and so did Shane. *Shit, the murder house is connected. Vengeful ghosts are one thing, but demons? What the fuck did we get ourselves into?*

"Now...tell me about Hayden Montgomery," Doc said. Lucas saw that, like the handcuffs, a line of finely etched runes along the blade blazed. "And I want to talk to Kenny, not the demon possessing him."

"It wasn't supposed to go like this," Kenny said, sounding miserable. "Julie and I went to Hayden's 'Maximize Your Potential' masterclass four years ago. It was at a retreat center in the North Carolina mountains. That's where we were when the Events happened. All of a sudden, none of us could go home."

Sadness colored Kenny's features. "Hayden was wonderful about taking charge. Everyone worked together, and we managed to turn the resort into a self-sustaining commune. What else could we do?"

"You were at a business retreat and ended up demon possessed?" Shane echoed, incredulous.

Kenny shrugged. "More of a self-actualization, motivational intensive small group workshop."

Lucas chuckled. "Wow. I haven't heard that many buzzwords since the bombs hit."

Shane rolled his eyes. Lucas grinned, completely unrepentant. "So what happened next?" Lucas prodded.

"Part of the original event was supposed to be about discovering our hidden psychic abilities," Kenny said. "Mostly like learning to trust your intuition, paying attention to your dreams. So everyone there had an interest in that sort of thing. But after the Events, people started to find that their abilities really were getting stronger."

"It wasn't just you," Shane said. "Same thing seems to have happened everywhere we've been."

"Hayden did his best to guide us. His specialty was dreams. And for a long time, things were good." Kenny looked down. "Then a fever hit the commune. This was about two months ago. Hayden died. So did several others. That's when Elliot took over."

Lucas heard the shift in Kenny's tone. Elliot clearly wasn't someone Kenny liked.

"Hayden was a good person. Elliot isn't. We didn't realize that at first. Maybe he kept that hidden, to stay on Hayden's good side," Kenny said. "But after Hayden died, Elliot got obsessed with pushing our psychic gifts to be stronger, especially the people who could see or talk to spirits. That's what Elliot can do. He said he wanted guidance from Hayden."

"And?" Doc prompted.

Kenny sighed. "Elliot channeled what he said was Hayden's ghost. I was there. I saw it. He channeled something. But I can't swear that it was Hayden."

"Let me guess—this ghost told you to come to Mountain Cove," Doc said in a dry tone.

"Yeah. Elliot had us packing up and moving out fast enough to make your head spin. He wouldn't listen to anyone else. The people who didn't want to go got left behind. I wish to hell I'd stayed with them," Kenny said.

"How did Julie die?" Doc asked.

Kenny looked down. "Elliot wanted more power. He said it would give him 'a better connection to the afterlife' to bring back Hayden and the others. Told us that Hayden had revealed a path to him." He swallowed hard. "Elliot chose four people—Julie was one of them. He asked them to 'help' him with the ritual, that it was a real honor to be chosen. He found this house, and kept the rest of us outside, far enough away so we couldn't see what was going on."

"And?" Doc prodded.

Kenny took a deep breath. "I think he must have drugged them. We didn't know until it was over that he'd killed them. I swear, we didn't know. I wouldn't have let her go if I had known."

Doc and Lucas looked to Julie's ghost. No one could mistake the anger in her expression, coupled with grief.

"Then what happened?" Doc sidestepped any comment on Kenny's guilt.

"Everything got strange. I thought maybe Elliot had drugged all of us because it was trippy." Kenny licked his lips nervously. "We got a glimpse of these...things...that just appeared after Elliot had been in the house for a while. And then one of them forced his way inside me—"

Everything about Kenny's visage and posture changed abruptly. "And then I had a new body to wear." Red eyes flashed, Kenny's mouth twisted into a sneer, and his body tensed, ready to fight. "He told you the truth about the brand. I'm here to stay. 'Til death do us part."

Doc had a blade against the man's throat before the man had a chance to move. Its sharp edge drew blood. "I want to hear from Kenny."

Out of the corner of his eye, Lucas saw a man he didn't recognize come from the inner section of the library. He held a pitcher in one hand and something clasped in his other fist.

"Why Mountain Cove?" Shane asked. "What did Elliot intend to do when you got here?"

Kenny raised his head, temporarily himself again. "It's all about the hotel. Elliot says that Hayden is waiting for us in there, and if we work together, we can bring him back and the others as well, and we'll all live forever, and the hotel will strengthen our abilities. Even Julie. He told us that their deaths didn't have to be permanent. We could all be together again."

Lucas could see the reaction on the other men's faces. "Shit," he muttered. "This is not going to go smoothly."

He couldn't decipher the look that passed between Doc and Royston, and Lucas hadn't forgotten the issue of the request that brought them to Ansted. Neither topic seemed appropriate to discuss in front of Kenny.

Shane turned to Kenny. "What were your orders, coming here?"

"We saw you two ride by," Kenny replied. "Elliot wanted to know who you were. We knew there were people here in the library, but not why they were here. Elliot wanted me to find out."

"That's it? Just recon?" Shane pressed.

Kenny looked away. "Elliot said that if I saw a way to scare you all off, I should do it." Lucas had a feeling his orders were much less benign.

"What are we going to do with him?" Royston asked Doc.

"Well, we can't send him back," Doc mused.

"But we can try to send him on," the man in the doorway said. "I might have left the priesthood, but they say the priesthood never leaves you. We can try an exorcism, and if that fails, we can release Kenny as a mercy."

"I have the keys to the jail," Doc said. "I can add some sigils so he won't make a break for it. We can put him in there and let you do your thing."

"Happy to help," the ex-priest said. "I brought some holy water and my rosary, got the prayer book in my pocket. We're good to go."

"And when you get him locked up, we need to have a little discussion about why we're here and how, exactly, we were invited," Lucas said, glaring at Doc.

"Yeah, I figured that was coming. I promise, I'll answer all your questions."

Lucas didn't feel like chatting while Doc and the other scholar were gone. Royston cleared his throat and left the room for a while. Lucas looked to Shane.

"Well, guess we got our answer on the murder house."

"Yeah. I was really hoping it wasn't connected."

"You and me both."

CHAPTER THREE

As much as Shane knew both of them wanted to discuss the pretense that brought them to the mountain, he didn't want to be overheard, so they sat quietly until Royston reappeared to let Doc and the other scholar in after they had been gone for about an hour. The former priest spoke quietly with Royston, then headed back down the hall.

Royston and Doc came back to sit at the table.

"Alright—shoot. What do you want to know?" Doc said.

Lucas leaned forward. "Why the hell did you bring us here? Because the coven asked us to come out here months ago—before some of those 'abilities' you mentioned came to be. So, spill."

Doc sighed. "Mama Jean had a vision a couple of months ago, about two 'warriors' with special powers who could set things right. Her visions may be cryptic, but they're never wrong. Eddie got talking to a pair of those wandering IT Priests, who mentioned the two of you. Eddie felt certain you were the ones from the vision. You'd have to ask him how he got word to the witches in Bedford. I did my best to pass the word through the ghosts. Obviously it worked, because here you are."

"We're nearly ready to transfer the final materials to the hotel and move our people inside," Royston said. "But Doc says that there's something not right about the hotel's energy. We need to fix that before we get settled."

"You're going to try to...live...in there?" Shane's eyes widened in concern.

"It seems safer than trying to continue to live out here," Royston said with a sad smile. Shane remembered all the movies he'd seen where a doomed alien race packed their vast knowledge into a spaceship and sent it to the stars on the eve of their own destruction. He had never expected to confront that scenario in reality.

"If you try to live inside the hotel, what are you going to do for food and water?" Shane asked, equal parts intrigued and horrified. "What if you get in and can't get back out?"

Royston shrugged. "So far, getting in and out hasn't been a problem when the hotel is 'phased in' here."

"When it's elsewhere...I'd hate to take a chance on where or when you might turn up," Lucas added.

"Fortunately, we haven't had the need to test that," Royston replied. "We've been moving in food and water along with the archives. Doc and Eddie and Mama Jean have promised to resupply us at intervals. If or when that fails, well, we'll deal with it as it comes."

"And you're sure the hotel is empty?" Lucas pressed.

Royston's gaze shifted. "Of living people? Yes. There are ghosts. So far, they haven't bothered us. There's an exceptionally strong spirit who still seems to take his duties at the front desk very seriously. He's never bothered us. But there are parts of the hotel that don't feel comfortable, like something isn't right. Doc says there's a dark presence, but he's not sure what it is."

Shane and Lucas exchanged a glance. Shane could see that Lucas had concerns about the scholars' plans.

"That could become a problem," Lucas said, leaning forward and resting his forearms on the table. "The ghosts might not object to your coming and going—since at the end of it, you don't stay. That might change when you move in. Ghosts can be protective—and territorial."

Royston nodded. "That occurred to me. Ansted's history is worryingly full of people who were said to have 'suddenly vanished' or 'went mad.'"

"You think that might all be linked to the anomaly?" Shane asked.

"It's not too late to re-think your decision to move in," Lucas said. "I understand wanting to store the materials there. But why would you want to try to stay there?"

Royston leaned back in his chair. "We think that time works differently inside the hotel. Right now, the building phases in and out every three days. That interval has held steady for the past few years. If you're inside the hotel, what feels like a couple of hours is only minutes on the outside."

Shane noticed that Lucas seemed to tune out of the conversation for a few minutes. That usually meant he was listening to Rocky. He wondered what the elemental spirit had found important.

The shift in Lucas's expression told Shane his partner had pulled himself out of his thoughts. "The people who plan to live inside the hotel with the archives—how did you pick them?"

Royston looked surprised at the question, then resigned. "When we first started collecting materials, right after the Events, we had a lot of people who wanted to help. Over time, most of them drifted away. Now, there's a handful of us for whom the archive is our legacy, our mission."

"None of us are young, or in particularly good health," Royston said with a self-deprecating smile. "And the hospital in these parts couldn't get supplies and shut down. Doc and Mama Jean—a folk healer back in the hollow—can only do so much for us." Shane noticed that he said that last word "holler."

"Best I can guess is that four of us might have a year left, and the others maybe a little more than that."

"But inside the hotel, the time you have left lasts longer." Lucas met the man's gaze as if daring him to contradict him.

Royston didn't look away. "Yes. We figured we would go inside, set up the archives, and leave a record for future researchers. Make the most of the time."

Royston leaned toward them. "That's why we're not real worried about getting back out. If it all goes sideways...well, we were planning to take some guns and ammo with us. The hotel may be closed, but we can still check out any time we want."

"Eddie told us he was an earth witch. Is that true?" Lucas asked.

"Yes," Doc answered. "He's very powerful. Eddie and Mama Jean and I, we act as 'anchors' to help stabilize the hotel."

Lucas turned back to Doc. "You didn't call us here to be hotel bouncers. What do you know—and how the hell do you know it?"

Doc pursed his lips as if thinking about how best to answer. "There are malignant entities that have found their way into the hotel. They're parasites, not just feeding off its power but gradually poisoning it. Joseph—the scholar who used to be a priest—and I suspected one of those might be a demon. Now, after what Kenny told us, I think we can be certain of that. It sounds like the entity in the hotel duped Elliot into believing—at least initially—that it was Hayden. Probably got Elliot to allow himself to be possessed. Then once Elliot was possessed, he made sure the others were too."

"So why don't you and Joseph take care of the problem?" Lucas asked, still not mollified.

"Given the nature of my abilities, I dare not enter. Neither can Eddie or Mama Jean. And it wouldn't be safe for Joseph to force a confrontation by himself. But you could," he said, meeting Lucas's gaze.

"Why is that?" Shane felt his heart speed up. He and Lucas had intentionally avoided witches and others with magic because they feared what might happen if anyone figured out about Rocky and Quentin. If they'd have known this situation involved witches—or demons—they wouldn't have come.

It might be too late to keep their talents from being exposed, but if he and Lucas didn't like what Doc told them in the next few minutes, they could be gone by daybreak.

Doc looked Lucas in the eye. "You can see and talk to ghosts, but you can't summon them—easily. And you have a second spirit within, so you can't be possessed." He turned to Shane. "You hear the daemon song—and you have a wolf. Joseph and I have no second spirit. We could be possessed—and the result would be disastrous."

"Let me get this straight. You want me to go into a disappearing hotel and get rid of an...entity?" Lucas challenged. "How the hell am I supposed to do that?"

"I believe you have dealt with spirits before," Doc said. "Your daemon will help to protect you. And with the rituals Mama Jean and I will teach you, I think you're the only one who can do it."

"I don't like being lied to." Lucas had his back up, and Shane knew it would take some good handling to smooth his hackles.

"How could we tell you the whole truth—when you didn't know it yourselves yet?"

Shane watched Lucas's jaw work, a sure tell that he was grinding his teeth. Now that Lucas knew the full story about the archive and the scholars' plan, Shane knew his partner wouldn't walk away.

"We don't know enough about the hotel, or what we might be going up against," Lucas said finally. "Before I do anything—we need more information." He glanced toward Shane. "And it has to be something all four of us agree to," he added, including Rocky and Quentin.

"Do you have any books, diaries, or materials about the hotel itself?" Shane asked. "I'd like to read them. It would help us help you."

Royston nodded. "Yes. Give me a few minutes, and I'll get them for you."

He left them in the break room. Lucas gave Doc a look that meant he was trying to figure out his agenda.

"So Eddie is a real witch??"

Doc nodded. "There have always been witches with 'elemental magic'—people who could manipulate air, water, earth, and fire."

"Wasn't there an old cartoon about a bald kid who could do that?" Lucas quipped.

Shane rolled his eyes. "Yes. We watched the whole series while we were babysitting that witness in Dayton who ratted out the Mob's top banker. Remember? The hotel that only got four channels on TV?"

Lucas gave a sad smile. "You know, four channels doesn't sound so bad now."

"Yeah. I guess it's all relative."

"Eddie and the Mysterium are a counterbalance to the anomaly," Doc replied. "As are Mama Jean and I. But with the entity in the hotel, the skills that serve us out here would be liabilities in there."

"How does Quentin feel about that plan?" Lucas asked Shane and smirked like he could guess.

"He says I owe him a steak—or a whole deer."

"Yeah. I figured. Rocky isn't sure about the idea of hanging around either. I should take another look at that first creepy cemetery. When we passed by, I couldn't tell if they were troublemakers—or sentinels."

"They are both."

Lucas and Shane turned to look at Doc.

"You heard me say that I am a medium. I'm also a guide. I help spirits move on to where they are going."

"You're a psychopomp," Shane said. "I've read about that ability."

Doc nodded. "Very good. The ghosts in the cemetery help us watch over the hotel. They make good sentries—and they can do a lot to keep out casual trespassers. And they alert me when someone is more than 'casual.'"

"If the 'folded energy' is a natural occurrence, then why did it wait so long before it made the hotel disappear?" Shane asked. "I get the idea of psychics and sensitives locating a building where they wanted to hold meetings over an energy well, or near a helpful genius loci. But why pick a place that's unstable?"

"Maybe the psychics thought that if the Veil was thinner there, with the energies all strange, that it would help them see across to the other side. It doesn't sound like they wanted to take anything away from the anomaly. They just wanted to ride the wave, so to speak," Lucas said. "Probably what made Elliot think the hotel could bring back the dead."

"We believe that the building's disappearances and energy are being disrupted by the malignant entity," Doc said. "Ridding the hotel of the parasite energy might not make it completely solid again, but it may spread out the intervals."

"Royston told us that the area near the hotel has a reputation for people disappearing or going mad," Shane said.

Doc looked pained. "The anomaly increases latent abilities. The Spiritualists expected that and wanted it. They had studied about psychic gifts and welcomed having them manifest. They usually did fine. The people who struggled—and who disappeared and went mad— had never considered that they had abilities. Some of them believed such gifts were of the devil. They weren't Spiritualists, and they had no training and no guidance. They feared what was happening to them, and when they couldn't control the power—their abilities destroyed them."

Lucas watched him with a wary look. "I still don't like that you knew more about us than we knew ourselves."

"I'm sorry," Doc said. "We were desperate. We fear that the entity has done real damage to the hotel and that if it isn't reversed, not only will the scholars not be safe, but the hotel might become lost forever.

And now, there's the added threat of the demons. We can't let them gain access to the hotel."

Lucas didn't say anything, but Shane knew that look. It might take a while for his partner to admit it, but they were staying—and Lucas intended to fight. Shane resigned himself to learning as much as he could, so he could protect Lucas—and the hotel.

"I need to be going," Doc said, and stood. "I should check on our prisoner—and bring him dinner. I'll let you know if Joseph has had any luck getting more information out of him. I will see you again soon."

Lucas and Shane sat quietly after Doc left, deep in their thoughts. Royston returned a few minutes later with a cardboard box that had what Shane thought of as a "used book store" smell of musty paper.

"This is what we have on the Mountain Cove Hotel, that old amusement park, and Eddie's place before he bought it," the scholar told them. "Some stuff about the Spiritualists, too."

Shane looked up at their host. "After the Spiritualist community disbanded, were individuals still drawn here? People interested in understanding 'the world beyond'?"

Royston perched on a corner of the table. "Sure. Some wanted to legend trip the hotel. A rumor went around for a while that there was some kind of 'magic artifact' buried in the foundation of one of the houses from the old community. Had a lot of people digging up the woods before the sheriff put a stop to it."

How did they stand being there long enough to dig something up? Shane wondered. Just riding past had given him a headache and made his wolf extremely out of sorts. *The hotel itself isn't evil. But if it has attracted other entities over the years, there's nothing to keep something evil from sneaking in.*

Quentin had thought he'd caught the scent of wolves and possibly wolf shifters. It would be good to know if they were friend or foe.

"When you and the other archivists go into the hotel, will there be anyone left in Ansted besides Eddie, Doc Swanson, and Mama Jean?" Lucas asked.

Royston shook his head. "Not that we know of. Wouldn't surprise me that there are folks at the back of the hollers that haven't come out in generations. If they wouldn't come out for movies, TV, flush toilets, and running water, they won't bother now."

Shane could grudgingly admit the logic in that.

"Doc told us that he was a psychopomp, a sort of jacked-up medium —and that he guides spirits to the afterlife. Did anyone suspect that, before the Events?" Lucas asked.

"Doc's been here a long time," Royston hedged. "It's quite a drive to the nearest hospital. Short of major surgery—the big stuff—Doc took care of it all. But everyone said he was at his best when someone was passing on. Got so that people who didn't want a priest or a minister, still asked for Doc at the end. Folks said that Doc seemed to smooth the way when someone was dying, made it easier on them."

Something's going on here that we're not seeing—and I don't think the scholars are seeing the whole picture either. Three human guardians, the cemetery ghosts, and the creatures Quentin sensed. Can't be a coincidence that they're all here near the hotel and the anomaly. But why? To keep something out—or lock it in? Maybe the anomaly and the vortex are too powerful or too important to risk allowing it to fall into the wrong hands. Or is it something else entirely?

"We usually do supper around seven," Royston told them. "Tonight is smoked venison with potatoes and carrots." At their expression of surprise, he chuckled.

"Part of that whole provisioning thing. We made sure we shot some deer, then smoked or jerked the meat so it would keep. We've had a garden since before things went bad. Plenty of root vegetables keep. Chickens and goats we plan to take with us for eggs, milk, and cheese. Brew some pretty fine beer too, if I do say so myself, and we've laid in enough moonshine for the duration." He grinned. "After all, this is West Virginia."

"It sounds amazing," Lucas replied wholeheartedly. "We haven't had a meal like that in a very long time."

Royston brightened. "You'll also have a chance to meet the rest of the team. We don't get a lot of visitors these days. They're looking forward to talking with you." He thumped the box of papers with his hand.

"I'll leave you alone to read. If the light changes, there's an oil lamp on the counter, and you're welcome to more of the tea in the big jar," he offered. "We're grateful for you coming out this way. Food and shelter are the best we can offer—for you and your horses—but you won't go away hungry."

"That's more than enough," Lucas assured him. "Thank you."

———

THE NEXT FEW hours went past quickly, with both Shane and Lucas engrossed in the materials Royston brought. Shane paged through old newspapers, yellowed letters, and a few journals kept by people who were amateur historians.

"There's a lot here. How's it going?" Shane asked after a while, taking a break to stretch and yawn.

Lucas pushed back from the table, rubbing his eyes and cracking his neck. "Slow. I hadn't really expected there to be quite so much. I found old articles about the people who died at the hotel. Interesting that someone bothered to keep them."

"So, what happened? Love triangles? Cheating spouses? Embezzlers?"

Lucas shook his head. "Surprisingly, no. The first suicide was one of the Spiritualists who founded the 1870s community, Benjamin Bowers. Part of the reason the community began to fall apart were allegations that he and the other medium, Phillip Carson, were abusing their authority and mishandling the money that was supposed to provide for the common good."

"Were they?"

Lucas took a long drink from his tea. "Carson might have been, but the coverage I've read was sympathetic to Bowers. Maybe he was naive, or just so focused on his mission that he couldn't see that he was being bamboozled by his partner. Or, as some of the accounts hint, he might have been either a jilted lover or rebuffed one to many times."

"Trouble in paradise, huh?"

"Yeah. So when it all began to spin out of control and Carson didn't deny the allegations, I guess Bowers reached his limit. He'd been the driving force behind building the hotel. It had been his dream to fill it with seekers and students who would flock here to learn how to use their gifts or find enlightenment. He loved the place, and now it was all going to go down the drain," Lucas recounted. "Bowers walked up to the top floor suite where the view was the best and ate a bullet."

"And the other suicides? Were they related?" Shane asked.

"Not all of them." Lucas reached to riffle through the old pages. "Carson's wife collapsed from heart trouble, which she hadn't had before. The gossips thought she might have taken foxglove, unable to face the scandal. Carson slunk off. He was never prosecuted and didn't seem to feel any remorse. Sort of like those crooked televangelists who bankrupted their flocks and ran off to the islands with all the money."

"I guess that's nothing new." Shane frowned. "But the hotel's site is located on a real energy anomaly. We've both felt the psychic impact of the location. Why would a site like that draw fake spiritualists?"

Lucas let his head fall back and put his drink on the table, pausing to rub circles on his temples, as if holding off a headache. "I don't think Carson and Bowers were fake. They might have even started with good intentions. Somewhere along the way, Bowers doubled down on the mission, and Carson spotted an opportunity to line his pockets that he couldn't pass up."

"Real psychic abilities, weak personal ethics," Shane summarized. "Guess that's not so unusual."

"Carson's wife didn't kill herself in the hotel," Lucas went on. "But there were other incidents that did happen there—people who weren't famous who died under questionable circumstances. After the Spiritualist community broke up, the hotel staggered on, mostly because of its great views and the state parks nearby. Management was a mixed bag— some good and some bad. By the end, it had fallen on hard times. The woman who bought it was supposedly a seer and renowned psychic from Russia, Roza Petrova."

"Let me guess—not really Russian?"

Lucas snorted. "Not only wasn't she Russian—she wasn't really a psychic, or her abilities weren't nearly as strong as she made them out to be. It was all parlor tricks and smoke and mirrors. She was a con artist of the worst kind, defrauding widows and bilking people out of fortunes with fake messages from their dead loved ones."

"Nice," Shane replied, his voice dripping with sarcasm.

"Right? There were also rumors about her being very harsh with the staff. She brought in teenage girls from the bigger cities to work at the hotel. Then they started to disappear."

"Trafficking?"

Lucas shook his head. "Even worse. She was killing them in some sort of ritual. When they caught her, she said it was what her 'spirit guide' demanded. Before they could arrest her, she got loose and stabbed herself. Bled to death in the hotel. That was right before it closed."

"Yeah, that's not good."

"I understand why Eddie and Doc want me to go in and try to set things right. It's just a bit of a stretch from what we did with the Marshals," Lucas replied.

"Everything we've gone up against in the last four years is a stretch," Shane said. "What else is new?"

THE NEXT MORNING, Shane and Lucas found hot coffee and oatmeal cookies waiting for them. They had met the other scholars at dinner the night before, which was a quiet and no-frills gathering. Royston's colleagues—all men in their middle years—had been curious but welcoming, and by the end of the evening, they were swapping funny stories over a bottle of moonshine.

"You notice that alcohol doesn't hit you quite the way it used to... when we were running on our original operating systems?" Lucas asked as they gratefully swallowed down coffee.

"Burns off faster," Shane confirmed. "I can get a buzz, and then it fades quickly. I hate to think how much I'd need to drink to actually get drunk."

Lucas looked distracted for a moment. "Rocky says it wouldn't be worth the effort. Something about borrowed energy in my case, and metabolism in yours."

"Nice to know."

Lucas had gone out to check on their horses before they went to bed, reporting back to Shane that their mounts had been fed, curried, and given water. This morning they walked out to the makeshift stable to take care of Red and Shadow and thanked the man who must have drawn clean-up duty that day. Shane couldn't help noticing that there were only two other horses, although six scholars lived in the library.

"Clara—the draft horse—we bought when one of the farmers sold everything off. She pulls the wagon to help us get materials into the hotel," Dennis, a scholar and the stable hand of the day, replied to Shane's question. "Doc said he'll give her a good home when we move on. Jack," he added, with a nod of his head to indicate a bay gelding, "is on loan from Eddie. In case one of us needs to go somewhere we can't walk. Eddie will take him back when it's time."

"You're all as set on doing this as Royston?" Lucas asked. He made the question sound curious, off-handed.

"I've beaten cancer twice," Dennis said. "And that was with everything modern medicine had to throw at it. How long do you think I'm going to last with moonshine and folk remedies?" He shook his head. "I get to be part of saving some of the world's knowledge, in case there's a future. And when my time is up, I'll be with my friends." He looked away. "I lost my family in the Events. So I don't have anywhere else to be, or anyone else to be with. This is more than I could have hoped for."

Shane could appreciate that. "We're going to do our level best to make sure you're safe in there."

"Thank you," Dennis said. "We're all pretty much in the same boat. We might squeeze in a bit more time this way, and we won't be alone. I know it probably sounds crazy to you—"

"It doesn't, and it's not for us to judge anyhow," Lucas cut him off. "We've got your back."

After they tended the horses, Lucas and Shane took a brief walk around Ansted, which gave them privacy to talk.

Shane tried not to think about the eerie silence. Daily life before the Events was never silent—the distant hum of airplanes overhead or cars on a nearby highway, the buzz of air conditioning motors or refrigerators, music on the radio, a TV in the background. Here, even the nature sounds seemed muted, as if the whole area was holding its breath.

"So what do you make of Royston and his gang?" Lucas asked.

Shane had been asking himself that same question, struggling to come up with an answer. "I get why they're doing it. And—assuming the hotel doesn't just totally vanish one day—it's not a bad idea."

Lucas nodded. "Pretty much what I made of it." He hesitated.

"You've been quiet about us getting invited here because of Rocky and Quentin—and me going into the hotel."

"Can I say how much I really, really don't like this idea?" Shane said, his voice sharper than he intended.

Lucas met his gaze, asking forgiveness but standing his ground. "You can. Duly noted. But there's a lot at stake. It's not just keeping the scholars safe—the entities in there could destroy the whole hotel, and the scholars and their archive with it."

"Entities, Lucas. Not necessarily ghosts," Shane emphasized. "Going in isn't the hard part. Whatever Elliot summoned is bad news—maybe a real demon. What's it going to take to get rid of the supernatural parasites?"

"Doc said that he and Mama Jean and Eddie can teach me how to dispel the entities. Rocky agrees that there's danger, but he seems to think that he and I together can do it."

"Then I'm coming with you." Shane lifted his chin and crossed his arms. Lucas's jaw twitched, a sure sign he intended to argue.

"I'm going to need you more outside," Lucas said. "The cemetery ghosts can only do so much, and Quentin might be able to call in reinforcements from the wolves and shifters."

"I don't like this," Shane grumbled.

"I know." Lucas met his gaze. "I can't say I'm thrilled, either. But I don't see another way around it."

Neither did Shane. And he figured that Lucas wouldn't commit to going in if Rocky had adamantly opposed it.

"All right," Shane relented. "But we'll be outside, watching your back."

Lucas smiled, an expression that said he understood Shane's reluctance and appreciated him going along with the plan. "I wouldn't expect anything else."

CHAPTER FOUR

"I swear the energy here is starting to fuck with me," Lucas said, as they walked back toward the library. "Rocky says he's okay, but from my end, it makes my bond with him feel all jangly."

"I know what you mean. Since we got here, Quentin's been closer to the surface. I feel like the lines are starting to blur, and I'm worried, a little, about keeping him on a short leash."

Lucas frowned. "It's not too late to leave."

Shane snorted. "You heard what Doc said. You're the only one who can fix what's wrong with the hotel."

"Remember all those movies we used to watch? Being the 'chosen one' was never a good thing," Lucas replied.

"What do you need to go inside?" Shane asked, shifting the discussion. "Because if the hotel has been phasing in every three days, it should be due again tonight."

"I'm expecting that Mama Jean, Doc, and Eddie will be there with you while I'm inside. Joseph can't really do much since the demons are locked in; otherwise, we could just have him exorcise the lot of them. If Doc really is a psychopomp, then he might be able to help deal with ghosts even if his magic keeps him from entering the hotel. Mama Jean and Eddie can help you make sure we don't get blindsided by Elliot and his murder house gang."

"

"I'd appreciate the backup," Shane admitted. "I still don't know what kind of creatures are in the woods. I'm not going to take someone else's word on whether they're friend or foe until Quentin and I can size them up."

"Fair enough." Lucas fell silent for a while. "It sounds like Eddie, Mama Jean, Doc, the cemetery ghosts...they've all worked together to protect the hotel and the anomaly. Even so, some bad 'entities' still got into the hotel. Now those entities are harming the hotel—and affecting its energy. It would be even worse if the crazy cultists took it over. So if we can dispel the entities and get rid of the demons, maybe the anomaly can go back to the way it was, and the scholars will be safe."

"And then the guardians can protect it the way that's worked until now," Shane replied.

"We can hope." Lucas chewed his lip as he thought. "I'm going to need salt, silver, and some of those dried plants we've been gathering—the ones that are good for protection. It wouldn't hurt to have some holy water, but I don't know where we're going to get that. I'll brush up on the banishment rite—take my book with me, just in case."

***

"We'll back you up any way we can," Royston told them, and the other scholars nodded.

"You can help us the most by contacting Doc and Mama Jean to make sure they're with us," Lucas replied. "And if you've got any extra salt, sage, or thyme, that would also help."

"I'll check for salt and the other things you mentioned," Dennis replied. "And if we don't have it, there may still be some left over at the market. We didn't move everything out of there when they up and left."

Lucas spent that evening huddled with Doc, Eddie, Mama Jean, and Joseph, going over what he needed to know to deal with the spirits and entities. Shane sat with the scholars who specialized in folklore, trying to narrow down what kind of entity Lucas might be facing inside the hotel. Hours later, they tended their horses and thanked the scholar who was on stable duty for managing to add a dried apple to each horse's feed. Then both men finally headed to their room, exhausted.

"We think that the entity is an *ala*," Shane told Lucas. "It's a type of

Slavic demon. We thought it sounded like the kind of entity that might have appealed to Roza as her abilities dimmed with age."

"Joseph went over a lot of demon lore. We can ask him if there's anything special I might need to know if it really is an *ala*," Lucas replied.

Shane helped Lucas gather what he needed from their bags.

"Once you go inside, you're going to be cut off," Shane said. "We won't know if you need backup."

"Doesn't matter if the scholars don't have the means to fight the entity and ghosts, and the rest of you shouldn't try to enter because it will fuck with your magic...power...wolf...whatever," Lucas replied with a wave of his hand.

Walking into a disappearing hotel to banish...maybe exorcise...a dark spirit scared the shit out of Lucas, and he suspected that Shane knew it. But handling the hard stuff because there wasn't anyone else to do it seemed to be the story of their lives.

Rocky, at least, wasn't quite as worried. Lucas didn't know how to feel about that. Rocky had assured him he wouldn't die so long as the elemental spirit remained as his co-pilot. Lucas feared there was a lot of potentially unpleasant territory between "being fine" and "not dead yet," and he didn't want to figure it out the hard way.

Neither man slept well that night. In the morning, Shane helped Lucas organize supplies and weapons. Iron and salt weakened or dispelled ghosts, while silver worked on many but not all supernatural creatures. Shotgun shells filled with a mixture of rock salt and iron shot would hold off a lot of paranormal predators.

"We're in luck," Shane said as he came back with two gallon jugs of water. "Joseph blessed the water." Shane held up a rosary. "And he blessed this too. So if we drop it in whatever water we want to sanctify, he thinks it will do the trick the next time we don't have a priest handy. He says he has a silver bowl and some other ritual things for you; I guess left over from his old job."

"Nice to know." Lucas pinched the bridge of his nose, staving off a headache. "We used to transport witnesses, chase down fugitives, serve warrants on mobsters. When did we become ghostbusters?"

Shane gave him a look of incredulity. "Right around the time you picked up an invisible hitchhiker, and I became a werewolf."

Lucas sighed. "Sometimes it's just a bit much, you know?"

A knock at the door made them turn, hands falling to their guns out of old habit. Royston stuck his head inside.

"Eddie, Doc, and Mama Jean are here. Come on out. We've got lunch fixed since you shouldn't go into a fight on an empty stomach."

Lucas hefted his pack and the two gallons of holy water, then followed Shane and Royston to the main lobby that had become more of a large living room.

Eddie and Doc stood with an older woman. "Marshals, meet Mama Jean," Eddie said.

Lucas sized up their new ally. Mama Jean had the sun-wrinkled skin of someone who had worked outside most of her life. She might have been in her seventies, but her eyes seemed much older. Her blue sweatshirt and jeans hung on her bony frame, practical, no-nonsense clothing meant for getting hard work done.

"Pleased to meet you," Lucas said. *What do you make of them, Rocky?*

I do not detect a threat. Their magic is very different. The woman's is most familiar as she draws on the energy of the world around her. The man who talks to ghosts feels like thunder and rushing water. The other man is fire and lightning. I do not know how else to describe them.

That's good. Thanks. Um, Rocky—going into the anomaly isn't going to fuck with your ability to keep me alive, is it?

I do not think so. I am older. It is...uncomfortable, but it does not change me.

"We'd best be going," Doc said. "Don't want to lose the light."

They rode out to the site of the hotel in the wagon, with Doc driving the draft horse and Mama Jean beside him on the front seat. Eddie rode in the back with them, but no one said much. Lucas stretched out his senses as he passed the old cemetery. This time, the ghosts did not seem to be judging him. Maybe they had decided he was another type of guardian. Or perhaps, he thought, they were focused on containing the hotel's unwelcome guests.

Lucas didn't feel the disorientation he'd experienced when they rode past the "missing" hotel, and Shane gave no indication that his headache had returned. "The energy feels different," he said.

Shane nodded. "Yeah, it's still jangled, but not nearly as loud or painful. The horses can feel a difference, too," he added, smoothing his hand down Red's neck. Neither horse had the wide-eyed, panicked look of that first trip.

"Wow. It's really there." Shane pointed, and Lucas looked up at the large clapboard hotel. It matched what he had seen in the old photographs. The hotel stood three stories tall, painted white with a slate roof and green shutters. It looked as solid as the mountain behind it, in spite of not being there just two days ago.

Lucas tried to read the hotel with the same "ghost sense" he had used at the cemetery. The connection felt wrong, filled with static and blurry as if it were constantly in motion. Even so, Lucas picked up a darkness that sent a chill down his back. He couldn't imagine how the scholars had come and gone without noticing—or without being attacked.

Now that Lucas stood in front of the old hotel, he could sense the push and pull of warring energies—or rather, Rocky could. The cemetery ghosts kept back weaker revenants, forming a protective cordon. That told Lucas that the malignant entity must have been strong to get past them—or perhaps carried in by someone.

Rocky sensed the magics of the three guardians and the familiar resonance that was Shane and Quentin. With their protection outside and the weapons he carried with him, this was as good an opportunity as he was ever going to get.

Lucas turned and gave Shane a snappy salute, then headed up the front steps to the Mountain Cove Hotel, half expecting to fall right through stairs that were only an illusion. But his feet connected with solid stone steps, and the boards of the wide front porch held his weight.

Up close, the hotel reminded Lucas of a Victorian seaside resort he had stayed in with his parents as a child. Even then, he had been impressed by the dark woodwork, the period furnishings, and the old-fashioned wallpaper and decorations. The Victorians had an over-the-top, too-much-is-not-enough love affair with velvet, beads, fringed lamp-shades, and elaborate knick-knacks, and his childhood imagination made the connection with all of the ghost stories he had ever seen.

The hotel lived up to his expectations. Spiritualism either paid well, or the community's founders had come from wealth, because the hotel felt more like a resort and less like an ascetic retreat. Or perhaps the people who came to refine their psychic gifts or seek the counsel of their dearly departed relatives wanted to do so in style.

The luxurious foyer had polished wooden floors and large area rugs. It seemed to take its inspiration more from the grand lodges of the Whitneys and Vanderbilts in the Adirondacks than from monastic retreats. Comfortable furnishings in the style of Gilded Era hunting resorts were grouped for conversation in front of large stone fireplaces. Tiffany lamps cast a warm glow on side tables, while chandeliers made with elk antlers hung overhead.

Lucas stopped to take the measure of the building, now that he was on the inside. He sensed more than one faint ghostly presence at a distance, as if the spirits were holding back, waiting to see what he would do. He thought of the suicides that happened here, the missing girls, and the psychic who had willingly sacrificed those young women for her own gain.

The energies are not poisoned, but they are unhealthy. Ghosts do not have the power to do that—at least, not by themselves. Something else is here. More than one something, Rocky said.

"Welcome to the Mountain Cove Hotel. How may we be of service?"

Lucas wheeled at the sound of the man's voice, shotgun racked and ready.

The man behind the counter looked like he had stepped out of a museum exhibit from the 1890s. The black frock coat and starched white shirt gave him a formal appearance, as did the carefully styled and Macassared hair.

"How are you here?" Lucas asked, not lowering his gun.

"Where else would I be?" The man's smile never faltered, and neither his voice nor his body language gave any hint of worry over the shotgun pointed at his chest.

He is not human. I do not sense danger from him. Curiosity. And... protectiveness. Perhaps wait to shoot him? Somewhere in their journey, Rocky had begun to acquire a dry sense of humor.

Lucas lowered the shotgun. "Let's start again. Who are you?"

The man's smile broadened. "That's more like it. I am Fenton Delacourt, your host here at the best Spiritualist hotel in the nation. At your service," he added with a shallow bow from the waist.

"I'm Lucas. I was told the hotel had a ghost problem."

Fenton looked distressed. "Oh my. I'm quite concerned to hear that sort of thing is going around—bad for business. Hard to meditate and reach your higher vibrations if you're worried about ghosts."

"My friends have been visiting. They said they saw you—and got glimpses of the ghosts."

Fenton gave him an appraising look. "Ah. The scholars. Always happy to have academics among our guests."

"They plan to become permanent residents. And...you're okay with that?"

"It's always been said that the hotel calls to those who need it," Fenton replied, his smile never slipping.

Did that include Roza Petrova, the fake Russian seer? Lucas wondered. *Or Bowers, the doomed co-founder of the failed Spiritualist community?*

"I'd like to have a look around," Lucas said. "I can help restless ghosts move on. Send troublesome spirits elsewhere. There's something here that is...twisting...the hotel's energy."

Fenton frowned. "We do not speak of that," he warned. "Some things are best not mentioned."

Lucas hadn't come to argue with...whatever Fenton was. "I promised my friends that I would look around and make sure everything was ready for them. I mean no harm to you or the hotel."

Fenton gave Lucas an incisive stare. "I believe you."

He can sense me, Rocky whispered in his mind.

Is he afraid of the entity?

It would appear so. Or perhaps, cautious. I pick up traces of a dark power, but I can't locate it yet.

Keep trying. I think Petrova might be the key to this.

Lucas hefted his bag and headed toward the public areas on the first floor and from there, to find the basement. He had a map provided by Royston, and he knew where the scholars had stored their archive materials. Based on that, he had already decided to save the top floor and Bowers for last. Given how much Bowers loved the hotel and the community, Lucas didn't think he was the source of the problem.

The hotel's large open dining room continued the sense of rustic luxury. The tables were set for dinner, with glassware and china place settings that glittered, not a speck of dust in sight. Lucas reached out to assure himself that the pieces were solid, although how "real" they were was a matter of debate. Here inside the hotel, at least, things were real enough to be dangerous. Lucas needed to remember that.

"What'll you have?" a familiar voice hailed him from behind the elaborate bar.

Lucas turned to see Fenton drying glasses, wearing a bartender's vest. The mirrored backbar reflected the glittering lights of the chandeliers.

"Fenton?"

"Can I make you a cocktail, sir? Or perhaps pour a few fingers of good scotch?"

Fenton either didn't recall their earlier conversation or had a reason for pretending not to. *Or maybe he's not the same Fenton. Rocky?*

I can't say for sure yet. Proceed with caution.

Lucas felt a prickle on the back of his neck that usually meant a ghost. He turned slowly, shotgun down but ready if needed. A faded figure sitting by the grand piano caught his attention.

"That's Irene. She doesn't bother anyone," Fenton said. "Been here for a long time. She just doesn't want to go home."

Lucas moved closer slowly. The woman's dress looked to be from the early 1900s, and she sat at a table near the piano, turned as if she were listening to music only she could hear. She didn't seem to notice him or to have heard the conversation. Lucas wondered if she was a "repeater" —a ghost whose energy had faded so much that it was like an image on a video loop, without sentience or the ability to react.

He turned away, willing for now to let Irene stay. When Lucas looked back toward the bar, Fenton was gone.

"Like that's not creepy at all," he muttered under his breath.

Lucas spotted a set of nondescript double doors in the back of the dining room used by the waitstaff. He slipped through them into a service corridor that ran behind the public rooms, linking them all to the kitchen and storage rooms for tables, chairs, and other materials.

If the stories about Roza and her bloody obsession were true, Lucas doubted she carried out her murders in places where guests were likely to hear or interrupt. Even the hotel staff might have objected to seeing some of their own gruesomely killed. That meant looking for the basement.

Lucas had a pack of matches and a candle in his jacket pocket and a lantern with extra candles in his pack since he had been unsure what he might find inside the hotel. By the time the hotel closed—and disappeared—in the 1920s, it had electric lights. Lucas hadn't been certain that the version that reappeared would be the most recent, or always be the same version, for that matter. He had learned the hard way not to take chances.

An unlocked door marked *"Basement"* led off the service hallway. While Lucas felt glad he didn't need to shoot the lock to get in, he noticed marks that suggested it had, at one time, been padlocked shut.

He opened the door and found a light switch. To his relief, a bare bulb glowed to life over the stairway. The cement stairs and metal pipe railing had clearly not been meant for guests. A musty smell rose from the bottom, the smell of damp concrete, mildew, and mold.

The main room at the bottom held the boilers, furnace, electrical panel, an ancient generator, along with pipes, ductwork, and conduits. As with the rest of the hotel that Lucas had seen thus far, the lack of dust and cobwebs made it look still in use. Lucas moved carefully, sweeping the room for threats, but saw no one. A dark hallway led off from one side.

"You really shouldn't be down here."

Lucas wheeled, only to find Fenton, dressed in workman's coveralls, standing by the furnace where, seconds ago, there had been no one.

"What are you?" he demanded, refusing to lower his shotgun this time.

"No one goes down the hallway," Fenton continued as if he hadn't heard the question. "It's off-limits."

"Oh yeah? By who? Madame Roza?" He headed toward the hallway, and Fenton moved toward the doorway as well.

Lucas turned the shotgun toward the mysterious man. "I don't want to shoot you—but I will if you get in my way. What's in the hallway that I'm not supposed to see?" Fenton didn't answer. Several possibilities churned in Lucas's mind, and he took a chance.

"That's where she kept the girls, isn't it? They died back there. And

I bet some of them never moved on. I'm not here to hurt them. I want to set them free."

For the first time, Fenton's expression changed from the pleasantly unreadable mask Lucas had seen before. He actually looked worried. "It's dangerous. She likes to visit them."

She. Madame Roza—or whatever she's become—is still torturing those poor spirits.

"I intend to stop her," Lucas told Fenton, who might be an unlikely ally but was the only chance for backup he had. "Can you warn me if she comes?"

For just a second, Fenton seemed frightened. *If he's somehow tied to the hotel itself, and Roza—or whatever "malignant entity" she's become— is feeding off the ghost girls, then maybe she's also leeching off him.*

"How about you just bang on a pipe if she shows up? That way she won't know," Lucas suggested.

Fenton nodded and moved back toward the boiler. Lucas found the switch for the second hallway and made his way forward carefully, feeling all his senses go on high alert.

Be careful. The energy in this area is unnatural. Something has tainted it. This is not part of the energy of the mountain, or what you call the anomaly, Rocky warned.

The first door opened into a stockroom filled with old tools and handyman supplies. The second held spare parts and odd bits of lumber and pipe. Lucas kept his attention fixed on the last door, which from its placement on the hallway, suggested it led to a somewhat bigger room. As with the main basement door, it looked as if a padlock and plate had been removed.

By now, his ghost sense screamed in the back of his mind, and gut instinct told him to run. Rocky held steady, so Lucas kept moving forward. The lights overhead flickered, and the hallway grew steadily colder as he moved farther from the main boiler room. At first, Lucas had chalked that up to being away from the heat from the furnace, but now he knew it was a sign of strong ghosts nearby.

He stopped and pulled out a canister of salt from his bag, then laid down a line across the hallway so nothing blindsided him from that direction. The corridor ended in a wall to his right, which meant he didn't worry about anyone coming at him from there. Then Lucas readied his shotgun and swung the third door open.

The stench of old blood and decay assaulted him. Lucas reached for the light switch and recoiled as the single bulb revealed the horrors inside.

Two filthy mattresses lay on the floor, soiled with blood and dark stains Lucas didn't want to ponder. A pair of manacles lay on the floor, and he saw a ring set into the stone wall where the chains could be fastened. A dented bucket stood in the corner, and a side table held what appeared to be surgical instruments. A gilded triptych hung high on the far wall as if to oversee the carnage.

Lucas swallowed back bile. He didn't need an imagination to fill in the details of how Roza kept herself busy.

The light flickered once more, and the air grew impossibly colder. Lucas felt a slight breeze where there shouldn't have been any.

"I came to set you free," he said to the empty room, knowing that spirits lingered even though he couldn't see them yet. "What she did to you was evil. I'll deal with her later. But if you're stuck here—I can send you on."

One by one, three faint images struggled to be seen. Lucas relied on his ghost sense, and that helped him make out more details. The three spirits were all teenage girls, perhaps seventeen or eighteen, he guessed. They looked emaciated, making it even more difficult to judge their ages. He felt relief that they had not manifested with their death wounds. Containing his rage already took a lot of his focus.

Lucas quickly set out four candles and connected them with a circle made from salt and other protective powders. He spoke the words to the litany Joseph had taught him to help stranded spirits find peace, turning clockwise as he did so to light the candles. Both Doc and the former priest had assured Lucas that the ritual elements actually helped to focus and transmute power and weren't just for show.

As Lucas lit the last candle, he felt sure that the energy in the room had changed. The air felt thick with power, and even the ghosts seemed to sense the shift.

Rocky?

Keep going. The doorway you are opening has nothing to do with the mountain. Something held the spirits here. Send them through, quickly.

Lucas had memorized the second incantation, words of blessing and release. "The path is clear, the way is shown. Leave the fetters of your ties here behind, and follow the light that calls you. Go to your rest, and be troubled by this world no more."

The energy in the room roiled as if two unseen powers struggled against each other in a clash that made his head pound and his stomach lurch. In the distance, he heard the clang of metal on metal. A pinpoint of bright light opened like a glowing spark in the middle of the room. Primal caution made him back up, even as the three ghostly women moved toward the glowing ember, which expanded in a single flare, forcing Lucas to shield his face.

When his vision cleared, the spark and the ghosts were gone. On a hunch, he strode across the small room and took down the triptych.

Lucas!

Rocky's warning made Lucas turn just in time to hear the clang of Fenton's wrench against the pipes and see a dark cloud rolling down the hallway toward him, blotting out the light.

Lucas turned and fired the shotgun into the dark mass. A shriek of rage and pain echoed from the walls. He fired again, and the cloud dispersed, but he knew it would be back. Reloading took seconds, and then Lucas dug in his pack for more supplies.

The cloud is not one being.

What does that mean?

I sense an angry ghost and several other energies that are not human —and never were.

Demons

Not daemons.

No, demons...infernal spirits from Hell?

I do not know of Hell.

Just my luck to get an agnostic daemon for a co-pilot, Lucas thought. *What kind of harmful not-human energies are there?*

More than we have time to discuss.

Lucas thanked all the video games and horror movies he and Shane had watched. The writers had done their homework, although they had probably never thought they would be writing a post-apocalyptic primer for hunting monsters. Those memories, coupled with the intense briefing by Doc, Eddie, Mama Jean, and Joseph, would have to suffice.

Lucas grabbed a piece of chalk from his bag and drew protective sigils on both walls on his side of the salt line, knowing Roza and other entities were gathering power once more.

"Rocky—can you talk to Fenton? Do you know what he is?" Lucas muttered, raising his shotgun once more.

I have been trying to figure that out since we entered. He is not exactly a daemon.

Lucas fired into the cloud, but this time, the black smoke parted, letting the shell pass through harmlessly.

"Fuck!" He changed his aim, swinging the barrel to one side at the last instant, and the entity shrieked as the salt and iron pellets ripped through it, then vanished.

"If he's not *exactly* a daemon, then what is he?" Lucas growled.

He is the soul of the hotel.

The soul?

That is the closest word in your thoughts. Such things can occur—

Save the explanation for when we're out of here. Can he help us?

Perhaps.

Lucas dug weapons and ingredients for the incantation out of his bag. "Gotta do better than that, Rocky. I don't want to be the next new ghost."

He pulled out the silver bowl Joseph had given him and hurriedly shook in holy water, as well as cinnamon and dried thyme the ex-priest found in an abandoned convenience store, and mint gathered along the roadside. As the black smoke began to build again, Lucas relit two of the candles he had used in the other room and pulled out a photograph from the box of memorabilia the scholars kept.

"Roza Petrova! Show yourself in your true form!" He dipped one corner of the photograph into the mixture in the bowl.

The smoke suddenly cleared. In its place stood an old woman. Age lined her face and silver streaked her dark hair, but the strong chin, high cheekbones, and sharp nose still held a cold beauty.

"Put that down!" she commanded, pointing imperiously at the photograph Lucas held.

Lucas had both his ghost sense and Rocky's energy to take the measure of the spirit. Roza was strong enough to appear nearly solid, and even at a distance, Lucas felt her power.

"Why did you summon the *ala*?" Lucas shot back. He held up the triptych, which confirmed what Shane and the scholars had guessed.

"I outlived my family, my lovers, my children," the ghost said, her Russian accent—real or affected—still thick. "And then, worst of all, I outlived my magic. Do you know what becomes of old women who have no one to care about them?" Her eyes narrowed. "They become prey."

"So, you decided to summon a demon and become the predator instead?" The blood-soaked room behind Lucas started to make sense in an awful way.

"I did what I had to do." Roza lifted her head.

Lucas's abilities let him see the ghost clearly. Rocky's power enabled him to see the shimmer of the creature beside her, glistening like black oil, a form that was in no way human. It reminded him of Shane's vision at the murder house and the black ooze that had filled Elliot after the sacrifices. A nighthawk perched on her shoulder, a creature the folklorists had said was likely a *zwodziasz* in disguise, a type of imp.

"And so your *ala* and your nighthawk helped you lure the girls, which you slaughtered to keep your bargain? What did you get out of it?" Lucas had suspected the triptych factored into either her control over the demons or sealed her deal—regardless of which it was, destroying it wouldn't be in her favor. From the way Roza's eyes tracked the relic in his hand, Lucas knew he had her weak spot.

"I would not have to die," Roza replied, and her voice still carried a sense of aristocratic condescension.

"Because you feared what awaited you?" Lucas couldn't help being curious.

"I am a survivor," Roza told him in a strong voice. "What I had to do, I am not always proud of, but still, I did what needed to be done. I am in no hurry to be judged."

Lucas wondered what crimes Roza had committed before coming to Mountain Cove, what in her history had created a woman of such indomitable will that she defied both Heaven and Hell.

"I came here, to the hotel, near the end of my powers. For several years, everything was very good. I liked it here. Then, my abilities began to fail. Some of the guests complained that I had not 'performed' to their liking—as if I were a circus animal for their amusement." She sniffed.

"The hotel was also dying, running out of visitors. Bowers's suicide was a blood sacrifice, although he didn't mean it to be. He gave his life wishing for the hotel to continue. The hotel itself might close, but the energy of the mountain was eternal. I realized I could tap into that current, extend my powers, buy myself time. I called on the *ala* for help, offering more sacrifices if it would keep me strong." Roza's voice held no trace of remorse.

"You became a parasite," Lucas replied. "To save yourself, you nearly destroyed the hotel and seriously fucked with the energy of the mountain."

She shrugged. "What is the saying? Ah, yes. Needs must, when the devil drives."

In the distance, he saw Fenton blocking Roza's escape—and another man Lucas could not see clearly, an older gentleman in a Gilded Era suit and top hat. He wondered how much the salt and iron he had fired into the dark cloud had drained Roza and her demons. Curious as he was about her story, Lucas had no intention of letting Roza regain her mojo.

Roza's eyes narrowed, and Lucas felt pressure against his temples as if she was trying to force herself inside his mind. The nighthawk took flight, and the demon slithered forward, both impossibly fast.

Lucas plunged the photograph into the mixture with one hand, as he smashed the triptych against the stone floor with the other. A red flame rose from the bowl of consecrated ingredients, and the broken relic burned with an eerie green fire.

He braced himself to feel the nighthawk's claws, but instead a transparent, glittering scrim of power rose from the salt line, stopping the imp like a bird flying into a glass pane. The demon backpedaled. Lucas felt Rocky's energy surge at the same instant that the salt circle flared with light.

"Roza Petrova—I abjure you and your dark instruments of infernal power. Your power here is broken, your spirit is banished, and your essence is anathema. Depart and never return."

Roza threw back her head, shrieking as the demon began to devour her and the nighthawk pecked out her eyes. The demon swallowed her whole like a huge snake, then consumed the imp as well, and went up in a surge of blindingly bright green flames.

When Lucas dared to open his eyes, blinking against the burn-in of the demon's flare, the hallway was empty, except for Fenton and the other ghost, who still remained as sentinels.

Are we safe? he asked Rocky silently, carefully gathering up his materials. Lucas removed the soggy photograph from the bowl, and then dropped the broken relic and the photograph into the rusted bucket from the other room, squirted some lighter fluid, and tossed in a match.

Rarely had he felt such satisfaction over a trash fire.

The Fenton-entity and the ghost do not appear to mean us harm, Rocky said.

Good. I've kicked enough ass for one night.

Technically—

It's just an expression, Rocky.

Lucas had expected Fenton and the well-dressed ghost to vanish while he packed up his gear, but to his surprise, they remained on guard as he walked down the hall toward them.

"Thank you," he said. "I have the feeling you helped keep that from being worse."

Now that he could make out the ghost's features, Lucas recognized him from the pictures. Benjamin Bowers, the ill-fated co-founder of the Mountain Cove community, the man who loved the hotel so much he chose to die there rather than see his life's dream fall apart.

Bowers looked Lucas up and down, then gave an approving nod and vanished.

"I guess he's one of the hotel's permanent residents, like Irene?" he asked Fenton as the coverall-clad version of the mysterious host walked back toward the stairs with him.

"Yes, he and a few others. They will not harm your friends. Now that the creatures and the one who summoned them are gone, the hotel —and the energy of the mountain—can heal," Fenton said. "We look forward to having the scholars move in. It will liven the place up," he added with a wink and a smile.

"I need to get back." Only now did Lucas remember the warning that time inside the hotel passed at a different rate than in the outside world. How long had he been in here?

"I'm afraid you can't leave just yet," Fenton said as Lucas reached the bottom of the steps. "Roza and the demon forced the hotel to phase before its time—that's the shudder you might have felt."

Lucas vaguely remembered feeling a disconcerting lurch back in the service hallway but had attributed it to the overall weirdness of the hotel itself.

"Am I trapped here? I thought you wanted the scholars to move in?" A surge of panic made Lucas's heart pound. Nice as the hotel was, he had no intention of becoming a permanent guest.

"Now that the parasite is gone, the hotel will adjust," Fenton told him. "Give it a couple of hours, and one of us will let you know when it is safe for you to leave. We are in your debt," he said, making that shallow bow again.

"In the meantime," Fenton suggested, "go see my counterpart in the bar. The liquor is quite real—and we have a nice selection. On the house."

"Are you really the soul of the Mountain Cove Hotel?"

Fenton gave an enigmatic smile. "That is as good a description as any. A combination of the residue of power left behind by many psychics who were even more talented than they expected, the mountain's unique energy, the ley lines beneath, and a man who believed in the hotel with so much passion that when he died, his essence sustained it."

"I'm pretty sure, after everything, I could use a drink," Lucas replied. "Thanks for having my back."

"Thank you for setting us free. You are not the usual visitor yourself."

"I may have been told that a time or two," Lucas replied with the twitch of a smile, and a friendly mental nudge to Rocky. "I'll be in the bar."

CHAPTER FIVE

Shane watched Lucas enter the Mountain Cove Hotel with a spring in his step. It was just like his partner to manage some swagger, even when heading into a building that wasn't always real.

Ever since they had faced down playground bullies together in elementary school, Shane and Lucas had been a team, and that meant Shane had been worrying about his best friend nearly his entire life. Knowing that the worry was returned didn't blunt the awful feeling in his gut.

He forced himself to turn away as the door clicked shut behind Lucas and looked at their new allies. "What now? Do we just stand here until he comes back out?"

Eddie chuckled. In his dark, old-fashioned suit, he really did remind Shane of a vampire, although seeing him in bright daylight disproved that theory. Still, Shane wondered if Eddie affected the look and mannerisms for protection, or whether they were just a remnant of days gone by.

"Now we make sure nothing goes in after him," Eddie told Shane. "Tell me—does the energy feel different from when you came?"

Shane shoved down his worry and forced himself to focus on what he heard in the song of the mountains' elemental spirits, and what

Quentin sensed around them. When he and Lucas had ridden into Ansted, the mountain's energies had felt so jangled that he could barely function, giving him a headache and making Quentin surly.

The pain and extreme uneasiness he and Lucas had felt when they passed by the empty hotel site on their way into town was gone, perhaps because the hotel was back. Just in case, Mama Jean had given them each spelled charms to wear. Lucas's hung from a strap around his neck. Shane's charm hung from a long leather cord that would still fit if he shifted to his wolf form.

Shane still felt off—the melody that he heard from the genius loci of the hills remained jumbled. Though where before it had sounded to him like many songs sung over top of each other, now the tunes were more like a round, interweaving and overlaying without discord. Quentin still paced, expecting an attack, but he didn't whine and scratch and growl in Shane's mind like a canine alert for imminent danger.

"It's better than it was," Shane replied. "Is it the hotel being here that makes the difference?"

"To a large part," Eddie said. "When the hotel phases out, the vortex and anomaly are out of balance, which causes discomfort for anyone with psychic sensitivity. We think the malignant entity's effect on the mountain's energy just makes it worse. The energy in this place has always been different. That's what called to so many people with special gifts."

"The hotel was supposed to be an anchor, built into the mountain-side." Mama Jean spoke up. She brought a willow broom with her, along with a large basket and a cloth-tied bundle. While Shane watched Lucas head into the old building, Mama Jean walked a few dozen paces down the road and began to sweep the surface clean, murmuring under her breath as she worked.

"Something's put the energies all catawampus," the witch said. "Like the hotel took sick. You get an infection, and it gets in your blood, makes it bad. There's something that's got into the hotel, infected its energy like bad blood. Fix the sickness, and the hotel won't ever be regular normal, but it will be back to its old self."

Mama Jean turned away and began to scatter a mixture out of the cloth bundle over the swept-clean area of the road. She did the same to the rest of the section of asphalt in front of the hotel, bidding her companions to move out of the way, until she had swept and sown a stretch that covered the whole area.

"There," she said, dusting off her hands. "That should help keep out any riff-raff that want to make trouble. Ward away bad intentions." She cocked an eye at Shane. "You have that charm I gave you?"

"Yes, ma'am," Shane replied, pulling at the neckline of his shirt to reveal the collar. "I made sure Lucas was wearing his too, before he went in."

She nodded, apparently satisfied. "Good. Don't take it off."

Whatever hesitation Shane might once have harbored over magic had been dispelled by the realities of the world after the Events. He didn't have to understand Mama Jean's protections to believe they provided another layer of defense.

Doc Swanson remained in a spot where he was nearest both the old cemetery and the hotel itself. He stood absolutely still, eyes closed, as if he had taken root.

"What's he doing?" Shane asked Eddie.

"Talking to the ghosts, asking them to help us protect the hotel, sending them out as scouts. He'll be like that the whole time we're here. Don't worry—he's fighting his own war, we just can't see it."

Mama Jean walked along the forested edge of the road, scattering the mixture from her bag and dropping small charms made from sticks, leaves, string, small bones, and pinecones, another level of warding to keep away troublemakers.

"Mama Jean understands the plants and roots—how to make medicine or poisons, how to use them to cure or kill. How to blend them to gather energy or scatter it," Eddie answered Shane's unspoken question.

He pointed to the hotel. "You and Lucas are sensitive to the elemental spirits. I perceive the energies of the deep earth. So I see a vortex here, all those subterranean currents fountaining up. But when a vortex happens in the same place as an unusually strong area of elemental magic, you get an anomaly. And that anomaly has been stained by whatever sickness has befallen the spirit of the hotel itself."

Shane had so many questions he wanted to ask. But his head had begun to throb just from being so close to the powerful energies in the cleft that held the hotel. Quentin seemed closer than usual to the surface of his consciousness, and the longer they stayed, the more restless Shane's wolf became.

"I can sense the wolves," he murmured, looking into the forest that stretched from the edge of the road to the horizon. He walked toward the shoulder of the asphalt, careful not to interfere with Mama Jean's wardings and listened to the songs of the genius loci, and to the sounds of the forest, which to Quentin were like a native tongue.

The rush of sensation through his bond with Quentin nearly overwhelmed Shane. Sight and sound took on a new level of definition, a whole new range he had never experienced as a "normal" human. He'd heard of people describing an acid trip as "expanding consciousness" and dismissed the description as junkie justifications. Now, he wondered if those altered states came close to the torrent of new colors, sounds, smells, and detail that assaulted him.

He turned back to Eddie. "There are other beings like me out there. Regular wolves. Wolf-shifters. Werewolves."

Eddie nodded. "The wolves began gathering after the Events as if the mountain called them home."

Shane concentrated, stretching out his senses in ways he had never tried before, both his ability to hear the songs of the daemons and his new wolf-mind.

"It glows." Shane's soft tone of wonder elicited a smile in response from Eddie.

"Beautiful, isn't it? Especially the first time you can see it as it really is."

In his mind's eye, Shane saw Mama Jean's protections as a shimmering spring green ring of light. He hadn't seen Eddie do anything witchy, but the area beneath their feet and the bedrock of the mountain behind the hotel had a deep blue inner light. Doc's magic looked like a spiderweb of golden strands. When Shane looked into the forest, he saw quicksilver flashes like light on water, and he knew in his bones they were the creatures that were not entirely normal. Creatures like him.

Then Shane looked at the hotel. A confluence of energies seethed and roiled beneath and around it like a private storm, a mingle of blue and green, shot through with an odd thread of gold. But a shadow cast across the hotel itself, dark despite the brilliance of the power surging around it, silent despite the cacophony of the anomaly's song.

"I see the hotel—and the stain. That's what Lucas needs to fix?" Shane wasn't sure his partner knew he had signed on for something so big.

"He need only remove the source of the poison," Eddie replied. "When that is done, the hotel and the anomaly will heal itself."

Pain spiked through Shane as if someone had rammed an ice pick through his skull. He cried out and folded in on himself as he collapsed. Eddie grabbed his arm, helping to break the fall.

"Shane!"

Eddie's voice sounded distant. Images came fast, like a TV montage almost too quick to follow. Elliot, back at the murder house, sacrificing the first victims, calling the demon, opening himself to possession. At the settlement in Hico, same ritual, new victims, only this time, the demons filled more bodies as Elliot burned the sigil-lock into their skin, trapping the demons inside and condemning the hosts to unending torment.

Strong hands gripped Shane's shoulders, shaking him. The voice calling to him wasn't Lucas's, and it took Shane time to remember the man in the strange, old-fashioned clothing. In his mind, Quentin snapped and paced, restrained by the thinnest, fraying control.

"I'm okay," he managed, as memories flooded back.

"A vision?" Eddie surmised.

"Yeah. Unpredictable—except for the part where it's always at a bad time." Shane let Eddie help him to his feet and guide him to sit on the back of the wagon while the earth witch dug out a chunk of dried meat and a full wineskin from a bag.

"Always eat after magic. Replenishes what the power takes out of you," Eddie advised. He waited as Shane followed his advice, even though Shane wasn't entirely sure he could keep the food down.

"I saw the cultists—the ones from Hico," Shane said as soon as he could manage his thoughts. "Elliot and Kenny weren't the only ones who were possessed. I think they all are now. The demons took their bodies and...hijacked their abilities. Demon witches," he warned, with all the urgency he could muster. "They've got magic—and demon strength. And Elliot branded them, so exorcising the spirits won't work. We're going to have to kill them all."

Eddie opened his mouth to respond, then shut it without saying anything and raised his head, as if scanning for danger.

Shane felt the mood shift between one breath and the next. In his mind, Quentin's hackles rose, and the wolf began to growl. Doc Swanson did not move, except to raise both hands from his sides to bend at the elbow, out in front of him. Mama Jean lifted her head as if she could smell trouble on the wind. With a crafty smile, she went back to walking and singing, tossing out more of the mixture from her bundle from time to time.

"Get ready," Eddie warned.

Shane forced himself to stand, taking a position beside Eddie. "Ready for what?"

The area where Mama Jean had sown her protective mixture flared with white light. Although the barrier absorbed the attack, Shane sensed the hostile magic skirting around the edges of their defenses, looking for a weak spot.

"They're here. The cultists," Eddie said.

Quentin surged against Shane's inner restraints, eager to get out and join the fight. Shane had to focus his will on keeping Quentin inside.

We don't know what we're up against, Shane argued with his wolf.

Enemy. Fight.

They're demons and bad witches. They could set our tail on fire.

Not if we bite first.

Down, boy. Maybe later. Can you sense the others like us, in the forest?

Yes. They are coming.

Here?

To fight. We go too?

Not yet.

No fun.

Shane was still adjusting to being able to communicate with his wolf side. Most of the time, Quentin rested quietly inside Shane's skin without causing trouble. Now, it took conscious thought to keep him restrained.

"How can I help?" Shane asked Eddie.

The wardings flashed as the attackers tried their energy against it, reminding Shane of electric bug zappers. Streaks of green light showed where the demons lashed out at the protections, but Mama Jean's perimeter held. She had stopped walking, but the song and chant never paused.

"Call to the creatures. You're one of them. Bring them in behind the troublemakers," Eddie suggested.

"I've never done anything like that. I've only had Quentin for about a month."

Eddie raised an eyebrow. "Interesting. You have surprising control for one so newly turned."

Shane wasn't willing to share that Rocky and Lucas helped to anchor him and guided his transition. He felt their absence keenly and glanced up at the hotel as if he could will Lucas to join them.

"I'll try. Quentin wants to make some noise. Maybe this will keep him happy."

Those other creatures—can you draw them closer? Box in the bad people?

Quentin gave a satisfied growl. *Let me out, and we howl.*

Shane did not want to shift, not here without Lucas and Rocky to help. But the longer the cultists assailed their protections, the more Shane could feel his precarious control begin to slip. He wasn't sure he trusted Quentin—trusted himself—without his partner to anchor him.

A song is just a different kind of howl, Shane thought, seizing on an idea. He took a deep breath to center himself, trying to ignore the impatient wolf that paced in the back of his mind. Instead, he remembered what he had seen earlier, the flashes of silver amid the forest. He focused on those quicksilver images and leaned into the songs of the mountain daemons.

Shane had never tried to influence the songs he heard. Now, he sent a rush of images, hoping that the elemental spirits behind those songs were as sentient as Rocky. He pictured the hotel under attack. And then he turned it over to Quentin and brought his own wolf song, letting it surge up from deep inside.

He felt...something. The darting silver flashes stilled, listening. A howl sounded in the distance, then another, and another, until the forest resounded with the howls, yips, and barks of creatures that were more than they appeared. And Shane felt the song shift as if the mountains howled along.

The quicksilver flashes became a tide, coming to hunt. *It's working.*

"They're coming," he managed. The cost of the effort hit him, and Shane fell to his hands and knees as his whole body trembled, fighting to keep his wolf inside his skin, struggling to remain human and in control.

The temperature dropped steadily, and Shane wondered if Doc had called in the ghostly cavalry. The bug-zapper bursts of light against the wardings had slowed. Beyond the protections, Shane heard growling, the snap of teeth, and human screams. He thought he caught a glimpse of gray spirits, beyond the curtain of magic that shielded the hotel's defenders.

"Let's see if I can shake things up a little," Eddie muttered, and Shane felt a surge of power flare as the witch gathered his abilities against the attackers. The ground under their feet trembled, and then beyond the green perimeter, rocks lifted into the air and pelted the attackers as Eddie lunged forward, hand outstretched, palm open. The cultists scattered, shouting as a hail of rocks hit hard enough to draw blood. And then, silence.

The wardings glowed solid, but the attacks abruptly stopped. The creatures were out there, Shane could feel their power bleeding through his weakening control, but they had backed off, keeping their distance.

Shane heard a rumble like thunder, despite a clear blue sky. Without warning, hot agony surged through Shane as if every bone had been crushed at once and his body were being turned inside out, skin flayed. He gasped and panted, barely holding onto consciousness let alone keeping Quentin under control. But his wolf had retreated, whining in fear and pain.

Mama Jean's song rose in defiance, and Shane recognized the old hymn about blood and spirit and redemption. He shivered as the legion of ghosts swept past them, flowing back to Doc and then beyond, seeking shelter in their graves.

What the fuck is going on? The wardings are supposed to keep out magic.

As quickly as the assault came, it vanished. It took all of Shane's strength to keep himself up on his hands and knees and not just collapse onto the roadway. Quentin had retreated to the back of his mind, but

Shane knew there was a moment there when his control hung by a thread.

That was close. Too close.

He froze. The Mountain Cove Hotel had vanished.

That's what we felt, the hotel ripping loose and floating away to wherever it goes. God, I thought it might kill me. If it was that bad out here, what was it like for Lucas, inside?

Shane turned to help Eddie, who had collapsed beside him. The witch was pale, and one cheek was scraped where he had gone down hard against the road, but he was breathing and had begun to move.

Fuck. What do I do now? How do I get Lucas back? When the hotel returns, will he still be alive?

Eddie's hand closed around Shane's arm, startling him. "Help me up," the witch said, sounding a little woozy. Shane pulled the other man to his feet and supported him with an arm around his shoulders as Eddie swayed.

"Day-um. Just as I sank my power down into the ground to shake things up for those cultists, the hotel went and pulled a runner." Eddie looked up at the huge bare spot on the mountain where the building had been not long ago.

Shane didn't feel too steady himself, not after the whiplash of energies that had zinged through his mind and body, or the tug of war with Quentin. Now that the hotel was gone, the energy felt more like it did when he and Lucas first rode by the site, jangly and fractured, although the charm from Mama Jean definitely helped.

Eddie nodded, taking a step to indicate that he could stand on his own. Shane let his arm drop but remained watchful.

"The cultists, they're gone?" Shane asked, looking to Mama Jean and Doc.

"They're gone alright, but it wasn't us who scared them off, not completely." Mama Jean stood with both fists on her hips, staring at the mountain as if she meant to give it a piece of her mind.

"This might have been a scout team, sent to see what new capabilities you and your partner brought. They didn't figure on the hotel throwing in a surprise of its own," Eddie added.

"What about Lucas?" Shane asked, fixing his attention on the empty space as if he could will the building back into place. "Is he..."

"We won't know until the hotel comes back," Mama Jean replied. "Best you can say is that he went in ready to fight a supernatural enemy, and that's more than others have."

"But the hotel had just reappeared. It hasn't been here for three days yet. It shouldn't have been ready to phase out. It changed its schedule." Shane felt like the hotel had somehow violated an unspoken contract.

"We never have known what set the frequency of the hotel's coming and going," Doc said. "Might be that the hotel does as it pleases."

"You talk about the hotel like it's sentient." Shane fought down fear and panic. *I knew I should have gone in with him. I was hardly useful here, and I almost couldn't control Quentin. At least if I'd stayed with Lucas, someone would have his back.*

"There's been a lot of debate over the years about that," Eddie responded. "No one knows for sure. Me, personally? I think it's become more than just a building. Can't tell you why or how—just a hunch."

"How do we know when it will come back?" Shane had no idea how to mount a rescue if the building wasn't there anymore.

"We don't," Mama Jean said.

"Lucas is in there!"

"And there's not a blessed thing we can do for him right now," Mama Jean replied. "We're just going to have to wait."

Shane looked around himself, then back at Mama Jean. "This area is still warded, right?" She nodded. "Then I'll wait here. Should be safe enough."

"The cultists will be back," Doc said.

"Then I'll shift and sleep in my fur. I'm not leaving without Lucas."

A silent conversation seemed to stretch between Doc and Eddie in a shared glance and Doc nodded. "How about I take the wagon to Ansted, bring back bedrolls and food and firewood, and we set up camp, right here, for the duration? Mama Jean can patch up the warding after Clara and I go out, and after we come back in."

Eddie nodded. "I agree. We shouldn't leave the hotel unguarded, and we have no way to know when it will return. We'll keep a vigil until it does."

"What about the road?" Shane asked belatedly. "We've cut off the town if anyone needed to get through."

Doc chuckled. "We've been out here for most of the day, and there hasn't been a soul yet that needed to go through. Don't think you need to worry about that." He headed toward where he had left Clara and the wagon. "I'll be right back. You just sit tight."

Eddie sat down cross-legged on the roadway, facing the forest. Shane sat next to him. Mama Jean went to fix where the edge of the warding got broken by Doc's departure, then walked the perimeter again, singing and chanting.

"Doc and Mama Jean are from around here," Shane finally said, breaking the silence. "So they can't compare how their magic was before being near the hotel and afterward. But you came from somewhere else. You said this place drew you here. Did it change your magic over time?"

Eddie stared off into the woods, although Shane couldn't see anything out there except trees at the moment. "It's a gradual thing," Eddie said, finally. "Like the way you adjust to shorter days and longer nights in the winter. Sometimes, you don't even know anything's changed until all of a sudden, something you never used to be able to do just opens up as a possibility."

Eddie shot him a side glance. "I imagine for you, with your bond with your wolf so new, the anomaly is making it hard to stay in control."

Shane hesitated, then nodded. "I came way too close to losing control of Quentin."

Eddie looked back toward the woods. "That's one way to look at it, I guess. What would have happened if he'd forced you to shift? Would he have attacked one of us? Eaten someone? Run off into the forest to chase the demon?"

Shane looked down at his hands. "I don't know. That's what scares me. But...I don't think so. He wanted to howl and rally the other crea-tures." He had never shifted without Lucas and Rocky to back him up, and they had promised that they wouldn't allow him to become a threat.

"He's still you," Eddie said. "Maybe a little more impetuous. If you don't lose your man-mind when you're in your fur, then it's really about gaining new senses from the wolf, not losing who you are as a human."

Shane sat with that for a moment. The hybrid shifter-werewolf that bit him had been the product of government experiments to create a super-soldier. It had been following orders when it attacked because Shane was firing on the rogue scientists and the dark witch that were the creature's masters. *He didn't attack me at random. He was still on task, carrying out his mission.*

That hadn't occurred to Shane before, and he almost gasped with the realization. *Those soldiers didn't already have the ability to hear the daemon song. They didn't have Lucas and Rocky to keep them on track. And even so, they followed orders.*

Maybe Quentin won't go feral, even if the mountain's magic breaks my control.

In his mind, Quentin raised his head from his paws, gave Shane as close to an eye-roll as a wolf could manage, and went back to sleep. Shane resolved to rest while he could. Perhaps he had gotten accustomed to the energy around him, or maybe Mama Jean's charm had even more power than Shane expected. But it seemed to him that the uncomfortable dissonance had eased, and the remaining jangle did not seem as painful.

A few hours later, Doc returned with the wagon, laden with supplies. Mama Jean fixed the wardings after he entered, and Doc drove Clara and the wagon into the center of the warded space.

"Got everything we might need to sit this out for a few days," Doc told them. "Food, water, whiskey, coffee, blankets, bedrolls, and a couple of tarps, in case the weather turns." He started unloading the firewood, as Shane and Eddie rose to help him.

The sunset painted the sky in rich shades of orange and pink. Shane and Doc got a fire started, while Eddie and Mama Jean sorted through the provisions to roast a simple supper of potatoes and sausages in the fire, with some dried fruit for dessert and moonshine to top it off.

Shane glanced over his shoulder at the empty mountainside, but the hotel had not reappeared. He shoved down his worry for Lucas, hoping that his partner would be safe and be able to get out of the hotel, and he wondered if Lucas's mission had been successful.

"You said that we didn't really run off the cultists in their full power," Shane said when they had eaten and were still seated around the fire, each with a cup of moonshine. "If what we did wasn't enough, how can we beat them when they return?"

"We don't know how it would have ended if the hotel's phase-out hadn't run them off," Eddie said after he'd taken a sip of his drink. "More of the creatures turned out this time to lend a hand because of you."

"More ghosts too," Doc added. "Your partner had a talk with them, I guess," he said with a look toward Shane. "That made an impression."

"If Lucas can heal the hotel, then its energy begins to heal too," Mama Jean said, picking a stray bit of meat from between her teeth. "We don't know what that will mean in a fight, but I wager it's something."

CHAPTER SIX

"I'm so sorry you didn't have the chance to experience dinner here with us," Fenton said from behind the Mountain Cove Hotel's front desk. "Come back any time."

Lucas hefted his gear bag and headed for the hotel's main doors, wondering how long he had been gone in "real" time. The hotel hadn't stayed its usual three days before vanishing—although barkeeper-Fenton assured Lucas that was more a fit of pique on the part of the establishment than a matter of habit.

Now, he wanted to get out while the getting was good and move the scholars in before the damn place picked up and left again.

He flung open the front door—and nearly collided with Shane, who approached the entrance with his gun up, ready for a fight.

"Whoa! Hold up. Don't shoot! It's me," Lucas said, putting his hands up in surrender and staying perfectly still.

"Lucas?"

"It's me—and Rocky too," Lucas replied. "Don't believe me? Ask Quentin."

Shane watched him warily, then his expression went blank for a moment, and Lucas knew his partner was checking with his ride-along wolf. Shane blinked, and smiled broadly, pulling Lucas into a backslapping hug.

"What the fuck, man? You scared me half to death. This was supposed to be the Overlook Hotel, not the TARDIS."

Lucas grinned at the geeky reference. "Yeah, well, let me tell you—it's even bigger on the inside." He hurried Shane down the steps, not willing to trust the hotel to stay put.

"You decide to take up camping?" Lucas asked, looking over the scene in front of the hotel.

"We had no idea when the hotel would come back, or how long it would stay when it did," Shane answered, nervously glancing over his shoulder as if the big building might be listening. "And we fought off some demon-witch scouts right after you went in, so we didn't want to leave the place unprotected for them to get in."

"Scouts?"

"I'll tell you all about it," Shane said, clapping him on the shoulder and looking ridiculously glad Lucas was back. "We have food. Come on and eat. That way you can tell everyone what the hell happened in there."

Lucas wondered whether the top-shelf scotch bartender-Fenton had served him was real, since he didn't feel any buzz.

It was real while you were inside the hotel, Rocky supplied. *If that helps.*

Lucas gratefully accepted the greetings of Doc, Eddie, and Mama Jean, as well as a plate of eggs and sausage and a cup of fire-brewed coffee. They held off questioning him while he ate. The sun had just risen above the treetops, and Lucas wondered how long he had been gone.

"About twenty-one hours," Shane answered his unspoken question. "You blinked out around nine o'clock yesterday morning, and got back right around six this morning."

Lucas just stared at him. "You've got to be kidding. That means I'd only been inside for an hour before the hotel vanished?"

His three companions nodded. "Shit. Time does move differently in there. With everything that happened, I was sure it had been at least three or four hours before the hotel vanished."

"You felt it?" Eddie asked, curiosity sparking in his eyes.

"It's not something I could have overlooked," Lucas replied and finished up the rest of his food. "I just didn't know what it was until the hotel wouldn't let me leave."

Once he had a refill of coffee, he recounted his story. The others listened without interrupting, fascinated at his tale.

"So you got rid of the ghosts and two demons and stopped off at the bar for cocktails?" Shane questioned.

"Fenton makes a really nice martini," Lucas said with a shrug. "You know how long it's been since I bellied up to a bar and ordered a drink?"

Shane's skepticism turned wistful. "Yeah—probably since that hotel in Cleveland on our last witness assignment."

Later, Lucas intended to have a long talk with Rocky about the "feel" of the hotel's energy. Just with his mostly human senses, Lucas thought the atmosphere inside felt lighter after Roza and the demons were gone.

"I sensed when you dispelled the ghosts," Doc said, after taking a long draught of his coffee. "Thank you for sending them on."

"It was past due. They had suffered far too much." Lucas figured his experiences would be new fodder for nightmares.

"The hotel packs a wallop if you're outside when it comes or goes," Shane said. "But the 'jangle' is a lot less since you got rid of the entity, and with Mama Jean's charms. And it's definitely better when the hotel is 'home' than when it's away."

"So Bowers has become a guardian," Eddie mused aloud. "That's interesting. Then again, perhaps he loved the hotel more than anything else in his life. So maybe it's not a stretch."

"He didn't want to leave," Lucas spoke up. "Neither did the other ghosts, like Irene. They can move on whenever they choose."

"Where did the demons come from?" Shane asked. "Did Roza summon them?"

"Spirits are around us all the time," Mama Jean replied. "Roza might have done a spell—she seems like the type. But if she was willing to kill those poor girls, then maybe those dark spirits were with her for a long time, and she just fed them enough to take shape on their own."

Lucas stretched and moved to refill his coffee. "When we've got the demon-witches handled, the hotel is ready for the scholars. Fenton confirmed that they were welcome to move in permanently—that they'd 'liven up' the place."

"Fenton sounds like an interesting guy," Shane observed. "How can a hotel have a soul, anyhow?"

Mama Jean gave him a thoughtful look. "You know, we talk about the spirit of the mountains, and the valleys, and the rivers. You can call them daemons, or genius loci, or elementals, but most folks call it the soul of the place." She leaned against the wagon, drinking her coffee and turned her gaze out over the horizon.

"I don't know if all those are the same energy. Don't know if it rightly matters. If you can have a daemon with you," she said, looking straight at Lucas, "and a wolf in you," she added with a glance at Shane, "then why can't the hotel have a spirit of its own? Especially in a place with such unusual energy."

That might be as close to an answer as we ever get, Lucas thought. *And if the hotel is happy, that's all that matters.*

Doc straightened and set down his coffee cup. "They're coming. The ghosts have spotted them."

"How many?" Eddie asked, as they all stood and quickly gathered up their things, leaving the fire burning within the circle of rocks that contained it.

"Two dozen, maybe a few more," Doc replied with a far-off look as he listened to his ghostly scouts.

"I've been thinking about the fight yesterday," Eddie said, as Doc retreated to the place he stood before, calling to the ghosts, and Mama Jean made a circuit to strengthen the wardings. "And I have some ideas to serve up something the demons won't expect—and maybe keep us from getting knocked on our asses again."

"How come everyone has a costume since the Events?" Lucas grumbled. "The IT Priests. Those knights we met up with. Now we've got gray-robed dark lord wannabes."

"You're just jealous," Shane teased, trying to hide his nervousness. "I mean, we used to wear our Fed suits."

"Yeah, and good riddance. Because if there's one thing I don't need after a fuckin' apocalypse, it's a suit coat and necktie."

Ominous figures stood outside Mama Jean's perimeter, massing silently in a creepy attempt at intimidation. Lucas felt like he'd been dropped into one of the video games he and Shane used to play to pass the time while they were babysitting witnesses. *Except if that were true, I'd have a way-cooler outfit.*

"You want to do it now, or later?" Lucas asked his partner.

"Might as well be done with it," Shane replied and headed off behind the wagon. A moment later, Lucas heard the heavy clink of a belt buckle against wood as Shane threw his clothing into the bed of the wagon, staying where he could shift to his wolf form with a bit of privacy.

Quentin padded out, looking rather pleased with himself, and let out a long, loud howl. He walked up to stand beside Lucas, who reached down to scratch him behind the ears. Quentin rumbled in warning, a familiar response to Lucas's intentional provocation.

Other howls answered. As long as the wolves and the other shifters remembered which side they were on, Lucas welcomed all the help they could get.

The loud crack and flare of light made Lucas jump as the cultists lashed out with the demons' power and their own hijacked magic against the protective wardings. Red fire streaked across the spring green glow of the protections, like bleeding gashes.

He could see the ghostly protectors Doc Swanson rallied. The spirits wove their way among the cultists, passing right through some of the robed attackers. Those that could manifest with more strength hurled rocks, clawed at arms and faces, or pushed and shoved, shrieking and keening in an ungodly caterwaul sure to raise gooseflesh and take a toll on concentration.

Quentin howled again, and Lucas imagined his partner as a wolf general, directing the shifters, calling them to battle. Lucas glimpsed dark blurs of motion, attacking behind the lines. That forced some of the cultists to turn their attention away from the warding, to avoid being mauled. Unfortunately, more robed attackers stepped up to take the place of those who tired or fell to the shifters and were-creatures.

"Remember—the real people are in torment, with demons locked into their flesh," Eddie called out. "Killing them ends their pain. It's a mercy."

Mama Jean walked slowly around the perimeter, chanting and singing. Lucas wondered how long she could sustain the wardings.

Not forever. I believe that is their goal—to exhaust her and make the walls fall.

How can we help?

My energy sustains your life. I can spare only small amounts without harming you. I can help you see more, if that would help. And you have your weapons. Be ready.

Lucas already had his shotgun locked and loaded. He added a couple of knives from his gear bag and stuck a Colt 1911 into the waistband at his back.

"Can I shoot through the warding, or will it ricochet?" Lucas called out to Mama Jean. He hated to interrupt her chant, but getting shot by his own bullet wasn't high on his list.

"The warding is one-way," Eddie answered for her. "We could step through it if we wanted—wouldn't recommend it. Fire at will." He grinned. "Give me a minute to do something, and that way you won't waste bullets. I've got a few tricks they haven't seen yet. This ought to get their attention."

Green and red flashes lit the forest like cursed neon lights. Eddie found the place where the cultists threw their energy hardest against the wardings, looking to make a weak spot. He raised one hand to focus his magic, limned in a blue glow as his power rose.

Eddie called out a word of power and clenched his fist. The ground beneath the witch-demon's feet trembled and then gave way, creating a sinkhole that sprawled for several yards and sent many of the attackers falling into the void. Those lucky enough to jump out of range now found themselves with a yawning chasm keeping them from getting close to an entire stretch of the warding.

"And I hope it goes all the way down to Hell!" Eddie shouted for good measure. Lucas figured that if the brands kept the demons from being exorcised, they might also trap the demons inside the corpses of those who fell into the pit.

While the attackers' attention was on the sinkhole, Lucas started shooting. He braced himself, ready to duck on the first shot, but when the rounds passed cleanly through the warding, Lucas grinned.

"Just like shooting womp rats," he muttered. When this was over, he and Shane would have to do another "re-watch" of their favorite movies —by taking turns recounting the storyline, complete with all the dialogue and details they could remember.

The wolves harried the attackers from behind the lines, crowding them toward the sinkhole or into the steady fusillade Lucas kept up. Some of the demons turned to lash out with their power against the shifters or ghosts, with little effect.

Eddie set his sights on another area farther down the perimeter, where the demon-witches continued their attack on the glowing green protective barrier. He repeated the spell, creating another sinkhole and sending more of the cultists tumbling into the opening.

Eddie staggered and would have fallen if Lucas hadn't grabbed him by the arm.

"Thanks," Eddie managed, looking exhausted by the effort. "Even with the vortex to draw on, that kind of magic kicks my ass. I don't want to undermine the road and make us fall in too, and I'm not keen on setting off a rockslide." He sank to the ground. "I'm going to need to catch my breath before I do something else."

Lucas stepped in front of him, protecting the witch, and resumed firing. He had no idea what Shane conveyed with his howls, but with the way the sounds varied, he knew some kind of communication was taking place. The wolves and shifters certainly had no trouble staying clear of Lucas's shots.

Lucas knew that the cultists couldn't all evade his bullets without making a full retreat. He varied his targets, never shooting twice into the same area, hoping to keep them on edge and kill as many as he could.

As the hours passed and the siege continued, Lucas knew they needed to find a way to up their game. Reinforcements had arrived for the cultists, but the defenders had no one else to call on since the scholars had neither the magic nor the weapons to provide backup.

Quentin's "voice" sounded strained, but he kept up the yips and barks that coordinated the wolves' assault. Mama Jean looked haggard and had stopped pacing to rest on the edge of the wagon, working up a mixture of some kind from her large basket and the cloth bundle inside. The wardings had held so far, but Lucas didn't know how long they could go on like this.

A flash of red, brighter than most, seared across the warding, and a figure surged forward, trying to cross the protective border. Quentin crossed the distance in a few leaps before Lucas had even focused on the threat.

"No teeth!" Lucas shouted, just as Quentin attacked since the last thing they needed was a newly turned demonic were-witch. Quentin's jaws snapped shut, and his claws slashed down through the seeker's shoulder. The demon-witch sent a streak of energy crackling toward Quentin. The wolf dodged, but the strike caught his hindquarters and sent him tumbling, with smoke rising from his fur.

Lucas shot the demon-witch in the head, then ran closer and swung his knife to decapitate the corpse. Mama Jean hurried to fix the breach in the warding, with Eddie right behind her, drawing from his magic to open a fissure beneath the feet of the cultists crowding forward to force their way through the protective barrier.

"Shane!" Lucas ran to check on his partner. Shane had remained in his wolf form, despite the injury. The smell of singed fur made Lucas choke. Quentin permitted Lucas to check on the injury to his hindquarters, which left a red, angry burn.

"You okay?" he asked, hoping that with tempers battle-short and a fresh wound, Quentin didn't forget his human side.

Quentin's yellow eyes met his, and the wolf gave a solemn nod. "Okay. We'll patch you up once we're done here. Maybe Doc knows a good vet," Lucas teased, relieved the damage hadn't been worse.

Quentin managed to curl his lip at Lucas's joke. The wolf tried to stand, but his injured leg gave way, and he collapsed, panting at the pain.

"Tell him to stay in his wolf form for a while," Eddie called. "His metabolism is higher from his shifter magic. He'll heal faster."

"You hear that?" Lucas asked. Again, the wolf nodded, then tossed its head toward the warding, as if to shoo Lucas back to work. Then Quentin let out a long howl that sounded like a battle cry.

Lucas crossed back to where Eddie and Mama Jean knelt over a pottery bowl filled with a mixture of fragrant plant leaves and powders, as well as other ingredients he didn't recognize.

"I'm just mustering some more power to help hold the gates," Mama Jean said, glancing up when Lucas joined them. "My mother, and her mother, and her mother's mother were all witches who are buried in these hills. We swear an oath to come if our descendants call on us with this ritual. They'll help carry me through."

Lucas could see that the effort of sustaining the wardings had gone hard on the older woman. A glance at Doc told him that rallying the ghosts was causing him strain.

"Can you and Doc team up? Would that help?" Lucas suggested. "Share the load and all?" He turned to Eddie. "Do you think there's any way what you can do with the vortex might be able to connect with my daemon and the anomaly to do more together than we can alone? I've still got a fair amount of ammunition, but it won't last forever."

"Maybe," Mamma Jean said. "Might be worth a try." She took her things over to where Doc stood, and Lucas turned his attention back to Eddie.

"Like she said, can't hurt to try," Eddie replied. "There are more of them coming. We can't do this all night, and we don't dare let them storm the hotel."

"How long until their reinforcements get here?"

Eddie's expression went blank while he checked with his magic. "Maybe half an hour. I'm sorry I can't just open up a pit big enough to swallow them all, but that would probably take us with it, along with half the mountain."

"That's okay," Lucas assured him. "But maybe we can gather enough help to take them all out at once."

"You know, if it doesn't work, we'll have probably run ourselves dry," Eddie warned.

"If it doesn't work, we'll have sped up the inevitable, but we're going to run out of juice sooner or later," Lucas said, sparing a worried glance toward where Quentin lay partly sheltered by the wagon, trying to rest and heal. Clara, the cart horse, had either been remarkably trained or—more likely—was under a calming spell to not react to the strange noises and lights all around them.

"Are you two scheming something?" Mama Jean asked when she returned from conferring with Doc. "'Cause me and Doc have our part ready—and maybe a bit more, if things turn out."

"We're ready," Lucas said, and Eddie stood, still looking worn but at least on his feet. Quentin wasn't asleep, and he gave a yip of encouragement.

"Whatever you see out there, don't let it bother you none," Mama Jean said. "There are even older protectors in these woods than the granny witches and the shifters—things as old as the daemons and the vortex. They don't like to be woke up, but I think we've got good reason to do it."

She walked back to Doc, and Lucas looked at Eddie. "You have any idea what she's talking about?"

Eddie's eyes narrowed as he thought. "They say there are some real strange creatures in these forests, much stranger than shifters. Most people think they're just folktales, but then again, they say that about magic too."

"Let's do this." Lucas took a deep breath and let it out again, refusing to think about how tired he felt. He reloaded all his guns and checked the supply of remaining bullets. It should be more than sufficient—unless the demons just didn't stop coming. Lucas had never tried to pair his connection to Rocky with a witch's magic. Hell, he'd only had Rocky onboard for a short time, and until now, they had tried hard to stay clear of both other hunters and people with magic, for fear of how his new co-pilot might be perceived. When Shane got turned, that gave the partners even more reasons to stay away from anyone who might be able to read the truth about them.

If they had known in advance about Eddie, Doc, and Mama Jean, Lucas wasn't entirely sure he and Shane would have come, fearing the worst. But they had found acceptance and support. Lucas wasn't naive enough to expect that from everyone, but it did mean he and Shane needed to have a discussion—assuming they lived through this fight.

"We need a physical connection. Put your hand on my shoulder," Eddie instructed. "And I'll do the same."

"Feels like senior prom, all over again," Lucas said, as he found himself at an awkward arm's length from Eddie.

Eddie chuckled. "Not much of a dancer? That's alright. We don't have to move. Just don't break the connection, got that?" Lucas nodded. "So go call up your daemon, and I'll tap into the vortex—and we'll see if we can wake up the neighbors."

Lucas shut his eyes and focused on his link with Rocky. *Can you do anything else with a little boost from Eddie? Because we're stretching pretty thin on our own.*

I can't leave your body without killing you. But perhaps I can see if any others of my kind can hear me.

What about the anomaly? I feel like we're on top of a huge source of energy and we aren't using it.

The anomaly is unstable. But now that the hotel is back, and healing...let me see.

Lucas felt vulnerable without a gun in his hand, as the cultists gathered along the warding and resumed their assault.

He caught motion out of the corner of his eye and saw that Shane had dragged himself behind the wagon to get dressed. He emerged in human form, limping toward the gear bag to get his gun and shotgun, noticeably dragging his wounded left leg. Shane caught his eye and gave him a nod and a cocky grin. Moments later, steady gunfire provided cover for Lucas and the others to make their move.

Lucas's hand tingled where he gripped Eddie's shoulder as if he brushed against a live wire. He felt Rocky's energy shift the way it did when he "spoke" to the other elemental spirits in the parks, mountains, and special places where the genius loci were strongest.

The tingle grew into an uncomfortable burn, as Eddie channeled the vortex's vast energy. Lucas felt Rocky draw back from the other daemons and wrap his essence around the bright blue flow of Eddie's earth magic. That core of energy rose through Lucas's body from the soles of his feet, burning like fire in his veins, filling him with a rush of power and a flood of images from eons of awareness.

Lucas felt the energy build until pain filled him, and his body seemed too small to contain what they had summoned. The staccato beat of gunfire melded with his own scream and Rocky's stern voice as the power tore through him and then released, sending a shudder through the ground that made him stagger and that sent trees swaying and rocks tumbling.

He opened his eyes and looked past the green light of the warding. Fewer of the robed attackers remained, and those who did battled ghosts, wolves, and creatures the likes of which Lucas had never seen.

One of the beings resembled horror movie hellhounds—a fierce black dog-like monster the size of a pony, with red eyes and wicked fangs. In the distance, a faceless white creature with the shape of a large man lumbered toward the cultists, who scurried to get out of his way.

Two more creatures came into view, both nearly the height of a man but moving all wrong. One had a muscular profile, with hunched shoulders and a larger than normal head. It waded in among the attackers, swinging its huge fists, smashing them out of his way. The other looked like a sci-fi movie alien, with a robed body and a pointed cowl or helmet where its head should have been, glowing a lava-red color from within.

Lucas's head throbbed, and fever burned through his body. He heard Rocky shouting in his mind as his knees buckled, and then he fell to the ground, landing hard on his ass, the connection with Eddie broken. He barely helped to break Eddie's fall as the man collapsed next to him, unconscious.

Shane kept firing. *How many of them are there?* Lucas wondered, wincing as the noise assaulted his aching head.

Doc and Mama Jean were leaning on each other, and while they might have been sharing their energy and magic, it looked to Lucas like they were holding each other up.

Beyond the shimmering wardings, some of the demon-witches lobbed balls of energy that impacted and spread like a wound over the green protective curtain of light, while others attacked the monstrous protectors Doc and Mama Jean had raised.

Eddie groaned, and Lucas checked on him, finding the witch awake and trying to sit up. Lucas steadied him and went to get them both water from the provisions in the wagon.

"This isn't looking too good for our side."

Lucas shifted, and that brought the hotel directly into view. "I should have thought of it before," he muttered to himself. He let go of Eddie and lingered just long enough to make sure the other man could stay upright.

"Stay here." With that, Lucas sprinted for the steps to the hotel and sincerely hoped he had not read Fenton wrong.

"Welcome back to the Mountain Cove Hotel. Lovely to see you again," Fenton greeted him from behind the front desk.

"There are dozens of crazy demons out there who want to take over the hotel and use its power," Lucas explained breathlessly. "We've been fighting them all day, but we're losing. There are too many of them. We've done everything we can do—including call up the Old Protectors —but it's not enough. If those demon-witches get inside, it'll make Roza and her *ala* look like a Sunday picnic by comparison—and they'll tap into the vortex and the anomaly, which will make them damn near unstoppable."

Lucas hoped he had made his case. Fenton needed to understand the risks. Outside, Shane's sustained gunfire sounded like a rapid heartbeat.

"Another threat to the hotel, you say?" Lucas spun to see Benjamin Bowers's ghost descending the broad staircase. "That's unacceptable. We just got rid of that Russian fraud and her unsavory companions."

"If you and the hotel can do something—anything—to defend your-selves, now is the time," Lucas begged. "Because my friends and I are half-dead, and we can't go on much longer. We need your help."

Bowers went to the front window, looking out over the battle-grounds, and down into the valley. Lucas remembered that the man had been a powerful psychic, back in his day, and that he had loved the hotel more than his own life.

"I have not seen the Old Protectors go to war in a long, long time," Bowers mused. "The snarly yow and the White Creature do not rouse from their slumber easily." He turned toward them. "You know what we need to do," Bowers told Fenton, who nodded soberly.

"Go back to your people," Fenton said, looking at Lucas. "We appre-ciate all that you have done to safeguard the hotel. Gather your friends and have them amplify the song of the mountain in their own way, and together, we will defend her."

Lucas had no idea what Fenton was talking about, but he nodded. "I'll tell them. Better do what you're going to do soon. Good luck."

With that, he headed back outside, running as fast as his exhausted body would go to rally the others. Lucas quickly relayed what Fenton and Bowers said and saw a mix of resignation and hope in his compan-ions' faces. They all knew that if this didn't work, they would die, the hotel would be overrun, and the scholars and their archive would be doomed.

"What did he mean—amplify the song as we know how?" Shane asked, finally falling back from his non-stop fusillade, although he kept his gun loaded and his eyes on the cultists who remained at a careful distance beyond the warding. Lucas could see that the green glow of the protection had faded badly. They were nearly out of time.

"Our magics," Eddie said. "Tune into them, in our own ways. Like we've been doing, only with the hotel joining in too. Throwing everything we've got at the cultists, all together."

"It could burn us up," Mama Jean noted. "You need to know that."

Doc Swanson smiled sadly. "Doesn't really matter if those demon-witches get through, we're burned up anyhow."

"I'm in." Shane met Lucas's gaze, and Lucas swore he saw a flash of wolf yellow in his blue eyes. He knew from the set of Shane's jaw that his partner had made up his mind.

"Hell, yes," Eddie said, looking exhausted but resolute.

When I told you that you might become immortal, I expected you to still have a body, Rocky warned. *I cannot promise what I can do if you burn up.*

Understood.

They turned back to Mama Jean. She flashed a broad, snaggle-toothed grin. "What are we waiting for? Let's throw down and be done with this nonsense."

Lucas looked back at the hotel. *We're ready,* he thought, wondering if Fenton or Bowers could read his mind.

He and the others formed a circle, joining hands. Lucas focused on the warmth of the skin of the two people on either side of him, on the regular rhythm of his breath—in and out—and on Rocky, a silent, powerful presence.

The irony of surviving the Events only to be killed in a battle between a cursed hotel and a bunch of demon-witches didn't escape him. Surely they hadn't come through so much for it just to end here.

He snuck a glance at Shane, whose expressions he knew as well as he did his own. Lucas could read the tension in his partner's shoulders, in his response-ready stance, and the squint of his eyes. The others looked equally stressed and resolute.

Now, a voice said in his mind, a voice that wasn't Rocky. Lucas braced himself, surrendering to fate.

A blast wave of power rushed through Lucas like he was trying to contain the whole of the ocean within himself. The storm surge of energy blew his abilities wide open, full strength. He saw the restless ghosts of the mountain, and he heard the songs of the genius loci from all the neighboring hills and valleys. This was the anomaly and the vortex mingled, and it felt like mainlining the raw, primordial forces of creation.

Lucas tightened his hold on the hands on either side of him, not daring to open his eyes. The shred of consciousness he retained that was still Lucas knew that the currents flowing through him were not meant for fragile human comprehension.

He heard the crash of falling trees and the roar of rockslides, wrapped in the howl of the wind as if the Titans themselves had awakened. As quickly as the blast began, it ended. Lucas swayed on his feet like he had been leaning into a strong wind that suddenly vanished. Their joined hands remained clasped white-knuckle tight, holding them up.

I'm alive. At least, I think I am. Heartbeat. Breathing. Holy shit—I survived!

We're still intact. Let's not do that again, Rocky said.

Lucas opened his eyes, almost afraid to look. The green warding was gone, and none of the gray-robed cultists were anywhere to be seen.

"Look." Shane pointed, and his voice held a combination of awe and fear.

All of the trees in a semi-circle moving out from the cleft of the mountain lay flattened, pointing away, as if Lucas and his friends were ground zero. *Like that meteor strike in Russia, a long time ago.*

He felt a tug and realized he still had his companions' hands trapped in his own vice grip and loosened his hold with a chagrined smile of apology. They all looked as shell-shocked as Lucas felt.

A glance over his shoulder revealed Fenton and Bowers standing on the hotel's wide porch. Fenton met his gaze, smiled and nodded, and then he and the ghost went back inside. Lucas wondered how long the hotel would hang around this time. Did it need to retreat somewhere to recharge? Or was its true home here in the cleft of the mountain with the anomaly and the vortex?

"Well, that's sorted," Mama Jean observed, dusting off her hands. "Don't think we'll see any more trouble, not for a while."

Doc Swanson nodded. "I suspect that you're right."

Eddie stared out at the flattened trees. Lucas wondered how much the land witch's experience had differed from his own since Lucas was linked to the daemon of the mountain, while Eddie's connection was to the forces of the earth beneath.

"It's a lot to take in, all at once," Eddie said. "Going to need to sit with it for a bit, I think."

Lucas agreed whole-heartedly. The others began to make their way back to the wagon, where Clara the cart horse stood, patiently waiting. Lucas wondered what spell Mama Jean had put on her, because she seemed to be taking this whole thing far better than the rest of them.

"You okay?" Shane asked, giving Lucas an appraising look.

Lucas managed a shrug. "We're still here, alive, in one piece, not burned to a crisp or stark-raving mad. I'll take it as a win."

Shane gave an unsteady laugh. "Yeah. Just another day on the job, staring down the maw of the universe."

"Getting to be the new normal," Lucas said, slapping him on the shoulder, a gesture that said everything they didn't need words to express. *We're alive. I'm glad you made it. Scared the fuck out of me. Damn, that was one hell of a ride.*

When they reached the library, the scholars rushed out to meet them, all of them asking questions at once. Lucas and the others did their best to answer, but all they could really manage was to assure the academics that the threat had been eliminated, the hotel was safe, and that Fenton confirmed that they were welcome to finish moving in.

"If you need me, you know where to find me," Doc said, leaving Clara and the wagon for the scholars to use and heading home on foot after bidding them goodbye with a wave.

"I'll be in my garden," Mama Jean added. "You take care moving into that hotel, you hear me? This rescuing stuff is hard on my joints." With that, she reclaimed her horse from the stable and rode off.

"You held up your end of things," Eddie told Lucas and Shane, shaking their hands. "Not bad for being the new kids," he added with a grin. "I imagine I'm going to have hell to pay to untangle some of the ley line energy back at the Mysterium, but it's a small price for setting things right. Stop by if you're in the area again. Preferably when you don't need to save the world." He headed for the stable to get his mount.

"We have a pot of rabbit stew ready for dinner, with biscuits and baked apples," Royston said. Lucas could see the scholarly curiosity that burned within the other man's eyes, but thankfully Royston held off with his questions for now. "And I imagine you'll need some moonshine to take the edge off. You both look like you've gone six rounds with a drunk grizzly bear."

Lucas and Shane looked at each other in the same instant, synchronicity born out of years on the road together, and then both of them broke out in unstoppable laughter.

"Sometimes you eat the bear," Lucas managed, laughing so hard it hurt to breathe as all the tension of the last several days finally reached a breaking point.

"And sometimes the bear eats you," Shane finished, tears coming to his eyes as he shook with the laughter that purged away the hardship, exhaustion, and terror.

Royston just stared, then finally gave a what-the-hell smile. "Come on in. I guess you've got quite a tale to tell—after you get fed and cleaned up. And if you're still not up to snuff then, the moonshine'll put you right."

CHAPTER SEVEN

"WHAT THE HELL IS A SNARLY YOW?" Shane asked as they helped the scholars load the last of their boxes into the wagon. A few days had passed since the battle, which gave Lucas and Shane a chance to heal and rest before heading back on the road.

"It's a big black dog—somewhere between a hellhound and a grim," Royston replied. "Those Old Protectors you say Mama Jean and Doc conjured up; they're the legends people tell their children at night to keep them out of the woods. That White Creature is one of them—big, burly shape but covered with smooth white skin and no features. The other two would have been the Grafton Monster and the Flatwoods Creature. They're West Virginia's versions of Bigfoot."

"They were real," Shane protested. "At least, real enough to do damage."

Royston shrugged. "Don't get my academic friends started on a debate about the nature of reality," he warned with a smile. "It could be that Mama Jean and Doc created a mass illusion. Or maybe they really did wake up ancient spirits to rise and protect the land. There are plenty of legends to that effect. Then again, maybe they were real because you believed in them—sort of like a tulpa."

"I don't think I have to tour Eddie's Mysterium in order to see the laws of the universe turned inside-out," Lucas muttered. "If someone told me the story we just told you and I hadn't seen it for myself, I'd have said they were tripping balls."

"I'm quite looking forward to getting to know more about this Fenton character—in any and all of his roles," Royston said. "But just in case he decides not to share his bar with us, we're taking an ample stash of moonshine and our still." He grinned. "It pays to be prepared."

Lucas and Shane offered to help the scholars unload at the hotel, but Royston assured them they could handle it, and Shane noticed that Lucas didn't insist.

"Thank you," Royston said, shaking their hands. They had already said goodbye to the other scholars, whom they had gotten to know from shared meals and help with research. Shane wished them well but felt equally relieved that he was not going with them—and resolved not to go anywhere near the Mountain Cove Hotel, ever again.

Shane and Lucas saddled up and headed onto the road. "Where to?" Shane asked. The scholars had replenished their supplies and packed enough trail rations for them to last for a week or more, their way of thanking them for saving the hotel. That spared Shane and Lucas from foraging for what they needed, at least for a while.

Lucas shrugged. "Probably ought to end up back in Gettysburg before too long to check in and see if anyone's requested us. But after everything here, I wouldn't object to finding somewhere quiet—without vortices or elemental spirits or disappearing hotels—and taking a little time off. Read a few books. Go fishing. Play some Frisbee with the wolf. That sort of thing."

Shane grinned. "I don't think that's too much to ask. Royston gave us a bunch of new novels I'm looking forward to reading, and I'm betting we can find a nice cabin to squat in on a lake somewhere. Quentin wants to do a little deer hunting, but he says he'll share."

"And Royston did send us on our way with a nice supply of moonshine," Lucas added. "I think we're due for some R&R. Let someone else save the world for a week. We'll be back on the job soon enough."

TO BE CONTINUED...

SHUTDOWN CREW

SHUTDOWN CREW
A WASTELAND MARSHALS NOVELLA
GAIL Z. MARTIN
LARRY N. MARTIN
U.S.
MARSHAL

CHAPTER ONE

"Best two out of three?" Lucas Maddox asked when Shane Collins sank the 8-ball after running the pool table.

"Sure. Rack 'em up," Shane replied.

Only the clack of pool balls and the soft snuffling of their horses broke the stillness in the empty roadside bar.

"I saw what you did." Lucas fished the balls out of the pockets and arranged them for the next game. Four balls were missing, only one cue was worth using, and the table had warped from nearly four years without heat or air conditioning, but this was still going to be the best "night on the town" he and Shane had for a long time.

"What *I* did?" Shane countered in mock objection. "And what was that?"

"You shot from the right side of the table." Lucas leaned over to eyeball the felt-covered surface, which was no longer level. "It's flatter."

"I'm amazed the table's in as good condition as it is, considering." Shane walked over to the bar and poured himself another finger of whiskey.

"Just our lucky day, I guess," Lucas replied. "About time. We've been overdue."

"Overdue" was probably the understatement of the year.

"It's been a long while since we found a place in this good shape," Shane said. Lucas joined him at the bar and refreshed his drink.

"The owners boarded it up tight, and from the outside, it doesn't look like much." Lucas looked out over the empty bar. "And the name—Adler's Filling Station—doesn't scream 'bar.' Plus, we're in the middle of nowhere. Doubt there's been a lot of traffic through these parts since the Events."

"Can't imagine there would be."

Four years ago, the world ended. Or at least, close enough that nothing would ever be the same again. Terrorists turned the nuclear countries' own warheads against them in a simultaneous strike, taking out the capitals and governments with only a few minutes' warning. That touched off earthquakes, tsunamis, and volcanic eruptions. Chunks of the power grid failed. Financial markets and the supply chain collapsed.

Major cities were either destroyed in the fires that followed or swamped by storm surges. Ash in the atmosphere altered the weather, bringing violent storms. Supplies grew scarce, impossible to replenish. Hunger and disease killed many who had avoided the blasts and radiation. People fled, eventually coming together in small fortified enclaves well inland from the coast.

Anarchy and chaos did more damage than the bombs, but the military and law enforcement units that survived the initial strikes and the aftermath were stretched too thin to maintain the peace. Now what remained were mostly local sheriffs, park rangers, and for the tri-state, the last two US Marshals—Shane and Lucas.

"Almost like old times," Shane said wistfully.

"Yeah. Almost."

Lucas rested his back against the bar, elbows behind him, and looked out over their home for the night. Adler's hadn't been a fancy place; it looked as hard used as the people who lived in this corner of West Virginia. The candles and kerosene lantern Shane and Lucas had brought with them did the interior a kindness with dim light that hid the dirt and wear. An old-fashioned jukebox sat against the wall, forever silenced. Framed photos showed off prize bucks or big fish, bowling tournament winners, and "grip and grin" pictures with local politicians.

Anything close to larger cities had been looted by desperate survivors long ago. After those first, awful months, Shane and Lucas learned to stick to the back roads, where it was easier to find a store, warehouse, or abandoned home that hadn't been picked clean.

"The horses seem to like it here." Shane nodded toward his roan gelding, Red, and Lucas's black stallion, Shadow. They had fed and watered the horses before bringing them inside, safe from danger, and filled a beer cooler for them with water from a hand pump out back.

"It's got four walls and a roof that doesn't leak—what's not to like?" Lucas replied, savoring his drink. The cement block walls and small barred windows beneath plywood provided one level of protection against wild animals and roving gangs. The salt lines across the openings coupled with protective sigils chalked onto walls and doors repelled an entirely different sort of predator.

They set their drinks aside and headed back to the pool table for the third round, joking and trash talking like the old days.

"Good game,' Shane said when Lucas won the round. "And you didn't even cheat."

"Pretty sure the slant in the table cheated for me." Lucas hung the cue back on the rack.

Shane walked over to the wall and pulled darts from the dartboard, still in place from where they'd been thrown on the last night before everything changed. "It's this or karaoke," he joked.

"We wouldn't want to scare the horses."

"Pretty sure they've heard the worst we can do."

Going anywhere now took far longer on horseback, so to pass the time, Shane and Lucas recounted favorite books, TV shows, and movies, or sang songs as best they could remember. Long evenings passed with dice, worn decks of cards, or the few favorite novels and role-playing games they managed to carry with them.

The Before was never coming back, but Shane and Lucas did their best to honor what they could hold onto with memories.

"I could really go for some Buffalo wings and an order of nachos," Lucas remarked.

"Yeah, me too," Shane agreed. "Beer nuts. Pizza. Fried pickles."

Talking about food from the old days was as close as they were likely to get to having it again.

Lucas threw the darts in rapid succession. One hit the bullseye, and the other two sank into the next ring.

"Nice throwing." Shane retrieved the darts and sent them flying with a few flicks of his wrist, scoring two bullseyes.

"Not too shabby yourself," Lucas replied.

"I figure we were lucky that the owner cleaned out the perishables before leaving." Lucas left the darts in place and headed back to the bar. "Place wouldn't be nearly as nice to stay in if they'd been rotting this whole time."

"He didn't take the alcohol," Shane pointed out, pouring them another drink. Having the safety to relax, even a little, was a rare luxury.

"Bottles are heavy and bulky," Lucas observed. "His loss, our gain." He avoided looking at the personal photos near the register or anything else that made the owners and customers real in his mind.

"We can't carry all of it—even if we had a pack mule," Shane observed.

"Don't need to," Lucas said with a shrug. "Take a few bottles, board everything up like it was, and stop through the next time we come this way. Our own personal stash."

"Sounds good to me. One of the perks of the job." Shane's chuckle had a bitter edge.

They sipped their whiskey in comfortable silence, each looking out over the empty bar alone with their thoughts and memories. After all these years, Lucas didn't need to talk to have a good idea what was going on inside Shane's head.

They'd grown up together, then gone into the Army, and after a couple of tours of duty in various locations, left the military and joined the US Marshals. Now they were the only family either of them had left.

The whiskey loosened muscles tight from riding and warmed Lucas in a way that was far too elusive nowadays. Even with precautions, they didn't dare drink too much—the dangers they faced Before paled in comparison to the threats that had crawled from the shadows after the Events.

"I'll take the first watch." Lucas knocked back the rest of his drink. "You need your beauty sleep," he added with a smirk.

Shane had a blond, blue-eyed All-American cowboy "aw shucks" appearance that worked great for questioning witnesses. Lucas's dark hair and eyes gave him a bad boy vibe that made it easy to play "bad cop." They were both the same height—nearly six-foot-two—but whether they were an exact match had been a matter of debate between them since they hit their last growth spurt.

"Fuck you," Shane replied without heat. "See if Rocky plays as good pool as I do."

Shane made a last check on the horses before grabbing his bedroll and a jacket for a pillow and stretching out on the pool table.

Lucas walked the perimeter to assure himself that the locks were set and the salt line remained unbroken, then headed to the small kitchen to look for any remaining staples that might still be useful. He emerged triumphant a short while later with a sealed pack of coffee beans, a new bar of soap, and two cans of tuna, all of which had been overlooked in the back of a cupboard.

You are happy tonight. The ancient, immortal elemental spirit that rode shotgun inside Lucas's mind made itself known for the first time that evening.

Hiya, Rocky. You're late to the party, Lucas replied silently.

Something about this place affects your mood. You are pleased and sad at the same time. Mostly pleased.

When a feral robot electrocuted Lucas during a job gone wrong, he would have died if Shane's desperate plea for help had not brought the help of a curious genius loci. Nicknamed "Rocky" for the nearby state park, the spirit agreed to coexist with Lucas and keep him alive with its primal energy. Lucas and Shane had grown used to the curious entity.

It's nice to get a taste of how things used to be. But that makes it sadder to realize those times are gone.

My mountain changed very little over a long time, Rocky replied.

Some changes can be good. The Events weren't. Lucas cleared his throat, ready to move on to a new subject. *Can you sense anything going on outside we should be worried about?*

Rocky was silent for several minutes. Lucas still didn't understand how his copilot functioned, although he was grateful to be alive and thankful for the abilities Rocky brought to their dangerous job.

No one expected two US Marshals to rid their territory of evil. Instead, they got called in on problems too big and potentially catastrophic for what remained of local law enforcement to handle. Increasingly, those cases involved the supernatural, since after the Events, ancient beings re-emerged from the shadows to lay claim to what remained.

I thought I sensed something earlier, but if so, it has gone, Rocky said.

Good to know. Lucas had told himself that he wouldn't look at the personal items behind the bar, but without a way to brew the coffee he had found, moving around seemed to be the best way to keep from drifting off.

He winced at the family pictures—kids, parents, and dogs, snapshots of vacations and summer days. Given how deserted the surrounding area had been when he and Shane rode in, those people were long gone. One faded black and white photo of an old clapboard church caught his attention.

Someone had taped a caption beneath the picture, "How far we've fallen!" Lucas realized that the concrete foundation and cellar beneath the church looked exactly like what had been repurposed as the bar.

What happened? Fire? Tornado? Something destroyed the wooden structure, and the locals made good use of the remaining basement. Lucas grinned.

Wait until I tell Shane we're probably on consecrated ground. And a good bartender hears his share of confessions. No wonder we both felt safer than usual here.

Lucas turned back toward the main area and froze. The air suddenly turned colder, and he saw the gray figure of a man perched on one of the barstools, nursing a drink. He looked like he was probably a regular, and Lucas wondered why the spirit lingered here of all places.

Did he get mugged in the parking lot? Have a heart attack in the men's room? Something about the expression on the man's face suggested another alternative. *Maybe he belonged here, with his people.*

The spirit didn't acknowledge him, and Lucas saw no cause for alarm. He felt an odd kinship with the ghost. Given the constant travel that went with the responsibilities of a US Marshal, life hadn't left time for a family, and the ever-present danger precluded forming friendships. Without Shane as a best friend and partner, Lucas didn't have to use much imagination to see himself in the ghost's place.

Shane's sudden cry of alarm had Lucas sprinting across the room to where the other man jolted upright, eyes wide. For a few seconds, Shane looked panicked and disoriented, then seemed to recognize his surroundings.

"Dream or vision?" Lucas fetched a canteen from his pack and handed it to Shane, who took a long gulp to steady himself.

"Vision, pretty sure of it." Shane took a long gulp from the canteen before giving it back with a shaking hand. "I saw two men in the woods dressed like hunters. No one I recognized. Something big and pale chased them—I couldn't get a good look through the trees at night. From the screaming, I think it caught them."

"Did you see anything to identify where it happened?" Lucas pressed.

Shane closed his eyes, and Lucas guessed he was reviewing what he had seen. "Nothing unusual about the landscape. But the mountain's song sounded like a woman wailing."

Shane's ability to hear the song of genius loci was a talent that had grown stronger since the Events, as had Lucas's talent for seeing ghosts. It had taken Shane a while to figure out what he was hearing and how to use his ability to navigate toward safe places, and away from areas where the elemental spirit was hostile or twisted. That gift had enabled Shane to reach out to Rocky and save Lucas's life, so while Lucas didn't completely understand how it worked, he was grateful for the advantage.

"Rocky? Does that sound familiar to you?" Usually Lucas carried on a silent conversation with the elemental, but speaking aloud also worked, and kept Shane included in the conversation.

I have not encountered that song. But now I will listen for it.

"He's got bupkis," Lucas relayed. "But now that you two know what to watch out for, maybe it'll mean something when we find it."

Shane slid off the pool table and stretched. "I'm not going to fall back to sleep any time soon. How about letting me take watch for a while?" He walked over to the bar and poured another finger of whiskey into his glass.

"It's a pity that stuff doesn't work on either of us like it used to." Lucas crawled up on the pool table and settled in. "Sometimes I wish it would."

Rocky's energy kept Lucas alive since his injuries had been too severe to fully heal. The elemental also altered his body in ways they were still discovering, including making it nearly impossible to get drunk. Shane's heightened metabolism after surviving a shifter attack gave him an equally high tolerance.

Figures now that booze is hard to get, neither of us are cheap drunks, Lucas thought as he drifted into a fitful sleep.

CHAPTER TWO

"Don't run off, Quentin, or I'll get you a leash!" Lucas called after the large wolf as it loped ahead on the road.

The cool fall breeze ruffled his fur, and the smell of nature—so muted to human senses—made the wolf's sensitive nose twitch. Quentin, Shane's name for his wolf side, happily ignored Lucas's shout but was careful to remain in view.

It had only been a few months since a fight that went sideways changed Shane's existence permanently. Without a cure for a genetically-engineered shifter's bite, he had been ready to die. Lucas had argued for another option—hunting together using Quentin's enhanced senses. Rocky had promised to help Shane keep control of his new wolfiness, tapping into Shane's innate ability to sense the song of the elemental spirits called daemon or genius loci.

So far, the shift in perspective had worked out better than anyone had dared hope.

Shane still had a lot to learn about his new wolf nature. The hybrid shifter that bit him was a weaponized creature created by a secret government project. Since the hybrids had been designed as ultra-soldiers, they retained their human consciousness even in wolf form, although they gained the senses of an apex predator, which always lurked at the back of his mind.

Shane had nicknamed his wolf form "Quentin." When he shifted, he could run faster, move silently, and fight with tooth and claw. Sight, hearing, and smell were enhanced beyond human capabilities. Shane had already discovered the benefit in being able to hunt for their dinner without using scarce ammunition.

He could shift at will, without the influence of the moon cycle, and he gained strength and endurance. He was still learning the extent of the changes, but the support and acceptance from Lucas and Rocky made a life-or-death difference.

He cocked his head, listening for the strange song he had heard in his vision. Elemental spirits could be attached to any natural feature. Most were passive and not particularly strong. Rocky had been an exception, as had a few other daemon they had found.

After a while, Quentin padded back to Lucas and the horses. Lucas stopped and tossed a bundle with Shane's clothing to the wolf, who caught it in his teeth and walked into the bushes. Shane emerged a few minutes later in human form.

"Anything?" Lucas asked as Shane swung into his saddle.

"Lots of rabbits—we won't go hungry."

"Good to know. Pick up any weeping-woman elementals?"

"Not yet. We've still got a while to ride before we get to the Green-brier," Shane pointed out.

"Rocky thought something was following us for a while, but it's gone now. So keep your eyes open," Lucas said. "How's Quentin holding up? I'm sure we'll find more Frisbees somewhere."

Shane rolled his eyes. "He's doing fine. And a ball will do if you can't find a Frisbee."

He knew what Lucas was really asking—whether Shane was finding it easier to maintain the balance between his human self and the wolf-soldier instincts that tried to come to the fore during times of stress or danger.

His shifted form wasn't a separate entity since he kept his memories, human reasoning, and sense of self. At the same time, the changes affected his body in a fundamental way, and forced an adjustment in his thinking to reconcile the new abilities and carefully control the primal urge to settle matters with force. Naming his wolf-side had started as a joke, but it helped Shane wrap his mind around the huge and permanent alteration that had been made to his mind and body without his permission.

I remember hearing that some rock stars with stage fright created and named a persona version of themselves they could "become" when they went on stage. Quentin is a "side" of me, but still me.

Silly as it might seem, burning off extra energy by hunting their dinner or loping alongside the horses—or chasing a Frisbee—helped Shane stay in charge of his new wolfiness. And since diversions were scarce, finding something new was a plus.

Lucas looked out over the empty road and then into the distance across the West Virginia mountains. "I always wanted to go to the Greenbrier—Before. I'd read so much about the not-so-secret bunker from the Cold War underneath such a fancy resort. I guess better late than never, right?"

Shane heard the wistfulness in his partner's voice. "I suspect the food was probably better then. If we had a way to not let the meat go to waste, Quentin could bring down a deer to have venison steaks. Cows are harder to come by."

"Do you think there'll be any requests for us?" Lucas kept his gaze on the mountains, a sure tell that he felt conflicted about taking on a new assignment.

"Probably. Shit isn't going to get any less fucked up as time goes on. And we're the only ones on call."

Two Marshals couldn't be everywhere. Requests for their help reached the larger forts and enclaves through the spotty internet and shortwave radio connections that had survived. The decision about which—if any—of the requests to accept was entirely up to Shane and Lucas.

"It's NOT TOO late to go looking for a nice cabin," Lucas said. "Something on a lake with fish in it, and woods all around. Let someone else handle the aftermath of the apocalypse."

"You'd get bored," Shane replied, used to the familiar debate.

"Not if the fish were biting."

"We took time off before the gig with the creepy hotel in Ansted,"

Shane reminded him. "That was our getting-to-know-the-new-wolf vacation."

"They say it's a good idea to have downtime when you get a new pet."

"Quentin's not a pet." Shane sighed and shook his head, used to Lucas's humor.

Banter had always been a way he and Lucas talked around difficult issues, going all the way back to being kids together. When necessary, they were both capable of addressing problems directly, but teasing served as a check-in and response without becoming too serious. Shane knew that Lucas was still adjusting to having a partner who could turn himself into a wolf, and that it would take a while to get used to, despite Lucas's whole-hearted support.

"There isn't a guide to our kind of weird," Lucas said. "I think we get to make up the rules on the fly. And besides, we take downtime after most jobs."

"To heal. Not exactly a vacation," Shane pointed out.

"It's more time off than we used to get, unless one of us was in the hospital."

"Yeah, well. We *had* hospitals back then. Push too hard, too fast now, and there's nobody to pick up the pieces," Shane answered.

"On the other hand, we don't break as easily. We heal faster. Were-wolves—or hybrids, or whatever—live longer than regular people, and with Rocky on board, I might be sorta immortal," Lucas mused. "So we're probably the best people for the job."

"If we're not entirely human, I'm not sure we count as 'people.' And we sure as hell aren't completely sane."

"Both of those things might count as upgrades."

"Hadn't thought of it that way," Shane admitted.

This part of the road passed through a thick forest. Shane usually enjoyed riding through wooded areas, but today he fidgeted. The darkness beneath the tree branches added to his unease, reminding him that they needed to find a place to stay for the night soon.

Lucas spotted an abandoned house near the road—one-floor, brick, 1950s design with small windows and an attached garage. They let the horses graze and drink from a nearby stream, and then Shane led them into the garage while Lucas made a sweep of the house.

"All clear." Lucas stuck his head through the doorway between the garage and house. "Just don't open the fridge," he added, wrinkling his nose.

By this time, anything still in the refrigerator had probably mummified, but Shane took the warning to heart. "I'll get water," he replied, grabbing their bucket. "You can figure out what we have left to eat."

Shane went around the corner of the house, heading for the woods. Weeds stood hip-high in the yard. A swing-set and other plastic toys peeked from the tall grass, faded and forgotten. The stream lay at the bottom of a small hill, just inside the tree line.

At the edge of the forest, Shane froze, and his wolf senses howled a warning in his mind. *That song,* he thought, hearing the faint but clear sound of a weeping woman from the daemon of the forest.

He saw a flash of white, and then something big, powerful, and putrid tackled him, taking them both to the ground. Shane bashed his attacker with the bucket, twisting to keep its sharp-toothed maw away from his neck.

The creature reared back, bleeding above one ear where the bucket had cut into the sensitive skin.

A shot rang out, passing through the attacker's rib cage, splattering Shane with blood and gobbets of flesh. The creature listed to one side and fell to the ground beside him.

"Shane!" Lucas came running, shotgun in hand.

Shane pushed himself up and tried to scrape the worst of the gore from his face and clothing.

"Did it bite you?"

Since Shane was covered in the thing's blood, he figured Lucas had a right to be worried.

"No. But it sure wanted to. What was it?"

Lucas walked carefully around the carcass, keeping his shotgun trained on it, although half the chest was missing. "My guess? A rougarou."

"I thought they were only in Canada."

"Newsflash—no one's on border patrol anymore," Lucas replied. "Some of the legends say it's a curse on a human who becomes a cannibal. Desperate times, man."

Shane suppressed a shudder. "You want to stand watch while I clean up in the stream? 'Cos otherwise you're going to be smelling rougarou funk all evening."

"Go. My eyes are watering from the stench."

Shane took the dented bucket with him, careful to scoop water for them to drink before he started to clean himself off. He sluiced off the worst of the blood from his skin and hair, then used a stick to scrape the bigger chunks off his jacket. He pulled a rag out of his pocket, soaked it in the water, and did his best to scrub away the bloody mess.

When he headed back up the hill, he was shivering from the cold water and the cool breeze, but at least he could stand to smell himself.

Lucas eyed him skeptically. "You're still staying downwind," he said, although the concern in his voice took the sting out of his words.

"Yeah, yeah." Shane grew serious. "Thanks. You saved my bacon. I'm not sure the bucket would have held him off much longer."

"It was Rocky's idea," Lucas snarked. "He wanted you to stick around so we could teach Quentin new tricks."

Jokes aside, Shane knew that playing games when he was in his wolf form helped him get used to moving in his fur and learning his new abilities—and limitations. That Lucas enjoyed it as well was a bonus. "Ha, ha. You're so funny," he replied dryly because he knew Lucas expected a retort.

They walked back to the house, and Shane gave himself credit for remembering to bring the bucket of water with them.

"Rocky thinks that's what was following us," Lucas said. "Must have caught our scent and waited for a chance."

"I'm still stuck on 'cannibal'—and a little nauseated too." He paused. "If it bit me, would that have had an effect?"

"I don't want to find out," Lucas replied. "Maybe not, since you're not 'factory-installed' human anymore, but I wouldn't want to risk it. Even the lore isn't consistent."

They headed back into the house. Lucas locked the door, and Shane double-checked all the windows and the back door, then laid down a line of salt.

"I guess it makes sense," Shane said. "Hard times. People go hungry. Eventually, someone snaps. I'm a little fuzzy on how the curse hits them. Last I heard, all of the Donner Party stayed human."

Lucas shrugged. "As far as we know."

"You've got a point."

Two DAYS LATER, they arrived at their destination. The Greenbrier Hotel in White Sulphur Springs was legendary for luxury, which made it a favorite of the Washington D.C. upper-crust. During the Cold War, a huge secret bunker was built beneath the hotel with the intent of being a fallback for the government in case of a nuclear attack. Although the bunker was never used, it remained untouched over the decades until a reporter eventually disclosed its existence to the public. After that, the Greenbrier made it a tourist attraction.

Then the Events happened. No one in Washington had a chance to flee for safety. When the scope of the catastrophe became clear, the hotel declared itself to be an independent enclave, giving sanctuary to its workers, local residents, and students at nearby colleges who had nowhere else to go. They erected a fence, planted crops on the lawn, and finally put the bunker to the use for which it had been built.

"Personally, I'm looking forward to staying in a hotel that still has running water," Lucas said. They reached the gatehouse in front of a high stockade fence that enclosed the hotel and its grounds. Armed guards stepped out to accost them.

"US Marshals Maddox and Collins." Lucas flashed his badge. Shane did the same, although the government that legitimized their authority was long gone.

"We've been expecting you," one of the guards said. "Ride up to the entrance, and someone will see to your horses."

Shane and Lucas rode abreast up the wide driveway toward the Greenbriar's grand main entrance. Shane had seen photographs of the resort back in its heyday, before hard times replaced the flower beds with vegetable gardens, and fenced livestock pens enclosed parts of the golf course.

The building looked as solid as ever, though in need of paint. The columns and arches of the six-story white central section evoked the style of antebellum Southern mansions. Its sprawling side wings and additional buildings made for a huge complex capable of housing thousands of people. Its generators, furnaces, wells, and mechanical systems made it possible for the enclave to function when the world beyond its fence had come to a stop.

"It's a step up from our usual digs," Lucas observed.

Shane thought back on all the abandoned houses and mold-ridden ruined buildings where they had taken shelter for the night. "Just a little," he said, deadpan.

Back in the day, Shane figured that the Greenbrier valets all probably wore fancy uniforms. Now, two boys in jeans and t-shirts who didn't look older than high school age stepped forward when they reached the front of the building.

"We can take your horses to the stables," the taller one offered. "We'll make sure they're fed, watered, and curried, and store your tack."

Lucas's eyes narrowed. "Where are the stables?"

"Over yonder," the shorter boy said, pointing toward a large barn in the distance. "They'll be safe and plenty comfortable. Someone's on duty 24/7 too."

"No one rides them but us," Lucas specified, reminding Shane of how particular his partner used to be entrusting the keys to their SUV to parking attendants.

"Absolutely," the taller valet replied. "We'll take good care of them."

Lucas and Shane removed their saddlebags and weapons, then handed over the reins after giving their mounts a reassuring pat and murmuring promises of treats later. Lucas watched the valets as they led the horses off toward the barn, and the set of his jaw made it clear that he didn't like entrusting Shadow to anyone.

"We'll go down after dinner and check on them." Shane bumped Lucas's shoulder to nudge him from his mood. "Maybe we can find apples or carrots. They get a chance for a little luxury too."

Reluctantly, Lucas grabbed his gear and the two men entered through the main arched doorway. Inside, more changes became apparent. Desks and work areas filled what had been shops and a grand foyer. Shane guessed this was the hub of the resort's security operation.

A man in what appeared to be a bellman's uniform repurposed for a military appearance came away from the office area to greet them.

"Marshals. Welcome. I'm Captain Landers, senior security team. We heard you were in West Virginia, and we hoped you would stop here before moving on."

"Even after the apocalypse, word gets around," Lucas said. "I'm guessing that means you've got requests for us?"

Landers nodded. "I do. But before we get to that, let me give you a quick tour on the way to your room."

"I've got to ask," Lucas interrupted. "Do you still have a casino? What about the big indoor swimming pool and bowling alley?"

Shane sighed and shook his head, wondering how long ago Lucas had considered a visit.

Landers chuckled. "I see our reputation precedes us," he replied as they began to climb the steps. "The casino was repurposed for additional housing. The swimming pool has been retooled as a cistern for drinking water. We did keep the bowling alley, the basketball court, and an outdoor pool, plus hiking trails and a few other amenities because people need elbow room and a way to blow off a little steam."

Shane looked around as they walked. The dining rooms were now set up more like college cafeterias with long tables to serve a large, permanent population efficiently. Large areas of the opulent gathering areas and lounges had been partitioned off for other uses.

"We've finally put the bunker to good use," Landers said. "It's our Command Central, where the operating team runs the whole complex."

"Sounds like you've got a great setup here," Shane said, appreciating the building's architecture and what remained of its faded glory.

"We were lucky," Landers confessed. "I was part of hotel security back Before. Because of the bunker, we had a plan in place for dealing with an attack—even if it didn't end up being the sort they expected. We were built to be self-sufficient for power, water, sewage, and extra capacity was put in when the bunker was built. Thanks to all that, we're the largest enclave in West Virginia still functioning outside Charleston and Wheeling."

Landers stopped in front of a door and used his key, then swung it open for them and stepped back. "We keep a couple of rooms open for official visitors—mostly the IT Priests or messengers from Fort Getty. Not much other travel going on. Most folks got where they were going and stayed there, if they were smart."

Other than being a little more hard-used than in its glory days, the room was unchanged, offering two queen-sized beds with clean linens, a small sitting area, and its own bathroom. The electric lights worked and might still power the TV although there were no channels left to watch.

"This is fantastic," Shane said. "Thank you."

Landers smiled. "It's a small 'thank you' for all that you've done, but we're happy to provide it. Once you've had a chance to rest and get cleaned up, I've set up a private dinner to brief you on the requests we've received, and such news as there is. A couple of our senior people will be there with us, as well as two IT Priests who arrived a couple of days ago to work on our system."

Lucas thanked him and pulled the door shut. Shane hesitantly flicked the light switch and watched the overhead light turn on. What had been commonplace not that long ago now seemed miraculous.

"Hot water," Lucas said with a grin like he had won the lottery. He toed off his boots, slung his jacket over a chair, and pulled a shirt from his saddlebag. "I wonder if they have a laundry room? Our stuff stinks as bad as we do."

"Even soap and a bathtub would be a step up from what we usually have for washing clothes," Shane pointed out. Staying clean on the road given the conditions of the aftermath was a challenge. "They're still pretty civilized here. Wouldn't want to be the barbarians at the feast."

"Speak for yourself," Lucas said, grinning. "Barbarians usually have all the fun."

Lucas disappeared into the bathroom, and Shane eyed the beds, trying to remember the last time they had stayed somewhere with a real mattress that hadn't been left to the elements. He sat in a chair rather than risk dirtying the comforter, since his jeans were streaked with dust from the road.

Most of the time, they shoved the memories from Before down and locked them away. Even after four years, there was too much loss, too much gone forever. Sometimes, like last night in the old bar, they let some of the best things slip back out, to be cherished and protected so that the past didn't fade away entirely.

Right now, in a room that looked like nothing had changed, Shane felt overwhelmed, like the dam of memories might break and drown him in the floodwaters.

He knew that taking a run in his fur would help dispel his mood, but Shane didn't want to risk anyone finding out his secret or taking a shot at him. In the months since he had been bitten, Shane had come a long way toward accepting the change.

Lucas and Rocky had given him unconditional acceptance, and Shane's ability to hear genius loci had also made it possible for Rocky to lend him silent reassurance. Because they believed in him, Shane was doing better about not thinking of himself as a danger, something to be hunted. He'd never looked askance at Lucas after his symbiosis with Rocky, and he appreciated them returning the same stalwart belief.

Might as well enjoy what we've got here while we can, Shane thought.

Lucas emerged wearing a clean shirt and his other pair of jeans, with his short hair spiked with water and face freshly scrubbed. "There's plenty of soap, so I washed my clothes while I was wearing them, and then did it over again, just me. Seemed to be the most efficient way."

"If something works, don't knock it." Shane grabbed his stuff and closed the bathroom door, reveling in how entirely normal a steam-filled bathroom used to be. He and Lucas had shared plenty of hotel rooms babysitting witnesses, although never in a place as nice as the Greenbrier.

He followed Lucas's advice and hung his wet clothing over the shower rod when he finished, surprised at how good it felt to be clean by the standards of old-normal.

When Shane came out, Lucas was toying with the TV. "I figured it couldn't hurt to try," he said with a shrug. "No signal. I imagine it would be too much of a drain on their generator if people were watching old videos."

"Easier to use a projector in a ballroom and do a movie night, if they've got the DVDs. Use less power, boost morale," Shane replied, although he couldn't help a pang of disappointment. Watching anything on TV would be a welcome reminder of days long past.

"Better get moving if we don't want to be late for dinner," Lucas said. "They might serve us real food along with the briefing."

Shane grinned. "I think Quentin is offended. I'm pretty sure the rabbits I bring back when I'm in my fur count as real."

"And I'm grateful for them," Lucas answered. "But it's nice to eat something now and again that isn't roasted on a stick over a fire."

Shane chuckled. "It's a little unnerving that the whole cooking thing doesn't seem nearly as important when I'm a wolf."

The guest room floors showed little outward change, although Shane suspected that entire families now lived in those rooms. The shift in the resort's purpose showed most in the common areas, but despite it all, the Greenbrier still retained an aura of faded glamor.

Signage directed them to the main office, where Landers was waiting for them. "Everything work okay in your room?" he asked.

Both Lucas and Shane laughed. "Way better than okay," Shane assured him.

Landers smiled. "Glad to offer a small respite. Now if you'll come with me, dinner should be ready—and I know our team is eager to talk with you."

They followed Landers through a ballroom and stared at the once-secret door that had been concealed behind a section of the wall. Shane couldn't help the shiver of excitement he felt.

"I've always heard about the bunker here, but I never had a chance to see it," Shane said, and a glance at his partner told him that Lucas shared his interest.

"Once the bunker was no longer secret, it became one of our best attractions," Landers said, leading them into the underground warren. "It really is an engineering marvel, and thanks to what they installed all those years ago, we've been able to protect a lot of people."

Shane wasn't embarrassed to play tourist, looking from one side to the other to take in the Cold War-era architecture. "They tried to think of everything," he murmured.

"It might not have been luxurious by politicians' standards, but now that we've actually had the end of the world, I'd say it's pretty cozy," Lucas observed.

"They were more optimistic than they realized," Landers replied. "There was a whole TV studio, so they assumed that most people would be able to tune in."

He led them to a dining room where four other people were waiting. "Marshals Maddox and Collins, I'd like you to meet Patricia Higgins and Donovan Eckart. They're our two most senior operations folks." Shane and Lucas shook hands and exchanged greetings, then turned to the other guests.

The two men looked to be in their late twenties, both wearing academic robes and each with a necklace of Mardi Gras beads. A battered action figure of Iron Man dangled from the taller man's necklace, while a similarly scuffed figure of Captain America hung from the other man's beads.

The whole IT Priest thing had started as a joke, a comment on how since programming and engineering students didn't have time for fun and supposedly didn't get laid—and would be poor forever thanks to student loans—they might as well join the priesthood. Then the world fell apart, and those same students found that their majors had become their livelihood. Now, they rode a circuit visiting the places that housed and protected the remaining internet servers to maintain what was left for as long as possible.

"Let me guess," Lucas said. "Tony and Steve?" They had met IT Priests before who chose their good-luck avatars to match their names.

The taller man laughed. "No. I'm Conrad and that's Jim. We just liked the characters."

"Nice to meet you," Shane replied, as Landers gestured for them all to have a seat.

Bowls of baked potatoes and carrots sat in the center of the table, along with a platter of what Shane thought smelled like venison, roasted with plenty of onions. A loaf of bread and a container of butter sat to one side, along with what looked like an apple crumble. Compared to their usual meals, it was a feast.

"Thank you," Shane said. "This all looks so good."

"The compound is self-sufficient," Landers said. "We do well with our crops and livestock, and there's plenty of game in the forest, plus a lake that's full of fish. There are a lot of mouths to feed, so every resource helps."

They dug in while the food was hot, and Shane bit back a moan of utter bliss at the taste. The Greenbrier's chefs might not cook for presidents and celebrities anymore, but their skill showed even in such simple but satisfying dishes.

When they finished, fresh coffee provided the perfect match to the apple crumble. Shane and Lucas had grown tolerant of grounds boiled over a fire, the best they could do when they were lucky enough to happen upon a supply. Now, as he savored the mellow flavor of a properly brewed cup, Shane realized he had almost forgotten what it was supposed to taste like.

When they finally pushed their empty plates to the side, Shane grinned. "Thank you. That's a meal to remember."

Landers grinned. "Never let it be said that the Greenbrier disappointed."

Lucas leaned forward, and rested his elbows on the table. "What news have you heard? And what messages do you have for us?"

Patricia pulled a folder from her beside her place setting and opened it. "Several reports of bandits waylaying travelers, two requests for help hunting creatures that shouldn't exist, and a petition from an enclave near a nuclear plant outside of Pittsburgh that says something unnatural is making people disappear."

Shane and Lucas exchanged a glance, and Shane didn't have to ask to know they agreed. "The nuclear plant," he said. "The others can be handled by local authorities."

Patricia nodded. "I figured that's what you'd say." She slid the folder toward Shane and Lucas. "Here's what they were able to email."

Thanks to the universities and the IT Priests, the internet still worked—some of the time. Outages were common and the infrastructure was fragile, but tireless jury-rigging kept the system going.

Shane and Lucas reviewed the printout. "Penn State Beaver?" Lucas said, glancing up at the others. "There were two nuclear plants near there."

Conrad nodded. "The Shippingport plant shut down before the Events, and the Beaver Valley plant nearly did a Three Mile Island when the power grid went down." He shrugged. "I was a nuclear engineering student."

"So—what do you make of the request?" Lucas asked Conrad. "What are we walking into?"

Conrad and Jim exchanged a glance that Shane recognized contained an entire conversation. "Conrad's the engineer. I grew up in Hookstown, so I heard all the scuttlebutt about the plants," Jim said. "My dad owned a bar where the guys from the plants would stop for a Boilermaker or two after they got done with their shifts. Back then, I didn't believe half of it. Now, I'm not so sure."

Shane held his coffee cup between his hands, savoring every sip. "What's not to believe?"

"Some of the stories are more far-fetched than others," Conrad warned. "Any time there's a big plant like that, there's a lot of dangerous waste to get rid of. That stuff was expensive and difficult to dispose of, which was a big incentive to cut corners."

Shane and Lucas had come upon plenty of illicit waste dumps in the years since the Events. They were one more nasty surprise and deadly hazard in a hostile landscape. "What kind of scale are we talking about?" Shane asked.

"Depends on who was telling the story," Jim answered. "One of the regulars at the bar swore that train cars full of waste had been sealed over with concrete and pushed into abandoned coal mines. That area had problems with sinkholes and mine subsidence before everything went to hell. I can't imagine that all the earthquakes since then made the situation any better."

Conrad took up the story. "When the Events happened, the Beaver plant went on emergency generator power to circulate the water in the cooling ponds for the core rods. Once the stash of diesel fuel ran out and there wasn't more to be found, the electricity went off and the pools overheated, which started a meltdown.

"They sent in a shutdown crew to do whatever they could to contain the radiation. It was a suicide mission, and the men who volunteered knew that. They brought in truckloads of cement and covered everything they could before they died. They never came out. People say that their ghosts stand watch over the plant."

"Even before everything went to hell, there were stories about strange creatures in the woods near the plants," Jim said. "Some of them were bogus, but I heard too many first-hand accounts from people I trusted to dismiss all of them. The old timers called them 'hellhounds' or the 'dogs of war.'"

Shane would be willing to bet money Lucas's thoughts had gone to the same place his did. *Dogs of war. Genetically-manipulated werewolf hybrids? Maybe adding some radiation to the drugs?*

"There were military installations not far from there, right?" Lucas asked.

Conrad nodded. "Not a full base, but a training facility that also housed missile silos and a World War II-era bunker. They'd been abandoned for quite a while before the Events. The scouts from the Beaver campus say that there's a prepper enclave that took over, and they're blockading access to the nuclear plants. No one's been able to figure out whether they're keeping people out to hide something or steering them away because it's dangerous."

Shane finished the last of his now-cold coffee. He thought about how he and Lucas could go through pots of java while guarding a witness, something that now seemed like an extravagance.

"Preppers," he said with a sigh.

The word Lucas muttered under his breath was decidedly less polite.

"We've run into folks like that more than once," Lucas said. "It doesn't usually go well."

Long before the sequential catastrophes that broke the world, groups had worried about an impending cataclysm and tried to prepare for it. Most hadn't been friendly to outsiders even before shortages became dramatic and permanent. The groups tended to be well-armed, suspicious, and hostile.

At best they kept to themselves and refused to work with others. At worst, they became small cartels trafficking scarce supplies and robbing travelers. Lucas and Shane's encounters with preppers up to now had always ended bloody.

"Everything we heard about the enclave was rumor. We didn't know anyone who had actually met the group, so there's no telling what's true," Conrad said. "But we figured you'd want to know they're out there."

"What do the people at the Beaver campus enclave think we can do about the situation?" Shane asked. "Hunt the hellhounds? Because taking on a prepper fortress or sealing up a leaking nuclear plant is a bit much to ask from two Marshals."

Conrad cleared his throat. "Actually? None of that. There were whispers that some of the hard-core types who worked at the facility were part of a secret government agency that wanted to create super-soldiers." He colored with embarrassment. "I know that sounds like the plot of a dozen action movies, but it wasn't entirely fictional."

No it isn't, Shane thought. *And the things they created killed Lucas and changed me.*

"This hush-hush agency have a name?" Lucas asked.

Both of the IT Priests shook their heads. "Not that I ever heard," Jim said. "And apparently, some sort of crazy cult took over a campground and might be up to no good. People are going missing. Sounds like the kind of thing people might call the Marshals about."

Shane looked to Lucas. "What do you think?"

"Worth checking out," Lucas replied. "Tell them we'll come—but if the situation isn't something we can fix, we aren't going to stick around."

"Fair enough," Landers replied, and the Greenbrier operations folks who had been listening in silent concentration nodded their agreement.

"The Greenbrier's bunker isn't the only government secret that eventually came to light," Patricia said. "We've heard tell of a number of classified projects that didn't stay hidden once everything changed."

"We've run into a few of those ourselves," Lucas said, and Shane knew his partner was thinking about the feral artificial intelligence robots at Raven Rock and the souped-up werewolves at Fort Detrick.

"We'll relay your message," Conrad said. "And before you leave, we'll also make sure you've got the latest information on the route that we can find. The team at the Beaver campus enclave says they have more intel for you and a place for you to stay, so head there first and then strategize next steps."

With the big issue sorted, conversation turned to lighter topics until the antique grandfather clock struck ten. They thanked their hosts and retreated to the room, as Shane went over the discussion in his mind.

"You know, I feel like I should take two or three more showers, just because I can," Lucas joked.

"Yeah, I was thinking the same thing. Although once I hit that mattress with real sheets, it could be hard to get me out of it in the morning," Shane replied, eying the bed on the left that he had claimed.

"Too bad we can't take them with us. But I imagine the horses would complain."

Shane chuckled at the mental image of Red and Shadow carrying the mattresses like they'd been strapped to the top of a car. "Probably not a good idea." He unlaced his boots and sprawled in an armchair. "So what do you think of the new 'assignment'?"

Lucas sat on the end of his bed and let himself fall back, arms splayed wide. "I think it sounds like a mess. Devil dogs, crazy cultists, batshit preppers, and guardian ghosts. Why do we always get the nut jobs?"

"Because we're the last Marshals standing—and we're not completely human."

"There is that," Lucas allowed. "I don't want to go anywhere near the nuclear plant without seeing what Rocky picks up from the local daemons. I have the feeling we only know half the story—and what they really want our help with is even worse than the part they told us about."

"Isn't that the way it always is?" Shane wondered whether the minibar was stocked and then remembered that it wouldn't do him much good anyhow. "But I agree—whether the folks at the campus know it or not, my gut says there's something bigger going on."

"Jokes aside, we've got more protections than regular people," Lucas said. "Between Rocky and Quentin, we've also got abilities that could come in handy. So I guess we're the best ones to send."

Shane could hear the weariness in his partner's voice and understood what he didn't say. *We're the only ones who can do it. But I wish we weren't.*

CHAPTER THREE

"Rocky says that the closer we get to the nuclear plant, the stranger the other daemons are," Lucas said as they rode along the empty highway. They avoided the main interstates whenever possible, feeling less exposed and closer to resources on the smaller state routes.

"Strange, how?"

"Our lives are weird when the fact that we can sense elementals isn't bizarre enough," Lucas replied. He was grateful for everything Rocky had done for him and for the times he had helped to save both Lucas and Shane. To be honest, he had come to enjoy Rocky's company, and having him along for the ride made the wilderness less lonely.

"Do you remember the twisted daemon we ran into at South Mountain Battlefield? The others elementals aren't as bad as that one, but Rocky says the ones near here are tainted, and if the stain takes hold they could become more dangerous," Lucas added.

"Can I just say that even as Quentin, I'm not thrilled about the prospect of hellhounds and devil dogs?" Shane said. "Not a family reunion I'm looking forward to."

"Do you think it's the radiation affecting the daemons or something else?"

Shane shrugged. "I think there's more going on here than we know yet. Nuclear plants had problems all along the seaboard, but we haven't heard tales of the same kinds of things."

"It could have happened, and we didn't hear about it," Lucas said. "Not like we can watch the six o'clock news."

"Maybe. But the IT Priests hear from everyone. You know they talk to their counterparts anywhere they can get a signal. I think we'd have heard something if it was widespread," Shane argued.

"What is Quentin picking up?"

Shane spent part of his time each day as his wolf while they traveled to the campus enclave. He had told Lucas that physical exertion helped to burn off the wolf-side's twitchiness and penchant for violence, making it easier for Shane's human mind to remain firmly in charge.

"Besides squirrels and rabbits? There are supernatural creatures in the woods. But not hybrids or werewolves—I'd know. I think whatever I'm sensing might be more of those paranormal beings that used to bother hiding." Shane nudged his mount to keep up, and Lucas was glad that the horses had finally gotten used to sensing Shane's wolfie side.

"Is this something we can fight?" Lucas asked. "Maybe this is end-stage evolution. I mean, humans got our shot as top-of-the-food-chain, and we fucked it up. The changes to the genius loci and the creatures—are they doing something that's actually wrong, or adapting to the new 'normal' after the Events?"

"You're asking the wrong person. That's way above my pay grade," Shane replied.

They broke up the long ride rehashing old movies and recounting the plots of books they had read. When they lapsed into silence, Lucas tuned in to what Rocky had to say about the area around them and anything he might pick up from the nearby elementals.

They gave the horses a rest in the shade near a stream, and Shane went wolf for a walkabout. By the time the horses had time to eat, drink and cool down, Quentin was back with the carcasses of two sizable rabbits dangling from his mouth. He dropped them at Lucas's feet, then spat out something else—a stained tennis ball.

"Seriously?" Lucas said with a laugh, but Quentin managed to have puppy eyes despite being a larger-than-normal wolf. Lucas threw the ball, and Quentin bounded off, coming back with his tail wagging.

"Don't swallow it," Lucas warned. "I'd have to Heimlich you and that wouldn't be pleasant—for either of us."

They played fetch until Quentin finally called an end to the game by refusing to give up the ball. Lucas gave him Shane's clothing and then took the ball and put it in his saddlebag for safekeeping. When Shane emerged, a sheen of sweat and the flush to his skin remained from the exertion.

"Thanks for that," Shane said. "Since I got bit, I have trouble with the extra energy. In my wolf form, running it off is fun." He swung into the saddle.

"I didn't sense anything worrisome," he continued. "But there were territory markings that didn't smell normal and some paw prints that weren't anything I could match with animals that should be in these parts."

Lucas looked out over the wooded hills and valleys. "Meaning what?"

Shane shrugged. "Don't know. There have always been stories about strange creatures in the area, long before the Events. I mean, look around. There's a whole lot of woods and not many people. It wouldn't be a stretch to think there were cryptids out there in places even the deer hunters didn't go."

"I can believe that," Lucas said. "We never really had a reason to spend much time outside cities with the Marshals, so I don't think I realized just how much...nothing...there is between places."

"Turned out to be a good thing in the long run," Shane replied. "The 'nothing' fared better than the cities."

The state route wended through valleys and ran alongside streams, then climbed steeply and offered a twisting ribbon of asphalt in the switchback descent. The views were breathtaking, but the nip in the air and the hint of fall color in the trees at the highest peaks warned that winter would soon follow. The sheer drop on one side, steep road, and exposure to the wind wouldn't be fun—or safe—once bad weather started, and the temperature fell.

Back roads offered more places to hole up for the night, another reason Shane and Lucas stuck to the byways. Defensibility overruled comfort. Tonight they found a mom-and-pop convenience store with barred, narrow windows and concrete-block walls. Gray-white paint peeled from the cement, and a windstorm had torn the sign on the roof nearly in two.

Lucas picked the lock on the door while Shane kept watch. The little market probably had made more money selling cigarettes and lottery tickets than it had food. The shelves were stripped bare and so were the coolers, but it didn't look looted. *Maybe the owners provisioned their neighbors when everyone moved out. Not everyone's a selfish asshole.*

He and Shane rearranged the empty shelving to make a corral for the horses, which left half the store for them. Once their mounts were cared for, Shane and Lucas headed outside with the spoils of Quentin's hunt. A small, overgrown park to one side of the building had a warped picnic table, a rusted grill pit, and an ancient hand pump that brought up clear water after some vigorous pumping.

Lucas went looking for firewood while Shane skinned and gutted the rabbits and filled their bucket with water to boil over the fire. Once the fire blazed, they roasted the meat on sticks. Lucas tried not to compare the gamey, tough meat to the memory of their dinner at the Greenbrier.

"We should be to Beaver Falls tomorrow," Shane said over a mouthful. "We've been in Pittsburgh several times." He paused, frowning. "What do you think the people at the campus aren't telling us?"

Lucas shrugged. "I guess we'll find out. But they have plenty of nuclear experts, so they don't need us for that. If the preppers are too big of a problem for the enclave's security team, I don't know what they think the two of us can do. So it's got to be something supernatural."

"I don't like going in blind." Shane finished the last of his rabbit and picked the stringy bits from between his teeth.

"We either find out the whole scoop, or we walk away," Lucas said. "I've got no desire to test how indestructible we are. Just because Rocky and Quentin can help pull our nuts out of the fire doesn't mean we should put them at risk for no good reason."

Shane nodded. "Good. We're on the same page."

They reached the fortified campus just before sundown. The buildings had been repurposed to hold a larger population and the grounds adapted for farming and livestock. Since larger schools had their own power plants and water supply, they were logical choices for enclaves.

Most of the students had nowhere to go after the Events, so they stayed on, and their majors suddenly became their professions. Athletes were recruited to augment campus security, and the school administrators worked with the town leaders to bring the two communities together for safety. Townspeople who didn't flee the area found shelter and a role helping to keep the enclave running smoothly.

"The Greenbrier said you were coming. Glad to see you got here safely," Dr. Damon Bauers said when he greeted them at the main gate. He vouched for them with the guards and then led them toward a barn erected on what had once been a grassy park.

Stablehands took Red and Shadow. The rare treat of apples meant the two horses didn't spare a backward glance for their riders, much to Shane's amusement.

"Don't worry—our folks will take good care of them," Bauers assured them. "You had a long trip."

"Feels longer on horseback than it did in a car." Lucas turned to get a look at the grounds in the fading light. "Looks like you've made a go of things here."

"We're not white-knuckling it every day like in the beginning, so I guess that's progress," Bauers said. "After they accepted that the Events were permanent, people...adapted."

Lucas knew what the man wasn't putting into words, that no one really "got over" the cataclysm, but with time they either resigned themselves to the new normal or self-destructed.

"It's not as fancy as the Greenbrier, but everyone's got clothing and shelter, and no one goes hungry."

"That's as good as it gets these days," Shane agreed.

Bauers led them to the administration building that now housed all the functions of enclave government and headed down the stairs into the basement.

"Thank you for coming. I know your help is in demand. As you've probably guessed, our email left out some important details best shared in person," Bauers said.

"Two IT Priests at the Greenbrier were from this area," Lucas said. "So they gave us some background. But since we're not nuclear experts, I don't think you wanted our help with illegal waste storage."

Bauers sighed. "No. You're right. Our people are monitoring the nuclear plants. But the real threat is something that we don't know how to handle."

"Tell us." Shane gave a sharp look that Lucas knew meant Bauer had better make a convincing case for their services.

"I think it will be easier if I show you."

Bauers led them to a section of the lower level that had been converted to a jail. The guards nodded as they passed, and the duty officer walked with them to an interrogation room, then headed back to retrieve the prisoner.

"Let me take the lead on this," Bauers cautioned them. "Stand back and listen. We've had Paul Campbell in custody for a month, and the problem isn't getting him to talk—it's knowing what to make of what he says. Let me wind him up, and you'll get an earful."

Shane and Lucas hung back at the far wall as the officer brought in a handcuffed man in his mid-thirties. He had short hair and a defiant set to his jaw, and his blue eyes blazed with anger.

"Why are you bothering me?" the prisoner said. "I've told you the truth, and you won't listen. What's different now?"

Bauer inclined his head toward Lucas and Shane. "They're new. Don't you want to tell them what you told me? Maybe they'll listen better."

Campbell tilted his head with a crafty gleam in his eyes. "You brought out the crazy monkey to dance for your guests."

"I guess you're a fraud like we always said you were," Bauer said with a shrug.

Campbell surged forward, jerked to a halt by the shackles around his ankles. "Don't say that! They can hear you. They hear everything!" He looked wildly around the room. "Forgive me for being in the company of the faithless. I believe! I believe!"

"You believe in fairytales," Bauers replied, cold and mocking. "Delusions."

Campbell stilled and fixed Bauers with a frighteningly focused glare. "It's all real. Faeries—that's just what we called them. Their language—so beautiful, nothing like ours. They name themselves something our tongues can't pronounce. But I've seen them," he said, eyes fervent. "They sing in my dreams."

"What good are your imaginary friends?" Bauer taunted, and Lucas knew the man was provoking the prisoner to get a reaction.

"They're not imaginary! They live beyond the rift, and when we're ready, they'll take us through," Campbell argued with a rapturous expression.

"And are there unicorns there too?"

"Don't you get it?" Campbell jumped to his feet, chains clattering. "They can take us back. Before the skies burned. Before everything changed. And once we're there, we can warn everyone. We can stop this, make it like it never happened."

Lucas edged closer. "Faeries? *Real* faeries?"

Campbell gave Lucas a shrewd look, as if he was trying to figure out whether he was being mocked. "That's what we call them, not what they call themselves. No wings. Not tiny. They're powerful, beautiful, filled with light. Pure."

Lucas doubted that any alien life form was "pure"—whatever that meant. He also distrusted unknown creatures offering to do favors, because there was always fine print that went bad.

"They offered to send you back?" Lucas's mind reeled at the possibility. *Could something actually do that? And if people could be sent to the past, could they possibly change the future and stop the Events from happening?*

"Preacher said they can. He's the one they talk to, but we saw a glimpse of them, and they are so beautiful," Campbell replied, enraptured at the memory.

"Preacher?" Shane nudged.

"Ed Johnson," Bauer answered. "He was one of the senior operators at the plant. Then he got religion and started his own little End Times cult."

"Liar!" Campbell rounded on Bauer like he would have swung a punch if his hands had been free. "He sees the truth beyond."

"Let's just take it easy," Shane said, raising both hands in accommodation. Lucas immediately recognized the "good cop" tone in his partner's voice, something that had always worked well for them over the years. "I want to hear more."

Shane smiled and moved a little closer. "Ignore him," he told Campbell, with a nod of his head toward Bauers. "Talk to me. Who's Ed, and why is he special?"

Relief showed in Campbell's face. "Finally, someone who'll listen." He glared at Bauer and then at Lucas, who kept his face neutral, allowing Shane to take the lead.

"Ed's a good guy. The best. We all worked together before the Events—long shifts, late hours, had some close calls," Campbell said.

"Ed's the reason our team got out alive before the meltdown. He knew something was wrong before the alarms went off, and he evacuated us. He could have been fired for that if he'd been wrong, and he did it anyhow to save us. The guys who waited to verify—they didn't make it out."

Shane nodded, never taking his eyes off Campbell. "So you trust him. And he's got good hunches. He protected you. When did he become 'Preacher'?"

While Shane worked the suspect, Lucas turned inward to Rocky. *Can you pick up anything weird? Like a rift through time?*

I have never encountered such a thing. I wouldn't know what it felt like. But I don't sense anything especially powerful. Except—

What?

There is a large area where the land is very sick. Poisoned. It is uncomfortable to sense.

Lucas nodded. *That's the nuclear plant. Plenty of radiation contaminating the whole area.*

There is also something...irregular. A strange energy vibration. It comes and goes.

Like a nexus? Lucas asked, worried. They had encountered a particularly strong "well" of energy, and closing it had nearly gotten them killed.

Not the same. Not a genius loci. Not entirely natural.

That got Lucas's attention. *If it's not natural, then how did it get there?*

I do not know. But we should find out.

Lucas tuned back in to Shane's conversation with Campbell. The prisoner was more than willing to talk now that he had an attentive audience.

"—thing like that happens, you do some soul-searching. Ed's a smart guy, and he's deep. Thinks about stuff real hard," Campbell was saying. "At first, he just got our heads out of our asses when the whole world was fucked. We found an old church camp and fixed it up, lived there since then."

"Was he Preacher back then?" Shane's patience amazed Lucas, how he just kept on, slow and steady, until he'd gotten what he wanted, like reeling in a fish.

Campbell shook his head, looking surprisingly relaxed for a guy in handcuffs and ankle shackles. "No. The first years, we just tried to stay alive. Then last winter, Ed started having weird dreams."

"Of the rift and the creatures?" Shane asked, sounding sincerely fascinated with Campbell's account.

"Yeah, but he didn't know what it was then. It took a while to figure out. You know, like in those Bible stories? Where God spoke to the prophets but they were all like, 'you talkin' to me'?"

Shane chuckled at the reference. "You think it was God?"

Lucas and Shane had grown up together, shared the same suburban memories, including Sunday mornings in the pews at a middle-of-the-road Methodist church where the minister told people to be honest, work hard, and spread kindness.

Given what they both witnessed in the army and later as US Marshals, Lucas had come to deeply doubt his beliefs. Then the Events happened, leaving no room to call any entity "good" that could have saved the world and didn't.

The few times he and Shane had talked about such things, he knew that Shane's disillusionment ran as deeply as his own, but it seemed to weigh heavier on Shane, perhaps because he had believed harder in the beginning.

"Not God," Campbell said in such an earnest voice that Lucas didn't doubt the man fully believed what he was saying. "Something else...old, wise, powerful. Beautiful."

"What did it want?"

"It wants to give us paradise," Campbell replied.

"What do you have to do to get it?" Shane pressed.

"We have to be patient," Campbell told him, pitching Shane like a prospective convert. Beside Lucas in the back of the room, Bauer looked like he was chewing nails. "It isn't strong enough to rescue us yet, but Ed

—Preacher—has seen the rift in his dreams. It will open, and we can step through it and leave all this behind."

"You said something about going back in time, before the Events. Did the faeries tell Ed they could do that?"

"Ed says that he got a look through the rift, and it was everything we could want. What do we want most? To go back, before everything happened. With our families. Maybe stop it from happening," Campbell told him, tears glistening in his eyes.

"Does Ed know when the rift will open? Or how?"

Campbell shook his head. "Not yet. The time isn't right. But soon. And then we can all go home."

Part of Lucas wanted to smack some sense into Campbell for falling for whatever con the "faeries" were running. Another part understood the bone-deep grief for the "old normal" that would never exist again, and the people lost with it. *Desperate people have always been easy marks.*

"Thank you for telling me," Shane said with an understanding smile. He stepped back, signaling an end to the interview.

"You could join us." Campbell leaned forward, hitting the end of his restraints like a dog on a chain. "We take in new people if they're the right type. Willing to work. Open minded. I'd vouch for you."

Just for an instant, Lucas saw emotion flicker across Shane's face before his expression closed off into a cop's expressionless mask.

"Thanks, but I've got a job here," Shane replied.

Bauer signaled to the guard who came in and grabbed Campbell by the arm. "Time to go," he told the prisoner.

"Think about it," Campbell said as he passed by Shane before the guard hustled him out of the room.

Bauer led them back to his office and motioned for them to sit down. "Well? What do you think—now that you've seen the crazy up close."

"I think Preacher Ed's being manipulated by some kind of entity that definitely isn't going to send them to find their heart's desire," Lucas said. "So the real question is—what does the entity want?"

Shane chewed on his lip for a few seconds, a sure tell that he was thinking. "I agree that the entity is real...and maybe so is the rift. But I don't think crossing through it is going to work out the way Campbell expects."

Bauer gave a crisp nod. "That's what I think too. But you did a much better job of drawing him out than I did. Guess that's why you're a Marshal."

Shane just chuckled. "Years of practice balancing out Lucas's more 'direct' approach."

Lucas looked to Bauer. "Do you have any intel on this 'church camp' where Preacher Ed and his Waco wackos are holed up in?"

Bauer nodded. "Yeah. Camp Calvin used to be a Presbyterian family camp. It's been around since the 1950s and was on its last legs—people didn't do that kind of thing anymore. The Events just sped up the inevitable."

He reached for a folder on his desk and handed it over. Lucas opened it and held it so Shane could see. Inside were color brochures for the camp, along with a map of the grounds.

"I heard about places like this when I was a kid, but we never went." Lucas looked at the pictures of smiling families.

"Apparently the 'camping' part wasn't too strenuous," Shane observed. "There's a dormitory, an auditorium, dining hall, swimming pool. Not exactly a tent revival."

"We interviewed folks who grew up around here and remembered the camp," Bauer said. "So we have a pretty good idea of the stuff that isn't on the brochure, like the mechanical systems. It was never a big place—probably could hold one hundred people max counting staff and guests."

"How big a group does Preacher Ed have?" Lucas was already running scenarios in his mind. "I don't know what the light-up creatures are, but I've got a gut feeling that letting Crazy Eddie and his band of merry men go through that rift is a bad idea."

"From what we could tell, best guess is no more than thirty," Bauer replied. "Campbell wouldn't confirm."

"Armed?" Shane questioned.

"Not that we ever saw. We had them on drone surveillance for a while and didn't see any weapons or drills."

"You've got a drone?" Lucas looked up, impressed.

"Had," Bauer said. "Before the preppers shot it down."

"The preppers and the cultists—" Shane started.

"No," Bauer corrected. "They're not working together. I don't think there's any love lost there."

"How did you capture Campbell?" Shane asked.

"He was proselytizing outside the main gate." Bauer wrinkled his nose. "Can you believe it? Just like those annoying street preachers."

Lucas started to laugh. Shane and Bauer just stared at him, which made Lucas laugh harder.

"Sorry," he managed in a strangled voice, wiping the tears from his eyes. "It's just—those assholes were always going on about how the end was near because the world was so evil. So now that we've actually had the fucking end, their recruiting pitch is to go back to the old evil world because it was so much better?"

Shane and Bauer chuckled at that. "You've got a point," Bauer conceded.

"Where does the nuclear plant come into this?" Shane asked.

Bauer shook his head. "We don't know. After the meltdown, the shutdown crew entombed it as best they could. It's more Three Mile Island than Chernobyl, if that's any comfort. It can't function, and it's deadly to go past the perimeter."

"But all that waste is still inside—and hidden in those mine tunnels, right?" Lucas mused. "So there's energy there, just not easy to access."

Bauer frowned. "I guess...although for the plant itself, I'd say that wouldn't be humanly possible."

"Not everything is human," Shane remarked.

The look Bauer gave him confirmed Lucas's suspicion that the administrator knew that the real problem was supernatural.

"Theoretically, is there any way the plant or the stored waste could explode?" Lucas asked.

Bauer leaned back in his chair. "A number of our people worked at the plant. We've run plenty of scenarios and simulations. It would take a one-in-a-million lineup of all the right things at the wrong time."

Lucas met Bauer's gaze. "One-in-a-million odds is pretty much how the Events happened. So that doesn't mean 'impossible.'"

Bauer grimaced. "Point taken. But the fact remains—people couldn't set off what's left."

"I don't think that what Campbell sees on the other side of the rift is 'people,'" Shane said.

"What about the preppers?" Lucas asked. "Have any of your team approached them?"

"They're not exactly the trusting sort. We've made overtures. They shut us down every time."

"Maybe your people didn't ask the right questions—or offer the right incentives," Lucas said, as the beginnings of a plan formed.

Bauer leaned forward with his elbows on his desk. "We've worked damn hard for the last four years to build this enclave and save as many as we could. I've heard that you two deal with things that can't be explained. I'd like to have you meet with Claire Palmer, the head of our coven-in-residence."

Lucas nodded. "We've worked with covens before. I'd like to hear their take on this whole 'faerie' thing."

"Claire's group has real power—but even they wanted to call in back-up. I'll let her share the details," Bauer replied. "I don't claim to understand. Just...protect my people."

<hr>

Lucas and Shane shared a dorm room originally meant for two students. The cramped space was much better than many of the ruins they had squatted in, even if it fell far short of the Greenbrier's luxury. Still, the beds were clean, and the shared bathroom at the end of the hall had plenty of hot water.

"Look at the bright side—at least it's not bunk beds," Shane snarked as he sat on the edge of his twin mattress.

"I'm grateful for small favors," Lucas replied. "And hot showers." Shane gave him a look Lucas recognized from long years together. "What?"

"You've got a plan."

"Not much of one," Lucas admitted. "I want to talk to the witches. If they sense Rocky and Quentin, they may tell us more than they've shared with Bauer. Then I want to see the preppers. As a hostage, if that's what it takes."

Shane shook his head and sighed. "Why did I figure you'd say that?"

"Because you've known me since the third grade."

"Fair enough." Shane cleared his throat. "I'm pretty certain that

Campbell will get me into the cult camp if we can persuade Bauer to let him go. If he thinks he's converting me, maybe they'll tell me what they're up to, and then Quentin can get me out of there."

Lucas stilled. "Are you sure?"

Shane frowned. "What's that supposed to mean?"

"It sounds good, doesn't it? To go back, before. Would you?" Lucas knew Shane heard everything he didn't say.

"Not without you, asshole. Who's going to be my best friend if I left you here?" Shane rolled his eyes as Lucas sat down across from him.

"Seriously? Go back to Before, knowing how it ends? Counting down every day to annihilation while everyone around me goes about their business? Knowing that even if I tried to warn the Pentagon, the White House—no one would believe me? Living through the Events again—and the last four years? How is that any kind of paradise?" Shane's voice rose with each challenge.

Lucas reached over to clap him on the shoulder. "You're right. I'm sorry. It's just—the whole idea has me a little crazy."

"Believe me, I get it." Shane paused and looked down. "I'm not wild about the thought of you walking into the prepper camp and giving yourself up."

"Says the guy who'll be pretending to join a doomsday cult."

"The cultists aren't heavily armed, and they won't be expecting me to leave as a wolf if it comes down to that," Shane pointed out. "How are you going to get the preppers to let you go?"

"My charm and good looks?" Lucas snarked, since he hadn't figured that part out.

"Then you're totally screwed," Shane joked, then sobered. "Seriously—what's the plan?"

Lucas grimaced. "I don't have one. Get in, find out what they're about, see what Rocky picks up in the area. Create a diversion; play it as it goes."

"That's not a plan."

"It's the best I've got at the moment."

"I hope I don't have to save your ass," Shane relayed.

"Rocky hopes no one pushes you through a rift."

"I guess that makes us even," Shane said with a sigh. "Alright—time to figure out the nitty-gritty details."

BAUER ARRANGED the meeting with the coven. Shane and Lucas had worked with witches before, and they had also fought people who misused their "extra" abilities.

Lucas didn't know what to expect. The woman who entered the meeting room with Bauer looked remarkably ordinary.

"Marshals." Claire Palmer looked like every minivan mom Lucas had ever met. She wore a band t-shirt and jeans, but Lucas recognized the protective metals and gemstones in her jewelry. Even more to the point, Rocky acknowledged the power he felt from the stranger.

"Nice to meet you," Lucas replied, taking her measure.

"Likewise." Claire's faint smirk as she regarded Lucas, and puzzled frown when she turned her attention to Shane, made him wonder what she saw in them. She might recognize Rocky's daemon energy, even if she hadn't considered the possibility of one "possessing" a human. But the hybrid shifter/werewolf whose bite transformed Shane wasn't a naturally occurring species, which might be more difficult for her to recognize.

They sat at the table in the conference room. Shane and Lucas took their seats, and aside from Claire, Bauer was the other one present.

"We understand that you're the one who requested us," Shane said.

Claire nodded. "One of my coven had a vision. In it we were warned that we can't win the coming battle without the two of you."

Shane fought to keep his expression neutral. "Coming battle?"

Claire spread her hands, palm up. "We don't know the details yet. But it has something to do with the nuclear plant, the people who have taken up residence in the old army base, and the cultists at the old campground."

"You've talked with the guy they've got locked up?" Lucas asked.

"Yes. Both directly and through dream-walking," Claire replied. "What my coven sister was able to read from his dreams was far more frightening than what he told us."

"Faeries?" Shane sounded skeptical.

She shook her head. "Energy bleeding through from…somewhere else. Maybe sentient, maybe not—but still dangerous. It would be bad enough if people were pulled in against their will, but the cultists have created their own myth about the energy, which makes them its willing helpers. People have done many horrible things in service to a powerful force they thought could give them their hearts' desire."

Lucas didn't like the sound of that at all, but he needed to know more before he was ready to commit. "Tell us about your magic."

Claire sat back in her chair. "Have you ever heard of cannel coal?"

They shook their heads, and she smiled. "That's okay—a lot of people haven't. Everyone knows about anthracite and bituminous coal—at least, people in these parts do. Cannel coal is a very special sort that isn't nearly as plentiful. Our magic connects to the cannel coal, and that weaves our power through the mountains."

"Coal magic?"

"Cannelmancy," Claire replied. "As old and true in these parts as granny witches. For generations, our men have gone down into the bones of the Earth, and the women worked magic and sang spells to bring them back from the underworld."

Shane raised an eyebrow. "Interesting. Any relationship to geomancy?"

Claire nodded. "A related sub-specialty. Coal as a mineral is associated with increasing one's powers and reversing negatives. We draw on the seams of cannel coal like ley lines."

"You're worried about the nuclear plant. Where does your magic come in?" Shane asked.

"Seams of cannel coal run all through the rock beneath the two plants," Claire replied. "We have drawn on that to contain the radiation and keep the condition of the facilities from getting worse. Some of us have the ability to scry—see things across a distance. That lets us see into places where it wouldn't be safe to go, to help keep an eye on things."

"We use the coal in our rituals," Claire continued. "It strengthens the spells. We have witches who can read patterns in the dust for divination, and the smoke is used for scrying."

"Are you connecting with the coal—or with the daemons of the land where the coal exists?" Lucas asked.

Claire smiled, and the glint in her eyes told Lucas that she had either figured out their secrets or had strong suspicions. "A very good question. I believe it's both. When we are in physical contact with cannel coal, our magic is more focused, and our power is amplified. Some of us have sensed the daemons, and we do what we can to help their energy heal where the radiation has sickened the land. That's a process that will require generations of witches."

Lucas noticed the polished black pendant that hung from a braided cord around Claire's neck. A sigil he didn't recognize was carved into the stone's smooth surface.

"Yes, it's made from cannel coal." Claire answered his unspoken question. "Everyone in our coven wears one for protection. Having it next to skin and close to the heart helps us to anchor our magic, and the sigil is one miners have used for centuries."

"What do you think is going on?" Shane asked.

"There's a threat to the nuclear plants, but it's not completely human," Claire replied. "And there are creatures drawn to this place that are friend and foe. My coven knows the lore and can work powerful magic, but we aren't warriors. Whatever this is, we can't fight it alone."

Shane could practically see the wheels turning in his partner's head.

"How did you figure we could help?" Lucas replied. "And why do you think we count as warriors?"

Claire gave them a considered look. "You have both gained new abilities that make you better able to stand against a threat like this. The enclave has a security team, but they don't understand magic or the entities involved. If they get sent to deal with this, they will die, and the result could be catastrophic."

"You're afraid something intends to sabotage the nuclear plants?" Shane asked.

Claire nodded. "We don't have all the details yet—and we're hoping you can help us with that—but yes, we think the plants are at risk. And if that happens, it will kill everyone in the contamination zone, and release a cloud of radioactive particles that will destroy thousands more."

She looked to Shane and then to Lucas. "Please help us. There's no one else we can ask."

CHAPTER FOUR

"Wʜᴀᴛ ᴀʀᴇ ʏᴏᴜ ᴅᴏɪɴɢ?" Paul Campbell hissed when Shane unlocked his cell in the middle of the night.

"Busting you out." Shane gestured for Campbell to follow him, and they crept down the deserted corridor. Shane had arranged the "jailbreak" with Bauer, but Campbell didn't need to know that.

"Where are the guards?" Campbell whispered. Shane handed him a jacket.

"I paid them off. Hurry." Shane had memorized the quickest way out of the building and the most direct route to leave the compound.

Once they were outside the wall, Shane turned to Campbell. "I thought about what you said—being able to go back before the Events. I want that. I'm ready to join."

Campbell smiled. "I knew you were different from the others. I could tell that you hadn't hardened your heart against the truth."

"Do you think Ed—Preacher—will be okay with me?" Shane did his best to seem nervous.

Campbell nodded. "We're always happy to have new additions. Come with me. It's not far."

Keeping a brisk pace warmed them in the cool autumn air. A full moon lit their path. Shane had a gun tucked into his waistband in case they ran into trouble. He listened to the night sounds, straining to hear

"

the songs of nearby genius loci, both to mark his route and to gauge the condition of the land around him.

The faint music that caught his attention sounded oddly out of tune. That was worrisome but not as clearly dangerous as some of the more twisted and malicious elementals they had encountered.

"Not far" was several miles. Shane noted landmarks. Even when he wasn't in wolf form, the enhanced awareness lingered at the back of Shane's mind, and he felt certain he would be able to get back to the campus.

"What made you change your mind?" Campbell asked after they had walked for a while. "Your partner seems like a real hard ass."

Shane chuckled. "He can be. Lucas is a good guy, a good Marshal. He's made his peace with everything that happened. Me....I miss how it used to be." His words held just enough of a hint of truth to sound believable. Campbell seemed to accept the explanation without qualms.

They turned off the road into a gravel drive that led back into the woods. Overhanging branches had been cleared so that moonlight lit their way. The forest around them was dark but never silent. Shane tensed with apprehension and Quentin's awareness of prey and predators nearby.

"We're here." Campbell stopped in front of large chain-link gates. A dinner bell on a post stood beside the entrance. He yanked on the rope, setting up a clatter that echoed through the night.

"Paul? We didn't think you were ever coming back!" A bearded man in a stained canvas jacket held up a lantern on the other side of the fence, leaning closer to confirm Campbell's identity.

"I wasn't sure I'd get the chance, but he helped me get out." Campbell jerked his head toward Shane, who stood a couple of paces behind him. "He wants to join up. How about letting us in?"

The clank and scrape of the chain sounded too loud in the stillness of the forest. Campbell led the way, and Shane followed, then the other man locked up behind them.

"I'm Brian," the bearded man said. Shane shook his hand and introduced himself.

"Do I still have my room, or did you give me up for dead? And can you find Shane somewhere to crash for the rest of the night? We can talk to Ed in the morning." Campbell asked.

"Sure thing," Brian agreed. "I'll let the night shift know you're back with a friend."

The dormitory looked weather-beaten even in the dark. Brian stopped at a table just inside the door to light a candle for a second lantern, which he handed off to Campbell.

"Your room is just like you left it. We can drag a bed in there for Shane if you want, or there are open rooms on the second floor, toward the end of the hall. If they're not occupied, the door isn't latched. Help yourselves. Bring Shane to breakfast, and Ed will send someone over for you. Good to have you back." Brian clapped a hand on Shane's shoulder.

The old building held the cold and smelled musty. Shane was glad for his warm coat as he wondered how—or if—the "campers" heated the dormitory in the winter.

"I can't remember how I left my room, so let's go up to the second floor. Then tomorrow you can have the room all to yourself, unless—"

"That's fine. I'm used to splitting a room with Lucas. Thanks."

Worn wooden stairs creaked under their weight. Shane followed Campbell until he stopped at an open door. "There are bunk beds in each room—we keep several made up in case we get new people. Pick which one you want. I don't care."

Shit. Sneaking out to have a look around is going to be harder if we're sharing a room. Shane took the bottom bed and stretched out fully clothed except for his boots. The wool blankets were scratchy but warm, probably Army surplus. He put his gun under his pillow and drifted into a light sleep.

Sunlight streamed through the dirty glass window, catching on dust motes in the air. Shane had a moment's disorientation until he remembered the middle-of-the-night trek and his reconnaissance mission.

Campbell was already up, looking entirely too chipper without coffee. "Come on," he urged. "I'll show you around on the way to breakfast."

Shane followed, managing to slip his gun into his jacket pocket without being noticed. Just in case.

Time had not been kind to the campground, which was a sad shadow of the idyllic family getaway pictured in the old brochure. Neglect and the harsher weather since the Events had damaged the buildings, and weeds had long ago taken over the flower beds. A faded and tattered flag still fluttered from a rusted post in the center of the courtyard between the main buildings.

"We've got chicken coops, so plenty of eggs," Campbell told him as they walked. "Got sheep and goats for milk and a couple of pigs. The camp had some apple trees, and we put in a garden, so that means oats and wheat, plus fresh vegetables in the summer and fall. Plenty of deer in the woods and fish in the creek, so we don't go hungry much."

Much.

When they reached the dining hall, everyone seated at the long tables looked up as they entered. Campbell waved. "Hey, everyone! I'm back. This is Shane. I'm glad to be home."

Mumbled greetings welcomed them, although no one looked up from their food for long. Shane followed Campbell to where a man in an apron stood beside two big cauldrons. He grunted at Campbell in what Shane guessed passed for "hello," and ladled a portion of scrambled eggs and something that looked like thick gruel onto plates for them.

They picked up forks at the end of the table, and Campbell gestured toward an urn with cups next to it.

"Help yourself to what passes for coffee. It's made from grain, but it warms you up, which is what counts. You get used to the taste."

In their travels as Marshals, Shane and Lucas had visited many different enclaves. Those built around Amish farms, living history museums, or college campuses were able to make the transition and provide both necessities and a bit of comfort to their residents.

He had never seen an enclave quite this hard-scrabble. Shane assessed the others in the room while trying not to stare. No one looked emaciated, but they all were a bit too thin. They wore patched and stained clothing, but everyone was adequately dressed for the weather. Something about the tables of men bent over their plates reminded him of old photographs of coal miners from a century prior, tired workers in dangerous conditions.

Still, despite the privations, Shane did not pick up a sense of despair. Quiet conversations resumed, and the two dozen or so residents seemed at ease.

"Is this everyone?"

Campbell looked up from where he was already half finished with his eggs and glanced at the other tables. "Mostly. Some are on kitchen duty or out in the barn or on patrol. We're a few less than when we started—been some hard years since then. But almost everyone here worked together at the plant back in the day. Got a couple of walk-ins. Clarence." He nodded toward the big man who had served their food. "Brian at the gate was on his own and asked to join up. And now you."

"Why did you stay? The Beaver campus isn't that far." *And it has a lot more resources,* Shane thought.

"At first, Ed thought we should be close enough to do something if things got worse at the plant. After that, I guess we just got used to being here," Campbell answered. "We had worked together for so long it was hard to trust strangers."

The eggs were fresh, and the warm gruel filled his belly. Shane wrinkled his nose at the smell of the ersatz coffee, and Campbell chuckled.

"It takes some getting used to."

Shane braced himself and took a sip. The bitter mixture didn't taste like java, but it wasn't as bad as some of the burned sludge Shane had forced down during long nights as a Marshal. "I've had worse."

As they finished, a man approached the table. "Paul, Ed's ready to see you and your new friend. He's waiting for you in his office."

The camp office building was a one-story, three-room cottage with faded paint and broken shutters. For the headquarters of a doomsday cult, shabby normality wasn't what Shane had been expecting.

Once inside, the illusion of "normal" ended.

Crudely drawn art covered three walls like something out of a psychological thriller. Strange symbols looked unlike anything Shane had encountered in their work with the covens or that he had found in the lore books. Murals of strange, white beings reminded him of UFO movies. A jagged yellow line painted next to the aliens separated them from rolling green hills and familiar houses, and Shane guessed that was the pre-Events past Campbell and the others staked their hopes on.

An altar of sorts was set up against the fourth wall. A roughly embroidered cloth covered the table, which was decked with half-burned candles, scavenged trinkets, and a bowl with the ashes of what smelled like sage. Above the offerings was another painting of the glowing rift, this time augmented with a mosaic made from broken glass, chipped pieces of yellow ceramics, and chunks of costume jewelry.

A circle with symbols inside it was painted on the wooden floor. A similar circle with the placement of symbols reversed mirrored it on the ceiling.

Is it a portal? A summoning circle?

"Is this your...church?" Shane asked.

Campbell shook his head. "Oh, no. This is where Preacher prepares to receive guidance from the faeries. Can't you feel that it's a sacred space?"

Shane's sense of the genius loci songs provided him with a comparison to the truly sacred. The discordant music seemed louder here, jangled and unpleasant. It would have been a place to avoid if he'd had a choice. Not necessarily evil, but different and powerful enough to cause trouble.

"I can feel it," Shane murmured, letting Campbell draw his own conclusions.

A door opened, and a bald man in his early fifties emerged. Shane had been expecting someone in the flowing robes of a guru, or the black cassock of a priest. Instead, Ed looked very ordinary, except for the tangle of embroidered symbols stitched onto his canvas jacket.

"Thank you for bringing Paul home," Ed said. "You must be Shane."

"You're welcome. Pleased to meet you."

Ed didn't look crazy, and since they had brought Campbell back to familiar territory, he had lost the wild glint in his eyes as well.

"I hear you want to join us. Why?" Ed gave Shane an assessing look.

"I've been a soldier and a US Marshal. I've seen the worst both before the Events and after. I'm tired," Shane replied, drawing from a version of the truth. "Paul said the beings who speak to you can take you back in time, to the way things were?"

Ed nodded solemnly. "They are beautiful and powerful. Light and life. Ancient and wise. All my life, I went to church. I sat in the pews and listened to the scripture. None of it really made sense. And then when I saw the...faeries...suddenly everything fell into place."

Ed's quiet, assured voice made him easy to trust. Shane didn't sense any falsehood, an instinct honed from years dealing with professional criminals. Ed believed what he was saying. Whatever he had seen fit into the familiar narrative of miracles and wonders he had learned in Sunday School, making old faith alive in a new way.

"You're fortunate that they chose you," Shane said. "I mean no disrespect, but do you know why?"

Ed spread his hands, palms up, and shrugged. "I did nothing to deserve this favor. Maybe they knew that my people trust me to care for them, and our spirits are flagging here."

Dammit. I want to dislike him, out him as a fraud, but he's a true believer. Whatever the "faeries" are, he's bamboozled by them just like the rest of his followers.

"When will it happen?"

Ed shook his head. "I don't know, but it will be soon. The visions come more often, and when I'm seized by one, everything feels real. I can see through the rift, and on the other side is everything that we lost. Just like it used to be—waiting for us to step through and reclaim it."

"Forgive my doubt, but having been in law enforcement—I was trained to be skeptical," Shane replied. "How do you know that what you see is true?"

He wouldn't have been surprised if Ed had snapped at him or berated his lack of faith. Instead, the older man fixed Shane with a look of compassion that touched him unexpectedly.

"You and I don't have the history together that I do with my team," Ed replied. "Brian is also a newcomer, much like you. It took time for him to accept the revelations, but he came to know the truth."

The truth is the truth because it's true, Shane thought. *I'm not going to get anywhere like this.*

"Why do the faeries want to help? What's in it for them?" The words sounded sharp as he said them, and Ed winced at the tactless question.

"Because they've taken pity on us? Who can know?" Ed shook his head. "As for what they gain—perhaps they're not like us. Maybe for them, everything isn't a transaction."

Ed said all the right things and clearly believed them. That meant he was as suckered in as the others.

"I want to believe," Shane said, meaning the words more than he intended.

"Tonight, I will pray to them," Ed said. "They have nothing to hide. I will call our people together and relay what they tell me." He clapped a hand on Shane's shoulder, fatherly and reassuring. "You will under- stand. You all will."

Shane and Campbell headed back toward the dormitory, taking the long way so Shane got a look at the rest of the campground. "It's not what it used to be, but we do the best we can," Campbell told him.

"Who did you lose?"

Campbell didn't need Shane to explain the question. "Everyone except this team," he said, looking away. "My wife, our children, my parents. Friends. Cousins. We all did. If Ed hadn't brought us here, given us the challenge of making this place livable, I don't know if I would have lasted very long. And I know I'm not the only one who felt like that."

In daylight, Shane could see that although the old buildings were hard-worn, essential repairs had been made. Campbell showed off the gardens, livestock pens, and farm field with obvious pride.

"We trade with the farmers around here for what we can't make," Campbell told him. "Cheese. Beer. Corn whiskey. We worked together to make a mill to grind flour. Nothing big, but it's enough."

The old campgrounds didn't look as shabby to Shane now that he understood what had gone into bringing it back to life. Campbell and the others valued things differently, but although they had done what they needed to do to survive, they had never accepted the finality of the Events. Their true home was somewhere long gone.

"You've put a lot of work into it," Shane said.

"We never could get the swimming pool to work right," Campbell said wistfully. "But that's okay, because we won't be here much longer."

Shane spent the afternoon shadowing Campbell on his chores, lending a hand wherever he could. The work was hard, but it kept Shane from thinking too much about the encounter with Ed and the promises—or lies—the "faeries" had shown him.

He felt Campbell watching him when they headed back to the dormitory to clean up for supper. "Are you okay? You've been quiet."

Shane walked over to the window and looked out across the forest. "When there's no other option except to keep putting one foot in front of the other, that's what you do. But the idea that it might be possible to go back to how it was before...that's a whole different thing."

He hadn't expected to feel conflicted. Shane thought he had made his peace with the way things were after the Events, as much as anyone could. The grief and trauma were never going to heal completely, but he'd learned to compartmentalize. He had Lucas for a partner, and they had a purpose, and it was enough.

Shane didn't believe that Ed's "faeries" could make good on time travel, especially since it seemed that Ed had inferred that outcome more than gotten an actual promise. But the thought of being able to return to a version of the world before the cataclysm created a stronger pull on his emotions than Shane had been prepared to face.

"You know what I think?" Campbell confided, dropping his voice although they were alone in their small room. "Maybe the faeries have been watching us, and they realized that we needed a reason to keep going."

His eyes were alight with the shared secret. "It's been tough. We've talked about joining up with a bigger group like the one at the Beaver campus, but after being on our own, we weren't sure we could fit in or do things their way. But staying here...well, we do the best we can. I think we were starting to wear thin; you know what I mean?"

"And the possibility of going through the rift gives you hope?" Shane turned to look at his companion.

"Yeah. Seeing the people we've lost, being back the way it used to be, maybe being able to save the world if we can stop the Events—what could be better? And if the rift dumps us out somewhere else...well, anywhere's better than here," Campbell replied.

I'm not so sure about that.

The group in the dining hall buzzed with excitement at the prospect of receiving word from the creatures beyond the rift. Shane ate his bowl of venison stew in silence, listening to the conversations around them.

"—first thing I'm gonna do is go see my little girl."

"—gettin' a pizza before I do anything."

"—gotta get back to my wife. We had a baby on the way."

Shane's heart ached for the men who had pinned their hopes on Ed's visions. He felt sure that everyone who had survived the Events had thought about what they would do with one more day before the end came. But these men believed that fantasy was almost within their grasp, and the cruelty of it made Shane clench his teeth.

Whatever or whoever these "faeries" are, they're either lying to Ed or he's reading his own wishes into what he's seeing.

Shane and Lucas recently dealt with a hotel in Ansted that phased in and out of existence thanks to a badly damaged genius loci and some freaky demon magic. Even it hadn't offered a gateway to a different destination in time, just a doorway to nothingness. *If that hadn't been a ride to the Before times, I don't think there's such a thing to be had.*

Shane thought about trying to talk Campbell out of staying, but he knew the man would be unlikely to return to an enclave that held him prisoner. *Dammit! If they cross the rift, I'm pretty sure they'll die. And if they don't and the whole thing falls apart, will they have a reason to go on?*

Shane did his best to smile and match the party mood of his companions. His head hurt like a storm was coming, and his skin tingled as if lightning had struck nearby. Shane listened to the song of the nearby genius loci, worried that the discordant jangle seemed to be getting worse. His wolf-side's enhanced senses were muted, but Shane still felt restless.

The energy is shifting. I don't know whether that's good or bad, but it's hella powerful.

A bell rang, deeper in tone than the one at the front gate. Campbell grabbed his empty dishes and stood, beckoning for Shane to come with him.

"Time to go. Ed's ready for the ritual."

They walked across the campground, joined by more residents as they went, and Shane noticed several men he hadn't seen before. Apparently, a vision was an all-hands event.

When the group reached the camp office, candles flickered in a half-circle around the front. The windows glowed with lantern light, and the smell of sage and incense hung in the air.

Ed came to the doorway after they assembled just beyond the candles. He wore the embroidered jacket, which Shane guessed was his version of holy vestments. "Welcome, friends. I will call to the faeries, and ask them your questions. We will learn more about the rift and how it can bring us home."

The sense of excitement and anticipation lit up the weary faces of the men around Shane. As skeptical as he was, he couldn't help being caught up in the mood.

What if Ed is right? What if it's really possible?

Ed left the door open so the others could see into the room with the murals and shrine. Candles lit the interior, with four more positioned at the quarters of the circle on the floor.

Preacher Ed walked first to the altar, lit a dried leaf from a candle, raised it toward the markings on the ceiling, then poured wine from a pitcher into a chalice he carried into the circle.

He knelt in the middle of the markings and lifted the chalice toward the sky. Shane couldn't make out the words of Ed's invocation, only the tone and cadence, but it conveyed reverence and hope. The look on Ed's face mirrored the expressions of the men around Shane, all of them betting everything they had despite the long odds.

The discordant song of the damaged genius loci grew painfully loud in his mind, shrill enough to make him wince. He wanted to howl. His wolf senses picked up an energy shift that made him uneasy.

The men around Shane seemed unaffected by the song, while Ed appeared to be caught in rapturous bliss, eyes staring at the ceiling, mouth open, and body taut.

White light flared inside the small building. The others shielded their eyes, but Shane forced himself not to look away. In that instant, before the room went dark again, Shane glimpsed something that wasn't human and sure as hell wasn't a faerie.

The light blinked out, leaving a red imprint in Shane's sight. The men outside had gone quiet, waiting for answers.

Ed slumped forward, shoulders rounded, head down. Shane wondered what it took out of the man to call down a visitation from the beings that had answered. After a few moments, Ed straightened and stood, then turned toward the anxious crowd outside the door.

"My friends, did you see? The faeries came. And very, very soon, they will open the way for us to travel to our heart's desire."

The men burst into a cacophony of questions but stilled when Ed motioned for silence. "One at a time. I will tell you everything that I have learned."

"When can we make the crossing?" Campbell spoke up. The others murmured in support, and Shane guessed that was uppermost in their minds.

"When the moon is right," Ed replied. "At the Equinox. That is when the Veil is thinnest. We must wait and prepare. They will return for us and take us to the place we came from."

The others called out questions. Ed calmed their worries, repeated the hope for returning to the past, and encouraged them to be patient.

Shane's head throbbed, and his eyes stung from the bright light. He no longer felt the urge to howl, but he was still unsettled with a strong desire to shift and run. The song of the damaged elemental no longer shrilled as loudly, though it hadn't faded altogether.

I need to get out of here. I've learned all I can. Time to go back to Lucas and strategize.

"What did you think?" Ed asked after most of the others drifted away, leaving only Campbell, Shane, and a handful of others.

"I was impressed," Shane replied, not exactly lying. "I want to bring my partner with us. We've been best friends all our lives. If he could see, he would believe."

Shane had no intention of bringing Lucas to the compound or returning without a plan and backup. But right now, he needed to play along.

"I'm afraid that can't be permitted," Ed said gently. "After what happened to Paul—being kidnapped and held against his will—we can't take the risk. You could miss when the rift opens, and once that happens, it won't open again. Trust me. You're safest here. Your partner made his choice."

Shane knew better than to argue. But he still had questions. "It's going to take a lot of energy to carry us all through the rift. Are the faeries strong enough?"

Ed looked away, past Shane toward where the old nuclear plant hunkered against the skyline. "If we need more energy, it's there for the taking."

Shane's breath caught as Ed confirmed his fears. "But that would mean an explosion, radiation—what about the people who would get hurt?"

Ed placed a hand on his shoulder, a gesture full of comfort—and warning. "Those who are worthy will be permitted to return to the golden times. A remnant will be saved. The others could not cross because their minds are too narrow. I'm sorry about your partner. But the faeries have chosen."

Shane forced his expression to be neutral. He nodded but did not speak. Campbell guided back to the path to the dormitory.

"I know it's a lot to take in since you're new," Campbell said once they were away from the others. "But you came at the perfect time, which proves you are meant to be among the remnant. And once we're home, it will all be worth it."

"Just trying to get my head around it all," Shane replied, which was the truth but not how he knew Campbell would take it.

"It's big, right? I mean, faeries! A split in the sky that takes us to the past. Like something out of a movie," Campbell said.

"Maybe I just need to sleep on it," Shane said. "Things always look clearer in the morning."

Campbell seemed satisfied by Shane's reply, and they walked back to the room talking about what they wanted to do first when they got to the past.

"I want a chili dog, with all the toppings, and a mound of French fries," Campbell said. "And ice cream. After I see everyone. But still— can you imagine being able to order a pizza again? Or watch TV? I'll never gripe about what's playing at the theater again."

Shane and Lucas talked about such things often on their long rides, but with the acknowledgment that those cherished memories were gone forever. Campbell's hope and his stalwart trust in Ed and the faeries broke Shane's heart in places he thought it would never break again.

"Yeah, I miss pizza," he replied. "Cherry pie. Hamburgers with extra cheese and onions. A really good steak—from a cow, not a deer."

"Now you're talkin'!" Campbell encouraged, slapping Shane on the back. "Ed says that the more we picture what we want, the easier it is for the faeries to bring us to the right moment in the past."

Shane didn't know what the faeries were, but he hated them with a passion for abusing the trust of Campbell and the others.

Back at the dormitory, Campbell hung his coat on a peg and put his boots by his bed. "Better get some shut-eye," he recommended. "Going to have a lot of chores to do tomorrow."

Shane made a show of unlacing his boots, but he kept them on, as well as his jacket. "Gotta pee," he said as he headed for the door.

"Be quiet when you come back," Campbell warned. "I'm going to be asleep as soon as I hit the pillow."

"Good night," Shane replied, knowing he wasn't returning. "Sleep tight."

The hallway was empty, although Shane could hear voices from behind closed doors. He moved quietly to the shared bathroom, relieved to find it empty. Shane had already scoped out the exits, including a window over the porch roof that made for an easier descent.

He opened the window and went into a stall to strip down. Then he rolled his clothing into a bundle with his coat and tied the laces of his boots together. The boots were heavy and clunky, but there was no helping it—replacements were hard to get.

Shane listened closely, but he didn't hear or scent anyone nearby. He shifted, then took his clothing bundle and the laces of his boots in his mouth and loped to the window. Once he assured himself that no one would see a wolf bounding from the dormitory window, Shane leaped over the sill, landing as silently as he could on the porch roof before jumping to the ground.

He kept to the shadows, easily avoiding the patrols. When Campbell had shown him around earlier, Shane had spotted where water had dug a swale beneath the fence. It didn't take much for his wolf to make the hole large enough to fit through, even with the objects he carried in his mouth.

Shane took a deep breath with a sigh of relief when he reached the other side. No one from the campground seemed to note his escape. Once the campground was out of sight, Shane stopped in the woods to shift and put on clothes.

"US Marshal Shane Collins, returning from reconnaissance," he told the guard at the Beaver campus gate. Shane didn't care that it was well past midnight. He wanted a hot shower and a glass of whiskey, and assurance that Lucas's mission had also been successful.

When he reached their room, it was dark and empty. A note from Lucas lay on the desk.

"Went to the prepper camp. I'll be back as soon as I can. Might be a couple of days, especially if they make it hard to leave. Hang tight, and I'll see you when I see you."

The note was dated two days ago, the same date Shane had gone to the campground.

Lucas still hadn't returned.

Something had gone wrong.

CHAPTER FIVE

Two days prior

WHAT ARE YOU HEARING? Lucas asked Rocky as he walked along the road toward the prepper camp.

You are nervous about meeting these people. They might be danger-ous. And you worry about Shane.

Lucas chuckled. *Yes, all of that. But I meant—what are you hearing around us? The other genius loci? Spirits?*

The daemons here are sickly, not evil. They have been poisoned like the land. Until the poison wanes, they will not be right.

Since the poison in question was radioactive, it could be ten thousand years before the land was clean again. The elementals didn't die, so they could wait for purification, but people might be long gone.

Anything that could be the "faeries" the cultists are raving about?

The energy in this place is unstable. It attracts broken things.

I think we're all broken these days, Lucas replied. *Or did you mean twisted?*

Yes. Dark damage. The vibrations around the poisoned place are all wrong. Perhaps humans mistake that for magic?

Lucas knew what the stories said about faeries. He remembered that in the old tales, faeries weren't nice. They were often petty, arrogant, territorial, and cruel. They stole children, switched babies, kidnapped people, and offered deals with a malicious twist.

Never eat their food or drink their wine. Never owe them a debt. Don't ask for favors, and stay away from their special places. Before he left the Beaver enclave, Bauers took him to the campus library, and Lucas gave himself a crash course in dealing with the fae.

Iron was the best protection, so along with his gun and a steel knife, Lucas carried a short, sharpened piece of rebar. He considered that to be insurance, but Lucas didn't believe the creature offering the cultists a free ride to the past was actually fae.

Maybe Shane's recon would give them a better idea of what they were up against and how to stop it. Lucas disliked splitting up—something proven to be a bad idea both on the job and in past D&D games—but he had to agree that they were more likely to infiltrate the cult and the preppers going solo rather than as a team. He just hoped they both got back safely.

Up ahead, he saw the sign and gatehouse for the nuclear plant. Mindful of the warnings about the radiation levels, Lucas had no desire for a closer look. Movement caught his eye, and Lucas peered at the hazy figures of the ghosts that blocked the driveway.

Are they the guardians? The spirits of the shutdown crew that died sealing off the plant?

The revenants stood like sentries, shoulder to shoulder. Aside from the enclaves, there didn't seem to be many people around to guard against, but Lucas figured that looters who didn't understand the dangers might try their luck to find anything they could use or sell.

Rocky yelped a warning, and Lucas pivoted just in time to see an unusually tall, wizened old man with a mane of white hair and a long scraggly beard standing close behind him. Before Lucas could draw his gun or either of the knives, the man's arm shot forward with unnatural speed and a gnarled hand gripped his shoulder so hard that Lucas thought the fingers would pierce his skin.

"What are you?" Lucas panted, finding himself unable to move.

"Hmm...what are *you?*" the man asked, fixing Lucas with a stare that seemed to see down to his bones. Piercing blue eyes looked out from beneath shaggy gray brows, and for a heartbeat, Lucas thought the eyes swam full of stars.

He is a forest spirit, ancient and very powerful, Rocky supplied. *I have not seen his kind since the mountains were new.*

"A human with an elemental inside? Or an elemental, wearing a human? This is...interesting."

Lucas felt the creature's power and froze, praying that its attention moved on.

The air grew cold as the guardian spirits slipped away from their post to gather around them. Now that they were closer, Lucas saw them in detail—men in coveralls and hazmat suits, gray-faced and sober-eyed.

Leave him alone. He is mine.

Lucas couldn't tell whether Rocky used his voice to speak aloud or if he only needed to mind-speak to draw the creature's attention. It worked, because the forest spirit nodded and released his grip. Freed from its spell, Lucas barely managed to stay on his feet.

"You do not come to cause harm. I see you are a guardian, like them," the creature said with a look toward the ghosts. "I will not take you away."

With that, the shaggy-haired man-creature turned and walked off, disappearing into the forest as the ghosts drifted back to their sentry post.

What the hell just happened? Lucas's knees still felt wobbly after the confrontation and the way the strange being had gotten into his head.

Forest spirit, remember? Very powerful.

Stronger than you?

Hard to say. Different...skills.

Before Lucas had a chance to ask more questions, he heard the click of a gun's safety.

"Stay where you are. Put your hands up," the stranger commanded. "Now turn around—slowly. And give me a reason not to shoot."

I guess I found the preppers.

Lucas faced three men with guns, all of whom looked like they could put up a fight he might not win.

"I'm US Marshal Lucas Maddox. I wanted to find the preppers in the old military enclave, ask them some questions."

"US Marshal? Didn't think there were any left," the man in front said.

"Not many. Just my partner and me. We do what we can."

"And what brings one of the last two Marshals to our humble abode?" the leader asked.

"Do we have to stand here freezing our nuts off? I talk better when I'm warm," Lucas replied, hoping his snark covered how off-kilter he still felt from the confrontation with the forest spirit.

"Suit yourself." The leader gave a jerk of his head, and his team fell in around Lucas.

They're ex-military. Or cops. They've been together for a while, and they were professionals.

"Where did you serve?" Lucas asked as they walked.

The leader gave him a look. "Why do you care?"

Lucas shrugged. "Takes one to know one."

"Hot spots, wherever they needed me," the stranger said. "Special ops. You?"

"Mostly Middle East. More action than I ever really wanted to see," Lucas replied. "Before I went into the Marshals."

"And you're still out there, doing your job? What can two men do against all that's wrong in the world?" The leader had a weary tone that Lucas recognized too well.

"More than you'd think."

The abandoned outpost still had the chain-link fence with warning signs and a small, crumbling guardhouse. They headed for the gate, and two sentries let them in while others hung back protectively.

"This way." The stranger led Lucas farther into the compound. The cement block buildings had peeling paint and faded roofs, but the yards were weeded, and while old, the structures had been maintained.

"Is it true that you've got a missile silo and a bunker?" Lucas asked. "Because that's pretty badass."

The stranger snickered. "Yeah. Both, actually. But the missiles are gone, and the bunker stinks."

When they reached a squat white building that looked like the base office, he stopped. "In here. Then it's time to talk."

He lit a lantern, which barely illuminated the small room. "Sit."

Lucas sat in the only chair, hands clasped between his knees.

One of the team stood near the door on watch. The second man took a position in the back corner, another line of protection. The leader sat behind an old army-issue desk that looked like it was from the 1950s.

"Who are you?" the man asked.

"Told you already. Who are you?" Lucas shot back.

"Captain Chris Thomas. And the people here are what's left of my command."

"How'd you become a bunch of preppers?" Lucas sat back in his chair, taking control. "Would have thought you'd have something better to do—like protect people instead of hiding."

The man in the corner started forward, but Thomas raised a hand, and he stopped immediately. "Who says we're not protecting people?" Thomas challenged.

"From what I hear, you blockade the road, run off travelers, maybe shake them down or make them disappear." Lucas shrugged, performing to get a reaction. "And then hide behind your fences and your guns."

"Then you hear wrong," the guy in the corner snapped before Thomas silenced him with a look.

"What business is it of yours?" Thomas asked, staring at Lucas as if he was a puzzle to be solved.

"The Beaver campus enclave requested my partner and me because they were worried about a threat to the nuclear plant," Lucas replied, dropping the banter. "They weren't sure who was more dangerous—the armed yahoos playing soldier of fortune or the crazy religious people who might drink their Kool-Aid with a side of radioactive waste."

"What did you plan to do about the threat?"

"Shut it down."

Thomas stared at the ceiling for a moment, then seemed to come to a decision. He settled forward, placing his elbows on the desk, and peered at Lucas. "We're not the ones you need to worry about."

"Says the guy who's holding me at gunpoint."

Thomas rolled his eyes, then nodded at his team, who holstered their weapons. "Better?" he snarked.

"Yeah, actually. Thanks." Lucas studied Thomas, trying to figure out his game. "Now you were saying that you're the good guys?"

"We're not 'preppers.' At least, not in the way most people mean it. We didn't hoard food, and we didn't stockpile a bunch of weapons waiting for the end of the world. We're military. We know how to scavenge and how to forage. But we didn't do it before the Events. Only after, when there was nowhere else to go."

Thomas met Lucas's gaze. "We didn't try to set the record straight about not being crazy survivalists. Figured if that helped to keep people away, it made less work for us."

"Why here?" Despite everything, Lucas found himself liking Thomas. The man didn't seem crazy. He had learned to trust his instincts, and his gut said Chris Thomas was telling the truth.

"My dad worked at the Beaver Valley plant. My grandpa worked at Shippingport. When the Events happened, my team was stationed at Fort Letterkenny in Chambersburg. We were an air defense unit, but we still never saw the strikes coming," Thomas said with a bitter note.

"For the first while, we stayed with the base, tried to help. But there was no support, no direction from the top. We were cut off and everything we had trained for no longer mattered because we failed," Thomas continued, the burden of guilt clear in his expression. "Little by little, people just...walked away."

"You didn't fail," Lucas said. "Or at least, you didn't fail any more than we all did. No one saw it coming."

"I try to tell myself that. Haven't listened yet."

"How did you get here?" Lucas asked.

"Most of my team members had family in the areas that were hardest hit. They didn't have anywhere to go. So I told them to come home with me," Thomas replied. "When we got here, we found out that my family was gone. I still don't know what happened to them. But we heard people talking about the nuclear plants and how they were afraid people would do something to them to make things worse."

Thomas paused and rubbed his temples. "We realized that no one was guarding the plant. This was something we could do. If the wrong people got access, they could do real harm. The guardian ghosts couldn't protect the plant on their own."

Lucas believed Thomas, but he felt sure the other man hadn't told him the whole story. "Does the phrase 'dogs of war' mean anything?"

Thomas's head snapped up. "What do you know?"

Lucas considered the other man's reaction and realized he'd hit a nerve. "Government experiments. Trying to create the perfect hybrid soldier. Werewolf, shifter, and human. We've run into them before. Got a tip that you might have seen them too."

Thomas looked at Lucas for a long moment, clearly deciding what and how much he wanted to say. "When we first came to the base, it was like something out of a horror movie. We found a dozen corpses, and even though they'd been dead for a while, there was plenty of evidence to suggest they had been clawed, bitten, and ripped apart by large, strong wild animals."

"I thought the base was abandoned."

"So did everyone. Apparently there was more going on here than just a skeleton crew maintaining the equipment," Thomas replied. "Once we got a good look around, it was clear that some kind of scientific work was in progress when the Events occurred. We found lab and medical equipment that was much newer than the original base. A lot of it had been smashed, but nothing had been looted. And there were more bodies."

Lucas didn't like where the story was heading. It sounded far too much like the experiments at Fort Hood and Dr. Richardson's violent hybrids.

"We were attacked. Man-sized wolves. Two of my people were killed." Thomas passed a hand back through his hair, and his gaze was shadowed.

"They were so fast, so strong. Nothing but a head shot stopped the creatures. We didn't know what we were up against," Thomas recalled. "Or maybe, we didn't want to know. We killed one with a machete and watched the body turn human again."

He blew out a long breath. "After that, we had a new mission. We hunted those monsters."

"What about the creature that looks like a crazy old man?" Lucas asked, watching closely to see Thomas's reaction. He mentally filed away their reaction to the hybrids so he could warn Shane.

The man's head snapped up. "You saw it?"

"Pretty sure I have a bruise on my shoulder from the way he grabbed me," Lucas replied. "What the fuck was he?"

"We think he's a Leshy. Slavic forest spirit. A lot of folks from Eastern Europe settled around here and brought their beliefs with them. Leshy have a reputation for being tricksters—and for eating people," Thomas replied.

"There were more of the werewolves—dogs of war, whatever you want to call them. We captured one and found out that they were

Grade-A, government-issued monsters, like something out of a bad movie," the captain added.

"We needed help, but we were on our own. We couldn't bring this down on the Beaver campus people. One night, we all prayed to whatever powers we believed in for help. The next night, the Leshy revealed itself."

"How did you tame it?"

Thomas gave a harsh laugh. "Tame? You don't 'tame' an ancient forest spirit. We made a deal with it. It doesn't eat us, and we let it have the troublemakers that show up between the camp and the nuclear plant. Mutually beneficial."

"So that's what he meant when he said he wouldn't take me. Good to know it wasn't my day to get eaten," Lucas replied. "I'm guessing he took care of the rest of the hybrid war dogs."

Captain Thomas nodded.

"He seemed to have an...understanding...with the guardian spirits at the plant entrance."

Thomas raised an eyebrow. "You're full of surprises. You can see them?"

Lucas shrugged. "People have come up with all kinds of surprising new talents since the Events. I caught glimpses of ghosts Before. Now I see them more often. No big deal."

"None of us got a visual on the ghosts, but any time we went near the entrance, we could feel that something wasn't right."

"It was too cold, your skin got prickly, and you had a strong urge to leave?"

Thomas nodded. "Yeah. It felt creepy, like we weren't wanted."

"And you weren't. The ghosts are the men who died in the meltdown and the shutdown crew that volunteered to seal things up afterward, knowing it was going to kill them," Lucas replied. "They're heroes —and they want to make sure no one comes along and fucks up what they died to fix."

"Anyone who goes past the fence around the plant isn't going to live long to enjoy whatever they steal. One of our guys rigged up a Geiger counter from spare parts before we settled in—wanted to know we weren't going to glow. We're far enough away here to be okay. The driveway past the gate is a couple of miles long, but the meter starts pegging even before you're close enough to see the plant," Thomas replied.

"What do you know about the crazy cultists in the church camp?" Lucas saw a flash of surprise in Thomas's eyes at the shift in topic.

"We leave them alone, and they don't bother us. They've been there for quite a while. When we checked them out, they seemed nutty but harmless."

Lucas shifted in his chair. "I'm not too sure about that. Your folks didn't freak out meeting a Leshy. Have you run into anything that might pass for the fae?"

"Fae?"

Lucas sighed. "Faeries. Like elves only meaner."

"You're fucking kidding me, right?"

"Wish to God I was. The Beaver campus people captured one of the cultists who was playing street preacher outside their gates, and we questioned him. Their leader has visions of creatures that promised to take them through a rift in the sky—back in time to before the Events. He called the beings 'faeries.'"

Thomas's eyes widened. "Faeries. Time travel. A hole in the sky. Did they eat some funny mushrooms?"

"It sounds nuts until you realize that they're all nuclear plant workers camping a stone's throw away from the biggest power source on this side of the state, in case that portal to the past needs a jumpstart."

All humor drained from Thomas's face. "You think they're a threat to the plant?"

"My partner went to find out. Much as I'd like to write off their boss man's visions as a bad trip, it doesn't matter whether these 'faeries' are real or not. Plenty of people have done terrible things because the voices in their heads said so," Lucas replied.

"Shit. Could they actually sabotage the plant? I thought it was sealed."

"There are mine tunnels filled with radioactive waste not far from the plant that are unstable. Plus, the containment team didn't stop the meltdown—they just smothered it in concrete. It's still burning underneath all that. If anyone knows how to pop the cork, it's the guys at the camp."

Lucas knew he was going out on a limb trusting Thomas, but he'd been silently checking in with Rocky all along, and his co-pilot was comfortable with the "preppers"—after they no longer held Lucas at gunpoint.

"They'd need something powerful to kick off either of those things," Thomas said, which reminded Lucas that the captain had family members who worked at the plants.

"After the Events, all the natural disasters shifted the resonance of the land in places," Lucas said. "It's hard to explain. Where the energy is tainted, it can be dangerous—and used by people with bad intentions."

Thomas met Lucas's gaze with a skeptical expression. "Sounds to me like you're talking about magic."

"Magic, energy—two names for the same thing depending on who's doing the explaining," Lucas replied.

"Are all Marshals as weird as you?"

Lucas grinned. "Since there's only me and my partner left, the answer is 'yes.'"

Thomas sat back in his chair, closed his eyes, and pinched the bridge of his nose. After a silent moment, he took a deep breath and looked at Lucas as if giving him one last chance to admit that this was all a joke.

Lucas watched denial battle with the details Thomas knew to be right, and it was almost as if he could see the confusion clear as the pieces slotted into place in the other man's mind.

"This isn't actually the craziest thing I've ever heard that turned out to be true," Thomas said. "What was that quote about 'three impossible things before breakfast'? So, Marshal Maddox—what were you expecting when you came here? Help storming the campground? Because it's a bit overkill, don't you think?"

"If the cultists have some sort of...connection...to whatever it is they think are faeries, and the power is real, then we don't know what they can do," Lucas said. "My partner is putting his life in danger to infiltrate the camp and find out what we're up against."

"You think it's actually faeries?"

Lucas rolled his eyes. "No. But seriously—you can believe in a Leshy, but you choke on the idea that *something* might have been misinterpreted to inspire those stories about the fae?"

"They didn't exactly cover mythical creatures in Basic Training. That must have been at Camp Hogwarts."

"Shane should be at the Beaver campus when I get back. If he's confirmed that the threat is real and has intel about whatever the 'rift' and 'fae' are, then we can make a plan." Lucas tamped down his worry over Shane's recon. "Even if their leader is a total nut job and dreamed the whole thing up, we can't let the cultists breach the containment on the reactor. Because whether or not faeries are real, we'll all be dead."

Thomas looked at Lucas for a few moments without saying anything. Finally, he gave a curt nod. "Okay. Let's hear what your partner has to say. In the meantime, you can stay the night here. The chow won't kill you, we all bathe regularly, and since the base was built for a much bigger crew, there are plenty of extra bunks."

Lucas gave him a wary look. "Just to be clear—am I a prisoner?"

Thomas glared at him. "Do you *want* to head back alone in the dark? The Leshy isn't the worst thing out there. You're free to go."

"Then I'll take you up on your offer," Lucas said, with a grudging smile which Thomas returned.

"Smart man." Thomas looked to one of the guards by the door. "Liam, take Marshal Maddox to one of the open rooms and give him a kit so he can clean up."

He glanced back to Lucas. "You've got about an hour until dinner. Liam will come to get you—the base layout takes a while to get used to. You're Army, so you'll understand when I say that even though you're not confined to quarters it's not a good look to go wandering around unescorted."

"Message received," Lucas replied, "and thanks for listening."

"We don't get much excitement around here. You can earn your dinner with stories from the road."

LUCAS PAID attention to the route as Liam led the way down corridors painted a sickly shade of industrial green. The dim glow from bare bulbs lit the way, and Lucas noted that many of the overhead fixtures were empty, presumably to save electricity from the base's generators. When they reached his room, Lucas thanked his guide.

"I'll be back to get you in time for dinner. The bathroom is two doors back the way we came. The lights work in there—just turn them off when you leave. And the water pressure is good. Rest if you want to—I'll pound hard enough to wake you up," Liam promised with a smirk.

"See you in a few," Lucas replied.

The room's utilitarian accommodations had a mid-century Army surplus look. A metal bunk bed sat against one wall, the double desk with two chairs took up most of the floor space, and two small closets with built-in drawers flanked the door. The single bulb overhead illuminated a surprisingly clean, relatively dust-free space.

Much as Lucas's curiosity urged him to explore, he had no intention of getting on the wrong side of his host since he had a feeling they'd need Thomas's help with the cultists. He found the dormitory-style bathroom, which had obviously been designed to take care of a crowd, and washed away the dirt and sweat from his journey. He felt reasonably safe here, but not enough to risk the vulnerability of taking a shower.

Maybe if we survive, I can talk Captain Thomas into giving Shane and me a tour—I'd like to see the bunker and the missile silo. The place is in better shape than I expected. We'll find out tomorrow if Thomas is telling the truth about letting me go, but so far, they're not as nuts as I thought they might be.

He knew that although Rocky had been mostly silent, the elemental was always present. *Anything you notice that I ought to know?* Lucas asked as he combed his fingers through his hair to look presentable.

The energy here is better than with the last soldiers you met.

Lucas grimaced at the memory. *Because those assholes were trying to kill us. They were crazy—and dangerous.*

Did I not say that? Rocky replied.

Lucas still wasn't sure how much his unlikely co-pilot understood of humor, or whether his dry observations were unintentionally funny. *I guess you did. Nice that these guys are different.*

Liam showed up on time and guided Lucas through the dimly-lit corridors to the dining hall. "What do you know about the base?" Lucas asked.

"It basically babysat the missile silos and the bombs they stored in the bunker," Liam said, "which was part of the Cold War plan to defend Pittsburgh and its manufacturing infrastructure. From what we could piece together, there were about thirty soldiers stationed here, so it was more of an outpost than a base."

"Kind of amazing the places you find now that everyone's run off and left them," Lucas mused.

"The bombs and the missiles are long gone, so we're not really sure what the soldiers did after that. Probably some kind of communications monitoring, given the equipment that's left. Of course, until the Events, this was all still government property," Liam replied.

"Obviously some of the stuff still works."

Liam nodded. "The site was decommissioned but not abandoned. Mothballed, I guess. It got enough maintenance to keep everything in working order in case they ever needed it. Sometime after that, another group moved in, like Captain Thomas told you—medical experimentation, we figure. That was a mess to clean up, but it meant all the systems were upgraded and running. Lucky for us. The generator and the water treatment system both work and so does the heat. No AC. It's enough to make the place livable."

Fifteen men and women in fatigues sat at a long table in the dining hall. They looked up when Lucas and Liam walked in, and Lucas figured guests were an unusual occurrence. After giving him the once-over, the former soldiers went back to their conversations, and Lucas followed his guide to line up at a pass-through at the kitchen. He could glimpse at least two people at work near the stove. As he and Liam reached the opening, the cook pushed filled plates across the shelf to them.

Some kind of meat in a brown gravy accompanied boiled potatoes and carrots. It smelled good, and Lucas was hungry.

"A couple of the guys have some real talent when it comes to making food that tastes great considering what we have to work with," Liam said as Lucas followed him to join the others at the table. "We do the best we can, hunting and trapping. Plenty of game to hunt now that there aren't as many people nearby. We put in a garden, and we barter with the farmers who are still around. It's enough."

"So tell us about what you've seen, Marshal," a female soldier with her dark hair pulled back in a bun asked after Liam and Lucas got settled. Lucas noticed that Thomas's people still stayed close to regulation in their appearance, although four years had passed since there was anyone official to care.

"Mostly, there's a whole lot of nothing out there," Lucas said.

"People left where they were and went somewhere else. There's hardly anyone outside the enclaves. Everyone liked to talk about being self-sufficient, but the Events made that a lot harder."

"Surely you've seen something interesting," one of the others said. "Remember—we don't have cable, and we've read all the books we could find."

Lucas came up with the best stories he could think of, leaving out anything about his near-death and Rocky or Shane's new wolfiness. When he finished, Lucas looked at the others as an idea took shape.

"You know, at the Beaver campus, there's a whole university library," Lucas said. "Maybe if there was a proper introduction so that they don't think you're crazy preppers, you could work out a lending arrangement."

He saw the excitement in the eyes of several of the soldiers and understood first-hand how tedious the boredom on a base could be. Lucas had a feeling that with better information, Bauers would change his mind about the outpost. Maybe the two groups could work out something that would help both parties.

"So it's just you and one other Marshal?" Liam asked.

"Shane and I have been friends since we were kids. Went through the Army together, joined up with the Marshals afterward. We were on assignment when the world ended. Since then, we just kept on doing what we do," Lucas replied with a shrug.

"And you cover how large an area?" The soldier who asked about the books looked curious.

"Western Pennsylvania, Eastern Ohio, and Northern West Virginia," Lucas replied. "Give or take."

"At least you don't have to go into New York. There's a camp at Chautauqua that's run like a frickin' fortress," the man across from Lucas said. "Everyone says the guy in charge is a real hard ass. People leave them alone."

"I'll keep that in mind," Lucas replied. "Can't imagine anything that would send us up that way, but then again, it's not like we'd be infringing on another Marshal's territory."

Lucas helped clean up after dinner and stuck around for a few friendly hands of cards afterward, mostly to observe what the group was like without Thomas present.

They seem to get along just fine. I don't get the feeling anyone is being kept here against their will.

The energy among them is good—strong enough to overcome the vibrations of this place, Rocky replied.

What's wrong with the base?

The stones remember. Fear, anger, destruction. Those are the reasons this exists. When it was empty, that faded. Now, they help it heal, Rocky added.

So there's a daemon here at the base?

Not exactly. All places have energy. Not all energy is aware, Rocky answered.

"Breakfast is at oh-six-hundred," Liam's voice broke Lucas from his thoughts.

Lucas raised an eyebrow. "Dude. You know the end of the world happened, right? You don't have to still get up that early."

Liam laughed. "Tell that to the boss. There are chickens to feed, eggs to gather, gardens to tend, and potatoes to peel. Captain Thomas believes that routines and purpose create resilience."

"You say that like it's something you've heard before," Lucas joked.

"All the time—even before the Events. And...he's right. Everyone here is still alive because of Captain Thomas," Liam said. "He kept us from panicking, gave us focus, and created a family for a bunch of people who had no one else left. Like what you and your partner created for yourselves."

"That makes sense."

Liam gave Lucas a measured look. "What you offered, about the library—you didn't have to do that. But, thank you. You have no idea how much that would mean to us. We go a little stir crazy. There's only so much poker even I can play before I need a break."

"When we're done stopping the crazy cultists, I'll be glad to introduce Captain Thomas to the guy in charge at the campus. I think your two groups could work something out. Maybe in more ways than just books. But the library is a start."

They reached Lucas's room, and Lucas grinned. "If you want me up at oh-dark-thirty, you better pound extra hard."

"Challenge accepted."

CHAPTER SIX

"Do you think it can work?" Shane asked Claire, looking up from the list of ingredients she handed him.

The witch chuckled. "I think the odds of it working are better than those of it failing spectacularly, or I wouldn't risk my coven."

"Fair enough." Shane realized his leg was bouncing beneath the table and willed himself to stop. Moments later, his fingers started to drum as if his hand had a mind of its own.

"You're worried," Claire said.

"He should have been back by now." Shane glanced toward the windows of the repurposed classroom building as if he could spot Lucas from here.

"You both agreed to two days and nights before deciding a rescue was needed, right?"

"Yeah, but I came back early—I was afraid that if I didn't take my chance, I'd be stuck there," Shane said.

"Give him a while longer. I don't sense danger around him."

Shane struggled to trust in the witch's clairvoyance. He guessed it wasn't too different from his own ability to hear the songs of the genius loci and gain warnings or help from them. But unfamiliar magic made Shane nervous, especially when Lucas's safety was on the line.

With a sigh, he forced himself to turn back to the task at hand. "What does your coven make of the cultists?"

Claire met his gaze. "A few think that we shouldn't get involved, but the rest realize that you need our help to succeed, whether we like this particular battle or not."

Shane got up to pace the length of the library conference room. "Believe me, if there were another way, I'd take it. I really thought the campground people weren't that bad until Ed pulled a Hotel California on me."

"It's very possible that the leader—Ed—has been deceived by whatever entity wants help to bring victims through the rift," Claire said. "Maybe he was a decent guy before it got its hooks in him."

"I couldn't tell whether he was so happy to be important that he'd sell off his folks for fodder or if he actually believed that the...faeries... could do everything he promised."

The door opened, and Lucas strode in, followed by Bauers. Shane crossed quickly to intercept his partner and gave him a head-to-toe scan, looking for injuries.

"I'm okay," Lucas said. "You?" He returned the assessing look, making sure Shane hadn't been hurt.

Shane nodded. "Yeah. I'm fine. But I've got a hell of a story to tell you—and Claire's worked out a lot of missing pieces."

"I want to hear what you found out—and I might be able to give you a run for your money on 'strange.'" Lucas clapped a hand on Shane's shoulder, a silent affirmation that they had both returned in one piece.

Bauers and Lucas sat at the table. Now that Shane knew Lucas was back safely, he could sit without fidgeting, and the bristling feeling under his skin from his wolf side calmed.

"How did you get away from the preppers?" Shane asked. "You don't look like you fought your way out."

"Didn't have to," Lucas replied. "Turns out they were pretty normal —except for the deal they made with the Leshy to eat trespassers."

That got everyone's attention. Shane and the others hung on every word as Lucas told them about his encounter with the creature and the guardian ghosts, his time inside the base, the secret project and dogs of war, and the request for access to the library.

"My gut tells me Captain Thomas is a good guy, and his people seem solid," Lucas finished. "I told them about the threat, and they're willing to help."

"Interesting," Claire replied. "That kind of backup will come in handy."

Everyone's attention turned to Shane. "How did things go with the crazy campers?" Lucas asked.

"Even crazier than I expected."

Lucas and the campus security chief listened intently as Shane recounted what had happened, culminating in Preacher Ed's ritual. Claire had heard his story already, but she paid close attention, perhaps looking for details missed in the first telling.

"I told Campbell that I wanted to go through the rift with them to make them trust me," Shane said. "But at the end, when I said that I needed to come back for you, they told me I couldn't leave. So I had to sneak out." Shane knew that Lucas would know what the others didn't—that shifting to his wolf form had been his ticket to freedom.

"Go back to the freaky ritual." Lucas leaned forward and rested his elbows on the table. "He had a bunch of symbols and murals and an altar." His eyes cut over to Claire. "I'm guessing you and Shane already went over whether the sigils were real or just nonsense?

She nodded. "A few come from pagan sources, and they were used in a lot of TV shows and movies. The rest of the symbols come from Hollywood."

Lucas looked at her sharply. "So they're fake?"

Claire frowned. "Yes—and no. Most of them don't come from real-world magical traditions. But magic is a combination of talent, belief, and intent. With enough belief and intention—and a smidge of talent—'made-up' sigils can channel real power. It's one of those cases where if people believe hard enough, they can work a kind of magic that is *focused* on the symbols but doesn't happen *because* of the marks—if you get what I mean."

"You think Preacher Ed has a little magic?" Bauers asked, clearly perplexed.

"Charismatic leaders usually do, even if they don't recognize it as such," Claire replied. "For the most successful televangelists, con artists, and politicians—their ability to manipulate people isn't entirely natural.

So it wouldn't be impossible for Ed to have a touch of magic if he's held his group together through all this."

"Is a little magic like a little knowledge—a dangerous thing?" Bauers asked.

"It can be," Claire replied. "I suspect that Ed's ability allowed him to 'tune in' to other energies."

Lucas turned his attention back to Shane. "Tell us again what you saw in the white light."

Shane rubbed his eyes, trying to remember. "It was only for a second. And the light was bright enough to hurt, so I was squinting. But in that instant, I thought I saw thin, pale shapes moving around."

"Did they have faces? Pointed ears?" Lucas prompted, and Shane made a face at him.

"No—but I get how someone could see what they wanted to see in those shapes," Shane replied.

"I've heard that energy can be sentient without a body," Lucas said offhandedly. Shane felt certain that Rocky was the source.

Claire fixed Lucas with a suspicious look. "That's true—but relatively rare. Still, it's probably at the base of a lot of urban legends and 'sightings.'"

"I'm lost," Bauers admitted. "What made the rift? Can the...things... inside it travel through time? And if they can't, why did they lie to Ed?"

Claire sat back and took a sip of her now-cold coffee. "I have a theory that I'm pretty sure is right, but...."

"What does the coven say about it?" Shane asked.

"They think it's solid. But the thing is, we can't know for sure until we confront the energy. So we need a Plan B, in case I'm wrong," she replied.

"Lay it out, and let us hear what you've got," Lucas urged.

"There are places where the fabric of reality is weak. Ghosts appear more easily, people see visions. Sometimes *things* slip across. The sites get known as holy spots and draw pilgrims, or people avoid them as evil. The land where the campground stands is one of those locations," Claire said.

"The native tribes considered that land to be 'touched by spirits,'" she continued. "They didn't build on it, but they did visit to seek guidance from the other side. Sometimes those visits involved intense meditation, dancing to exhaustion, and naturally occurring psychotropic drugs."

"Sounds like one hell of a Saturday night," Lucas said with a smirk.

"Heaven, hell, the past—it's all in the eye of the beholder," Claire said, ignoring Lucas's smart-ass remark. "When someone with a touch of talent and a lot of intent is in a place of power —especially on an auspicious date—a little bit of magic can cause a whole lot of trouble."

"Like the Fall equinox? That's coming up, right?" Calendars no longer mattered as much as they once had, but Shane thought he remembered the date.

"It's considered to be a good date for magic," Claire confirmed.

"How does the radiation from the plant and the damaged natural energy play into it?" Lucas asked.

Shane knew they were talking about a twisted daemon. He wondered if Claire knew it too and had figured out about Rocky and Quentin.

"When someone trances, it alters how the brain works," Claire continued. "If a thin place opens during that trance, the person can see the energy on the other side. But human brains don't know what to make of that, so they 'see' familiar patterns. Angels. Demons—or faeries."

"What happens if someone actually goes through the thin place?" Shane asked.

"Nothing good. They could be burned up in the energy flow. Or if the energy is sentient, consumed."

"Ed was willing to blow up the plant to level-up the rift enough to take them all to the past," Shane said.

Claire grimaced. "If they do that, we won't be around to care anymore—and they won't be either. Feeding the rift their life energy plus the explosion of the plant might be even worse than the meltdown itself. They won't end up in the past—and they'll kill a lot of people on their way out."

Shane turned to look at Claire. "How do we stop it?"

"Bringing in Captain Thomas and his people takes care of one problem—rounding up the campers," Lucas said. "That lets us focus on Crazy Eddie."

Claire slid two carved pendants toward Shane and Lucas. The cool, slick cannel coal was smooth to Lucas's touch, and he felt Rocky startle at its resonance.

"Please, wear these. Humor me," she said with a knowing smile. "I carved them myself, with intention. Cannel coal has been used for centuries by shamans and mystics. It holds power. The amulets will offer some protection and allow you to better control your talents," she said, with a look that said she suspected that Lucas and Shane were out of the ordinary.

Can't you feel it? The coal knows the witches' power. Rocky was clearly impressed.

Does that mean something? Lucas couldn't help being skeptical.

Possibly. The coal connects you to the witches and the witches to what lies beneath.

"Veins of cannel coal run all through the land beneath the camp," Claire added. "It's part of what makes that area special. My sisters and I draw magic—Cannelmancy—from that coal—and I'm willing to bet that the rift energy can't. So...we ask the guardian ghosts and the Leshy to protect the plant. The preppers round up the cultists and keep them from interfering. My coven uses the cannel coal to strengthen our magic and contain the rift while the two of you stop Ed—or anyone else—from going through."

"Can't the rift just open up at another time?" Lucas asked. "Because there have been stories for a long time about faeries taking people and animals across to their realm. So these rifts must be able to come and go without having someone on this side summoning it."

Shane recognized Lucas's narrow-eyed glare. It was the face he made when he was thinking hard, trying to poke holes in the logic.

"The natural energy of places—whether you call them daemons, elementals, or genius loci—vary in strength," Claire said, with a look at Lucas and Shane that Bauers didn't seem to catch. "Fortunately, they don't all coincide with thin places, so rifts are fairly rare. When they do occur, it's probably where our faerie legends originated. I think what we've got here is a 'perfect storm'—all the worst-case factors in one place."

"That makes sense," Shane replied, mulling over what he'd heard. "And don't forget—since the Events, the supernatural things in the world have gotten bolder—and stronger. That might change how common these sorts of things are."

"Lucky us," Lucas muttered.

"If no one is summoning it, the rift can't open far enough to be dangerous on a large scale by itself—or it would have done so long ago," Claire replied. "If people are foolish enough to go near the thin places, the energy can reach them in their dreams or cause visions if they've got a bit of talent. So we deal with Ed and burn down the camp, put up a fence, and try to keep anyone else from doing the same thing."

Shane looked over to Lucas, wondering what Rocky made of all this. Shane had stopped pacing, and since he didn't feel like howling, Shane figured his wolf-side senses hadn't picked up on anything. "What do you think?" Shane asked.

"I think we're in way over our heads, as usual," Lucas replied. "Unfortunately, I can't come up with anything better. It's an utterly batshit plan. But it just might work."

Shane turned back to Claire. "All right. We're in. The equinox is only a couple of days away. If we're going to do this, we'd better hurry."

CHAPTER SEVEN

"It's go-time. Let's show 'em we've still got what counts," Captain Thomas said to his team as they headed out from the rendezvous point. Their camouflage fatigues let them blend into the moonlit forest, while training and experience enabled them to silently close in on their target. They carried handguns and automatic rifles, but Thomas assured the Marshals and Claire that their goal was to subdue as many of the cultists as possible without firing a shot.

Lucas silently doubted things would go that smoothly, given the camp residents' whole-hearted faith in their leader and their desperation to return to the world as it used to be. Still, he admired Thomas's desire to make this as bloodless as possible and hoped they would be able to make good on that goal.

Lucas and Shane hung back, staying close enough to see what was going on and keeping enough distance to let the soldiers plow the road before they moved in on Ed and his bodyguards.

"Looks like Captain Thomas and his team liked having a new mission," Shane said as they waited in the darkness.

"A mission—and a library," Lucas replied. "They lit up like Christmas. He and Bauers hit it off, so I think they'll figure out how to do more together. Too bad it took so long."

Claire and her coven sisters had been in position since dusk, hidden in the forest all around the base of the camp's hilltop location. Shane and Lucas waited just inside the tree line on the back side of the compound, near the place Shane had dug his way out from under the fence.

Lucas missed having an earpiece and a radio feed connecting the team and giving everyone real-time updates.

I can sense the presence of the witches if that's of concern.

Then again, Lucas had his own personal elemental, which was even better. *Good to know. Anything else?*

The ghosts are between the camp and the plant, instead of where they were before. And the creature roams the woods, Rocky replied.

Then I guess the gang's all here.

Shots rang out.

"That's our cue," Lucas muttered. He led the way up the hill, gun drawn, with Shane at his back.

It felt like old times, moving in sync and running toward danger. Not that they had ever really stopped, but since the Events, charging in with regular weapons was the exception. Lucas had come to feel more comfortable with a knife in his hand or a spell book.

Rocky—what are you picking up?

The energy is gathering. The witches may not be able to hold it back for long.

"Rocky says we'd better hurry, or the party will start without us."

"You sure you don't need me in wolf form?"

Lucas glanced over his shoulder. "So you can get shot by the soldiers? Nope."

Torches burned all around the camp, and what might have been festive under other circumstances now looked to Lucas like something out of a low-budget horror movie.

Two soldiers stood outside the dining hall where Thomas's unit corralled the rest of the camp residents. They waved Lucas and Shane on, indicating that everything had been swept except for the ritual space.

"This way." Shane moved in front, and Lucas fell in behind him as habit and training took over.

Lucas briefly glimpsed the camp as they ran, but what he saw corroborated Shane's story about the cultists and their rough existence. *They could have gone to the Beaver campus and been much more comfortable. But they stayed here, with almost nothing, for a lie.*

Shane slowed and gestured for Lucas to stop at the side of a building within sight of Ed's office. "I don't know if he'll have guards. I think that we need our 'other sides' here. I'll shift and take out any sentries that the soldiers missed. You and Rocky go after Ed."

"We can just shoot the fuckers," Lucas argued.

"Ed would hear. He'll be caught up in the moment. If I take down the guards quietly, you and Rocky can deal with Ed, and he might not realize you're coming."

"We could just shoot Ed."

"Not without knowing how linked he is to the rift. We have no idea what would happen if he died while he was connected," Shane argued. Lucas didn't like it, but he understood the danger.

"Fine. Just don't get shot."

"Don't get sucked through the rift."

Shane turned around and stripped quickly, then shifted in a process that never ceased to be miraculous to Lucas. Quentin looked up at him, wagged his tail, and then pressed a wet, slimy nose against the palm of Lucas's hand.

"You could have just said 'good luck,'" Lucas muttered as the wolf bounded off.

Dark shadows stretched between the torches, swallowing the light. Now that the soldiers had rounded up everyone except for those inside Ed's office, the deserted grounds were eerily still. Training came back like muscle memory from his Army days as Lucas slipped between the camp buildings.

The soldiers had steered clear of Ed's office by design since neither Shane nor the coven could be sure what magical protections were in place. The witches had their hands full blocking as much of the summoned magic as they could, which left it up to Lucas and Shane.

Quentin padded up to the office, staying several feet beyond the doorway. No sentries stood on the outside of the building, so he started barking and then let out a long, mournful howl to attract attention.

"Drama wolf," Lucas muttered.

One man stepped outside to see what was going on. Quentin rushed him from the side, knocking him flat on his back and biting deep into his leg. Lucas was there in a heartbeat, cuffing the man and shoving a rag in his mouth. Quentin woofed and tossed his head, signaling that he would circle the building.

Rocky, what's going on inside?

One man—and very unusual energy distortions.

"Fuck," Lucas growled. *Shield me the best you can—I'm going in.*

As Lucas plunged through the doorway, he felt a frisson of energy that twisted his gut and raised bile in his throat. The power felt terribly *wrong*. That might have stopped him in his tracks without Rocky's countering presence.

Candles lit the inside of the office, and their flickering glow gave the murals a sinister appearance. Incense hung heavy in the air, along with the smell of ozone like after a lightning storm. Amid it all, Ed kneeled inside the warded circle with a large bowl in front of him and a sharp hunting knife on the floor beside it.

"Ed—stop!" Lucas shouted, gun raised.

Ed looked at him with a bemused expression. "Not now. We're almost home."

"It's a lie. Whatever you think you see through the rift, it's not real."

"We're going back, and you can't stop me." Ed's utter confidence wasn't shaken even when he was staring down the barrel of a gun.

Lucas hesitated. *He's an unarmed civilian. But if he summons those creatures through the rift, he's just as dangerous as a suicide bomber.*

The painful decision became clear, and Lucas knew it would haunt his dreams. *I don't have a choice.*

Lucas fired, braced to see the bullet tear through Ed's skull. Instead, it vanished as it crossed over the warded circle.

Ed favored him with a tolerant smile. "I know what you're trying to do. I can feel other magics trying to hold the faeries at bay, but they won't succeed. Today, we are going home."

Can you get me past that warding? Lucas silently asked Rocky, knowing that time was running out. *Yes or no?*

Maybe.

Good enough for me.

Lucas surged forward as Ed dropped a match into the bowl. Green fire flared as a tremor rippled through the building. Sparks danced as the energy around them warped, and a small, glowing hole appeared in the charged air at the center of the warded circle.

He felt the protections try to hold him back, but they were no match for an ancient elemental spirit. Heat and pressure didn't deter him and neither did the sudden flash of blinding pain, and then Lucas was on the inside, and he pulled the trigger.

Nothing stopped the bullet this time. It blew off the side of Ed's skull, and Preacher fell forward, lifeblood pouring into the bowl.

"Shit." Lucas knew that mingling the blood with the ingredients in the bowl couldn't be good. Even worse—he was still inside the circle as the working powered up.

The hole in the air swelled, and Lucas backpedaled, but the protective barrier held firm even as the energy within the warded space felt like it would turn itself inside-out.

Get me out of here, Rocky!

Busy keeping you from getting sucked into the hole at the moment.

Brilliant light filled the hole, and Lucas threw his arm up to shield his eyes. Peering through slitted eyes, he saw motion inside but couldn't make out details. Lucas felt the pull of the rift and threw himself backward onto his ass, bracing his hands and the thick rubber waffle-tread of his boots to keep from being dragged away.

The bowl wobbled and tipped, spilling out blood and ash, then skidded across the floor toward the light along with the candles. Ed's corpse, caught in the undertow of energy, slid toward the rift, leaving a bloody streak across the floor.

Every movie Lucas had seen about black holes flashed through his mind as he felt the drag of the energy, and he knew that he couldn't hold out forever. He tried to scratch through the painted circle on the floor to break the warding, but it held fast.

Rocky!

Lucas thought his brain might melt between Rocky's struggle to withstand the rift and the siren-song of the luminous energy that twined with the hill's twisted daemon. In the distance, he thought he heard Quentin howl and an alien, answering shriek.

The bowl and then the candles tumbled into the rift, followed by Ed's body, pliant as a broken doll.

I'm next.

For a few seconds, the rift *wobbled*, and its hold on him waned. Lucas scrabbled away from the anomaly, pressing his back against the unyielding energy of the warding. The rip in the air grew larger, and the longer Lucas stared, the more his mind tried desperately to match the ever-shifting pulse to familiar images. Others might have thought they glimpsed faeries or home, but all Lucas saw was the deadly energy arc that had stopped his heart at Raven Rock before Rocky brought him back.

The tug of the rift drew Lucas's legs out straight, and he dug his heels in even as it yanked him onto his back. He flipped over, clawing at the floor, arms outstretched and toes braced.

Lucas feared he and Rocky were losing their fight and wondered if the traction would rip him apart before it pulled him in. He slipped an inch, and then another, and closed his eyes, expecting to die.

His eyes snapped open when the room began to shake. He heard a loud, deafening *crack* as the concrete beneath him split, creating a gap in the floor and breaking the circle. Long, bony fingers closed around his wrist with an iron grip, and the Leshy dragged Lucas to safety.

As soon as the warding was broken, Lucas felt the combined power of the coven sweep past him like a storm front, with Rocky's untrammeled energy joining in the surge. The force of it pressed down on him as if he were trapped beneath invisible waves, and Lucas struggled to breathe.

The Leshy let go of Lucas's hand and bellowed in rage, striding toward the rift. A freezing gust of wind followed the creature, and Lucas saw the ghosts of the doomed shutdown crew stream toward the rip in the air and then through it and into the light.

Did they choose to go through to stop one last threat? If the energy beyond the rift feeds on life, what happens when dead souls pass across?

The rift struggled to hold its shape as the light within waned and blinked.

The Leshy planted himself in front of the rip and spread his bony arms wide. Lucas felt Rocky lend his energy to that of the witches, channeling power through the ancient forest spirit. The creature curled his fingers as if gripping something and drew his hands together, dragging the edges of the rift toward each other, and closing the hole as the energy within struggled against the influx of ghosts. Then the Leshy brought his gnarled hands together with a clap like thunder that shook the building and nearly deafened Lucas.

The light vanished and with it, the rip in the air.

Lucas still lay on the floor where the Leshy had dropped him, and he stared up at the creature as it matter-of-factly walked past him and out the door. He felt punch drunk from the wild currents of energy that had flowed around and through him, like a bad moonshine hangover.

What the everlasting fuck just happened?

"Lucas!" Shane's voice broke through his torpor.

The next thing Lucas knew, he was being hauled to his feet and manhandled out the door. Belatedly, it registered that at some point, Shane had shifted back to human form and dressed.

"Need to get out of here. Thomas's team is going to handle the camp demolition. They're having entirely too much fun."

Lucas struggled to keep his feet under him. The throbbing in his head vied with his bruised wrist and wrenched shoulder from the Leshy dragging him to safety. He didn't think he could form a sentence if his life depended on it, and the most coherent thought his muddied brain could manage was *safe*.

CHAPTER EIGHT

L UCAS TRIED TO TALK, but all that came from his parched throat was a dry croak.

"It's okay." Shane held out a glass of water and helped Lucas sit up in bed. The campus health center was now the enclave's hospital, and Shane had strong-armed his stubborn partner into being held overnight for observation after their close call at the campground. "You got a little beat up, but nothing that Rocky and some pain meds won't fix."

Lucas lay back against the pillow, and Shane read his puzzled expression. "How much do you remember?"

"Not sure," Lucas rasped. "It was pretty trippy."

Shane barked a laugh. "That's an understatement."

Even though he had several hours to sort through his jumbled memories while Lucas slept off the meds, the whole incident felt too surreal to believe.

"Tell me."

Shane cleared his throat. "I can tell you what I know, but the coven and the soldiers have their own pieces of it. After I left you at the front of the office building, I went around back and found a second guard. Then I heard a shot and didn't want to waste time, so I bit his hamstring and came back for you."

He stared out the window, replaying the events in his mind. "By then, you were already inside the warding—what the fuck were you thinking? You shot Ed, and all hell broke loose. I wasn't sure that Rocky and the coven could handle the rift on their own. Since I hadn't shifted back yet, I went looking for help—the ghosts and the Leshy."

Shane looked back at his partner, and Lucas's raised eyebrow made his silent question clear. "I guess wolves can get their point across to a forest spirit when the chips are down," Shane replied.

"He caused an earthquake that split the concrete floor and broke the warded circle, then stomped in there like a boss and dragged you out. The shutdown crew ghosts went through to drain the rift's power. It needed to consume living souls to gain energy—at least that's what I got out of what the coven said. I think Rocky and the witches channeled all their power through the Leshy, and he used his mojo to force the rift closed."

"And the ghosts?"

Shane shook his head. "There's no way for them to return. Whether they can go on to anywhere else...like an afterlife, if there is one...there's no way to know. They sacrificed so much—again. Do you remember any of that? Claire said that being so close to all that power might have knocked you for a loop."

Shane had the doctor's assurance that Lucas was not seriously injured, but he worried about damage that couldn't be seen.

"Yeah. Sorta."

Shane nodded. "Good enough—for now. The soldiers brought the cultists down to the road, and then Thomas and a couple of others went back and torched the place. The cult members are under house arrest here at the campus until Bauers's security team and the enclave administration figure out what to do with them."

"Makes sense." Lucas leaned up for another drink, swallowing gratefully.

"You ended up with a badly wrenched shoulder—but it's not dislocated. And your wrist isn't broken, although it might feel like it. Leshies apparently don't know their own strength."

"Saved my ass," Lucas grated.

"That was more of a group effort," Shane replied with a humorless laugh.

"Thanks."

Shane gave an exaggerated shrug. "It would be boring without you." He paused. "How's Rocky? The coven said he did a lot to hold off the rift."

"They know?" Lucas yelped in surprise.

Shane nodded. "Yeah. About Rocky and my wolf side. Apparently, the coven picked up on it pretty soon after we got here, and they're okay with it. I had to do some fast talking to Captain Thomas and his team to explain why I wasn't like the 'dogs of war' they hunted."

Lucas looked concerned. "Are the soldiers a threat?" His expression darkened like he might drag himself out of bed to throw down.

"Claire and the coven vouched for me—and so did the Leshy," Shane replied. "Thomas and his team took a little persuading, but they agreed in the end. Might be a good idea to get a collar or something to make it clear that Quentin is me—just in case."

Lucas didn't look reassured. "I'll deal with them." He sighed, still clearly not recovered yet. "Rocky's alright. Maybe drained a bit, but still fixing me."

"Good." Shane drummed his fingers for a moment. "Once you're back in action, we've got an offer on the table. Bauers said we're welcome to winter here—make this our base. We could do jobs wherever we're requested, but we'd have a place to come back to that has heat and running water."

The first winter after the Events, with everything still in chaos, Shane and Lucas had holed up wherever they could find shelter. It had been cold and miserable, and Shane hoped they never had to live like that again.

Since then, one enclave or another had offered them somewhere to stay for the winter.

"You don't have to make a decision now. But it's something to think about. It would be nice to have a plan and not take what we can find at the last minute."

Lucas managed a tired grin. "Where's the fun in that?"

Shane flipped him off. "Can't spell 'fun' without f-u."

"Get any new requests?"

Having his usually talkative partner reduced to short answers was strange, but Shane figured Lucas would be feeling better before he had a chance to get used to the quiet.

"Nothing urgent. All within a couple of day's ride from here. By the way—Red and Shadow like the stables. They get apples."

"Bribes."

"Maybe."

"Okay."

"Okay—what?" Shane frowned, wanting to make sure he understood.

"We stay."

Shane grinned. "Yeah?"

Lucas tried to shrug and ended up wincing. "Food's good. Why not?"

"You forgot to mention showers and indoor plumbing," Shane joked. He felt the last of his tension and worry slide free. "I'll tell Bauers. I'm actually looking forward to us spending time with Claire and the coven. I think they can teach us a lot. Kinda nice to have people who know the truth and don't run off screaming."

"Yet." Lucas's sarcasm was the best indicator that he was on the mend.

Dangerous loose ends still remained. They probably hadn't seen the last of the hybrid "dogs of war," and one of their creators, Dr. Richardson, remained at large. He and Lucas were still discovering the possibilities—and limitations—that came with their newly altered state.

On the other hand, they had survived another confrontation and gained new allies. They had a home—at least for the winter. And they had both survived without major damage.

All in all, it was as good as it got, after the end of the world.

ABOUT THE AUTHORS

Gail Z. Martin writes epic fantasy, urban fantasy, and steampunk for Solaris Books, Orbit Books, Falstaff Books, SOL Publishing, and Darkwind Press. Recent books include *Vengeance, Sellsword's Oath, Inheritance, and Sons of Darkness.* As Morgan Brice, she writes urban fantasy MM paranormal romance. New books include *Loose Ends, Unholy, Leap of Faith, Kings of the Mountain, and Huntsman.*

Larry N. Martin is the author of the sci-fi adventure novel *Salvage Rat,* and the portal fantasy series, *The Splintered Crown, A Tankards and Heroes novel.* He is the co-author (with Gail Z. Martin) of the *Spells, Salt, & Steel: New Templar Knights* series; the Steampunk series *Iron & Blood;* and a collection of short stories and novellas: *The Storm & Fury Adventures* set in the Iron & Blood universe. He is also the co-author (with Gail) of the *Wasteland Marshals* series and the *Joe Mack - Shadow Council* series from Falstaff Books.

Find them online at www.GailZMartin.com, on Twitter @GailZMartin and @LNMartinAuthor, and at www.DisquietingVisions.com blog.

Gail is also the organizer of the #HoldOnToTheLight campaign at www.HoldOnToTheLight.com

Never miss out on the news and new releases by signing up for the newsletter at http://eepurl.com/dd5XLj

Join the Shadow Alliance street team so you never miss a new release!

Get all the scoop first + giveaways + fun stuff! https://www.facebook.com/groups/435812789942761

f facebook.com/winterkingdoms

BB bookbub.com/profile/gail-z-martin

g goodreads.com/GailZMartin

p pinterest.com/gzmartin